PAX
PACIFICA

ALSO BY STEVE PIECZENIK

Maximum Vigilance

Blood Heat

The Mind Palace

Hidden Passions

PAX PACIFICA

STEVE PIECZENIK

WARNER BOOKS

A Time Warner Company

Warner Books, Inc., 1271 Avenue of the Americas, New York, NY 10020

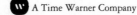 A Time Warner Company

Printed in the United States of America

First Printing: February, 1995

10 9 8 7 6 5 4 3 2 1

Library of Congress Cataloging-in-Publication Data

Pieczenik, Steve R.
    Pax Pacifica / Steve Pieczenik.
      p. cm.
    ISBN 0-446-51557-4
    1. Crisis management in government—Fiction.   I. Title.
    PS3566.I3813P39 1995
    813'.54—dc20
                                         94-7117
                                         CIP

Book design by Giorgetta Bell McRee

To Mel Parker, my editor and friend,
who persevered and inspired with gentlemanly grace
and unwavering professionalism.

To Birdie, my wife, who dared to venture
on the thousand-mile journey of life
with love, humor, and courage.

Acknowledgments

I would like to thank everyone at Warner Books, in particular Larry Kirshbaum, Nanscy Neiman, Jackie Merri Meyer, Harvey-Jane Kowal, Susan Moffat, Ellen Herrick, Liv Blumer, Nancy Wiese, and Alexandra Urdang, as well as Sharon Krassney and Ana Crespo.

Special thanks to my copyeditor, Fred Chase.

And once again I'd like to thank my friend and agent, Robert Gottlieb of the William Morris Agency.

PAX
PACIFICA

PROLOGUE

Li Peng, train engineer for *huoche* 217, a 30,415-pound diesel-electric locomotive, found the barren landscape of Pakistan forbidding. Even the placid luminescence of a moon-filled sky did nothing to alleviate his anxiety. Unlike the start of his voyage at the luscious Kashgar oasis of China's wild west, Li found this part of the three-thousand-mile trip from Sinkiang, China, to Zahedan, Iran, particularly uncomfortable. His sixth sense told him that nothing but danger lay along this dry, empty, godforsaken land. The *mujahedeen*, former Islamic freedom fighters who still operated along this long tail of the Hindu Kush mountain range, had driven the once formidable Soviet army out of this region with nothing more than shoulder-fired Stinger missiles. So it was not unreasonable that Li Peng was frightened of having his train, with its twenty boxcars of valuable cargo, hijacked, derailed, or destroyed by these religious zealots who owed their allegiance to no one other than Allah and their own pecuniary interests.

Wiping his brow and sipping a cup of cold green *chá*, Li opened the throttle and listened to the familiar straining sounds of the engine for any abnormalities. The roar reminded him of his fears of silence. By

2 *Steve Pieczenik*

nature he was extremely superstitious, believing that the potential dangers of the world could be warded off by the *chhi-lin*, an auspicious monster that represented both the favor of the heavens and the emperor's supreme virtue. In his mind, Li Peng was riding his *chhi-lin*, an animal with the body of a deer and the tail of an ox. It had horse's hooves and a single, fleshy horn. The hair on its back was multi-colored but its belly was bright yellow, just like his *huoche*. When it walked, it did not crush the grass. It spared the innocent but struck the guilty with its single horn. Li Peng wondered whether the *chhi-lin* would spare him as an innocent person if the monster knew what cargo his train carried.

Li Peng slowed his train as it rounded a curve. For a moment he sensed an unusual vibration in the hot, sticky compartment and thought of everything that could go wrong, from a faulty kingpin in the underbelly of the locomotive to the alternator on the main generator, which sat behind the turbocharger. But whatever the problem, he knew he wouldn't have any time to fix it. He had exactly six hours in which to arrive at his destination. And if he failed to deliver his cargo on time, for whatever reason, the consequences would be simple—immediate dismissal and incarceration in a prison labor camp somewhere in the frozen tundra of Manchuria.

At the same time that Li Peng was mulling over his destiny, a taut man with powerful arms was busy trying to derail the oncoming train. Slowly, he turned a four-foot T-shaped wrench counterclockwise, loosening the nut on the bolt that held the splice bar against the web of the outside rail. He could have used Primacord, a plastique twisted in the form of a rope, to blow away the outside rail, but that might have left incriminating evidence of sabotage. And his instructions had been quite clear: make the derailment look like an accident—and take pictures.

As he turned the wrench, he could feel the vibrations of Li Peng's locomotive along the rails and knew that in a few short minutes the train would become an uncontrollable missile, thrust off the curved embankment into the crystal-clear night like a projectile of destruction. He smiled to himself with the pride of belonging. His time-honored act of sabotage was not unlike that of his proletarian predecessors who had thrown their shoes into the factory machinery in order to protest the Industrial Revolution.

As the relentless sound of the train roared toward him, the man saw the expansion space between the abutting steel rails widen. At the same time, the spike that held the steel tie plate and rail anchor to the wooden tie popped up, lifting the railroad track from its ballast.

With only a few minutes left to clear the area, he ran up a hillock, crouched behind a large boulder, and positioned his Nikon. As expected, when the train rounded the bend, it hit the side of the hill, buckled into an accordion of twisted metal, and exploded into a bright ball of fire. The man watched as the pristine black sky became a Van Gogh palette of swirling yellow irises. He took a whole roll of film before being whisked away in a car by an accomplice whose mission was to make certain that those pictures were properly developed and sent to the Secretary of State, Department of State, Washington, D.C.

Holding the camera victoriously in the air, in a right hand decorated with the faded tattoo of an eel entwined around a sword, he was pleased that his pictures would put China and the United States on an irreversible course of mutual destruction.

Three hundred miles south of mainland China, U.S. Army Captain Jaime Nunez checked his side-looking radar, the sophisticated AN/APS-94F, which was carefully tracking the countless green blips traversing the elliptoid fluorescent screen. His OV-1D Mohawk twin turboprop combat aircraft was flying smoothly at fifteen thousand feet over the Chinese-controlled Paracel Islands in the South China Sea. His mission objective: document the Chinese People's Liberation Army's $5 billion buildup of recently purchased Russian military equipment. Evaluate the completion of an airstrip capable of accommodating Russian-built SU-27s. Photograph the docking points for the Russian-made KIROV-Class guided missile cruisers and the KONI-Class frigates.

Despite the ongoing cutbacks in the Defense Department budget, Nunez was confident of the sophisticated equipment on his Mohawk. Unlike most of the other army surveillance aircraft, the Mohawk was equipped with radar, photographic, and infrared sensors capable of monitoring enemy movement in daylight, darkness, and inclement weather. Eager to transmit his information, Jaime switched to his primary sensor, the AN/UPD-7 airborne radar surveillance, which in conjunction with a data link relayed the radar information to a ground-based receiving station. The station would convert the signals to film for real-time viewing analysis.

Squinting at his radar in disbelief, Nunez turned toward his co-pilot/navigator, Lieutenant Amanda Blake, an attractive redhead from Culpeper, Virginia. "Jesus Christ. Look what we have here."

"I'd say about twenty-eight FLANKERs," Blake said nervously. "And from my intercept of their radio traffic, it sounds as if all of the planes are being flown by Chinese pilots."

"Caramba, chiquita!" Nunez responded. "At least forty. I'll bet you one hundred dollars for every plane over twenty-eight."

"Jaime," Blake said, pointing to her right. "Check out one o'clock."

"I see ten Soviet Su-27s flying above us," he said, "and each one is carrying five missiles. Ten times five makes fifty missiles directed straight at us. Not very good odds."

Blake tried to remain calm, despite a gnawing anxiety that they were a slow-moving target on a nonofficially authorized surveillance. If intercepted they had been instructed to claim that they were merely "off course" and had "accidentally trespassed" into this highly restricted area. They were to offer their apologies and their desire to immediately fly back to their base.

"One of the FLANKERs is heading our way," Nunez said, taking evasive action by descending into cloud cover. But the Mohawk, already traveling at its maximum speed of four hundred miles per hour, was no match for the highly sophisticated FLANKER going at almost twice the speed of sound.

"They've locked in their missiles," Blake responded, punching in the code for distress. But she didn't fool herself. There was nothing anyone could do. As volunteers for this assignment, they were fully aware that they might become hostage to the superior technology of the Chinese People's Liberation Army. It certainly was no secret that China had been buying sophisticated military equipment from cash-strapped Russia for the past few years. And in a few seconds one of those missiles would surely hit them, she thought.

"Don't forget your chopsticks," Nunez said, banking the plane deeper into the clouds.

"*Xìexie ni*. Thank you." Blake responded nervously, reaching her hand out and squeezing Nunez's sweaty palm.

"Take care of yourself, Miss Culpeper High," Nunez said.

"I'm scared," Blake replied, biting her lower lip.

Within one hour of impact, the OV-ID Mohawk was reported as missing during a routine training exercise over the Pacific Ocean. Captain Jaime Nunez and Lieutenant Amanda Blake became the first unlisted American casualties of a nonexistent war at a location that had no coordinates.

CHAPTER ONE

The motorcade emerged from the State Department underground garage like black ants scurrying from their habitat. The bulletproof black Cadillac limousine, bracketed by two Range Rovers filled with armed Diplomatic Security Agents, sped down 24th Street, preempting the traffic at George Washington Circle with their flashing red lights and intimidating speeds. The three-car motorcade headed north toward Connecticut Avenue.

When the cars stopped in front of a nondescript converted ten-story apartment building, the DSAs rushed out of their Rovers and stood at their customary positions surrounding the black Cadillac, scanning the immediate environs for any potential problems. Once they felt comfortable that there was no immediate threat to the occupants of the limousine, they allowed the two men sitting in the back seat to leave their bathysphere of protection.

Both men, dressed in de rigueur State Department pin-striped black suits, walked by the DSAs without saying a word and entered the embassy, where they were immediately whisked to the ambassador's office on the second floor.

"Welcome to the Chinese embassy," Ambassador Guan Fugen said nervously. "Please come in." He motioned his two guests into a sparsely decorated office with furnishings deceptively American—a mahogany desk, several wingback chairs, a traditional sofa. Only a large handmade Tibetan rug gave any indication of ethnic distinction.

Ambassador Guan Fugen, a fifty-year-old career diplomat, had learned that bad news travels fast. But it was often delivered by a State Department desk officer. At most, an Assistant Secretary of State. The presence of both the Secretary of State and the Assistant Secretary of State for East Asian and Pacific Affairs meant that U.S.-Chinese relations were in serious trouble, if not at a major point of crisis.

"Thank you, Mr. Ambassador," Secretary of State James Moffat said in a controlled fashion, taking a seat on the velvet sofa opposite the ambassador. Moffat was a heavyset six-foot man with silver-gray hair who would have been perfectly cast as a diplomat by any Hollywood studio. "I am sorry to say that this is not a social visit so let us get to the heart of the matter quickly. We are here to officially protest the irresponsible action of your government in incidents involving American citizens."

"This is an official demarche," Assistant Secretary Desaix Clark added, as he took his seat next to the secretary, "protesting the fact that on two separate occasions the People's Republic of China has evinced behavior that the United States considers extremely dangerous to the maintenance of world peace, as well as showing a complete disregard for the sanctity of human lives." The tall, forty-eight-year-old diplomat, whose penetrating deep-set eyes were searing into Guan, was having a hard time restraining his own feelings. "Especially American lives."

Desaix, a psychiatrist with ruggedly handsome features, swarthy skin, and wavy salt-and-pepper hair, was a twenty-year veteran of the State Department who had made his mark as a hostage negotiator and crisis manager. He knew that like much of diplomacy, the demarche was simply another ritualized behavior that was scripted by centuries of diplomats who had to find a way of protesting the actions of a foreign government in a civilized, rational manner. For Desaix, an emotional Cajun from the bayous of Lafayette, Louisiana, this demarche was particularly hard for him to make. He felt indirectly responsible for the deaths of both Captain Nunez and Lieutenant Blake, having "unofficially" approved the Defense Intelligence Agency's request for the intelligence-gathering mission over the Paracels. Desaix had no doubt that the Chinese leaders had decided to teach the United States a lesson—do not meddle in matters that don't directly concern you.

"As the official representative of the People's Republic of China," Guan responded, "I must find out the precise nature of your government's official protest."

"A DF4 Eastwind locomotive," Moffat replied slowly and meticulously, giving Desaix, his friend of twenty-five years, time to cool down, "designated *huoche* 217, recently pulled twenty sealed cars carrying an assortment of short- and long-range ballistic missiles from its point of origin in Kashgar, China, toward its destination in Zahedan, Iran. The train was derailed in western Pakistan. The transmission of such dangerous weapons manufactured in your country is in direct violation of both U.S.-Chinese Accords and UN Resolution 732 prohibiting the export of nuclear weapons to terrorist nations—"

"My government protests such an allegation," Guan said, interrupting what he sensed was to be a long list of indictments. "We value our friendship with the U.S. and would not do anything that would jeopardize that relationship."

"I think that you would be interested in these pictures taken from our satellites," Desaix replied. He handed the ambassador a folder marked TOP SECRET/NO FORN/NO CON. Desaix made no mention of the fact that the photographs of the train wreck had been sent to the Secretary of State anonymously. Although it was not unusual for the State Department to receive unsolicited material, Desaix couldn't help wondering who had sent those pictures. And why.

Desaix's submission of classified material to prove a point was as much a part of the ritual of the demarche as was Guan's anemic denial of a problem. Guan, like most Chinese officials, often sprinkled his remarks with *tifa*, standard policy statements, like the one about the importance of U.S.-Chinese relations. From Desaix's experience with Chinese negotiators, he knew that the *tifa* were really intended to demonstrate the Chinese negotiator's personal loyalty to the current Chinese leadership and its basic policies. And Ambassador Guan was well aware that scores of Chinese officials would soon be reading the minutes of this meeting.

"As you can see from these photographs," Moffat said, "the People's Republic of China was shipping the following items to Iran: CSS-2 Intercontinental-Range Ballistic Missiles, "8610" Short-Range Ballistic Missiles, M-9 SRBMs, and M-11 SRBMs."

"Look here," Desaix said, pointing to specific objects in several pictures. "Restricted rocket motors, fuel systems, and guidance electronic systems were on that train as well."

"I find this most interesting," Guan said, more closely monitoring Desaix's facial expressions than the photographs he held in his hand. Of the two Americans, Desaix was obviously the one who could be most easily manipulated into making an outburst that would mitigate the impact of the demarche—at least for the official Chinese record. Guan wondered how he could create a scenario that would blunt the American initiative.

"What exactly do you find interesting?" Desaix asked provocatively.

"I see various parts of what you, Mr. Secretary, call missiles," Guan replied slowly, "but which I am not able to identify as anything more than twisted metal. At this moment I would have to take your conclusions at face value."

"Does that mean that you agree with the accuracy of our allegation?" Moffat pressed Guan, knowing that if he accepted even a scintilla of their demarche, Moffat could return to State and initiate retaliatory procedures against the People's Republic. Otherwise, Guan could stonewall them, contesting every aspect of the demarche by requesting a lengthy study period before his government could respond. And if that happened Moffat knew he would have a hard time convincing the President to mount a diplomatic initiative against China at a time when the American people were basically isolationists, more concerned with domestic issues than world events.

"Not at all, Mr. Secretary," Guan replied firmly. "Neither I nor my government agrees with any part of your allegations. What I find particularly interesting is that I see in these photographs an extensive amount of train damage. How exactly did that happen, I wonder?"

"We suspect that the train had mechanical difficulties," Desaix answered calmly, "and derailed as it came around a bend in the track."

"Very interesting, Dr. Clark," Guan said. "And how do you explain the fact that the Pakistani government reported to us that the rail bedding had been tampered with?"

"That I can't explain," Desaix replied, wondering how he could avoid being sandbagged by the ambassador into revealing his own suspicions about an act of sabotage. Clearly, whoever sent the pictures had also been involved in creating the train wreck. Desaix wondered who stood to gain from embarrassing the Chinese government. Another government? Some terrorist group?

"May I remind you, Mr. Ambassador," Moffat interceded, "that the principal problem the U.S. government has with the People's Republic of China is its manufacture and export of nuclear missiles to irresponsible nations that support international terrorism. We find the actions and policies of your government highly destabilizing to the U.S. government's efforts to maintain peace in the Middle East."

"Our government appreciates your exhaustive efforts at trying to maintain world peace," Guan responded, "but we must defer any comments at this particular point in time concerning your specific allegations."

"Thank you for your kind words," Moffat retorted. "But we cannot defer the matter of the death of two American pilots on a routine flying mission over the South China Sea."

"Mr. Secretary, let me facilitate our discussion," Guan said. "Your Mohawk plane was flying in a highly restricted military area. I would conclude that like the train, the Mohawk, an antiquated spy plane, must have had mechanical problems that led to an unfortunate accident in an area over which it should not have been flying."

"Are you telling me, Mr. Ambassador," Moffat asked, his face flushed red, "that there will be no apologies or explanations proffered by your government regarding either incident?"

"At least not for the moment, Mr. Secretary," Guan replied quietly, reflecting an underlying personal sadness. "It seems as if we have been discussing two completely separate accidents that occurred in different parts of the world, involving the deaths of both American and Chinese citizens."

"That was no accident over the Paracel Islands," Desaix blurted out. "That was a clear act of revenge."

Moffat flashed an angry look at Desaix, who had just ignored a primary rule of protocol: never directly accuse a foreign government of a transgression without incontrovertible evidence. Which in the world of diplomacy, of course, was a rare commodity.

"Whatever we say at this point I'm afraid will not be very productive," Guan said, standing up. "I appreciate your having come to see me. I can assure you that every attention will be accorded to your country's demarche, Mr. Secretary."

"Thank you for having seen us on such short notice," Moffat responded appropriately, walking toward the door. "Please give my regards to Prime Minister Lee Ann Wu."

"I certainly will, Mr. Secretary," Guan said, leading his guests into the antechamber. He turned to Desaix. "Remember, Dr. Clark, we have a saying that skillful warriors are able to be invincible, but they cannot cause opponents to be vulnerable."

Desaix smiled knowingly. "As I recall, one of your famous military strategists said that invincibility is a matter of defense but vulnerability is a matter of attack."

But despite his having had the last word, Desaix could taste the bitter venom of unsatisfied revenge in his mouth.

CHAPTER TWO

The G Street Club in downtown Washington, D.C., could be safely characterized as one of those last remaining bastions of WASP exclusivity. From the outside, the club seemed little more than a small white clapboard New England colonial with a white picket fence encircling a well-manicured lawn. But once inside, its wainscoted rooms, floor-to-ceiling bookshelves filled with rare first editions, scuffed leather armchairs, and Tiffany lamps were reminders that this house properly belonged to a bygone era when Charles Bohlen, George Kennan, Dean Acheson, and a handful of other State Department "wise men" developed American foreign policy after World War II. From this inconspicuous property, these men had established and maintained their rule over Foggy Bottom for a period of time in which the United States truly reigned supreme.

Greeted by the club manager, Moffat and Desaix were led through narrow carpeted corridors to a small, sparsely decorated dining room where a round table with a hand-stitched Venetian tablecloth and two place settings awaited. Clearly, Moffat had called ahead. This was where Moffat would take Desaix whenever he wanted to have an intimate, yet professional, discussion. When it was Desaix's turn, he could be relied on to counter with one of his lowbrow but discreet suburban hangouts that specialized in entertaining Washington luminaries with the same indifference it affectionately imparted to all its regular customers.

Desaix never liked the G Street Club, or any one of the other old-line, all-male social organizations that were frequently distinguished more by the types of people they excluded than by the personal accomplishments of their members. While Desaix was never one to pursue social causes, he still prided himself on being a believer in meritocracy. As the next to the youngest of five children of a physician father and socialite mother, Desaix grew up with the noblesse oblige of those privileged few who lived on Prytania Street in the fashionable Garden District of New Orleans. An iconoclast and rebel since childhood, Desaix had learned early on that he had to make his mark on a family that considered personal accomplishment and social responsibility the primary justification for their existence. When his older brother, Gaston, was about to become a general practitioner, Desaix had to become a board-certified psychiatrist as well as a Ph.D. in international relations, just to attract the praise of an emotionally distant father. Throughout his formative years, scholastic competition, rivalries, and sporadic outbursts of deviant behavior had marked Desaix's relationship with his siblings. Only his younger sister, Antoinette, an affectionate, sweet tomboy, provided him with the gentle kindness and understanding that he sought in his subsequent relationships with women. Although he was particularly close to his mother, a histrionic concert pianist who had given up a promising career to raise her children, Desaix often found himself in the emotionally precarious position of acting more like a surrogate lover and husband than a son. Early on, he had learned to distance himself from the suffocating maternal emotions that were identified as love, but which marked his dependency. He was, as honestly as he could describe it, a product of a typical upper-class professional American family—functionally dysfunctional.

In contrast, James Moffat had been the only child of a family who, for several decades, had lived in the privileged heart of old-money Philadelphia in a quaint brownstone town house off Rittenhouse Square. His father had been the principal managing director of a small but prestigious regional investment banking house, specializing in the relatively safe area of underwriting utility bonds. His mother, much more courageous and adventuresome, had broken with family tradition and opened up a women's lingerie store that eventually grew into a chain, requiring the underwriting services of her husband's firm. From his father, Moffat learned to be cautious, temperate, polite, and exceedingly appropriate, as might be expected from an established Philadelphia family. On the other hand, his vivacious mother had taught him that at key points in life, one had to be prepared to take high risks and make what appeared to be irrational decisions based on nothing more than intuition. Moffat's affinity for Desaix was based on what he had incorporated from his mother's teachings. Despite his outward protests, Moffat vicariously enjoyed Desaix's passions and occasional excesses, well aware that beneath his own composed, sober facade he, Moffat, was a man of both intense feelings and subtle machinations. A covert version of Desaix, if you will. Thus, his ascendancy to Secretary of State.

"Would you mind explaining your outburst to Ambassador Guan?" Moffat asked in a scolding manner. He nodded to the waiter standing in the doorway to begin serving the meal.

"Are we in the Mr. Secretary or the Jimboy mode?" Desaix asked, prepared for the obligatory dressing-down he was about to receive.

"Right now, you're talking to the Secretary of State at the distinguished G Street Club," Moffat replied with seriousness, but careful not to overplay the role. Otherwise, Desaix would be tempted to undermine his remarks with caustic sarcasm or simple silence. And that would not help them to resolve their professional differences. If anything, it would require them to tap into their deep reservoir of goodwill and friendship. And that was both time-consuming and costly.

"Mr. Secretary," Desaix responded somberly, as he started to cut into his *cordon bleu*, "it was obvious that the Chinese ambassador was trying to deny his country's responsibility for the murders of Nunez and Blake. And as I'm the Assistant Secretary of State for East Asian and Pacific Affairs, that made me mad."

"And as my Assistant Secretary of State for East Asian and Pacific Affairs," Moffat asked, carefully sipping his glass of white wine, "did you or did you not transgress your official role as a representative of the United States government?"

Desaix stared knowingly into Moffat's cold brown eyes, wondering how long this charade of formality would continue. He knew that Moffat had to reprimand him for his inappropriate outburst. That was part of his job. Gratefully, he was doing it in private.

"What made you commit such a foolish act?" Moffat asked again, hoping that Desaix wouldn't bolt from the room, as he had on previous occasions such as this.

"What do you mean?" Desaix asked, perplexed.

"Who gave you the order to authorize a covert action against the Chinese?" Moffat asked, meticulously dissecting the skin off his roasted chicken.

"What are you talking about?" Desaix asked angrily.

"Did you or didn't you order an off-line sabotage of that train?" Moffat asked calmly, placing his knife and fork down.

"Jim," Desaix responded, knowing exactly what it was that Moffat expected from him, "you know damn well that you asked me to get specific evidence on the Chinese transport of missiles passing through Pakistan into Iran. When I asked you if we would have to task the CIA and require a finding," Desaix whispered, leaning over toward Moffat, "you said to use my own discretion. And I did."

"What did you do?" Moffat asked, knowing that he was testing the limits of his friend's patience.

"Even though I had full legal authority to authorize a covert action against that train," Desaix responded in a controlled voice, "I went against my basic Cajun instincts for exposing hypocrisy and treachery, and instead tasked the NSA to electronically sweep the train from above. That was my entire involvement in the matter. You know damn well that I wouldn't do anything that might embarrass our government. I may be impulsive, but I'm not stupid."

"Then who committed that act of sabotage?" Moffat asked in a confused but now relaxed voice.

"I don't know," Desaix replied, "but I think we can assume that whoever sent us those pictures was also involved in derailing the train."

"Why do you think so?" Moffat asked, continuing to eat his food in his methodical way.

"Because the photographer knew exactly what he or she wanted to depict—embarrassing evidence of illegal Chinese activity."

"Who stands to gain from that?" Moffat asked, sipping his glass of water.

"Taiwan, China's principal rival, comes immediately to mind," Desaix replied, annoyed by Moffat's insouciant manner.

"Most unlikely," Moffat responded. "They have too large a trade balance with the mainland to risk a major confrontation with China over the issue of nuclear proliferation."

"What about Japan?" Desaix asked. "They are historical enemies."

"History also bows to the imperatives of commerce," Moffat replied. "At present they are involved in too many international joint ventures to risk their relationship over a few nuclear warheads."

"Israel?" Desaix replied. "They have a vested interest in making certain that nuclear weapons don't reach any of their hard-line Muslim enemies—Iran, Syria, or Iraq."

"In principle that might be true," Moffat agreed, "but in reality you and I know that Israel, for quite a while now, has been secretly helping the Chinese develop their nuclear arsenal. It's not likely that they would try to compromise their very important client."

"Damnit, Jim. Can we stop all this phony question-and-answer nonsense. What's going on? Do you know who did it?"

Moffat once again put down his knife and fork and took a hard look at Desaix. Theirs was a deep bond of friendship and affection. While Desaix was in the State Department as Deputy Assistant Secretary of State in various bureaus, Moffat was a national security expert in several administrations and agencies, including the National Security Council, the CIA, the State Department, and the Department of Defense. But no matter how many countries or levels of the bureaucracy separated them over the years, they had always maintained a close relationship filled with an uncanny blend of personal mischief and serious foreign policy. Despite their adolescent need to compete with each other, their friendship had withstood countless years of planning, scheming, and the political betrayal—of others. The friendship had also been marked by wide swings in attitudes, beliefs, moods, and emotions. At any moment, they could run the gamut from the very formal to the raunchy, from extreme rationality to complete absurdity, from trust to sudden paranoia. It was a relationship immersed in both contradiction and *bon amitié*. A relationship that Moffat would be saddened to give up.

Whenever they worked together they were known as the "Sec and Doc Show," two tough national security experts who could be trusted to get any job done. There were only two caveats: never interfere and never ask how. Moffat was the politician, the rainmaker, the bureaucratic turf-protector. He would have been the senior partner in a law firm who brought in the business, oversaw the process, and kept the client informed and appreciative. Desaix would have been the inside man, the fixer, the operator. He would be responsible for the nuts and bolts of managing the case—or in their situation the international crisis. He developed the analysis, planned the strategy, and implemented the tactics. It was a marriage of interdependency, familiarity, loyalty, and mutual respect.

"I wish I knew who did it," Moffat replied. "But it's something you might want to look into."

"Why didn't you ask me that right up front?" Desaix asked, bothered by Moffat's uncharacteristic coy manner. It seemed as if he were going out of his way to provoke him. "You still don't believe that I didn't do it. Do you?"

"I'm glad we understand each other, Desaix," Moffat responded, ignoring Desaix's question. "I hope you like your *cordon bleu*. I tried to have the chef prepare your favorite dish, *oysters bienville*. But I'm afraid he didn't know how to make it."

"Thank you for your kind consideration, Mr. Secretary," Desaix said sarcastically, disappointed that they had spent the last half hour doing nothing more than fencing.

"To return to our original discussion," Moffat said, trying to sound as if he considered his problems with Desaix over. "I hope that this will be the last time I will have to remind you about your professional conduct." After all, as Secretary of State he had to have the complete loyalty of all his subordinates—especially that of his best friend.

CHAPTER THREE

Revenge against the Chinese obsessed Desaix's thoughts as he walked briskly down the candy-striped corridor of the seventh floor of the State Department. What could he do to signal them that they could not get away with the wanton killing of Americans? Desaix had grown up with a basic rule of survival: *il faut tuer avant d'être tué.* Kill before being killed. A notion that went completely against his training as a diplomat, where reconciliation and avoidance of confrontation were considered paramount. Moffat's reproach had left Desaix with a clear sense that he was on probation. Even their long-standing friendship could not protect him against bureaucratic retribution if he were to do anything that might further inflame U.S.-Chinese relationships.

"You have a ton of messages waiting for you," William Toland said to his boss as Desaix passed him and entered his office.

"Come inside," Desaix replied, taking off his jacket and seating himself behind his large, cluttered mahogany desk. He liked the fact that his office always appeared to be in turmoil, covered with unruly stacks of memoranda, reports, and newsletters, both classified and un- classified, frequently intermingled. It allowed the uninitiated visitor to think that he was both unorganized and disorderly, a notion that could not have been further from the truth.

On the sides of his desk were the basic electronic accoutrements required of all assistant secretaries: a STU-3 secured telephone, a secured computer terminal, and a nonsecured fax machine. Attached to the wall, behind his desk, was an antique Mercator projection map, which distorted the land masses toward the pole, a purposeful reminder to him that so-called objective information was often fallacious, if not outright fictitious.

"Here's a NO DIS/EYES ONLY cable that I think you should read right away," Toland said, handing Desaix the classified paper. "Oh, and Mrs. Jaime Nunez has been waiting to see you."

Toland was a short, nattily dressed, flaxen-haired man in his mid-thirties. He was an extremely efficient FSO-2 whom Desaix had promoted to executive secretary above the protests of the Foreign Service Director General, who felt that the position should be filled by an FSO-1 with more experience. Although he couldn't prove it, Desaix suspected that the DG was really reflecting the not too subtle institutional pressure to keep Toland, the recently appointed chairman of the Gay and Lesbian Foreign Service Organization, away from a high-profile job.

Desaix knew that Toland was grateful to him for the time, energy, and political cachet he had expended on Toland's promotion, as well as for his behind-the-scenes work lobbying both the White House and Congress to eliminate the antiquated rules that prohibited avowed homosexuals from entering the Foreign Service. Armed with longitudinal studies showing that an avowed homosexual presented significantly less of a national security risk than a closet gambler or a sexually promiscuous heterosexual, Desaix was able to persuade the legislators.

"Tell her to come in," Desaix said, waving away the cable. "And would you please send those photos of the Chinese train wreck to the National Photographic Interpretation Center immediately?" NPIC was located in the old naval gun factory along the Anacostia River in Washington, only a few blocks away from the State Department.

"Any particular slug?" Toland asked.

"Task them to identify the source of origin," Desaix replied, surprised that no one in the intelligence system had made any type of notation on those pictures. But in all fairness to the intelligence community, Desaix thought, NPIC's principal job was to analyze the "take" of their own photographic reconnaissance aircraft and satellites.

"I know what you're thinking," Toland replied, thrusting the cables into Desaix's hands. "But sometimes SIGINT/ELINT intel does have greater priority over the human condition."

"Thank you, André Malraux," Desaix responded, referring to the French author of *Man's Fate*, a novel depicting the heroic exploits of Zhou Enlai during the Communist Party's 1920s uprising in Shanghai. Desaix pointed his index finger in the direction of the waiting room where Mrs. Nunez was sitting. "When a piece of paper becomes more important than a person, that's when I quit this job."

"At the expense of sounding callous, let me provide you with a précis of the cable," Toland replied.

"Toland," Desaix exploded, "if you're not careful you might end up as the new chargé in Ulan Bator."

"You're right," Toland responded unconvincingly, "I've become like all those terrible, officious functionaries who fight us all the way. Isn't it wonderful?" he asked sarcastically. "I've finally arrived."

"Forget it," Desaix said, walking toward the door. "I'll get her myself."

"A secret envoy from Taiwan just concluded five days of talks with his mainland counterpart in Beijing," Toland whispered to Desaix as they strode into the crowded front office.

"So?" Desaix asked.

"This is the first time since 1949, when the Communists defeated the Nationalist government and forced it to flee to Taiwan, that representatives of the two hostile governments have discussed their differences."

"What differences?" Desaix asked, piqued by the notion that enemies who had vowed mutual destruction for the past fifty years were now discussing a rapprochement without informing the United States. It was usually the other way around. If the U.S. made even an overture, let alone a deal with either China or Taiwan, Desaix would immediately be on the phone with a representative of one or the other country for fear of insulting someone's national sensibilities.

"According to this cable," Toland replied, "they discussed cooperating to fight crime and smuggling."

"There's got to be more than that," Desaix responded, spying a woman in her mid-thirties sitting demurely in the waiting room. "Both sides officially regard Taiwan as part of China, and each claims to be the legitimate government of China. Something big is going on."

"Oh, yes," Toland said. "I almost forgot. They did discuss something else."

"What was that?" Desaix asked brusquely, disliking Toland's annoying habit of stringing him along.

"They spent quite a lot of time discussing the issue of protecting private Taiwanese investments in China," Toland replied. "That amounts to one hundred billion dollars."

"Are you certain?" Desaix asked, perplexed by this last bit of information. For over twenty years the Taiwanese had been investing in southern China. But that was no different from their strategy of investments in Vietnam, Cambodia, Thailand, Latin America, and even the United States. It was the magnitude of the Taiwanese investment and the sense that they needed protection from the Chinese that struck Desaix as extremely unusual. It was comparable to the proverbial chickens in the hen house asking the fox to protect them from any predators.

"I'll double-check it," Toland replied.

"And don't forget those photos," Desaix added.

"Don't worry, boss," Toland said, walking away satisfied with himself for having notified an Assistant Secretary of State of a significant event that was previously unknown. It was worth at least two days of corridor conversation.

"How do you do, Mrs. Nunez," Desaix said, extending his hand to the attractive woman in the plain black dress. "I'm Dr. Desaix Clark." He wondered why he felt compelled to introduce himself as a physician. Was he concerned that he might have to hide behind his medical facade in order to maintain some modicum of control over their conversation? Or was there something about her that spelled potential confrontation which might best be handled by assuming the role of a physician rather than that of senior diplomat?

"Thank you for seeing me on such short notice," Mrs. Nunez replied, "but I couldn't find anyone at DOD who could really help me out." She fixed a doleful gaze on the man who was known within the national security bureaucracy as one of the few senior officials who really gave a damn about the "grunts," whether they were "civvies" or uniformed. He had the reputation of being someone who was accessible and compassionate. She was filled with so many mixed emotions—rage, sadness, pain, and desire for revenge—she didn't know what to say first or how to say it.

"I'm glad you could come to see me," Desaix said, leading her back to his office. "I was about to pay you a condolence call." He motioned to her to sit down on the leather couch, which he quickly cleared of papers. He chose one of the two wingback chairs opposite her. "Would you like some tea or coffee?"

"No, thank you," Mrs. Nunez replied, trying to keep her emotions in check. Grabbing her knees with both hands, she squeezed them tightly in order to prevent her hands from shaking.

"I can't tell you how sorry I am about your husband's death," Desaix said, trying to prevent his own voice from cracking with emotion.

"Some of the people at DOD told me," Mrs. Nunez said haltingly, "that I should see you. You would be able to help me."

"If there is anything I can do for you," Desaix responded, "please tell me what it is."

"I didn't want him to reenlist for those dangerous assignments," she said, her voice now containing a sharper edge to it. "He had already done three overseas tours so he was entitled to stay stateside for at least four years. But despite my imploring him to take a desk job at the Pentagon, he refused. He told me that he would rather die in the field doing his job than become one of what he called the walking dead, pushing papers and attending endless, meaningless meetings."

"I understand exactly how he felt," Desaix responded, waiting for her submerged anger to surface. "I do my best to get into the field as often as possible."

"He had a great respect for people like you, Dr. Clark," she said, her voice increasingly more brittle. "Everything he said or did was always prefaced by 'the Assistant Secretary of Defense said this' or 'the

Assistant Secretary for Special Operations said that.' I'm sorry, but I know that it doesn't really pertain to you directly. . ."

"That's all right," Desaix replied. "I understand."

"My husband wasn't really happy until he signed up for the army's special intelligence unit." She paused to catch her breath. "He called it the action junkie's delight. It was the one assignment that he really loved . . . and the one that cost him his life."

Desaix remained silent, waiting for the explosion. He hoped that whatever anger she felt would be directed toward him. If she didn't express her feelings about her husband's death, she would eventually internalize her anger, turning it into self-blame and precipitating what could become an intractable depression.

"Why did his military commanders let him go?" she asked angrily. "They knew it was a dangerous assignment."

"That was their job," Desaix responded calmly. "And I'm certain they felt that he and Lieutenant Blake were the ones who were best suited for that particular assignment." She was beginning to shake. "Do you have any children?" Desaix asked.

"Two teenage girls," she replied.

"How are your daughters handling his death?" Desaix asked.

"Fortunately, they are extremely busy," she replied, "so they don't have much time to mourn."

"I think it might be useful if you and they saw someone professionally to help you deal with his death," Desaix said softly, wishing he could cradle this hurting woman in his arms and assure her that she would recover. After much grief and sorrow. And time. But it would happen. Instead, he stood and walked over to his desk.

"I've already run out of my mental health insurance coverage," she replied, chagrined. "Jaime and I went to couples therapy to try to deal with some marital problems we were having."

"Don't worry about anything," he said, picking up the telephone. "Toland, come in here, stat." Desaix was not surprised to hear that the Nunezes had had marital problems. Over fifty percent of military and Foreign Service families had some type of mental health, marital, or drug or alcohol abuse problem. And Desaix suspected that Mrs. Nunez's husband might have been trying to escape an unhappy marriage by joining an assignment that took him overseas—alone. Most, if not all, action junkies Desaix had known were trying to escape from something—a passionless marriage, a nonstimulating job, a dead-end career, or a boring existence. They just wanted to erase the tedium in their life by acting out a fantasy of action and adventure. As a psychiatrist, Desaix could understand and empathize. But as a professional diplomat with serious responsibilities, he had to co-opt those individual psychodynamics and assist them in the most humane way possible to serve their country.

"I feel so ashamed telling you all this," Mrs. Nunez said, burying her face in her hands, "but I have no one to talk to. I have no family of my own and I don't get along with Jaime's family. Most of our military friends are dispersed throughout the world."

"Do you have a job, Mrs. Nunez?" Desaix asked, putting down the receiver.

"I've had lots of part-time jobs over the years," she replied, wiping away her tears with her handkerchief, "but I've always dreamed of joining the Foreign Service."

"You called?" Toland asked.

"I want you to prepare the necessary paperwork to make certain that Mrs. Nunez and her two daughters have unlimited mental health coverage," Desaix said. "Tell the director of Med to give me a call if he has any problems with that."

"Thank you," Mrs. Nunez said, blushing with embarrassment.

"Assume it's already done," Toland replied.

"And have Mrs. Nunez admitted to the Foreign Service Institute to prepare her for a permanent FSO position," Desaix ordered.

"But," Toland sputtered, "I think we're cutting back—"

"Toland," Desaix interrupted, "no ifs, ands, or buts. *Comprenez-vous?*"

"*Je vous comprends.* I understand." Toland responded with General Charles de Gaulle's famous statement to President Dwight Eisenhower in expressing Gallic condolences when the Russians had revealed the embarrassing U-2 reconnaissance overflights.

"I don't know how to thank you," Mrs. Nunez said, shaking Desaix's hand.

"There's no need," Desaix replied, escorting her out the office. "It's I who must thank you for your personal sacrifice. Your husband was a dedicated public servant who gave his life to his country. I would like you to find some consolation in the fact that when your husband died he was doing exactly what he wanted to do. Most people are not that fortunate."

"I'm so glad my trust in you was not misplaced. Thank you again."

"If you need anything, please feel free to call me," Desaix replied as he walked Mrs. Nunez into the corridor. He went back into his office and closed the door, glad he had been able to help her. Whenever an American military person died, he took it personally and felt that he had failed professionally. Toland would have to remind him from time to time that he was being unreasonable.

He picked up the ringing STU-3 telephone. "Yes," he replied, impressed by NPIC's unusually quick response. "The point of origin is where?"

CHAPTER FOUR

F ive hours later Desaix sat hunched at his desk pondering the NPIC technician's response. China! The pictures were developed in China. There was no doubt about it, the technician had said, from the granular quality of the paper, to the specific photochemicals used, the distinct watermark on the paper, and the poor resolution of the images.

Desaix scrolled down his monitor, quickly reviewing the options paper he was preparing for Moffat. But he was having a hard time focusing his thoughts on China's unexpected aggressive behavior. His eyes kept shifting from his monitor to the pictures that lay on his desk.

Who would gain most from disseminating pictures of a Chinese train wreck carrying contraband nuclear weapons?

His eye jumped back and forth between the little red stars on a map marking newly acquired Chinese military bases and a document marked TOP SECRET/NO DIS/CHINA'S REGIONAL ASSERTIVENESS: BEIJING'S ARMS PURCHASES AND EXPANSION OF MILITARY FACILITIES CREATE CONCERNS THROUGHOUT ASIA. He certainly could understand how from Vietnam to Indonesia and Australia, government officials, diplomats, and military analysts were scared. If war broke out, Beijing would conquer East Asia almost without a struggle and then defend her sweeping territorial claims in the South China Sea. And whoever controlled the sea would claim its extensive oil and mineral reserves and dominate Japanese shipping lanes.

Although many of the countries in the region weren't sure whether they should be more concerned about China or Japan, there was little doubt in Desaix's mind which of the two countries was a greater military threat. From Indonesia, the Chinese had negotiated the purchase of fifty refitted ships (a third of the former East German navy) for a mere $200 million, and the unusual right of the Chinese to patrol the territorial waters surrounding the capital city, Jakarta. And there was no doubt that tensions were extremely high between Vietnam and China because of the twenty new military bases and airfields and one million PLA soldiers China had placed along the eight-hundred-mile land border between these two countries. At the same time, there had been a series of minor naval skirmishes over the Paracel and Spratly islands in the South China Sea. But most worrisome for China's neighbors was the recent military buildup on Woody Island in the Paracels. From the data that Nunez and Blake had transmitted before they were shot down, Desaix knew that the Chinese had just completed an airstrip capable of accommodating Russian-built Su-27s as well as constructing the docking berths for frigate-sized ships. It was not hard to conclude that this event, along with new military facilities at Zhanjiang in southern China, enabled aerial refueling and would allow the Chinese to defend a claim over the entire South China Sea.

Desaix saved his options paper and brought up a document on his screen marked CHINESE WEAPONS PURCHASES. He was overwhelmed by both the magnitude and diversity of their recent acquisitions. Russia had sold them eighty-three Su-27 long-range strike fighters, with at least sixty of them delivered in the past month. At the same time, the Chinese had purchased from them forty-six MiG-31 long-range interceptors, with arrangements to manufacture at least three hundred more at Sheyang under license. They also had bought 794 T-72M main battle tanks, fourteen A-50 airborne warning and control aircraft and long-range early warning radar systems from Moscow. The People's Liberation Army was now in the process of acquiring eleven supersonic TU-22M Russian long-range bombers and was negotiating with Russian and Ukrainian officials to purchase the 68,000-ton carrier *Varyag*, currently under construction.

There was no doubt in Desaix's mind that China's ambitions and Russia's need for cash made for a potentially volatile combination. But what surprised Desaix the most was a highly classified piece of information that China had turned to Israel for an aerial refueling capability to extend the range of its fighters and bombers, as well as for advanced electronic warfare capabilities and a radar system for its J-8 II fighter under development in Shenyang. He wondered why the Israelis were helping to arm a country that had been shipping nuclear missiles to Israel's traditional enemies in the Middle East. But in all fairness, Desaix thought, how different were the Israelis from the U.S. government, which years ago had shipped massive amounts of airplanes, tanks, and ships to both China and Taiwan in order to curry favor with both countries.

On the other hand, if someone representing a foreign country had taken those pictures, why would they have placed themselves in the precarious position of developing the film in China? That could have been compromising and self-defeating. Perhaps his line of thinking had been misdirected. Perhaps someone or some group within China was trying to embarrass the present government. But who? And why? If Chinese were responsible, whoever did it had to be part of a very sophisticated intelligence network, Desaix concluded. They had to have detailed knowledge of military decisions and information to take corroborative pictures of the train wreck. Could it have been some unknown terrorist group, a vestige of the post-Tiananmen student dissident movement? Or could it be a political-military faction who opposed Prime Minister Lee Ann Wu, a ruthless, enlightened despot. But why now, he wondered. As far as Desaix knew, there had been no intelligence to indicate that she was in any unusual political trouble. But he also knew all too well that intelligence was extremely fallible. He wondered what Moffat would think about getting firsthand knowledge of the situation. A trip to China . . .

"Dr. Clark, don't you think it's time to go home?" Toland asked, sticking his head into the room.

"Do you have any more intel on that secret Taiwan-China meeting?" Desaix asked.

"As far as we can tell," Toland replied, "Defense Minister General Y. K. Chang and some of his PLA subordinates were the only senior Chinese officials involved, along with their Taiwanese counterparts."

"Prime Minister Lee Ann Wu wasn't there?" Desaix asked.

"There's no evidence that she attended any of the meetings. What do you think that means?"

"Given the important nature of the meeting," Desaix replied, "her absence is quite significant. On the other hand, Chang does work for her."

"There's been no previous evidence of this type of schism," Toland said, realizing that this might be one of those moments in the life of an FSO when what appears to be an inconsequential conversation with a senior State Department official turns out to be the turning point in a major policy analysis or decision.

"You're right," Desaix responded, "but that might only mean that our intelligence has been poor, or that a military-civilian tension was of too low an intensity for us to pick up, or that something else entirely is happening about which we know nothing." Once again, he thought of the pictures and how frustrated he felt being at the mercy of secondhand information.

"Or as you often like to say, pick letter E, 'all of the above,' " Toland said, quoting one of Desaix's favorite aphorisms.

"Not in this situation," Desaix continued. "I have a feeling that there is only one choice."

"Which one?" Toland said.

"I wish I knew," Desaix replied, punching the buttons on his terminal. "That may be the question of the day."

"Speaking of the day," Toland said. "If you don't mind, I'm heading home. Otherwise, I'm not going to be able to function tomorrow."

"Thanks for staying around so long," Desaix said, waving him away, "and congrats on the good pickup. If you're not careful, I may make you our ambassador to Taiwan."

"But we don't have one there," Toland replied, laughing.

"Precisely my point," Desaix said. "You're too valuable to have such a distinguished post. I need you around here, especially when I'm not around."

"Are you going somewhere?" Toland asked, his interest piqued again.

"Good night," Desaix shouted, "and pleasant dreams. Now get out of here."

When the door closed behind Toland, Desaix sighed deeply, wondering how he was going to get Moffat to send him to China.

CHAPTER FIVE

Desaix rushed down the seventh-floor corridor to the State Department Operations Center. A crisis in the Far East was brewing and Moffat's late-night call made it perfectly clear that Desaix was to be in charge of managing it. He handed his ID to the security guard and passed through the glass doors that separated the sanctity of discreet diplomacy from the hurly-burly of activity in the State Department's nerve center.

Unlike in the rest of the building, Desaix felt particularly comfortable within this oversized international emergency room. The din of junior Foreign Service officers shouting and motioning to one another in their own patois of gutteral utterances and peremptory demands filled the air. If he didn't know any better, he could be walking through the trading pits of Wall Street with young men and women barking out buy and sell orders, or racing down the patient-filled hallways of a hospital emergency room. The adrenal rush was the same. Dressed in khakis and sweaters, these FSOs reflected the defiant informality that had insidiously permeated the department, pushing aside the pin-striped formality of the past. Desaix liked to think that he could identify with the youngsters.

These FSOs were his kind of people, action junkies who were willing to thrust themselves into the seductive allure of uncertainty, risk, and personal accountability. Desaix was one of the few State Department officials who knew that they routinely listened in on their superiors' conversations routed through the Op Center's switchboard. On occasion, he would request some privileged intel garnered from their unauthorized eavesdropping of conversations between world leaders and senior State Department officials. In turn, tongue-in-cheek, he promised them immunity from prosecution for violation of section 2510 of Title 18 of the U.S. Criminal Code, or that he would report them to the Public Integrity Section of the Department of Justice, the graveyard of power abuse investigations.

Unlike the rest of the department, these FSOs represented a new breed of foreign policy specialists nurtured both on the immediacy of CNN and the pulsating rhythm of MTV. So it was not surprising to Desaix that these "dippers," as he called them, baby diplomats in diapers, maintained their manic level of activity by constantly manipulating the latest electronic gadgetry splayed out in front of each work station. The Op Center had become a virtual FAO Schwarz of foreign-made crisis management toys. Hong Kong–manufactured clocks were tucked in behind plastic panels. Multi-colored Philippine maps of the world were inscribed on panes of glass. Green-glowing Taiwanese fluorescent computer screens stood alongside Malaysian-assembled four-color printers. Japanese fax machines, Indonesian-assembled intercoms, and German STU-3 secure telephones decorated every other desk.

Desaix proceeded through another set of electronically secured doors and down a long, carpeted corridor toward the Office of Crisis Management, a dedicated area within the larger Op Center designed specifically for international crises. He had helped create it when Donald Westview had been President. Desaix had won some hard bureaucratic fights to get the subsequent President, Allison Bonner, and now Richard Bartholomew to reaffirm his exclusive position as the U.S. government's principal international crisis manager. And he had made himself indispensable to them by serving as the government's primary institutional memory and skill bank.

As he approached the office with the overhanging sign, S/S—

O/CMS, CRISIS MANAGEMENT SUPPORT OFFICE, Desaix felt unusually tired, on the brink of emotional bankruptcy. He had given up any hope that he could change his personality and allow himself to tolerate the tediousness of normal daily living, filled with its fair share of routine and boredom. Emotional commitments and long-term relationships had always been simply transition points that allowed him to weather out the protracted time between international crises. Four marriages. Countless liaisons. His latest live-in arrangement with Mary Dougherty, now Director of the Secret Service, had foundered because of mutual preoccupations with respective careers. Like most passionate lovers, they had never really wanted to give themselves the chance to live an ordinary life. It would have destroyed their respective raisons d'être. Ironically, it was only in the world of international relations that he could effect change of any kind. In that large arena, he could assert the one element of his personality that had caused him so much trouble in the past—the need to control everyone and everything around him. In the parlance of his cousins from the bayous, Desaix was a control freak who embodied the essence of every Acadian pantry's "Holy Trinity"—onion, bell pepper, and Tabasco sauce. It was said of Desaix that he would eat anything, including people, that wouldn't eat him first. On the other hand, only Desaix knew that his ruthless intensity was offset by his contradictory Cajun attitude toward life: *Laisser les bons temps rouler.* Let the good times roll. Like most of his high-pressured colleagues, he just knew how to work and play hard.

At the end of the carpeted corridor was a series of glass-encased rooms, each with several people milling about. Desaix entered the room marked TASK FORCE ONE/EAP BUREAU: U.S.—PACIFIC RIM CRISIS. In many ways this twenty-by-thirty-foot room duplicated the appearance and ambience of the front office of the Op Center. A major part was taken up by a long rectangular mahogany table outfitted with a bank of unsecured telephone consoles. Each console was identified by a handwritten sign that designated the State Department agency or department involved in the management of this particular crisis—Agency for International Development, Legislation, Public Affairs, Politico-Military Affairs, Diplomatic Security, Legal, Consular Affairs. Occasionally, a representative from the CIA sat on the task force. But in this case there was none. Too bad, thought Desaix, that relations between State and CIA were so strained. State's huge Intelligence and Research Bureau, INR, had been transferred to the CIA in a massive reorganization of the intelligence community. Desaix now missed the intellectual cross-fertilization.

At the ends of the table were places for the coordinator and deputy coordinator of the task force. Usually, Desaix chose either the office director or the country desk officer as the task force coordinator to run the day-to-day aspects of the crisis. On a table to the right of the coordinator's chair lay five different clipboards marked Incoming Cables, Outgoing Cables, Situation Reports, Press Releases, and Logs. Alongside the clipboards were two conventional unsecured telephones. One of Desaix's rules of crisis management required that someone keep these commercial telephone lines continuously open, for despite all the sophisticated satellites and electronic equipment used to monitor a crisis, the most reliable form of communication was still the ordinary telephone.

On the wall at the far end of the room was a large blackboard filled with a roster of names under three separate categories—Action Officer, Taskings, Deadlines. On the top of the blackboard were three clocks, each one set to a time zone involved in the crisis: Washington, D.C., Beijing, Greenwich Mean Time.

Next to them was a small glass-encased cubicle containing two STU-3 telephones. That was where the classified calls were supposed to be made. In truth, most calls, whether classified secured or not, were handled on the unsecured lines. And the reason, as everyone knew, was quite simple. Once the unsecured lines were tied up it was very hard to get a secured call into the same place, because an unsecured line was necessary to acquire a secured call. Circular reasoning at best, thought Desaix, but accurate.

Through Moffat's telephone call to him, Desaix had achieved the first tenet of crisis management: make certain that you are invited to participate. In most cases, managing a crisis was a highly coveted position because it was one of the few places where a normally staid professional diplomat could shine and receive the recognition he so desperately sought. And managing a crisis was the best way to impact on history in a noticeable way. More often than not, diplomats left no trace on the course of historical events. At best, they hoped to be a footnote in a doctoral dissertation, for historians reflexively ignored the self-effacing men and women who performed the daily drudgery of political reporting and maintaining social contacts that constituted the essence of diplomacy. Instead, the historian, like a Hollywood producer, sought out the most dramatic events and the most charismatic characters. So it was no accident that history was inscribed in the minds of children by warped tales of scintillating personalities and heroic events. And nothing motivated Desaix as much as his desire to be embraced by the hands of history. It was his fundamental contention that, like a beautiful woman, destiny beckoned only those who approached her without any hesitancy, shame, or remorse. Looking around the room, he asked the most important question of the moment: "Who wants Chinese food or pizza?"

"We've already placed an order for four pizzas, double order cheese with everything on it, including anchovies," Renee Rydell responded, a fifty-nine-year-old Deputy Assistant Secretary of State for Management. Despite her frail appearance, she scurried about the crisis center dressed in colorful jogging clothing, Reeboks, and an effervescent disposition. Rydell was considered the doyenne of the Op Center, indispensable to its daily operations, as Desaix had learned grudgingly. He never liked to depend on anyone who made himself an integral part of the system.

"In a crisis involving the Far East," Desaix replied, "I find it strange that none of my people in the EAP bureau ordered Chinese food." He looked at the familiar faces around the room, sheepishly nodding their heads in agreement.

"Don't worry, Desaix," Renee replied, handing him a Situation Report, "the way this crisis is playing out, I have a feeling that you will have time to order several Chinese banquets."

"What do you mean, Renee?" Desaix asked, reading the Sit Rep with skepticism. As in the beginning of all crises, facts and information were, at best, scarce, fragmentary, and misleading. Desaix considered these bits of information factoids, half fact—half fiction.

"Too much sound and fury signifying very little," she replied nonchalantly. "Too much sushi without any *wasabe* mustard. No punch to the bite."

"According to the National Security Agency's Electronic Intelligence and Signal Intelligence," Desaix said, reading intently, "the Japanese have mobilized twelve light infantry divisions, six hundred and fifty combat aircraft, sixty anti–submarine warfare ships, and sixteen submarines in the South China Sea."

"Keep reading," Renee said, calculating the cost per slice of pizza. "They're all over the place."

"Several of their troop ships and combat aircraft are heading toward three straits—Malacca, Sunda, and Lombok." Desaix glanced at the map of the world. "That means that Japan is heading straight toward Singapore, Indonesia, and Malaysia."

"Oil," Renee replied. "Ninety percent of Japan's oil imports come from the Malay Peninsula and the Indonesian archipelago, or have to pass through one of those three straits."

"Yet there is no evidence that they are in any way short of oil," Desaix said, scanning the Sit Rep. "Aren't their major suppliers in the Persian Gulf—Iran, Bahrain, United Arab Emirates, Saudi Arabia? According to this report they have a two-year storage overcapacity, not including extensive oil reserves in Mexico and Venezuela."

"Read on, Desaix," Renee said. "It makes less sense as you learn more. Damnit," she added, "these pizza orders always drive me crazy. There is an extra piece or a dollar short."

"ELINT and SIGINT reveal," Desaix read, "that the Japanese Self-Defense Forces, JSDF, have placed multi-headed nuclear H-2 missiles at Tanegashima Launch Facility, fifty miles off the southern end of Kyushu Island. SIGINT Telemetry has picked up Japanese targeting of three Chinese provinces of Manchuria: Heilongjiang, Jilin, Liaoning. Several JSDF armored divisions have been moved to the northernmost Japanese island of Hokkaido—within striking distance of China."

"So what do you think?" Renee asked.

"From this information," Desaix replied, "it looks as if Japan wants to precipitate World War III."

"Come on, Desaix," Renee replied laughingly, "aren't we being a little bit dramatic?"

"Edwin, has the Senate Foreign Relations Committee or the Senate

Intelligence Subcommittee been informed of any of this yet?" Desaix asked a mild-mannered FSO who was the Japanese desk officer.

"No," Edwin replied, busily working at his computer. "I'm proceeding on your standard SOP—reveal nothing to no one unless it enhances our strategic objectives. I'm trying to keep it in-house as long as possible."

"Good," Desaix replied.

"Whatever happened to the open democratic system?" Renee asked sarcastically, knowing full well that the name of the game was to make certain that the crisis was managed from the seventh-floor Op Center and not from one of the other competing crisis centers at DOD, CIA, or most devastatingly, the White House. Once it got to the White House Sit Room, the crisis would be permanently co-opted by the National Security Advisor or his designees, leaving State permanently out in the cold.

"At this point, Edwin," Desaix asked, "what would you think should be our objective?" He liked Edwin Rittenhouse, a pleasantly rotund man who had served in Beijing and Tokyo.

"Collect information, restrict dissemination and access," Edwin replied. "And try to figure out what the hell is going on."

"Does it make sense to you that Japan has suddenly gone on the warpath without any obvious precipitant?" Desaix looked around the room, making certain that everyone was busy at their respective work station. Idle hands made for idle minds and dangerous gossip.

"No," Edwin replied. "To do what they seem to be doing they would have to repeal Article 9 of the Japanese constitution, the one that prohibits them from warfare and the maintenance of an army. They are only allowed a self-defense force, which is deliberately proscribed from any offensive action."

"What about China's expansionism?" Desaix asked.

"As far as I can tell, China's aggressive behavior in that region has not yet presented itself as a direct economic or military threat to Japan," Edwin responded hesitantly. "But, of course, there could always be that possibility."

"Is there any Japanese public sentiment for a war?"

"If anything," Edwin replied, "the latest polls reveal that over fifty-five percent of the Japanese population want a significant decrease in the size of the Self-Defense Forces. They need to use the savings for a peace benefit, to get their ten-year sluggish economy going again."

"So I have what seems to be a military crisis developing without a political, military, or economic rationale," Desaix said pensively. "What do our people in Tokyo say?"

"Pretty much the same thing you're saying," Edwin replied, punching up the latest TOP SECRET/NO DIS/NIACT cables on his monitor.

"Why don't you contact the Agency?" Renee asked. "Maybe they have their own reading on it."

"How long will it take for you to get the pizzas?" Desaix asked, clearly annoyed by her question. "I'm sure everyone is hungry."

"Sorry I brought up such a sore subject," Renee replied, "but it's hard for me to believe that we don't talk to one another just because the CIA absorbed State's INR bureau."

"Christ, Renee," Edwin said chuckling, "how gauche can you be. Have you forgotten Desaix's three basic rules of crisis management: control, control, and control?"

"All right, the point is well taken," Desaix said. "Get me anything that the Agency may have produced on today's events that wasn't already published in the *New York Times* or *Washington Post*."

"Both the National Intelligence Directorate, NID, and the National Intelligence Estimate, NIE," Edwin replied, "are pretty bland on the subject, other than noting 'unusual Japanese troop movements.' "

"So much for fraternal cooperation," Desaix said, staring at Renee.

"You mean fratricidal competition," Renee responded, wagging her forefinger disapprovingly at him. "I hate to inform you that there is more to the U.S. government than a Secretary of State and a President."

"Renee," Desaix said brusquely, "I think I smell the pizzas burning in the oven. Don't you think you should try to get them out before there's nothing left?"

"I get the hint," Renee said, turning to leave. "Just remember, Desaix, crisis management is a team effort designed to prevent a crisis from happening. It's not an opportunity for the best and the brightest Lone Rangers to make their mark on history."

"You're right." Desaix laughed. "Crisis management has become the daily administrivia of managing a gradually defunct State Department."

"Something doesn't compute, Dr. Clark," Edwin interrupted.

"What's the problem?" Desaix asked, alarmed by the SIGINT and ELINT reports flashing on Edwin's screen.

"Two divisions of elite Japanese troops were flown into Harbin, Manchuria," Edwin said incredulously.

CHAPTER SIX

D esaix, you certainly know how to pick out-of-the-way places,"
Moffat said as he stepped out of the bulletproof Cadillac limousine.

"Welcome to my G Street Club, Jimboy," Desaix said, assuming
the good ole boy attitude. The crisis seemed to have abated for a while
and the two friends were out on the town for some relaxation. The
Japanese "invasion" of China had not presaged World War III. Rather,
it turned out to be a preplanned Japanese-Chinese military exercise
about which they had not informed the U.S.

Desaix waved away the hovering Diplomatic Security Agents who
were scanning the run-down area surrounding Hurricane Alley, a converted warehouse in a blue-collar suburb of Washington. "Remember,
we're here to clear our heads and enjoy ourselves for a few hours. Then
it's back to the Op Center for me, and who knows where for you. If we
don't talk politics and keep your DS boys leashed in some dark corner,
no one is going to notice us—even in that ridiculous outfit you're
wearing," Desaix said, laughing as he watched his six foot three
friend, dressed in blue jeans, plaid shirt, and cowboy hat, walk across
the street toward the building with the flashing pink neon sign. This
was the side of Moffat he enjoyed most.

"I can already see tomorrow's *Washington Post* headline," Moffat said apprehensively, waiting for Desaix to catch up and stop laughing. "Sec State caught in zydeco love nest with best friend, Assistant Secretary of State, Dr. Desaix Clark."

"Jimboy," Desaix said, placing his arm around his friend's broad, stooped shoulder. *"Ne t'inquiétes pas. Laisser les bons temps rouler."*

"I know," Moffat replied. "Don't worry. Just let the good times roll."

"How often have we been quail hunting together?" Desaix asked, referring to their frequent barhopping junkets in the pursuit of that great Cajun pastime, *chasser la femme*—chasing women.

"Enough to make my DS agents nervous," Moffat replied. "They've more than hinted that you are not exactly the best role model for me, pointing out your impressive history of marriages and divorces."

"Wait a minute," Desaix said, defensively grabbing Moffat's arm as he opened the glass door to the dance club. "During the past twenty-five years that we've been friends, I have been married and divorced only four times."

"That's right," Moffat said, "twice as many times as I have. That makes you twice as poor an influence on me."

"Didn't you ever tell anyone about the years you spent in China, Thailand, and Vietnam?" Desaix asked.

"Of course," Moffat responded. "As a former professor of Asian studies at Berkeley, I had to do a lot of extensive field studies."

"Right. But did you ever tell your DS agents about the in-depth field studies you conducted in the fleshpots of Bangkok, Hong Kong, Taiwan, Tokyo, and Shanghai?" Desaix smiled, relishing the banter between them.

"Your point?" Moffat asked, disliking Desaix's mind games as much as Desaix liked to play them. He had always wondered whether this was how Desaix had worked with his psychiatric patients. But the specifics of doing therapy was a topic he could never get Desaix to discuss. His medical-psychiatrist existence before joining State was something Desaix rarely brought into their conversations.

"My point," Desaix said, "is that whatever holds true for me is equally true for you. So there is no need for you to climb on your high stallion of self-righteousness. We both have a pretty poor history when it comes to long-term relationships. Other than our own, of course."

"My friend," Moffat said in a half-mocking, half-patronizing tone of voice, putting his arm around Desaix's shoulder, "my friend, what would I do without you?"

"You would do the same thing you're doing now—jollying me along."

"Let's go inside before we miss out on all the fun," Moffat said, ignoring Desaix's tone. Beneath Desaix's jesting and teasing, Moffat always sensed an underlying need to assess the basis of their friendship. Was it real or was it simply a matter of convenience? Everyone who knew Desaix was very much aware of the axiom he lived by: trust is good but control is better. It kept them both on their emotional toes. But Desaix's opinion aside, it also allowed Moffat to manipulate him.

"Oh, one more thing before we go in," Desaix said abruptly. "The anonymous train wreck pictures were processed in China."

"Interesting," Moffat replied. "Try to find out who sabotaged the train and who processed the film. I suspect they may be one and the same."

"I am," Desaix said. "But so far I've got nothing conclusive."

"Welcome to China, my friend," Moffat replied, his arm around Desaix's shoulder. "The land of the indeterminate and indefinable."

"*Laissons nous amuser.* Let's go in and have fun," Desaix said in his thickest Cajun accent as they entered the dance club, followed discreetly by the two DS agents.

For a weekday night Hurricane Alley was unusually crowded, thought Desaix, making his way through the couples bouncing jauntily to the two-beat zydeco rhythm. The large square room was little more than the shell of a converted military Quonset hut. Uncomfortable wooden booths lined two sides of the barracks-like room. A black Formica bar covered the third wall. From somewhere in the back, perky waitresses dressed in cowboy boots, short skirts, and cowboy hats brought the rowdy customers plates of spare ribs, corn on the cob, and cole slaw. On stage at the far end of the room, Rockin' Bopsie and the Zydeco Twisters, a black band from Louisiana, were playing a song that was a cross between country-western music and rhythm and blues. Unlike a more traditional zydeco band comprised of fiddle, accordion, and the metal washboard known as a frattoir, this group had a saxophone, drummer, and massive amounts of electronic equipment.

"This sounds like good old rock 'n' roll," Moffat yelled to Desaix above the music, insinuating his way toward the bar.

"It's a cross between Fats Domino and Clifton Chenier," Desaix replied. "It's not pure zydeco but what the hell. It's good enough for picking up women."

"I've got a confession to make," Moffat said as the bartender handed them two light beers.

"Don't tell me you're coming out of the closet," Desaix replied, raising his bottle of beer in a friendly toast. He glanced around the room and noticed that the DS agents had faded comfortably into the background. At the far end of the room, a group of young women, probably secretaries, were standing around waiting for someone to ask them to dance. He nodded his head in their direction. A tall unassuming blonde smiled back.

"No," Moffat replied, "but I don't know how to dance to this kind of music."

"Oh, come on," Desaix replied, distracted by the blonde's inviting smile. "It's as easy as walking, except you shift your weight from side to side. I assure you it's a lot easier than being Sec State."

"Show me," Moffat said.

"Are you sure?" Desaix asked, taken aback by Moffat's willingness to make a fool of himself.

"Of course," Moffat said, holding out his arms. "If you can do it, I can do it."

"A little competition there?" Desaix asked.

"Teach me!" Moffat said.

"Okay," Desaix said, shrugging his shoulders to the smiling blonde. "Place your feet apart and shift your weight back and forth on the balls of your feet."

Moffat followed Desaix's instructions perfectly. Although he felt silly, Moffat was determined to learn the dance step.

"Good," Desaix said. "Feel yourself balance from side to side."

"It's like warming up for one of our games of touch football," Moffat said, shifting his weight, feeling increasingly more foolish.

"Now," Desaix said, demonstrating the next move, "step with your left foot, tap with your right, step on your right foot . . . and then step . . . on your left. Shift your weight from side to side as you step."

"Hold it," Moffat said, trying to mimic Desaix. "I take two steps with my left foot, shift my weight, then take two steps with my right foot. Is that right?"

"No. One step with your left foot, then tap your right in place, and then step on the right foot and step on your left foot. And that's one half of the step." Desaix held Moffat's waist steady with both of his hands. "Remember, all the movement is below the knees, so don't sway your hips or your shoulders."

"Am I getting it?" Moffat asked, bobbing enthusiastically.

"Yes," Desaix replied, proud of his student. "Now, instead of tapping with your right foot, dip your body ever so slightly so that it looks something like this—step left, dip right, step right, step left."

"How's this?" Moffat asked, priding himself on being a quick study.

"Relax more," Desaix said, as he tried to prevent Moffat's hips from swaying. "The music is fast, so you won't have the time to take big steps or lift your feet very high off the floor. Wiggle your hips."

"Swing and sway with Sammy Kaye," Moffat said, moving his large body effortlessly to the rhythm of the music.

"Now you're ready for the next half of the step," Desaix said. "You're going to do a mirror image of the step you just learned but on the right side."

"Got it," Moffat said. "Step right, tap left, step left, step right . . . brush . . . step . . . step . . ." Looking up and beaming with the pride of success, he added, "You Cajuns make dancing so simple."

"We believe that life is pretty complicated," Desaix answered, "so if you can't improve on it, we say *ainsi soit-il*. So be it."

"Desaix," Moffat said laughing. "Who the hell do you think you're bullshitting?"

"What do you mean?" Desaix asked, surprised by Moffat's tone of voice.

"Whether it's Cajun dancing or crisis management," Moffat said, "you always choreograph the steps beforehand so that there are no surprises. Nothing is spontaneous with you, my dear friend."

"Christ, where the hell did that sermon come from?" Desaix asked, taking another sip of his beer.

"Just a friendly observation from a concerned friend," Moffat said, moving in place to the fast-stomping music.

"Bullshit!" Desaix shouted, slamming his bottle on the bar.

"Take it easy," Moffat said. "You're going to get my guard dogs all excited and who knows what might happen to you if you don't calm down."

"You're not threatening me, are you?" Desaix asked facetiously. If he didn't know better he might have thought Moffat was trying to provoke a confrontation.

"Of course not," Moffat said. "I want to make certain that you don't get too cocky just because you're my dancing teacher."

"And so the twin-headed dragon of envy and competition once again rears its ugly head," Desaix said, placing his arm around Moffat's shoulder. "God bless friendship. Nothing concerning human nature is simple. Is it?"

"No," Moffat answered, hugging his friend, "especially with two horny single men who are trying to have a good time but are straining at the bit to talk about the ongoing international crisis."

"Christ," Desaix said, relieved. "I was wondering which of us was going to continue to break our sacrosanct rule not to work when we go out in the evening."

"Am I a friend," Moffat asked jokingly, "or am I not a friend?" He paused to take another drink. "Look how far I would go to keep our friendship intact."

"You mean asking me to teach you to dance was a way to avoid breaking our rule too much?" Desaix asked.

"One of us had to preempt the other," Moffat replied laughing, "so it might as well have been me. Otherwise we would end up doing nothing but talking about today's crisis."

"You son of a bitch!" Desaix said, shaking his head in disbelief. Usually it was he who manipulated Moffat. "Do me a favor."

"What's that?" Moffat asked.

"Please don't make a habit of co-opting me," Desaix said.

"Agreed." Moffat shook Desaix's hand. "Unless, of course, it's absolutely necessary."

"I say we move toward that blonde and her friends," Desaix said, nodding his head in their direction, "to see how well you've learned your dancing."

"Wait a minute, that blonde is too tall for you," Moffat said. "You take the brunette standing next to her."

"I don't believe it," Desaix said, glancing at the short, svelte brunette in the sequined cowboy skirt. "You seem determined to one-up me on everything. What's going on, Jimboy?"

"Forget it," Moffat replied. "Your psychological antenna is on over-drive." He placed his hand around Desaix's shoulder and led him through the crowded room toward the smiling blonde. The brunette by her side seemed totally oblivious to their intentions, scanning the room as if she were looking for someone in particular.

"I couldn't help notice your beautiful smile," Desaix said, as he approached the buxom blonde.

"Haven't I seen you guys before?" she asked, trying to quickly assess which of the two men was more appealing.

"We do TV commercials for a local car dealership," Moffat answered, taking the woman's hand and leading her onto the dance floor.

"What the—" Desaix was surprised and slightly annoyed by Moffat's fast move.

"So," the brunette asked, "are you going to ask me to dance or are we going to stare at each other a bit longer?"

Her sullen defiance attracted Desaix. She reminded him of Mary Dougherty. Both were straightforward.

"Yeah, sure," Desaix replied, taking her hand and leading her onto the dance floor. "Why not."

"Hey, don't do me any favors," she replied, pulling back.

"Sorry, forget it," Desaix said, circling her waist and staying at the perimeter of the dancing couples. "You're a good dancer."

"Thanks," she replied. "I like zydeco. It's different, yet familiar, if you know what I mean."

"I grew up with that music," Desaix said, feeling a bit of déjà vu. His initial conversation with Mary when they first met at the White House was as awkward and inane as the one he was having with this woman. Desaix thought he heard her mutter some words of approval but he already was lost in thought. Was it really preoccupation with their work that had caused the breakup? After her much deserved promotion to Director of the Secret Service, Mary traveled over seventy percent of the time. And when they were together there was so much catching up to do that it seemed as if they were always making love with some clock ticking away in the background. Moments of tenderness turned into recriminations, with both unwilling to admit the basic truth: neither would free up the necessary time to make the relationship work. Could it be that Mary was one more example of Desaix's need to pick women with whom he could never really develop a complete and lasting relationship? Was he programmed to self-destruct with a woman? More frighteningly, he wondered, was he condemned to follow a pattern of self-delusion that he could control people and events, when he was, in fact, impotent to do anything but watch events and relationships unfold without having any impact on their outcome.

"Do you always fall into a trance when you hear this music?" his dance partner asked.

Before Desaix could grab her wrist, she started to walk away.

"Wait a minute," Desaix yelled to her over the blaring music. "I'm sorry if I've done anything that offended you."

"You didn't do anything," she turned and shouted back. "That's the problem. Maybe you should continue to dance by yourself. You seem to enjoy that best of all."

A commotion in the middle of the dance floor forced Desaix to look around just as the DS agents rushed into the crowd, pushing aside the screaming dancers. People were bumping into one another, trying to flee the frightening scene.

James Moffat was sprawled in the center of the dance floor covered with blood.

CHAPTER SEVEN

Whater happened?" Desaix asked, examining Moffat as he lay there with a one-inch gash above his left eye.

The DS agents had pushed back the curious dancers surrounding them, providing a protective circle around Moffat.

"I don't know," Moffat said, pressing a wet compress against his forehead. "We were dancing. Then a guy came up to me, cut me with a knife, and disappeared."

"Just like that?" Desaix asked, looking around for Moffat's dancing partner. "He didn't say anything? No one saw him?"

"Even though he was white, he said, 'This is a present from the Tiger Eels.' " Moffat looked down at his new plaid shirt and was surprised by the amount of blood he had spilled. "It all took place in less than a split second. I don't think I could even identify him if I saw him again."

"Close off the exits," Desaix ordered the DS agents, "and call the department for more backup. Make sure to keep the local police out of this one. We don't want any media coverage. Refer all calls to the State press office."

"Wait a minute," Moffat said, trying to stand. "Let's not make this into more than what it is—a simple assault. No need to call for more agents or anything else." He looked around the dance floor. "What happened to my blonde?"

"Good question," Desaix said, scanning the room. The brunette was nowhere to be seen either. "Could she have done this?"

"Not unless she had three arms," Moffat replied. "Listen, Desaix, I'm fine. Let's not make this into an unnecessary crisis. We already had one today."

"Do you think this incident might have anything to do with today's crisis or those anonymous photos?" Desaix asked as they walked out the door.

"Please do me one favor, Desaix," Moffat said, inhaling deeply the brisk night air. "No conspiracies. No retaliations. No coincidences. And no speculations. Leave it rest."

"Wait a minute, Jimboy," Desaix said, while they waited for an agent to bring the limousine around. "I'm not the one who cut you above the eye shouting something about Tiger Eels. And I didn't say a word about the little crisis with China and Japan we tried to leave behind us for a few hours. But when some mysterious man cuts your face shouting some slogan that clearly has significance to the Far East—"

"Could have been any malcontent," Moffat interrupted. "Someone who was turned down for a visa or working papers."

"Strange that no one in the room recognized you except this one malcontent," Desaix commented, opening the car door for Moffat. "And don't you find it equally strange that as soon as you were attacked your dancing partner suddenly vamooses out of the place?"

"The only thing I find strange is that we actually went to Hurricane Alley in the first place," Moffat replied, laying his head back on the seat so Desaix could examine it more carefully.

"Take us to the George Washington University emergency room," Desaix told the driver, who had turned on the flashing red light that would allow them to speed through the empty streets. He had already handed Desaix the emergency medical kit carried in each limousine and had radioed the ER in order to prepare them for the arrival of the Sec State.

"No," Moffat said. "I told you, let's not make this a bigger incident than it has to be. I have a small gash on my face and that's all I've got, so let's not get too dramatic about it. You know better than I do that any cut on the face looks worse than it is because the face is a highly vascular area." Pausing, he added, "Even though I know that we did everything possible to disguise our identities, including the use of fake names to make the reservations, I still don't want the *Post* to get hold of this incident and blow it out of proportion. If that happened, I would be restricted to only sensible activities in the evening, which would be unbearable. But you know how the President hates scandals."

"All right," Desaix said. "Just tell me again what happened. And please don't insist that this was some frigging accident. Not when Tiger Eels sounds like some kind of Chinese tong gang." Desaix cleaned the wound with Mercurochrome and applied a butterfly bandage.

"Listen, Doc," Moffat replied, "you're doing a great job with my healing process so let's not spoil a good thing."

"As you wish," Desaix said in a resigned voice.

"I don't believe it! Desaix Clark acquiescing so quickly and effortlessly. I think that's more of a shock to me than this knife wound."

"You know what I'm going to do the minute we return to your apartment," Desaix said.

"You'll go over to the department and insist that the duty officer let you into the restricted INR area so that you can refresh your memory about the Tiger Eels," Moffat said.

"You know me well," Desaix replied as he cleaned up the medical debris. "Especially when there's a strange American mystery wrapped within an Asian enigma."

"Okay, I'll make things easier for you," Moffat said. "The Tiger Eels organization, you remember, with its characteristic tattoo of an eel wrapped around a sword, was an underground nationalist Taiwanese group that was created to drive out the Kuomintang after they massacred thousands of Taiwanese on February 28, 1947. A generation of doctors, scholars, and political leaders were murdered. I'm amazed that you don't know that much about them."

"And the organization is still strong?" Desaix asked.

"Like most underground organizations at the time that were dedicated to driving General Chiang Kai-shek and his barbarous henchmen out of Taiwan, the Tiger Eels became just like their new KMT conquerors. They got heavily involved in the criminal underworld and even started to collaborate with the KMT." He sat up, looking recovered. "They're not as powerful as they once were. But they make themselves known whenever U.S. government policy is perceived to be tilting away from an evenhanded approach to Taiwan and China."

"Are they *Qingbao Ju?*" Desaix asked.

"We suspect they work for Taiwan Military Intelligence," Moffat responded.

"But why would they strike you in public like that?" Desaix asked, wondering how Moffat knew so much about this group. And how did the group know where Moffat was going to be that evening? Too many questions were swirling around Desaix's mind with too few answers.

"You remember the old Chinese proverb," Moffat said, "kill the monkey if you want to scare the tigers?"

"What do you mean?" Desaix asked.

"I have a strong suspicion that both China and Japan are about to invade Taiwan. And I think that the Taiwanese government feels that the President and I have forged a secret alliance with both countries to support them in the invasion."

"This all sounds crazy," Desaix said.

"Tell me about it," Moffat said. "That's why I didn't say a word concerning any of this until I received some confirmation of what was happening. Not until today when you sent me your Sit Reps did I realize that the SIGINT and ELINT reports I had been receiving from the NSA for some time now, describing this very scenario, were accurate."

"Jim," Desaix said, "how long have we been friends?"

"About twenty-five years," Moffat replied. "Why?"

"Am I your Assistant Secretary of State for East Asian and Pacific Affairs?" Desaix asked brusquely.

"As of this moment you are," Moffat replied. "What are you driving at, Desaix?"

"Remember that wonderful word the Chinese have for friendship? *Quanxi.* Or as we round-eyed heathens tend to pronounce it, 'guanshi.' "

"That's right," Moffat said impatiently.

"When two people are friends they share their secrets, thoughts, and emotions," Desaix said. "Since I know emotions are not your strong suit, I've never pushed that aspect of our relationship. Instead—"

"Wait a minute," Moffat interrupted, his face flushed red, "is this emotional accounting day? Because if it is, you can stop right now." Crunching his face into a grimace of pain, he added, "I've got enough problems without your telling me what I do or do not owe you. Remember, Desaix, without our *quanxi,* you've got nothing. Not even the privilege of my being angry at you for having been such an ungrateful friend."

"Hold on," Desaix said, placing his hand on Moffat's arm in a gesture of friendship. "This whole situation is getting out of hand."

"What would you have done differently to make certain that the situation wouldn't turn into a confrontation?" Moffat asked, pulling back his arm.

"Honestly?" Desaix answered hesitantly. "Nothing. I wouldn't have done anything differently." He paused to assess Moffat's reaction. "I don't know what the hell is going on. But I want to find out. Look at it from my point of view. I get called into a situation in which it appears that Japan is invading China. But now it turns out that they are probably both ganging up on one small helpless island, Taiwan, for reasons that are totally unclear to me. Then a mysterious person, allegedly acting on behalf of a Taiwanese gang, personally attacks the Secretary of State to scare him and other senior policymakers away from supporting the invaders. Worst of all, my best friend and I have a major blowup because we are unable to discuss, in a civilized fashion, the events of the day. What this tells me is that something in our discussion is very threatening to one of us, or both."

"Always a shrink," Moffat replied, sounding disappointed. "You've got to understand, analyze, intellectualize, and rationalize. Can't you just let go without having to understand or control it?"

"Don't skirt the issue," Desaix said. "I still don't understand why China, a country without any expansionist history, would suddenly become aggressive and cuddle with Japan, its historical enemy."

"There is the Co-Prosperity Theory of a Greater Asia," Moffat retorted, "which posits exactly that scenario. China in concert with Japan would dominate Asia in the twenty-first century."

"That fanciful theory has been floating around for over a decade," Desaix replied, summarily dismissing the faddish think tank idea. He believed that the historical animosity between the two countries as well as their marked cultural differences were two strong reasons why they would never be able to form an effective alliance.

"If you're so eager to find out," Moffat said, "why don't you go over there and find out. Play superman. Try to stop the crisis singlehandedly. If anybody can do it, I'm certain you can."

"Why don't you stop the car and let me out here," Desaix said, instructing the driver, "before we both say things we'll regret." He opened the door and turned toward Moffat. "Maybe I'll take you up on that visit to China. But you already knew that, since I'm a sucker for a challenge. And I'm just about finished with my options paper. I'll have it for you tomorrow."

"Take care of yourself, Desaix," Moffat said, motioning the driver to proceed.

Standing in the cold, brisk air, Desaix pulled up his jacket collar and looked around. He was still in Maryland, standing at the intersection of Connecticut and Georgia avenues. Although he felt tired and emotionally drained, he needed to go back to Hurricane Alley and find the blonde. She should be able to provide him with the answer to the one question that bothered him the most: who attacked Moffat with a knife? She must have seen his assailant.

As Desaix hailed a passing blue Barwind taxi and instructed the driver to head toward the dance club, he felt that strange sensation in the pit of his stomach which always frightened him—a cross between anxiety, nausea, and fear—a signal that he was not in control of his life. From the viewpoint of his most reliable survival mechanism, his intuition, the day's events were overtaking his ability to discern a pattern. Too much was happening too quickly and he sensed that they were not a coincidence.

He paid the taxi driver and was relieved to see that the dance hall was still bounding with activity. He nodded to the bouncer at the door and walked into the raucous room like a male predator on the hunt. He recognized a few faces from before, but there was no sight of the blonde or her girlfriend. Damnit, he thought, what made him think they would still be there? Curiosity, he concluded. The same reason that drivers slow down on a highway to gawk at a car accident. Desaix was betting that although the two women didn't want trouble, they would come back to capitalize on their newfound notoriety.

He prowled the room, but still found no sign of them. As he was about to stake out the women's restroom, he heard someone call out to him. "How's your friend doing?" the blonde asked, smiling. "I hope it was nothing serious."

"Thanks," Desaix said calmly, not wanting to reveal his excitement at having found her. "He's doing much better."

"Good," she said.

"Do you want to dance?" Desaix asked, trying to make it seem as if he had returned in order to have some more fun.

"Sure," she said, leading him onto the dance floor. "I figured you'd come back."

"Why?" Desaix asked, holding her thin waist tightly toward him. "What made you think that?"

"You have hawk eyes," she said. "From the very first moment you walked in here, I could see you scan the room as if you were expecting trouble."

"You're extremely observant," Desaix said, pressing his body against hers, swaying to the rhythmic music.

"I should be," she said. "I observe people for a living."

"What does that mean?" he asked.

"I'm a credit analyst," she replied proudly. "If I don't spot that something's wrong with a customer then I haven't done my job, because most people lie on their financial statement."

"Did you see anything wrong with my partner this evening?" Desaix asked, holding his breath.

"You bet," she said. "That's why I knew you'd be back to find out the real story."

"What do you mean?" Desaix asked, fearful of what he might hear.

"You've got one of those faces that questions everything and everyone," she said, holding Desaix tightly.

"What happened?" Desaix asked.

"Nothing, really," she replied.

"What do you mean nothing?" Desaix asked incredulously. "Someone attacked your dancing partner with a knife and ran."

"I'm telling you nothing happened," she repeated. "No one attacked him with a knife. He slipped and banged his head hard against the wooden floor. Then he told me to get the hell out of there because his bodyguards would think that I pushed him. So me and my girlfriend ran out of the place before his guards could catch us."

"Do you know who my friend is?" Desaix asked, not sure whether to believe what she had just told him.

"Should I?" she asked. "Is he someone famous?"

"No," Desaix answered. "Not really."

"Is there something wrong?" she asked, letting him go.

"Yes," he replied, distracted. "Something is very wrong," Desaix repeated to himself as he left the woman in the middle of the dance floor and walked out. "Except I don't know what it is."

CHAPTER EIGHT

W hy did Moffat claim that a member of the Tiger Eels had at-tacked him, wondered Desaix, as he showed his ID pass to the night guard at the C Street entrance to the State Department. And why did friendship have to be such a goddamn fragile entity, dependent on emotional variables he, Desaix, could not control? Maybe he should forgo friendship and stick to something he *could* control, like a crisis in the Far East. Every crisis in which he had ever been involved had become a part of him and his sense of possessiveness. For Desaix, a cri-sis was not an independent entity. It was either *his* crisis or someone else's crisis. And it was in the management of a crisis that he could bury all personal disappointments and hurts. He could be rewarded for his selfless dedication to saving lives while covering himself in a shroud of professionalism, accountability, and, most importantly, emotional exhaustion. A crisis offered him the institutional analogue of the adrenal rush, a magnificent high that staved off an underlying depression.

"Do we have another all-nighter, Dr. Clark?" the guard asked as he greeted Desaix.

"International troublemakers are never very considerate," Desaix said as he passed through the metal detector. He wondered if anyone had ever been caught trying to smuggle in a weapon. For the most part the metal detectors and X-ray luggage scanners State used were psychological deterrents, dissuading the ordinary person from trying anything foolhardy. But a few years ago a deranged employee shot everyone in sight as he came through the main diplomatic entrance, forced his way through the lobby barriers, and was finally apprehended and killed on the second floor only after a major shoot-out with over half a dozen security guards. So much for protective barriers, thought Desaix as he proceeded into the Op Center. He smirked to himself as he realized that their real purpose was, like the stone fence around a mental institution, to keep the "deranged" perpetrators of U.S. foreign policy away from the more innocent general public.

"What's been happening?" Desaix asked, sitting down in front of a computer terminal alongside Renee, who was munching a piece of cold pizza.

"The usual statements by all the principals reaffirming their desire for peace," Renee said, looking bewildered.

"Who said what?" Desaix asked, turning on the terminal.

"Prime Minister Lee Ann Wu said China is simply conducting military exercises with its close neighbor and ally Japan," Renee replied. "It's only two A.M. You struck out? None of the midnight beauties were tempted to eat Cajun catfish?"

"You know I have a deep abiding passion for older women who eat cold pizza in the middle of the night," Desaix replied, smiling warmly.

"It was that bad, huh?"

"Why are you so surprised to see me?" Desaix asked. "You know I'm always hanging around here whenever something's going on in my region."

"True," Renee said, "but usually when you and the Sec State go out for the evening you rarely show up this early. So I figured you must have kicked up a lot of sawdust on the dance floor without having anything to show for it."

"How did you know that I was out with Moffat?" Desaix asked, always intrigued by what Renee knew about everybody and everything that transpired within the building.

"You forget, my dear Assistant Secretary of State," Renee replied, "that as the day-to-day head of the Op Center, I have to know where all the principals are going in case I need to reach them. And unlike your negligent self, your friend checked out to a place called Hurricane Alley, which I discovered when I tried to reach him was a country-western dance hall."

"You tried to reach him this evening?" Desaix asked.

"Sure, through the DS agents," Renee replied with a perplexed expression on her face. "Didn't he tell you?"

"Tell me what?" Desaix asked, biting his lower lip, a nervous habit since childhood.

"The Taiwanese Interest Section called up the Op Center to find out where Moffat was because they were extremely concerned about intel reports that they had just received regarding—"

"The Tiger Eels," Desaix interrupted.

"Yes," Renee said. "Then he did tell you."

"In a manner of speaking," Desaix replied, thrilled to learn that Moffat had not lied to him. Someone had attacked Moffat, just as his friend had said, on behalf of the Taiwanese Tiger Eels. But why would the blonde lie?

"You look relieved," Renee said.

"I am," Desaix replied mischievously, "but don't even try to understand it." He laughed, grateful that he still had a close friend in politics, where expediency was an occupational hazard. How could he have doubted Moffat? What was it about his own character that allowed him to believe a complete stranger faster than a friend about an insignificant episode, blow it completely out of proportion, and use it as a litmus test of a twenty-five-year friendship? It revealed more about his screwed-up dynamics than anything else, thought Desaix.

"Are you all right?" Renee asked, concerned that Desaix had suddenly become so quiet.

"Better than ever," Desaix replied. "What did Prime Minister Sammy Mori say?" Desaix asked, flipping through the ELINT and SIGINT updates.

"The usual Japanese bull," Renee replied, finishing her pizza. "Japan has no territorial ambitions, blah blah blah. China and Taiwan are close friends of the Rising Run."

"And the Taiwanese?" Desaix asked.

"As usual, they'll wait until Uncle Sam makes his first response and then support it—strongly or moderately. You know the U.S. doesn't sneeze without Taiwan saying 'God Bless You.' "

"Has President Bartholomew made any statements yet?" Desaix asked, hoping the answer would be in the negative. He needed a few hours of sleep and reflection before going in to see Moffat with his position paper on the crisis.

"Come on, Desaix," Renee replied, surprised. "Since when does the White House release a statement about an ongoing crisis without our chop on it? And we've been as quiet as a mouse—standard operating procedures. I haven't detected any major news interest, certainly not from CNN or any of the other major networks."

"What about the *San Jose Mercury* or *Newsday*?" Desaix asked, concerned that the second string newspapers, which were far more aggressive than their larger competitors, had smelled blood and were in hot pursuit. The *Mercury* had broken the story on the extensive corruption in the Philippines that eventually brought down Marcos and his entourage. And *Newsday* had made the devastating revelations about Serbian death campaigns and their strategy of ethnic cleansing. If Desaix were to create a new axiom for crisis management, it would be to forget the *New York Times* and the *Washington Post* and concentrate on the quality regional papers.

"So far so good," Renee replied. "Zippo."

"Then maintain the clamp on the news," Desaix responded. "Any leaks other than the usual ones from the Sec State or Pres are strictly verboten."

"Funny how the big muckamucks are allowed to leak top secret information to the press to serve their own political agendas," Renee said, "but we working stiffs would be thrown into the can for violation of the National Security Secrets Act."

"Welcome to the inequities of international affairs." Desaix laughed.

"Desaix, why don't you get some sleep," Renee said in a maternal tone of voice. "You look exhausted. If something of importance comes up, I'll wake you."

"I just want to scan some intel, then I'll take a snooze." He typed in the code word KEYNOTE in order to access the highly sensitive, compartmentalized CIA information on Prime Minister Lee Ann Wu. "What?" he shouted, as he read out loud the response: RESTRICTED ACCESS/NOT AVAILABLE.

"Why are you so surprised? You know the Agency closes us off every time we have a crisis. You're going to get the same response on Prime Minister Mori, and any principal in Taiwan, China, or Japan. So stop beating your head against the wall and get some sleep. Remember, tomorrow is another day."

"Thank you, Scarlett," Desaix said, realizing she was right. He would get the information he needed through the NSA, NSC, DIA, and other agencies. In the meantime, he would get some rest.

"*Fais-do-do, mon cheri.* Go to sleep, my dear," Renee said, eager to practice her Foreign Service Institute French.

"Maybe I will," Desaix said, walking toward the alcove adjacent to the bathroom where there was always a prepared cot. He put on the eyeshades and earplugs resting on the pillow and tried to relax. Within seconds he could hear the *chank-a-chank*, the little iron triangles of the Cajun music bursting through the windows of his childhood home on Prytania Street in New Orleans. He wrestled with the conflicting sounds and images that flooded his dreams.

Tightly holding a silver tray stacked with Wedgwood teacups and saucers, he walked carefully through the sun-drenched living room of his family's Corinthian-columned house. The nine-year-old boy felt overwhelmed by the splendor of the fourteen-foot ceilings and Tiffany glass window panels etched with scenes of St. George slaying the dragon and maimed bodies pleading for salvation. Why did there always have to be human carnage associated with spiritual redemption, the boy wondered as his little hands tightened their grip around the lip of the tray. He yelled at his twelve-year-old brother, Gaston, to stop calling him "momma's boy." But Gaston wouldn't listen and called his three younger sisters to come and see what their brother was doing. Only sweet, affectionate Antoinette defended Desaix against their older brother's taunts. Marianne, as usual, couldn't take sides and Georgette cowered in the corner, desperately trying to avoid the altercation.

Torn between his desire to physically attack his brother and the need to avoid incurring his mother's wrath by dropping the tray, the small boy negotiated an agreement with his brother—until he could retaliate. When he walked onto the veranda, his physician-father was rocking quietly in his chair in the distance, completely ignoring the boy's presence. Desaix wanted to scream at his father to attract his attention, but all he could do was remain silent. Someday he would do something so important that his father would take note of him, Desaix swore to himself.

He laid the tray on the table and walked into the family's crowded flower garden to appreciate the waxen-barked crape myrtles with their airy blossoms of red, purple, pink, and white nestled alongside the sweet magnolia. As he bent down to smell the flowers a bee stung him on the back. He ran screaming onto the veranda, tears streaming down his cheeks, bumping into the table and knocking over the tray of china. The precious cups and saucers crashed onto the floor, shattering into tiny pieces. His father said and did nothing. He continued to rock back and forth, reading his paper. His brother and sisters laughed. His mother ran out of the kitchen screaming, "You broke china! You allowed it to happen. It was not a time to smell the flowers. The garden is swarming with bees."

Drenched in sweat, Desaix awoke with the feeling that his life was expendable. And that scared him.

CHAPTER NINE

H ow's the eye?" Desaix asked, walking briskly into Moffat's office.

"I fell in the shower, if anyone asks," Moffat replied in a businesslike fashion, pointing to the small bandage.

"About last night . . ." Desaix started, contritely.

"Forget about it. We know each other too long and too well to go in for apologies."

"Being a good friend means never having to say you're sorry," Desaix said sarcastically, parodying the words of a famous 1960s film.

"What we're involved in right now puts a gashed eye and a blonde in perspective," Moffat said as he walked toward his desk and picked up some papers. "The intel you have in your options paper is just not possible." He held the papers out toward Desaix, who stood before him, grinning like the Cheshire cat. Desaix always did have the disconcerting habit of making him feel inadequate.

"*Quanxi* or no *quanxi* with the Chinese, friendship or no friendship, the evidence proves otherwise," Desaix replied, glad that after a quick nap he had been able to work practically all night on the report. He knew that the assessment of the situation he had just delivered was what his Cajun brethren called a *coup de foudre*, a bolt of lightning.

"But China stopped its expansionism years ago," Moffat replied defensively. He walked around his desk, a sprawling eighteenth-century mahogany table covered with the standard accoutrements of power, a secure STU-3 telephone console, National Intelligence Estimates, National Intelligence Directorates, and countless numbers of blue-tagged Top Secret Action Memorandums.

As Moffat paced the room, Desaix was impressed as he always was by the sheer bulk of space that his friend could displace in a room three times the size of any normal living room. "Instead of zydeco," he said, "maybe you should take up ballroom dancing."

"What?" Moffat asked, as if he hadn't heard the question correctly.

"Grace, my friend," Desaix said provocatively. "You need more grace."

"Grace? What the hell does grace have to do with the fact that China is about to attack Taiwan?" Moffat asked angrily, now self-consciously pacing the room.

"You walk as if you wanted to discard parts of your body," Desaix said. "Jim, you've got to feel the beat here in your hips," he said, willing to sound silly at a most inappropriate moment. To make his point, Desaix began to sway to the remembered rhythms of last night's zydeco music.

"I've got a potential crisis on my hands, and what does my principal crisis manager discuss?" Moffat asked, incensed. "Analysis? Strategy? Tactics? No, he's criticizing my congenital flat feet. Very helpful, Desaix. Very helpful. I couldn't have asked for a better friend in a time of need."

"Remember last night's lesson: always make certain that your arms swing like pendulums . . ." Desaix continued, going out of his way to ignore his friend. "One . . . two . . . one . . . two . . ." He held his arms out in front of him, as if they were encircling *une belle fille*, a beautiful girl.

"Why are you giving me such a hard time?" Moffat asked, his face beet red, stopping in front of the bone white mantelpiece. The two bergère armchairs facing the fireplace set the graceful tone of the room.

"Are you ready to explode yet?" Desaix approached Moffat and placed his hands on his broad shoulders.

"Is that what you're trying to do? Make me mad?" Moffat threw Desaix's arms off in disgust. "Wasn't our fight last night enough?"

"It doesn't take much these days to make a reserved, quiet Secretary of State strike out at his best friend, does it?" Desaix walked back to his chair and sat down with his hands neatly folded on his lap.

"Your point?" Moffat asked.

"With the proper provocation—dancing lessons if you will—or whatever—even China can become aggressive again . . ." Desaix replied, pointing to his report on the table. "It's all in there."

"CHINESE CRISIS MANAGEMENT," Moffat read aloud from Desaix's report. He looked up. "Why the hell do you always have to bust my balls every time you give me the goodies I've asked you to prepare?"

"It's called love." Desaix blew Moffat a kiss.

"It's more like S&M," Moffat said, scanning the top secret memorandum once again. His frown turned into a smile.

"Come on, Jim," Desaix said. "Tell me how brilliant it is. I was going to call it CHINESE BEHAVIOR: A CRISIS IN AMBIVALENCE, but I thought that sounded a little too pretentious."

"It's brilliant," Moffat replied.

"No . . . no . . . more. Much more," Desaix said. "Make me purr."

"You are a real agent provocateur," Moffat responded.

"You're a perfect example of what I've always told you, Jim," Desaix said. "If sufficiently provoked, anyone will blow, no matter how understanding or psychologically sophisticated he or she might be. What you lack, my friend, is a little more grace under pressure."

"I'll wager you that Sammy Mori is behind this," Moffat said, distraught after another quick perusal of the memo.

"Maybe," Desaix said. "But since the 1989 Tiananmen Square episode, when thousands of dissident students were killed or arrested in full view of the world media, and later the death of Deng Xiaoping and his octogenarian Gang of Eight, China has continued to pursue its own expansionist foreign policy in Vietnam and the eastern part of Cambodia as well as its oppression of Tibet and their other so-called Autonomous Regions."

"That's all true," Moffat argued. "But for the past two years China's aggression has ceased, and Prime Minister Lee Ann Wu has channeled her people's manpower into building up the country's infrastructure."

"So explain to me why they've been transporting nuclear weapons to the Middle East and why they went out of their way to shoot down our Mohawk reconnaissance plane?" Desaix asked. "And, by the way, why are the Chinese on the verge of assaulting Taiwan, a sixty-year ally of the United States? Just when some meaningful U.S.-Chinese negotiations are being conducted."

"Perhaps Mori is providing the kindling," Moffat replied.

"Maybe your Empress Dowager—"

"Wait a minute," Moffat interjected. "Why do you call her 'my' Empress Dowager?"

"It's just a figure of speech," Desaix replied, surprised by Moffat's defensive question. "Is there something you haven't told me?"

"Like what?" Moffat asked, annoyed.

"Well, tell me about her," Desaix said, curious about Moffat's irritable response. "The CIA profile literally consisted of information compiled from *Time* and *Newsweek*."

"I've negotiated with her several times," Moffat said in a more relaxed manner. "She's an extremely attractive woman, even for someone in her late forties. I found her to be both gracious and shrewd. As you know, she has a doctorate in political economics from Berkeley, so she knows the American mind very well."

"You taught at Berkeley," Desaix interrupted.

"Yes I did," Moffat replied, "but at a different time and in another department. She knows that we Americans, as a people, are impatient, goal-oriented, and pragmatic," Moffat continued. "Like most authoritarian world leaders, she both admires our international support for democracy and despises our moral hypocrisy, as evidenced by the double standards we impose in the areas of human rights and arms proliferation."

"She does have a point," Desaix interjected.

"In any case," Moffat continued, ignoring Desaix's comment, "Prime Minister Lee Ann Wu is ambitious, willful, and manipulative. She has to maintain a delicate balance between her allegiance to the repressive army and the burgeoning democratic movement. She was elected by a plurality of the popular votes in the new, fragile democracy. For that reason, she finds herself in constant conflict with her Defense Minister, Y. K. Chang, an ugly, ruthless son of a bitch."

"He sounds like your typical military general in any Third World country," Desaix said, waiting to see if Moffat knew or would say anything about the secret meeting between Chang and his Taiwanese counterparts. He wondered whether Chang had anything to do with sending those photos to the Sec State. They were certain to embarrass the Empress Dowager.

"He is. In any case," Moffat said, "I believe she's still amenable to the proper personal handling."

"Is that a hint?" Desaix asked, suddenly feeling again that he was being manipulated into the position of having to do something he wanted to do anyway—go to China.

"We'll discuss that point after you tell me what you really think about the crisis," Moffat said.

"To start with, I think the Empress Dowager is responding to a lot of pressure points that are manufactured right here, in the good old U.S. of A." Desaix continued. "As you can see from my report, I identify several things that are contributing to this boiling Chinese cauldron. Let's begin with the fact that China lost its Most Favored Nation trading status with the U.S., thanks to the actions of a Congress that was rightfully upset by China's abominable record on human rights. Now don't get me wrong, I don't approve of their human rights record either, but, having their MFN status taken away forced them to find new trading partners who were more reliable and less demanding."

Desaix paused and scrutinized Moffat's face. There was a look on it that he had not seen before. Beneath Moffat's seemingly insouciant manner Desaix thought he saw a frightened Secretary of State.

"Desaix, I can't believe that my hard-nosed Assistant Secretary sounds like a goddamn apologist for the Chinese," Moffat said, trying to hide his anger, but not certain that his formative years at a Quaker boarding school in Bucks County, Pennsylvania, had been altogether successful in teaching him the merits of silence, good thoughts, and good deeds.

"Don't you believe in the good old Christian precept of forgiveness of sins?" Desaix asked.

"Proceed," Moffat said, becoming exasperated.

"China, along with their neighbor to the north, the former Soviet Union, has lost its direction," Desaix continued. "For all practical purposes they are operating with some chicken gumbo–like ideology, part Communism, part capitalism, part social nationalism, part Confucianism, laced with a heavy dose of repression and fear."

"I'd say that's a pretty vulnerable position to be in," Moffat said.

"*Oui mon cher,*" Desaix said. "But that's just openers. Overlay that basic Chinese vulnerability with our removal of Most Favored Nation status, forcing them to lose billions of trade dollars. Then, for a little bit of spice, add our trade representative imposing 301 sanctions against them for violating our intellectual property rights."

"That simply means that they will have to cease and desist their copyright piracy," Moffat retorted.

"I think you forgot a small matter of fines and trade restrictions," Desaix said.

"Minor point," Moffat responded.

"Then what do you make of our continuously badgering them about driftnet fishing violations in the northern Pacific?" Desaix asked.

"They were ruining our salmon industry," Moffat answered, beginning to enjoy the role of devil's advocate.

"To add insult to injury, U.S. customs officers have been raiding and closing down Chinese textile firms operating in the U.S.," Desaix continued.

"Goddamnit, Desaix!" Moffat shouted. "You're the one who ordered Treasury to shut down those twenty-two textile factories. Not to mention for the umpteenth time the fact that you personally closed one of their operations yourself." Pausing, he added, "And don't tell me you did it only because you don't like senior Chinese government officials who took bribes and kickbacks. No holier than thou speech, I beg you."

"Remember your Quaker background, Jim. Just try to practice a few minutes of silence." Desaix went on. "Let's add to the above list a U.S. embargo imposed on any Chinese goods that we think are made with prison labor, which as you and I know constitutes almost sixty-five percent of the manufactured goods coming directly from China and Hong Kong."

"The U.S. government has always been opposed to the exploitation of prison labor. You know that." Moffat found himself in the awkward position of sounding both defensive and sanctimonious. If nothing else, he, like Desaix, prided himself on being a political realist and strategic opportunist.

"Tell the Chinese," Desaix replied, "why we only pay our prisoners a few dollars a day when they make license plates or serve as human guinea pigs for our benevolently rapacious pharmaceutical companies."

"Desaix, get off your moral high horse. It's grating." Moffat was getting impatient with Desaix's overnight conversion from the Wild Cajun to the newly empathic moralist.

"Jim," Desaix said, "I'm not arguing theology or morality here. I'm simply trying to point out why our relationship with China has eroded precipitously over the last few years. If we don't understand Chinese sensitivities vis-à-vis the U.S., then how are we supposed to avoid military confrontation?"

"And now I suppose you are going to bring up the Maritime Affairs problem? Please don't, I've had it with that one," Moffat said, moving restlessly in his armchair.

"All right, I won't say a word about our having imposed stiff fines and restrictions on their flagships," Desaix replied. "Let's talk a little bit about how in the process of improving our relationship with Taiwan, we exacerbated our diminishing relationship with China."

"Taiwan has a formal defense treaty with us."

"No argument there," Desaix replied. "But did we really have to go out of our way to have Taiwan admitted to our select economic club—the General Agreement on Tariff and Trade—while we actively campaigned to exclude China?" Desaix did not wait for a response. "And please don't forget how we encouraged our NATO allies, the French and the Dutch, to send Taiwan surplus submarines and frigates while we increased our own arms sales."

"Christ! You were the one who formulated all that policy," Moffat exclaimed. "Are you telling me now that you might have made a mistake?"

"Maybe," Desaix replied contritely. "As I'm explaining this all to you I think I'm beginning to realize what a major screwup I might have made."

"So our little tête-à-tête becomes an awareness session for you. Terrific!" Moffat said. "Should I charge you for your therapy?"

Desaix didn't reply. He didn't know what to think. So many thoughts rushed through his mind. How could he have helped to create a foreign policy strategy that might end up in war? What was all this horseshit about his psychological sensibilities and insights that would give him the ability to manage confrontations, crises, and conflicts? Maybe he should carry a professional card that read: Have insights, will fight. For someone who prided himself on being a formidable strategist, he had forgotten to take into consideration one important factor—the long-term cumulative effect of short-range tactical policy decisions. For ten years, he had helped squeeze the Chinese into cooperating on a whole range of problems—putting pressure on the North Koreans to stop their nuclear proliferation program, restraining the Khmer Rouge from intensifying their internecine war with the other Cambodian factions, and making certain there was an orderly transfer of Hong Kong from British to Chinese rule. He had pressured the Chinese into helping the U.S. without ever really rewarding them for their efforts. Had he inadvertently trapped himself into the classic tunnel vision characteristic of those who manage a particular region of the world or a narrow spectrum of U.S. foreign policy for too long?

"Don't blame yourself too much," Moffat said. "I'm just as guilty as you are, if not more so. I should have been tracking the increasing tension."

"If you don't have a strategic overview of this bilateral relationship, then who does?" Desaix asked rhetorically. Unfortunately, he knew the answer all too well.

"Come on, Desaix. Don't tell me that you've gone completely senile on me. You know the answer as well as I do. There is no one in our government who tracks our long-term strategic interests." Moffat walked to his desk and raised a classified monograph. "Here's a one-million-dollar study done by one of our 'Beltway bandits' telling me what I should be concerned about for the next five years. But you and

I know that the government doesn't work that way. We're lucky if the President can plan one week ahead."

"I know, I know."

"And then we have the problem of continuity. No one from one administration to another remembers why a particular policy was ever initiated or who initiated it. So we're always reinventing the same wheel. I could go on. But I won't. Instead, I'll give you one week. Then I'll have to bring everyone else in. Get over there, meet with the Prime Minister, and try to diffuse this situation as quickly as possible." As Moffat spoke, he realized that he was simply stating what Desaix had maneuvered him into saying from the very beginning of their meeting.

"What about the President?" Desaix asked as he started to leave the room.

"Don't worry. I'll take care of him," Moffat replied. "But I can only stall DOD, the NSC, and the CIA for so long. You just worry about one thing."

"What's that?" Desaix asked, smiling mischievously.

"*Quanxi!*" Moffat yelled as he picked up the STU-3 telephone. "Get me the White House."

CHAPTER TEN

Desaix had instructed the U.S. embassy in Beijing not to send an official delegation to greet him at the airport. Highly unorthodox, but typically Desaix. His nonceremonial arrival allowed him the luxury of a few hours of freedom before the controlled formality of his position restricted his movements.

The crowded, sputum-infested subway had taken Desaix to what had become his most reflective spot in the city. Standing in the middle of an almost silent Tiananmen Square, he recalled the vivid television images of June 1989 when the bloodstained treads of the PLA tanks crushed countless bodies of screaming students into a silent pulp. Then, he found himself unable to comprehend or articulate the enormity of the crime that he had witnessed. Yet time had passed, group memory had dulled, and U.S.-China *quanxi* had begun. And then the story had repeated itself with the Cambodian leaders of the genocidal Khmer Rouge. Supported by the senior Chinese leadership, the Cambodian faction had been responsible for the slaughter of at least two million Cambodians. And the world had done little, if anything, to express its moral outrage. Several years later, Desaix had directly negotiated with those social engineers of destruction to decide whether they were to once again rule the country, this time with world legitimacy.

How was he to respond to perpetrators of mass murder? He sighed with the world-weariness of a man destined to bear witness to unrelenting carnage. His cynicism, nurtured through the mind-numbing practice of realpolitik, had taught him the art of the reflexive diplomatic gesture, bereft of substance or emotion. Instead of going with his instinct to scream Emile Zola's famous *J'accuse*, he had learned to transmute his feelings into a palaver of meaningless politesse, beginning with the ritual diplomatic formality of introduction: "Your excellency, your honor . . ."

He fixed his gaze on the imposing towers and gates of the Imperial City. On the northernmost gate, the Gate of Heavenly Peace, hung the popular, omnipresent portrait of Chairman Mao, an orange-colored, apple-shaped face with a receding black hairline and an avuncular smile. A meticulous rendition of a carefully constructed legend.

How ironic, thought Desaix, that the Chinese Communist revolution was born of Mao's compulsion to foment dissent against the status quo. Although an obviously strained comparison, Desaix identified with that incessant need in Mao to criticize and fault those in authority. The psychodynamics that had forced Desaix to forage alone in the tempests of adolescence were similar to those that found Mao refusing to accept his own family's Confucian values. Both men had ventured forth through uncharted courses of personal turbulence and self-discovery. But Mao had become a revolutionary leader of imposing proportions, while Desaix had become a participant-observer, studying men like Mao.

The two large red banners bracketing the picture of Mao, exhorting the masses to praise his achievements, were stenciled incorrectly with bold white Mandarin letters. Desaix smiled to himself. This pervasive imperfection was China's saving grace, he thought, along with its sense of mischief and humor. Together, they salvaged the country from the gruesome realities of its highly structured social order, with its mandates for conformity and obedience.

To his left stood the Great Hall of the People, a Radio City–like showcase of spacious splendor that could accommodate the ten thousand loyal party representatives who would arrive twice a year to play

out their roles as elected representatives of their provinces and ham-
lets. It was here, thought Desaix, that these delegates shamelessly
granted legitimacy to a political process that rested on the shaky ballast of fear and repression.

But it was toward the Museum of the Chinese Revolution, a vast
rectangular building with an awkward facade of lopsided marble
columns, that Desaix walked. A visit to this veritable orgy of Chinese
Communist ideology had become a ritual each time he visited Beijing. With time to spare before his meeting with the American ambassador, he decided to stroll through the museum.

Not surprisingly, he felt comfortable walking through the long
musty corridors, dark empty spaces, and drab green walls plastered
with faded pictures of heroes and martyrs. He had always felt an undefined kinship with those men and women who had given their lives
to the cause. Although their names blurred into an alliteration of un-
pronounceable consonants and vowels, Desaix could envision himself
as one of those brave men fighting the imperialist aggressors—the arrogant British, the duplicitous French, the persistent Germans—de-
fending their right to become a nation state free of foreign
intervention.

Desaix was offended by several pictures, one of which portrayed
British warships destroying the port of Shanghai during the Opium
Wars of the late 1800s. Like many righteous schoolboys with a solid
Christian education, Desaix had learned at St. Ignatius Middle School
that the Chinese heathens, bereft of the greater Judeo-Christian
virtues of abstinence and divine salvation, had brought the terrors of
opium addiction upon themselves. It had taken many years for him to
learn that under the rule of Tzu Hsi, the original Empress Dowager, it
was the British who had forced the Chinese to accept the shipments of
opium as payment for an unacceptable trade imbalance with England.

Far more disturbing were more recent pictures of sleek schooners
owned by prominent American merchant princes transporting opium
to Shanghai. It always amazed Desaix how the later generations of
American scions used the contrived altruism of philanthropy to wash
away their ancestral stigma of commercial opportunism and moral op-
probrium. For Desaix, America was still a land of unbounded promise
and indelible corruption. And with only a small stretch of the imagi-

nation, not all that different from China. It hadn't been too long ago that a Kennedy family member had funded the Department of Ethics at Georgetown University, just one of the family's repeated attempts to wipe away the imprint of a politically unscrupulous legacy left by the paterfamilias, Joseph Kennedy.

Looking at an exhibition of rusted steel medical instruments, Desaix felt the strongest sense of kinship with Dr. Sun Yat-sen, a practicing physician who became the leader of the Nationalist Party and the first President of the Republic of China. It was ironic that two of Sun Yat-sen's disciples, Zhou Enlai and General Chiang Kai-shek, became lifelong adversaries. Zhou became one of the leaders of the Communist Party while the General became the founder of the Kuomintang, eventually fleeing to Taiwan after his army was destroyed by Zhou's forces. For Desaix, the fact that Sun Yat-sen, a medical doctor like himself, could become the leader of his country held out the seductive promise of a long-cherished dream that had been squelched once he had decided to become a crisis manager. Fortunately, for both Desaix and the vast mosaic of American citizens, he recognized this spasm of envy as a product of infantile fantasies nurtured by a voracious childhood appetite for fictionalized biographies of world leaders accomplishing glorified deeds. Desaix had decided early on to live life as if it were an extension of the Mardi Gras, where costumed horseback riders followed their captain in a mad dash through the countryside. A difficult lifestyle from which to alter history.

"Did you know that Chinese lice are yellow in color and North American lice are dark brown?" An unkempt Caucasian woman intruded into Desaix's ruminations with her question.

"I beg your pardon?" Desaix asked as he surveyed this slightly overweight woman in her mid-thirties who had quietly sidled up alongside him. Peculiar, he thought, taken by themselves her features were not particularly attractive. But taken together, she definitely appeared inviting. Her angular face, and light blue cat eyes sitting beneath thin arches of meticulously plucked eyebrows, were strangely attractive. Her five foot six frame was tucked comfortably inside a loose-fitting bright red sweatsuit. A broad smile and brilliantly white teeth bade him an unconditional invitation to easy conversation.

"You know, those nasty little creatures that infest our hair and body parts cleverly adapt to their surroundings as they suck their host's blood," she continued with the enthusism of a college major in zoology.

"Are you an entomologist?" Desaix asked.

"No, I'm just a student of small and large parasites. I find that parasites constitute the better part of the world's animal—and human—population. So I thought it would be best to learn something about them." She added matter-of-factly, "Those parasites in blue uniforms, those soldiers over there with their flashing Nikons, are Japanese air force officers."

"I'm tempted to ask how you know," Desaix said, "but I have this uncanny feeling that you would give me some type of response that would force me to keep on asking you more questions, for which you would provide me still another set of profound non sequiturs."

"You're pretty astute," she replied, "but I'm going to have to disappoint you. I'm simply a professional dilettante who continuously undertakes self-improvement courses to learn all sorts of esoterica that allows me to comment on almost anything of an inconsequential matter at inappropriate times." Her face lit up with a warm grin, and she held out her hand to Desaix. "My name is Phoebe Hill."

"I'm pleased to meet you, Phoebe Hill. My name is Desaix Clark," Desaix replied, shaking her hand but taking his time to release his hold. He noticed that she didn't resist. He also noticed that she wore no rings on her fingers.

"Desaix? That's French, isn't it?" she asked, staring into his dark eyes. She liked the strong features of his face and wondered whether his salt-and-pepper hair was prematurely graying. Everything about him seemed to radiate a quiet self-confidence.

"Cajun," Desaix replied, wondering what type of reaction it would elicit. He was impressed with her spontaneity and her facility for subtly eliciting information from him, a trait he had admired in Mary.

"Buckwheat Zydeco, Beausoleil, Chenier. All the great ones," Phoebe responded.

"I'm impressed," he replied.

"Don't be. I told you I'm an expert at esoterica. In my misbegotten youth I spent some time in the bayous and rice paddies of southwestern Louisiana. It was my way of feeling part of my parents' hippie generation. Kind of an ersatz Vietnam. I thought if I helped the poor farmers down there harvest their crops I was making up for the Vietnamese countryside that my father had napalmed as a navy pilot."

"So Phoebe comes from Phoebe Snow, the folk singer?" Desaix asked, thinking that her bold, forthright manner reminded him of the 1960s hippies.

"Something like that," she responded.

"And Hill?" Desaix asked. "Where does that come from?"

"Four generations of native-born Californians who settled down around La Jolla and Del Mar," Phoebe replied. "My grandfathers clipped coupons and lived off their trust funds," she added with a laugh.

"What brings you to China?"

"Would you believe me if I told you that I was a tourist?" she answered, breaking once again into her winning grin.

"Should I?" Desaix enjoyed jousting verbally with her.

"*Kěnéng.* Maybe," she replied.

"*Hǎo ba.* That's fine." Desaix answered.

"So you speak Chinese?" she said.

"*Wǒr búhwày jyǎrng Hànyěw.* I don't speak Chinese. That's pretty much the extent of my knowledge." Desaix paused. "You never did answer my question."

"Suspicious type, huh?" Phoebe started walking toward the doors. "Do you mind if we get some fresh air? It's kind of dark and gloomy in here."

They walked down the museum's broad marble steps to the entrance of the building and watched three elderly white-haired men, dressed in the old-style Mao jackets, throw a red plastic Frisbee to one another in the square.

"Amazing what they can do with that plastic saucer," Desaix said.

They watched as each of the men performed a particular trick. One man made the Frisbee skip along the ground. Another threw it in the air and made it turn around like a boomerang. The third man put such a spin on it that as soon as it left his hand it immediately returned.

"They're purposely showing off for us," Phoebe offered. "You want to play with it? I'm sure they'll let us take a turn."

"No. I've got to get going," Desaix replied, as he checked his watch. "I'm late for a business appointment. And it's been a good twenty years since I played with one of those toys."

"So you are a businessman?" Phoebe asked.

"Yes. Import and export of heavy machinery," Desaix lied, suddenly becoming impatient with her questions.

"Fascinating!" she responded. "My dad was also in the import-export business. Actually, I'm an assistant professor of engineering at UCLA, over here on a faculty exchange program. I usually visit this museum to get away from my students. This is one place I know they won't follow me. They wouldn't be caught dead in such an 'ideologically regressive' institution. In case you're not aware, it's unfashionable in China right now to be politically correct. The only thing that they're concerned about is making money and living like a rich American."

Her change from tourist to professor somehow didn't surprise Desaix. If anything, it piqued his interest. He had an uncomfortable feeling that whoever she might really be, she had a side of her personality that was both demanding and officious. Quite a synthesis, he thought to himself, a seeming 1960s flower child in the persona of a no-nonsense professional woman.

"Listen, is there any way that we can get together later on, at a more convenient time?" Desaix asked, clearing his throat of the phlegm that had been rapidly building up. The combination of bituminous pollution and unrelenting dust always made breathing the Beijing air painful to him. Just looking at the stooped street cleaners, with their gauze-covered mouths, made him want to cough.

"Having a hard time breathing?" Phoebe asked, concerned. "It took me over six months to adapt to this crud."

"I always forget how polluted it is here. It's gotten worse over the years," Desaix replied, spitting on the step.

Before he had time to excuse his uncharacteristic action to Phoebe, an elderly woman wearing a red armband blew her silver whistle and began to wave her arms frantically at him. In an instant, four police officers appeared in their unshaped green uniforms, shouting all sorts of unintelligible orders at Desaix. The men playing Frisbee stopped their game to watch the commotion.

Desaix tried unsuccessfully to extricate his right arm from the tight grip of an officer.

"Don't do anything. Let me handle this," Phoebe replied calmly. "It's against the law to spit on this street. Not a street three blocks from here, but this street. It's the only way that they can manage to keep a few important streets clean." Phoebe walked over to the old woman and spoke to her in Chinese, in a firm tone of voice. Desaix watched as the old woman cowered, nodding her head in agreement. Phoebe handed her a twenty-five-yuan note and received a receipt in return. Within seconds, everyone had dispersed.

"Welcome to China, Dr. Desaix Clark," Phoebe said pointedly, handing him the receipt. "The Assistant Secretary of State for East Asian and Pacific Affairs should know better than to spit on Chinese soil."

CHAPTER ELEVEN

As Phoebe helped Desaix out of the tiny orange taxicab, a veritable tin can on wheels, she lowered her head in a mocking bow. "Welcome to the American embassy. As your official control officer and political counselor, I welcome you to American soil."

"Thank you, Ms. Hill. I'm deeply indebted to you for your deft handling of a very delicate situation. Of course, I'm certain that you will keep this unfortunate episode to yourself," Desaix replied, hoping that she would be discreet, but certain that the expectoration episode would attain a prominent place in the oldies but goodies legends of Foggy Bottom. It would probably rank along with the one about the Assistant Secretary of State who had been deliberately left on the runway of a remote South Pacific island as the Secretary's plane took off, to teach him a not-so-subtle lesson about keeping the Secretary waiting. Desaix wondered whether Phoebe had any lesson in mind for him.

As in most large bureaucratic systems, the State Department had its own unspoken rivalry between management and labor, and the seventh floor of State embodied that separation. Any personnel physically located on the sixth floor and below were considered potentially hostile adversaries by those anointed and appointed principals who had their offices on the seventh floor, where the Secretary of State was. Desaix's office was on the seventh floor; Phoebe would have been on the fourth.

"That furry-hatted creature standing at the gate, the one with the green jacket, red epaulettes, and yellow stripes down the sides of his pants, is none other than 'Genghis Khan,' our sole source of protection against any massive onslaught of the 'yellow peril,' " Phoebe whispered, hoping that her conspiratorial manner would dispel the tension that had permeated the cab ride to the embassy.

"I assume that he is a member of the Gongabu Guards from the Public Security Bureau?" Desaix asked. The Gongabu had been founded by Kang Sheng, a lifetime consort of Mao's nettlesome fourth wife, and had been fostered by the high technological assistance of Western Europe. In the 1980s the Bundeskrimalant, the German super-police, provided the PSB with a clone of the computer that reputedly had led to the capture of the Baader-Meinhof terrorist gang. Not to be outdone by their European Common Market partner, the French immediately gave the PSB automated fingerprint files to be used for the purpose of fighting drug traffickers. As far as Desaix was concerned, no country was free of guilt for helping to build the impressive Chinese security apparatus that had led to the Tiananmen Square massacre. Even the United States had provided technical security assistance that enabled the PSB to intensify its surveillance of Western diplomats, journalists, and Chinese dissidents. What goes around, comes around, thought Desaix.

"If he weren't, I think we would be in deep shock," Phoebe replied.

Desaix gazed at the drab, squat, three-story stone building and decided that Ambassador Wayne Cartwright III must get depressed every morning when he arrived for work. A huge cement walkway surrounded the building where grass should have been. The trees and cropped bushes that hugged the security fence lent no grace to the landscape. An austere feeling, thought Desaix. Perfectly suited to the image China sought to portray to the world.

Phoebe pointed to a large sign dominating the bicycle parking area in front of the embassy.

"DON'T EVEN THINK OF PARKING HERE," Desaix read aloud, laughing. Directly in front of the sign stood a row of at least 150 identical bicycles chained to one another. Thank God, he thought, if nothing else, the Americans, like the Chinese, are possessed of a sense of humor.

"That particular bicycle space—the one in front of the sign—belongs to Ambassador Cartwright. And you know what he's like . . ."

Phoebe and Desaix both showed their State Department identity cards to the Chinese guard, who nodded his head and allowed them to pass.

"I bet he nailed the sign up himself," Desaix said.

In the guardhouse they passed through a metal detector monitored by a crewcut marine corporal whose principal function, like that of his colleagues the world over, was to lend the U.S. embassy a facade of invincibility. Unfortunately, because of their extreme youth and inexperience, the Marines were often the first ones to panic in an emergency, and the first ones to be thrown out of a host country for unruly behavior. What could one realistically expect from a typical American teenager, thought Desaix, who had never been outside of Boise, Idaho? Chinese dumplings were a poor substitute for *hànbǎobāo*, hamburger.

"The sign was the first thing he did when he arrived here a few months ago," Phoebe continued. "Six A.M. promptly, he was right out there, hammer and nail, bang, bang, banging away. The Deputy Chief of Mission lodged a formal complaint with the Chinese until he realized who had put up the sign."

"Did he bring his twenty-two-speed racer with him, considering he knew that he was being assigned to the 'heavenly repository of all bicycles'?" Desaix asked, laughing.

"No, I think he realized that the best way to ingratiate himself with the Chinese powers-that-be was to buy one of their finest."

"The Beijing Pigeon or the Shanghai Phoenix . . . ?" Desaix didn't hear Phoebe's response. As they walked through the hallway of the embassy his attention was distracted by the black-and-white photographs of past American emissaries to China that hung on the faded green walls. They were all of white men bearing stern demeanors and upright postures, born and bred from the finest that America had at that time, the self-proclaimed missionary and the white Anglo-Saxon Protestant cave dweller.

"What do you think, honky?" came a booming voice from the top of the stairs.

"Given the fact that you cashed out of your company some fourteen million dollars ago, I would say that you bought the more expensive Shanghai Phoenix," Desaix yelled as he raced up the stairs and hugged the big, burly black man in the handmade silk pin-striped suit.

"Unlike you white Cajun trash, I buy nothing but the best," Ambassador Wayne Cartwright III replied, holding the friend who, on more than one occasion, had saved him from being thrown out of the Foreign Service for insubordination.

"How good it is to see you," Desaix said, examining him at arm's length. "Still as handsome and impertinent as ever?" Desaix's cavalier, breezy manner testified to the bond of years of mutual frustration and major disappointments. Cartwright and Desaix had fought some major battles together in the trenches of the Foreign Service. And Desaix had called in all of his political chits to have Cartwright posted to China. As in most of life's endeavors, it was not what you knew, but who you knew. In the State Department, like most bloated and underutilized bureaucracies, the ambitiously bright could always make themselves known one way or another. And when they finally achieved some modicum of power, they reached out for those who were like-minded. It was Social Darwinism at its best—or worst. Or in Desaix and Cartwright's language, it was simply a matter of *quanxi*.

"If they hadn't outlawed the concubine system here, I would easily have had two wives and four mistresses by now," Cartwright replied. "Right, Ms. Hill?"

"Yes, Mr. Ambassador. You would have been crowned Thrice Potentate by the Masons, but I don't think that your current wife would have liked it," Phoebe replied, enjoying the camaraderie she was witnessing.

"And tell me, my Cajun stud, are you still fornicating indiscriminately or have you seen the merits of serial monogamy?" Cartwright asked, assuming that Desaix's bio had been studied by Phoebe earlier in the week and so he was not being unduly indiscreet. Both he and Desaix had cemented their friendship when they realized that they both lived by the same Chinese proverb: "A wife can never be so desirable as a concubine, a concubine never so exciting as an illicit love affair, an illicit love affair never so maddening as an inaccessible woman."

"I have sworn off wine, women, and song. But I have just acquired a new and unusual vice, thanks to Ms. Phoebe," Desaix replied, his eyes twinkling.

"Now, Ms. Hill, all I told you to do was to keep an eye on my good friend here," Cartwright said. "To make sure he didn't get into any trouble."

"On the contrary, it was because she did her job so well that I might enjoy getting into some more trouble. Just so she can bail me out. She's quite a crisis manager, Wayne," Desaix replied as he watched Phoebe turn red with embarrassment.

"Am I to understand, then, that you will continue to act like some redneck white trash, spitting all over the sidewalks of Beijing?" Cartwright asked in a sarcastic tone.

"Christ, if you guys were only half as good in political reporting as you are in disseminating disinformation on us poor tourists, we would have one hell of an embassy," Desaix replied.

"Disinformation! My black ass," Cartwright shouted. "One of the flunkies from the Chinese Foreign Ministry is waiting outside my office to make a demarche." He turned to Phoebe: "Please take care of the situation. Desaix and I will see you later on."

Cartwright took Desaix's arm and led him down the narrow, cluttered corridor to his office and closed the door behind them. The room reminded Desaix of his high school principal's office. Cardboard file boxes lined the peeling ivory-colored walls. At one end of the room an American flag stood behind an immense wooden desk, 1940s vintage, covered three inches deep with reports and documents. At the other end stood a black leather couch that had given a few too many years of service and a sticky glass-topped coffee table. Two straightbacked wooden chairs faced the couch in an attempt to create a relaxed chatting arrangement. Desaix gave the shabbiness of the room a long searching look and wondered whether China was considered a hardship post among Foreign Service officers.

"We're in deep shit, aren't we?" Desaix asked, looking into Cartwright's troubled face.

"If it were any browner, I'd say we struck oil," Cartwright replied.

"Do you know anything about photographs of a Chinese train wreck involving nuclear weapons?" Desaix asked. "They were sent directly to Moffat."

"No," Wayne replied abruptly. "Forget about those photos. We've got more important things to concern us."

"I've only been out of contact for twenty-four hours—what the hell has happened?" Desaix asked, worried that the momentum of the crisis might be reaching a point beyond which he might not be able to have an impact.

"While you've no doubt been watching *Gone With the Wind* for the umpteenth time in your first-class seat over the Pacific, our new Empress Dowager has really stepped up her war dance," Wayne said. "Moffat sent you this cable, which, of course, no one is allowed to read, except for the hundred intermediaries who made the cable possible."

Cartwright handed Desaix an envelope. Only a few pretenses of secrecy still remained in this new age of open-access computer technology. One was the sealed envelope.

Desaix opened up the obviously resealed envelope and read the cable.

NIGHT ACTION IMMEDIATE; TOP SECRET; EYES ONLY; NO FOR-
EIGNERS; NO CONTRACT; NO DISTRIBUTION.

PROCEED IMMEDIATELY TO SEE PRIME MINISTER LEE ANN WU.
TRY TO DISSUADE HER FROM INVADING TAIWAN WITH HER
JAPANESE ALLIES. PLAY UP JAPANESE BELLICOSITY, HISTORICAL
HATREDS. EMPHASIZE THAT JAPANESE WAR MACHINERY CAN BE
EASILY DIRECTED TOWARD MANCHURIA, NOT TAIWAN, ONCE IT
IS IN PLACE.

INFORM HER THAT THE U.S. IS EXTREMELY DISTURBED BY U.S.
ELECTRONIC INTELLIGENCE AND SIGNAL INTELLIGENCE THAT
HAVE PICKED UP JAPANESE MILITARY EXPANSIONIST INTEN-
TIONS. TELL HER THAT JAPANESE SELF-DEFENSE FORCES HAVE

PUT IN PLACE MULTI-HEADED NUCLEAR H-2 MISSILES AT TANE-
GASHIMA LAUNCH FACILITY, FIFTY MILES OFF THE SOUTHERN
END OF KYUSHU ISLAND. OUR SIGINT TELEMETRY HAS PICKED
UP JAPANESE TARGETING OF THE THREE CHINESE PROVINCES OF
MANCHURIA: HEILONGJIANG, JILIN, LIAONING. EMPHASIZE U.S.
CONCERN THAT THE JAPANESE GROUND SELF-DEFENSE FORCE
HAS MOVED SEVERAL INFANTRY DIVISIONS AND ARMORED DIVI-
SIONS TO THE NORTHERNMOST ISLAND OF HOKKAIDO.

MAKE NO MENTION OF CHINESE MILITARY INVOLVEMENT. LET
HER SAVE FACE BY PLACING THE BLAME ON THE JAPANESE.

PLANT MISTRUST AND DOUBT IN HER MIND. STALL FOR TIME IF
YOU FEEL WE NEED TO EVACUATE PERSONNEL FROM THE EM-
BASSY.

IF YOU ARE NOT SUCCESSFUL, INFORM AMBASSADOR
CARTWRIGHT THAT ALL DEPENDENTS MUST BE OUT OF CHINA
WITHIN SEVENTY-TWO HOURS. THEN GET THE HELL OUT OF
THERE YOURSELF.

YOU ARE NOT, I REPEAT, NOT AUTHORIZED TO NEGOTIATE ANY-
THING OTHER THAN A CESSATION OF TENSIONS. UNDER NO
CONDITIONS ARE YOU TO INVOLVE YOURSELF IN THE INTERNAL
AFFAIRS OF CHINA.

BONNE CHANCE!
JAMES MOFFAT

P.S. DOD, CIA, DIA, NSC WANT TO KNOW WHAT THE HELL YOU
ARE DOING OUT THERE. ALL YOUR FANS ARE AFRAID YOU
MIGHT MUCK UP THEIR PLANS AND TAKE THE ACTION AWAY
FROM THEM. I CAN ONLY COVER YOU FOR A COUPLE OF DAYS.

"Is it time to show the Empress Dowager the airline guide?"
Cartwright asked, his face twisting into a squirreled expression of an-
ticipatory mischief.

"Come on, Wayne, be serious," Desaix replied, annoyed. In the parlance of the Foreign Service, to show the airline guide meant that the
U.S. was prepared to offer safe haven, usually to a corrupt world

leader, in order to avoid unnecessary problems or bloodshed. Former world travelers included Batista of Cuba, Duvalier of Haiti, Amin of Uganda, Mobutu of Zaire, Marcos of the Philippines, and several Latin American luminaries who had sensed they were no longer welcome at home. That was far from the case with the Chinese Prime Minister, who, from what little Desaix could fathom, held the upper hand in the country.

"All right. But you can't blame me for trying to sound like the Pillsbury Dough Boy," Cartwright replied, using the derogatory term for the old-line WASP Foreign Service.

"Wayne, you've told me that we are in deep shit. I know that you've read the cable. Standard operating procedure. But knowing you, you've already set up an appointment for me with Lee Ann Wu herself," Desaix said, counting on Wayne's usual meticulousness.

"We've got exactly one and a half hours to brief you before your first meeting with the Prime Minister," Cartwright said. "If you hadn't screwed around at the museum, we might have had—"

"I get the idea," Desaix interrupted. "So let's start on the light and sound show. And try to make it a little more interesting and informative than reading *The Economist*." Desaix spoke with a restlessness that had come with the unexpected urgent tone of the cable.

"If you recall the cable you sent warning me of your arrival"—as Cartwright spoke he grabbed two cans of Diet Coke perched on his windowsill and tossed one to Desaix—"I think you wanted to know about the Chinese missile proliferation problem, and an updated version of Lee Ann Wu's Political Profile and Operational Code. So far so good?"

"So far, no evidence of Alzheimer's," Desaix replied. As Desaix had with Moffat, Desaix and Wayne had developed a smart-ass communication system that was a testimony to their lengthy friendship.

"Here's the lineup for this afternoon," Cartwright said. "A little bit on missile proliferation because we felt that you should have some of the latest info on it . . . It's really scary . . ."

"Do you think their ten-year history with production could be fueling this military juggernaut?" Desaix asked.

"In part," Cartwright replied. "I think they got carried away with a false sense of superiority and invincibility because they have become the world's major producer of missile technology. But the rest of their self-aggrandisement rests with their Middle Kingdom Complex, which our Empress Dowager has been cleverly cultivating over the past years."

"You sound as if you've been talking to the 'sluts and nuts' department." Desaix was referring to the noncovert division of the Central Intelligence Agency that prepares the psychological profiles on world leaders.

"We'll get into that. I mean, what's a surgeon without his scalpel? And what's a political psychiatrist without his Profiles and Op Codes?" Cartwright asked, knowing full well that understanding the psychology of a leader's approach to conflict was the backbone of Desaix's expertise.

"Can you really deliver all that in time for our meeting with Her Highness?" Desaix asked skeptically.

"If you stop asking me so many questions, then maybe we would have the time." Cartwright pressed the button on his STU-3 telephone and summoned the first briefer.

Desaix sat back in the worn leather couch, concentrating on the only question that really intrigued him. What was really motivating the Empress Dowager to rattle her sabers?

CHAPTER TWELVE

N*ee hăo ma?* How are you?" Prime Minister Lee Ann Wu extended her thin, long hand to welcome Desaix. "Please call me Ann."

Accompanied by an entourage of eight civilian and military assistants, she escorted Desaix and Cartwright through the empty marble halls of the Great Hall of the People.

"It is an honor to meet you, Madame Prime Minister," Desaix said, stunned by the appearance of the infamous Empress Dowager. No State Department briefings or photographs could have prepared him for the woman who stood before him. She was tall and thin, and her finely sculptured features radiated an attractiveness that was more European than Chinese. She could have been an Italian model painted by the Renaissance Florentine artist Piero Della Francesca, with her high cheekbones, slightly slanted hazel eyes, aquiline nose, and long black hair drawn into a chignon. The elegance of her simple black Western dress forced Desaix to dismiss the popular Manichaean portrait of her as some female variant of the deadly Dr. Fu Manchu. If anything, he found himself irresistibly drawn to her, much as he would be to a classical work of art that dared the viewer to fathom its emotional subtlety and grace. Desaix sensed beneath her clean, stylish lines a reservoir of passion and emotional mischief.

Ann, Desaix, Cartwright, and General Y. K. Chang, her Defense Minister, walked together up the broad marble stairs to a small banquet room decorated with silk wall paintings from Suzhou, the Venice of China. It was clear to Desaix that Ann had chosen to hold their talks in this overwhelming granite mausoleum, rather than in the dilapidated International Building of Negotiations, in order to create a sense of her country's great tradition and future potential. Very clever of her, Desaix thought. She probably knew that this room might make Desaix feel relaxed, because the region of Suzhou in southeast China was very similar to the topography of Desaix's birthplace.

Desaix wondered which of several Chinese negotiating ploys Ann would test out on him. There was a time, just before her ascendance to power, when Chinese negotiators would play out a guilt game Desaix dubbed "protect your friends." It was used as a pressure tactic, and implied that unless the United States showed flexibility and gave in to Chinese demands, Chinese leaders sympathetic to the U.S. might get into political trouble. Or perhaps she would play the "we really don't need you" game to avoid appearing dependent in any way on a foreign government. Desaix remembered the pissing contest that almost erupted around President Nixon's first trip to China in 1971. Senior Chinese officials were determined to make it appear as if the U.S. had asked for the invitation, rather than having responded to one from Zhou Enlai.

"Isn't it difficult to believe that my critics call me Tzu Hsi, the Empress Dowager?" Ann asked, motioning to Desaix and Cartwright to be seated opposite her at the carved rosewood banquet table.

"Perhaps they are jealous of you," Desaix replied, taken aback by both her directness and her uncanny intuitive sense of what he was thinking.

Staring at the Defense Minister, Desaix thought of all the reasons why he shouldn't like him. Chang possessed all the features that Desaix associated with the Chinese warlord—a squat, unattractive, menacing-looking soldier whose very presence bespoke threat, violence, and the disproportionate power he wielded in Ann's autocratic government.

"Your Southern charm betrays you, Dr. Desaix Clark," Ann replied. "These people, of whom many are in your own government, consider me as depraved as Messalina, more cruel than Lucrezia Borgia, and more despotic than Catherine the Great."

"I have found that one sign of a strong, vibrant, effective leader is the number of derogatory epithets that are heaped upon him—or her," Desaix replied, as he sipped the cup of green tea that had been offered to him by one of the unobtrusive attendants standing at the perimeter of the room.

"You, too, are said to lead an exciting life, Mr. Secretary," Ann responded coyly. All that she had studied about Desaix had convinced her that he was a throwback to a romantic era of individualism and certainty that had existed in the U.S. around the turn of the century. Certainly, there had been no one like him at Berkeley during the time she was there, except for a few misbegotten radicals who confused emotional intensity with political effectiveness. Yes, Desaix was a rogue whom she could have a lot of fun manipulating—and being manipulated by.

"Those who inform you have a rich imagination," Desaix replied cautiously, "and perhaps they, themselves, lead an emotionally or intellectually impoverished life."

"Well said, Dr. Clark," Ann replied. She wondered which of the many facets of her personality Desaix, the psychiatrist, would find most fascinating. And which of her traits, as a man, he would find most enticing.

"Please call me Desaix if you wish me to call you Ann," he said, smiling at the forced formality that such occasions engender.

"Already we begin to bargain," Ann replied laughing. "So it shall be . . . Desaix." If they had met at a singles bar in the States, she decided, she would have definitely succumbed to his easy patter and charm. But as Prime Minister, she had to endure a certain amount of ritualistic give and take before she could even consider reacting to the essential substance of their talk. What a drag, she thought.

"Thank you, Ann," Desaix said, impressed with her facile repartee in English. Desaix suspected that her particularly bold style was enhanced, if not completely molded, by her graduate school years studying political economics at Berkeley. Without being offensive or too intrusive, she had acquired the direct manner of the typical American female graduate student. He also decided that she had a better sense of the American mentality than he had of the Chinese. But he would do his best to make sure she didn't know that.

"How ironic that of the two of us," Ann said, "you, the American, have the more interesting name, while I, the exotic Oriental, have the more prosaic name."

"Perhaps, like all stereotypes, we should discard them if we really want to understand each other," Desaix replied, pursuing the first rule of negotiating with the Chinese—personalize the relationship. Or as Moffat had instructed, develop *quanxi.* Chinese officials viewed politics as a highly human process, rather than the working of institutions.

"Am I to assume, then, that you will not expect me to act grateful and submissive or wear a seductive long silk dress with slits down both sides trying to entice you to commit unwitting, evil deeds?" Ann asked, her pear-shaped Modigliani face breaking into a broad teasing smile. She recalled those wonderful sexual encounters when her American lovers insisted on her dressing in the slinky costume of the Chinese *femme fatale.* It definitely was a turn-on.

"Not unless you want to play a part in a remake of a Charlie Chan movie." Desaix turned to the expressionless face and broad shoulders of General Chang and guessed that the General's ordinary green uniform studded with gold stars cloaked a man with great ambitions. But because of his lack of reaction to the conversation it was impossible to judge.

"Can I presume that I am not dealing with a typical senior State Department official who must request permission from his superiors every time he clears his throat and utters a few words?" Ann asked, noticing that Cartwright had not raised his head even once to caution Desaix as he had done on numerous occasions with other officials.

"I will leave that judgment to you," Desaix replied. "As you know, I am here to try to defuse what the United States considers to be a very dangerous situation."

As he spoke, several waiters dressed in starched white jackets approached the table with trays of food.

"Matters of state should only be discussed with a clear head and a full stomach," Ann said, directing the servers to pour a clear liquid from a crystal decanter. She raised her glass of *máotái j ŭu,* her country's 120 proof liquor, and proposed a toast. "May the storm clouds dispel as quickly as they appeared and may the sun continue to shine on the old and new friends of China."

"To the success of those friends of China who are working to dispel the storm clouds," Desaix countered, cupping his glass in both hands and pointing it toward Ann, at once inviting her to drink with him and accept his challenge of peace.

"*Gānbēi.* Cheers," Ann replied. She put her lips to the glass, threw her head backward, and then tipped the glass toward Desaix to show him that it was completely empty. Her gesture implied that she expected no less from him.

The Chinese toast of glasses, as Desaix knew, was more than a mere formality or quaint custom. It entailed an invitation to engage in a repartee of clever words, clear thoughts, and physical sobriety. In fact, a guest's ability to match his host's consumption of alcohol was the beginning of one of many intellectual and physical tests of mettle. The Chinese used food to foster an oral dependency between the supplicant and the host. Distrustful of impersonal or legalistic negotiations, they pursued their objectives through a variety of stratagems designed to manipulate feelings of friendship, obligation, guilt, and dependence.

This highly psychological approach to negotiation reflected a culture that stressed interdependency rather than individuality, and a political system that perceived politics as the interplay between superiors and inferiors rather than between equals. The DIA, NSA, and FBI counterintelligence files were very clear on the fact that Ann had gone to great lengths to collect information on Desaix's opinions and preferences, in addition to his politics. So Desaix was curious to see how Ann was going to use this information. Seemingly insignificant dinnertime conversation and sightseeing banter were always viewed by the Chinese as an opportunity both to gain new information and to cultivate a mood of "friendship." But Desaix knew that when Chinese officials spoke of "friendship," or identified a foreigner as an "old friend," it implied obligations as much as good personal relations.

From her Operational Code that he had developed from the National Security Agency's SIGINT and ELINT, Desaix was aware that Ann had highly mixed feelings about Americans. On the one hand, she admired and coveted the power and economic progress that she saw in the West. Yet she resented China's dependence for modernizing on the same foreigners who had mistreated her country in the past.

"I think that we must begin by referring to the first principles of negotiation. Is that not right, Desaix?" Ann asked coyly, knowing full well that someone of Desaix's psychological sensibilities would have studied the basic principles of Chinese negotiations. She nodded her head ever so effortlessly at the waiters standing silently behind each chair.

"And what might that be, Ann?" Desaix replied, equally coyly. If he didn't know better, he might think she was manipulating him into an adolescent mating pattern. He had the distinct impression that Ann, the sophisticated American graduate student, was using the facade of the imperious Empress Dowager to toy with him both intellectually and emotionally. He wondered to what end?

"Oh, come, come, Dr. Clark. As one of the world's preeminent crisis managers . . . " she began, appreciating the fact that he wasn't above playing the classic statesman role of acting self-effacing and incredulous. But unlike most of his colleagues, she thought, he must like the theater of innuendos and shadows.

"You flatter me, Ann," Desaix replied. His stomach started to churn as he recalled Mao's words: "The higher the monkey climbs the tree, the further he falls." He sensed that she was setting him up.

"Control . . . control . . . control . . . " Ann replied, laughing heartily. "Am I not a good student?" She wondered what he would have been like as her graduate thesis advisor at Berkeley. Perhaps he might have been too demanding, insisting on a more sharply defined thesis than the one she had written—"Chinese Political-Economic Expansionism in the Twenty-first Century."

"You are an extremely good student," Desaix replied, his voice suddenly serious. "Unfortunately, I am here because my government feels that the current situation is getting out of control, to make a poor joke. We feel that if China's course cannot be diverted we will all suffer the consequences."

"Oh, you talk of such heady matters," Ann said, "while I simply propose that you relinquish control of our discussion for one hour while I feast you in a manner that you will find quite entertaining." She decided there was something both disconcerting and attractive about Desaix's intensity.

Cartwright, who had purposely not intruded himself into the conversation, stared at Ann in disbelief. Something was wrong. Very wrong. Ann was not behaving in her well-known no-nonsense, matter-of-fact manner. If anything, her behavior was flirtatious. And far too saccharine. Artificial. He hoped that Desaix wasn't being co-opted by this Chinese Svengali.

"I see that Ambassador Cartwright III appears a little skeptical," Ann said, preempting any statement that Cartwright might make that would spoil the relaxed tone of the meeting.

"As usual, Madame Prime Minister, I am always enchanted, if not a little bit surprised, by your hospitality," Cartwright replied, passing a handwritten note to Desaix that read "Crock of shit."

"As Ambassador Cartwright was so kind to remind me," Desaix went on, looking up from the note, "time is of the essence. My government is not desirous of going to war. But as you know from our history, if we are pushed to the limits, which in this case means if China proceeds on her course to invade Taiwan, then we have no other choice than to stop you." As Desaix spoke, he scanned General Chang's wrinkled potato-like face. It remained unreadable. I wonder how well he understands English, thought Desaix.

"As a native of New Orleans, Desaix, I know that you are a gourmet," Ann continued, completely ignoring Desaix's military threat. "I've arranged for you to sample a variety of our specialty dishes."

"I certainly appreciate your concern and hospitality," Desaix replied, trying to be content with the thought that when Ann considered it the appropriate time, his concerns would be addressed. He picked up his chopsticks as the waiter placed the first dish in front of him, a fish cooked in a dark brown sauce.

"This dish is called *hong shao yu,* a delicacy of Shandong Province in North China," Ann announced as they all began to eat. "It is a fish caught in Bei Hai Lake and cooked with ginger, chile, pepper, sugar, and scallion." She was impressed with Desaix's dexterity in handling the chopsticks. She could tell that he was used to eating Chinese food. He was a "tamed barbarian."

"Tasteful," Desaix said. "A nice combination of sweet and sour." If she is as clever as she seems, he thought, she would understand that he was conveying the fact that their negotiations would be both painful and productive.

"Our next dish is extremely special," Ann said next. "I think you will find it both interesting and tasty." She smiled to herself. She liked the way he was using the simple act of eating to convey a diplomatic message. Very Asian. But very unnecessary. She knew better than he why he was here. There was very little she could do to short-circuit the necessary, ancient rituals of Chinese negotiations, especially with Chang by her side. He was watching her like a hawk.

"Sounds fascinating," Desaix replied, concerned by the mischievous glint in her eyes.

Cartwright passed another piece of paper to Desaix, which read, "It looks like the light and sound show is coming soon," and continued eating his fish.

When everyone had finished his first course a waiter rolled out a cart containing a large frying pan crackling with burning oil sitting on top of a portable stove. A second waiter rolled out a cart with a large tank of water on it in which a spirited yellowtail fish swam freely about. With a slight motion of her head, Ann instructed the first waiter to commence the necessary preparations for the next course.

Plunging his hand into the fish tank, the waiter pulled out the flapping twelve-inch fish and thrust it in front of Desaix's face, so there could be no mistake that it was alive. Then he took a wooden stick from the cart and beat the fish's body mercilessly, until it stopped flapping. He flung it into the hot pan and cooked it for several minutes, slicing it up. During most of the preparation, it was obvious that the fish remained alive, its eyes agape in silent agony.

"Enjoy your next course gentlemen," Ann said nonchalantly.

CHAPTER THIRTEEN

As Desaix watched the yellowtail fish die its slow, tortured death his facial muscles tensed. The sparkle of delight that he had felt at the beginning of the meeting disappeared.

Ann took note of Desaix's abrupt change and was amused. He was so typical of the self-assured Occidental who arrived at the Middle Kingdom, threatening her and her people, yet revolted by such a simple Chinese culinary delight as a live frying fish. How different, she thought, were the balanced ways of her people. Unlike the self-deluding Occidentals who thought they were all-powerful, the Chinese knew it was really Shou-lao, the God of Long Life, who fixed the time of a fish's—or man's—death, having inscribed it on his tablets at the moment of birth. Death was to be greeted with pomp and mirth, not with the bizarre Western expressions of remorse or sadness. That was why the dour black uniform of mourning of the early days had been replaced by a silk robe filled with the colorful tapestry and symbolic patterns of the Kangxi imperial court. For the Chinese, death was a welcome invitation to an even Greater Kingdom, not the end of some misbegotten earthly voyage. How much the round-eyed barbarians had to learn, she thought.

"You don't seem to be very hungry, Desaix," Ann stated with disappointment in her voice. At the same time, she felt sorry for him because he was trying so hard.

"I thank you for your concern. But quite frankly, I'm not certain that I can devour any delicacy that is neither dead nor alive," Desaix replied, certain that Ann was testing him. But for what, he wondered. Courage? Ruthlessness? Callousness?

"You are right," she proclaimed, clapping her hands and ordering the waiters to take away the fish. "How inconsiderate of me not to take into account your Western sensibilities."

"Madame Prime Minister," Desaix replied, "perhaps we can speak further about the difficult situation our two countries find themselves in."

"Madame Prime Minister?" Ann asked indignantly. "I thought we would reserve those formalities for our officials, General Chang and Ambassador Cartwright." She was surprised that Desaix could not see through her official title.

"Thank you," Cartwright replied, smiling at her insult. In the world of high-level diplomacy, indifference from a host country official could mark the end of a promising career. And if nothing else, he was a careerist to a fault. He had cultivated the right friends and had touched all the right State Department bases. His assignments to both European and Asian posts, and his excruciating tour of duty as executive secretary for Secretary of State James Moffat had earned him the right to be insulted by a head of state.

"You see, Desaix," Ann continued, "even your vainglorious Ambassador Cartwright III knows how to prostrate his dignity in the presence of, as he calls me behind my back, the 'wicked Dowager of Shandong Province.' "

"Ambassador Cartwright is a man of many talents," Desaix said, trying not to sound defensive, "and discretion is certainly one of them. I know that he has the greatest personal respect for you."

"Come . . . come . . . now . . . Desaix," Ann replied, as she beckoned waiters carrying yet another silver tray crowded with delicacies—camel's hump and bear's paw. Garnished with colorful vegetables, the platter of meats represented what many considered two of Mongolia's finest dishes. "Let us eat these delicacies before our bitter words tarnish our tastebuds." She admired his loyalty to his friend, a trait she was certain assured Moffat's complete confidence in Desaix's execution of the Secretary of State's intended agenda for China—and her.

"How strange that the camel and the bear must become almost extinct before they are considered a culinary treat," Desaix said as he picked at the strands of meat.

"Desaix, perhaps you can explain to us why it is that we tend to appreciate only those things that we no longer possess," Ann asked.

"Laziness and ignorance. We take for granted those things we have," Desaix replied, realizing that Ann was really referring to the deteriorating relationship between the U.S. and China.

"Strange, isn't it," Ann continued, "that loss and confrontation should sharpen our sensibilities."

"The real question," Cartwright interjected, trying desperately to swallow the tough overcooked meat, "is whether irreparable damage hasn't already been done."

Ann hoped that Desaix wouldn't be derailed by Cartwright's hostile words. "True bonds can rarely be ripped apart if there is goodwill and trust," she answered. "Principles of friendship should never change. Isn't that right, Desaix?"

"I would agree with that," he replied, thankful that they were again focused on the issue at hand.

From previous negotiations with the Chinese, Desaix understood the sequence of events. After seeking to build a personal relationship with Desaix in her opening moves, Ann would now seek to gain his commitment to general principles favorable to her objectives. The first principle she wanted Desaix to agree to implied that friends never turn against each other. No matter what their differences might be. Loyalty, consistency, and dependability were keystone attributes of that relationship. And Desaix had to admit that the United States was not seen around the world as a good ally. How many times during the management of a crisis would he hear from former allies that the U.S. had changed the rules in the middle of the game. Sometimes he wished he could forget his own involvement with the infamous Panamanian military dictator who had been arrested by U.S. officials for subversive activities that had been aided and abetted by the U.S. government itself.

"Can you and I agree, Desaix," Ann asked, "that the principle of normalization between our countries has been guided by the Shanghai Communiqué signed by President Nixon and Premier Zhou in February 1972? As I recall, it emphasizes 'respect for the sovereignty and territorial integrity of all states' and 'noninterference in the internal affairs of other states.' "

"Clearly, I think that we can agree to the Shanghai Communiqué as a good starting point," Desaix replied, impressed that Ann could quote the language of the communiqué. He noticed that General Chang was jotting down some notes on a pad he removed from his jacket. They would probably be kept to provide Ann with written evidence of inconsistencies in American foreign policy, if she ever had to prove that Desaix had violated the basic principles of understanding. Or perhaps he was keeping a record of her performance in the negotiations in order to report any deviations back to his colleagues in the Central Committee.

What a woman, Desaix thought. Subtle and elliptical in presenting her position, as well as masterful in her use of political symbolism. A seemingly harmless dinner had become a movable feast of metaphors. The only thing that was missing was a Greek Chorus to highlight the latent meanings scattered throughout the meal. Desaix's early days as a diplomatic novitiate were replete with solving the mystery of latent messages. When he had accompanied National Security Advisor Henry Kissinger on his first secret trip to Beijing in 1971 in the capacity of notetaker, Premier Zhou Enlai had hinted at conflict within the Chinese leadership by omitting the name of Defense Minister Lin Biao from a list of officials who wanted to thank Kissinger for gifts he had brought from the United States. And a year later, Zhou indirectly suggested to President Nixon that he, Zhou, was seriously ill by quoting from a poem by Chairman Mao Zedong about the evanescence of life. Desaix could fill a book with such indirect information. On one subsequent U.S. visit to China, Mao obliquely indicated that he did not support his wife's destructive political ambitions by telling Kissinger that China's women were "too numerous" and caused "disasters." Desaix wondered what Mao would have said about Ann. He probably would have considered her a "successful disaster."

"Now that we have agreed on the basic principle of noninterference in the internal affairs of a country, I fail to see how China's actions are in any way inconsistent with our principles of mutual understanding," Ann replied coldly, waving another group of waiters into the room. Desaix was far more contemplative than she had been led to believe, especially for someone who was allegedly addicted to action.

"The United States has substantial evidence to suggest that both China and Japan are about to invade Taiwan," Desaix replied with a directness he knew he couldn't avoid any longer. "As you know, we have both a moral and legal obligation to defend Taiwan against any external aggression and—" Desaix cut his sentence short as two waiters walked into the room carrying a glass cage filled with dozens of writhing snakes.

"What is this?" Cartwright blurted out.

"I understand that you grew up in the snake-filled bayous of Louisiana," Ann replied, ignoring Cartwright. She recalled how she had recoiled the first time she had seen live snakes at a dinner. But through self-discipline and denial, she had learned to accept these creatures as useful props in the game of diplomacy.

"You're quite right. I did grow up amid snakes. But unfortunately, I never learned to appreciate them," Desaix replied. What in God's name was she trying to tell him this time, he wondered.

"*Shur tzan* is an extremely popular delicacy here in Beijing," Ann said, motioning to the waiter who had grabbed a cobra with a gloved hand. He brought it over to Desaix.

"Madame Prime Minister, with all due respect, I find this completely inappropriate," Cartwright said, standing up, ready to leave. "Your message is loud and clear. We will cable the Secretary of State that your response to Dr. Clark's message is a resounding no."

"Sit down, Wayne!" Desaix ordered, impatient with Cartwright's ignoring of diplomatic protocol. How many times had they discussed that an American ambassador represents his country's best interests, not his own personal feelings. Diplomacy was the art of the possible in a world of conflicting interests, transparent machinations, and acceptable duplicity. The business of negotiating required an infinite amount of patience for the game of smoke and mirrors, reflections of nuances and innuendos refracted through a prism of ambiguity and uncertainty. There was no room for certitude or rigidity. Certainly not righteous indignation. The diplomatic game as played by China was, by its very nature, alien to the American temperament. Americans required clearly delineated distinctions and a definite outcome. Not symbols. Not snakes and fish.

Cartwright sat down reluctantly.

"I see that we share another principle of mutual understanding, Desaix," Ann said laughing. "It is harder to control one's subordinate than one's enemy." She liked Desaix's frankness and appreciated his willingness to discipline his ambassador in front of her, although a most uncommon practice. But his true mettle was yet to be tried.

Desaix felt badly when Cartwright winced, as Ann had intended, at her statement. "Ann, as you know, our time is limited. Every moment that we avoid discussing the problem is one moment that takes us further away from resolving an escalating crisis," Desaix said, annoyed that she did nothing to stop the waiter from playing with the cobra right in front of his face. Clearly, Desaix thought, she was continuing to evaluate his strengths. She wanted to see at what point he would break, just as Cartwright had broken. But Desaix was intent on disappointing her.

Desaix sat motionless as the waiter placed the snake on the table in front of him, and put one hand on the snake's head and the other on its tail. The second waiter took Desaix's right hand and ran it one third of the way down the length of the snake's underside, resting it on a protrusion called the bile sac. As Desaix sat with his hand on the belly of the snake, the waiter sliced into the cobra's skin with a thin stainless-steel knife, and with a quick movement of his fingers squeezed the bile sac from the body. He placed the sac on a small saucer and returned the snake to the crowded glass cage. As the first waiter left the room with the cage, the second waiter squeezed the brown bile from the sac, mixed it with *máotái jǐu* in two small glasses and handed the glasses to Desaix and Ann.

"*Gānbēi!* Cheers!" Ann said, raising her glass to her lips.

"*Gānbēi!*" Desaix replied, quickly swallowing the thick, brown liquid. He wondered what added significance this little theatrical event had for their negotiations. Was it a hostile message that the Chinese would one way or another "de-fang" the bilious venom of the dangerous U.S. snake? Or was this Ann's way of being conciliatory? Was she trying to tell him that he could neutralize the present crisis if he would be courageous enough to trust her?

"This drink," Ann explained, "is reputed to be good for your heart . . . "

"And for promoting virility," Desaix added, smiling as Ann flushed. Most unusual reaction for a woman who had spent several years in the States, thought Desaix. Could she be faking a false modesty?

"We Chinese do not like to beat up our friends," Ann replied, with a directness that she could see startled Desaix. "You Americans are the guilty party in this mounting crisis."

"In what way?" Desaix asked calmly, knowing that her statement was a classic ploy to apply pressure. He recalled a favorite Chinese tactic used around the time of President Gerald Ford's visit, a technique Desaix called "purposeful unpredictability." Without any explanation, senior Chinese officials would suddenly cancel long-standing scheduled meetings. Or they would refuse to confirm a senior U.S. official's appointment with his counterpart until the very last minute. But the tactic that Desaix appreciated the most was when Chinese officials would show extreme concern about the comfort of a newly arrived guest, only to follow it by an exhausting all-night negotiating session to both pressure and disorient the American.

"As you are Assistant Secretary of State for East Asian and Pacific Affairs, representing the United States of America, I can only blame you and your superiors for allowing this crisis to become uncontrollable."

Although Ann sounded stern, Desaix sensed that she was only mouthing the empty words of a prepared script. The Chinese were notorious for portraying themselves as the injured party in any negotiation, a tactic aimed at putting their adversary on the defensive.

"For over a decade you have been supporting and encouraging

the Democratic Progressive Party, the Taiwanese independence movement, and violating the mutually agreed upon principles of one China," Ann continued. "Over our continuous protests, the U.S. and its allies have been exporting arms to Taiwan—the French, naval warships, the Dutch, submarines, and the U.S., F-16s."

"Madame Prime Minister," Cartwright interrupted. "Senior Chinese military officials were duly notified. At the time of the arms shipments, none of your senior military officials objected."

"Please, Ambassador Cartwright," Ann replied, "I am fully aware of your explanations. As I'm sure you know, those senior military officials are no longer with us."

"I'm sorry to differ with you but—" Cartwright countered.

"I think that you've made your point, Mr. Ambassador," Ann replied, making certain that he didn't finish a sentence she would not have been able to contradict.

"Ann, tell me how else the United States has been at fault in this crisis," Desaix asked in an empathic tone of voice, hoping to decrease her intensity.

"We have made a demarche over numerous issues," Ann replied. "Illegal customs raids on legitimate Chinese businesses operating in the U.S. Confiscation of Chinese manufactured products because they were allegedly made by Chinese prison labor. Impounding of Chinese fishing boats in northern Pacific waters because of our driftnet fishing. And, of course, your withdrawal of Most Favored Nation status, which forced us to become noncompetitive in your consumer markets." Ann recited the litany of complaints in a monotone voice reminiscent of a Buddhist mantra.

Desaix was impressed by her list of grievances. It was almost as if she had been privy to his report to Moffat. He was certain as well that she had been fully briefed on his inappropriate outburst in the demarche to Ambassador Guan and, at the appropriate moment, would use it to embarrass him and his government. It was simply a matter of time.

"As far as I know," Desaix replied, sensing he was speaking primarily for General Chang's record, "various representatives of my bureau have been trying to work out those problems with your officials."

"But progress has been too slow," Ann replied curtly.

"Excuse me," Desaix countered, sounding equally indignant, "but these are issues that our government feels your officials have ignored or have been unwilling to address in a constructive way. And those are the issues that we feel have fueled the present crisis."

"And what might they be, Dr. Clark?" Ann asked, fearful that Chang would use it as evidence that the negotiations had failed.

"I think you know," Desaix replied. "Against our continuous protests, China has been exporting missile and nuclear technology despite the fact that you are signatory to the Nuclear Nonproliferation Treaty. In violation of the Bacteriological Warfare Conventions, you have developed a formidable biological warfare capability. We are equally disturbed by your violation of human rights principles—the incarceration of political dissidents, the repression of religious freedom, and the continued illegal occupation of Tibet."

"And you have evidence for these accusations?" Ann asked, glancing at General Chang, who screwed his potato face into a grimace of displeasure.

"Yes," Desaix replied. "We have evidence collected over the last three years that suggests that China has shipped forty CSS-2 IRBMs to Iran for a reported nine billion dollars. Iraq has received the "8610" short-range ballistic missiles with an estimated range of four hundred miles. And Syria has received from you the M-9 SRBM with an estimated range of nine hundred miles and a two-thousand-pound payload."

"Well, well, Dr. Clark. It seems as if the only country in the Middle East with whom we have not been trading has been Israel," Ann replied laughing. "We certainly don't want to be accused of being anti-Semitic."

"Of that," Desaix replied nervously, "you don't have to be worried."

"Well," Ann replied, "at least we're doing something right." At this point, she hoped he would end his diatribe against China and proceed on to the next point of proposed constructive measures to resolve the crisis.

"You and I both know that Israel has become your invaluable joint venture partner in the missile and nuclear technology you export," Desaix responded.

Cartwright looked at Desaix in anguish. What was he trying to do? For over twenty years the fact that Israel was helping the Chinese develop their missile capability was an extremely sensitive issue. Only a few of the senior decision-makers knew anything about it.

"Come now, Dr. Clark," Ann chortled. "You certainly have an active imagination. Have you ever thought of writing fiction?"

"I hold the same attitude toward novels as did Confucius," Desaix replied. "To me they represent the lowest of human endeavors, for the novelist starts with a lie around which he or she elaborates a fanciful story."

"So too with diplomacy," Ann replied. She wondered who his favorite authors were. They both probably enjoyed those writers who could describe the ambiguities and complexities of life in a forceful, dispassionate way in a world where it was difficult to separate evil from good.

"Except that Israel's participation in developing your M-11 SRBM missile for export to Pakistan and Saudi Arabia is unfortunately not a matter of fiction," Desaix replied.

"What conceivable reason could Israel, or we, have to sell armaments to her avowed enemies?" Ann asked. "It certainly is the ultimate of cynicism."

"It certainly is, isn't it?" Desaix agreed. "But it is an unfortunate testimony to both greed and power."

"How so?" Ann asked.

"I think the answer is obvious," Desaix replied, wondering why she was purposely opening up the Pandora's box that had contained the silent conspiracy. He berated himself for pursuing the issue further than he had to. Was he trying to torpedo his own negotiations?

"Please try to enlighten us, Desaix," Ann responded provocatively. If he wanted to hang himself, why not provide the noose, she thought.

"Israel sells missiles and technology," Desaix replied, "because they desperately need hard currency. Nothing more, nothing less. In the arms bazaar of the Middle East, there are no enemies or allies—simply financial interests and transactions."

"Very interesting," Ann replied, nodding her head in silent approval of his explanation. But why was he pressing the point?

"I would say it's outright scandalous if it is true," Cartwright interjected, making certain that the official record of the meeting reflected the fact that he was completely surprised by Desaix's disclosure. This would allow the U.S. government some meager measure of deniability.

"Well, perhaps someone in our government might know something about this matter," Ann replied coyly. She hoped he would pick up the clue.

"I suggest you ask your senior officials at the National Defense Science, Technology, and Industry Commission, the Ministry of Foreign Affairs, and at the most senior levels of the Military Commission." Desaix directed his comments toward General Chang.

"I certainly will," Ann replied, looking at General Chang, who squinted his eyes in disdainful approval.

From his last-minute State Department intel briefings, just before he took off to China, Desaix knew that Chang had a disproportionate amount of power in China. Chang directly commanded the People's Liberation Army, most of whom were personally loyal to him. At the age of eighty-one, he was the last remaining member of the Second Generation Leaders who had participated in Mao's six-thousand-mile Long March from Jiangxi Province to Shaanxi Province, fleeing his arch enemy, General Chiang Kai-shek.

General Y. K. Chang was the sole political and ideological bridge between the eight elders who had controlled China during the 1980s and early 1900s and the cadre of Third Generation leaders helping Ann rule China. The Third Generation leaders were in their early fifties and had played a minimal role in the early years of the People's Republic. But Desaix knew that although they were better educated and more cosmopolitan than their predecessors, these new leaders lacked the policy authority and political networks of the Second Generation. The crisis they were precipitating, thought Desaix, could be interpreted as a desperate attempt on their part to consolidate their power internally by expanding China's de facto hegemony over its Pacific neighbors.

But Desaix sensed that there was a tension between Ann and Chang. Maybe Chang was responsible for sabotaging the train and sending those photos to Moffat in order to embarrass Ann's government, thereby placing himself in the position of becoming the alternative "responsible" leader. Were Chang's secret meetings with senior Taiwanese officials part of an attempt to reach a solution that included the overthrow of Ann?

"Dr. Clark, you have impressed me with your knowledge and your desire to defuse this crisis," Ann said abruptly, fearful that the negotiations might deteriorate. "I am ordering General Chang to look into the matter. I give you my word that no military activities will continue as you and I attempt to assess the present situation and work out a solution acceptable to all parties. I expect your government and the Republic of China, Taiwan, to act accordingly."

"I will immediately cable the Secretary of State and the President the good news," Desaix replied, noticing that for the first time General Chang was smiling.

"Well, Ambassador Cartwright, what do you think of the wicked Empress Dowager now?" Ann asked as she shook his hand.

"I think that the Prime Minister is a shrewd statesperson who understands that war benefits no one except those who never wanted peace in the first place," Cartwright replied. What the hell is she up to? he wondered.

"Ann, I've enjoyed our meeting—and meeting you," Desaix said. "Now that we are working toward a common purpose, I hope you will again call me Desaix. Dr. Clark is so formal."

As they shook hands, Desaix could feel himself reacting to her as a woman rather than a Prime Minister. He sensed that beneath her cool exterior was an inviting sensuality that stirred all the fantasies he had ever had about Asian women.

"Let us walk downstairs together," Ann suggested, taking Desaix's arm and leading him down the marble staircase.

Outside the Great Hall of the People they confronted what looked like an anti-American demonstration. Phalanxes of green-uniformed policemen were trying to hold back a crowd of students shouting epithets in English. The students waved makeshift banners warning the U.S. not to interfere in the internal affairs of China.

Desaix smiled, sensing that the demonstration was orchestrated by Ann as a parting reminder to him that she had public support for any anti-American sentiment articulated during their meeting.

As Desaix stood next to her, listening to the screaming crowd, a student broke through the police barricade, aimed a pistol at Ann, and fired.

CHAPTER FOURTEEN

Her clothes soaked in blood, Ann's body slumped into Desaix's arms. Pandemonium broke out. Frightened demonstrators ran in all directions. General Chang shouted orders to the police, who apprehended the youthful assailant. Dozens of university students were whisked away, screaming obscenities as they fought back. Cartwright ordered his waiting protective detail of Diplomatic Security Agents to form a *cordon sanitaire* around Desaix and Ann, who lay inert on the steps of the Great Hall, where Desaix had gently eased her. He grabbed one of the agent's portable telephones and relayed the news to Phoebe Hill, instructing her to fax the information to the Sec State on a Night Action/Immediate/EYES ONLY basis.

"Ann, don't move," Desaix said as he ripped open her blouse to locate the site of bleeding near her left shoulder.

"Don't you think that you are a little bit too presumptuous?" Ann gasped, trying to laugh, obviously in shock.

"I think I found the bullet's entry point," Desaix said. He took off his red silk tie and wound it around her shoulder.

"I feel very lucky that you are a medical doctor . . . " Ann said, wincing as she pressed his probing hands against her breastbone to

counter the pain. "You seem so very certain in everything you do . . . "
She watched his face, intensely preoccupied with her well-being.

Desaix smiled at her, grateful that her assailant was a bad shot. The
wound was superficial and would heal quickly. The bullet had disturbed little as it entered and left her body. He could hear the distant
wailing siren of an approaching ambulance.

He helped her stand up, conscious of the pressure of her body
against him. His instincts told him that her closeness to him was for
more than support, but he hoped against all his experience that he
was wrong. A sudden trauma, a sense of vulnerability, and overwhelming gratitude frequently set the stage for a dependent patient
to idolize a seemingly omnipotent psychiatrist. In this case, an Empress who was on the borderline of inappropriate sexual enticement to
express her gratitude. Yet he couldn't deny his attraction to her lithe,
effortless femininity. He was being drawn to her against his better
judgment.

Desaix assisted her down the steps, passing through a phalanx of
her cheering supporters, toward the waiting ambulance. Cartwright
shook his head disapprovingly at Desaix, as if he had been privy to his
friend's private thoughts.

Ann sat in the ambulance while a Chinese military doctor ban-
daged her shoulder. She smiled and waved her good arm at the distraught members of her entourage, trying to assure them that she was
all right.

"Let us see whether we can get away from the prying eyes of my
Defense Minister," Ann whispered, squeezing Desaix's hand tightly.
His hands felt warm and reassuring.

Desaix remained silent, wondering what she meant. He sighed
with the resignation of an old warrior confronting a familiar foe. As
far as Desaix was concerned, sex and politics were inextricably inter-
woven. But always through the threads of manipulation, duplicity,
and self-delusion. He wondered how much of Ann's sudden coquettish
behavior was a continuation of the negotiation process.

Desaix continued his silence as Ann stepped out of the ambulance,
took his arm, and led him toward Chang An Boulevard.

"Go away!" she shouted, as she waved away her preoccupied protective detail to a discreet, yet accessible distance. Desaix was surprised

at how harsh she sounded with them when only a few seconds before she was so vulnerable and grateful.

"Now I truly appreciate the reputation that has preceded you, Dr. Clark. You have shown yourself skillful as a diplomat and comforting as a doctor. Just how much do you know about us Chinese?" Ann said with a teasing quality in her voice, thrilled that he was torn by his attraction to her and his need to be judicious.

She led him through the entrance of the Forbidden City, which had been closed to tourists since dusk, nodding to the two military guards standing casually beneath a red screen with golden calligraphy and the Chinese flag.

"I know that the Chinese follow two contradictory beliefs," Desaix replied. "Confucianism for the mind. Taoism for the heart. What we Americans call the id and the superego."

"You are quite right. They are not too different," Ann replied, brushing lightly against him as they walked down the empty paths. "Confucius was the practical philosopher for ruling a country efficiently, organizing society, and establishing patriarchal family life. On the other hand, Taoism embodied a deep pagan romanticism, a wordly-wise protest against the notion that man could make nature conform to his designs."

"You're beginning to sound like Huang Di, the father of Chinese civilization . . . " Desaix laughed. Like any good seductress Ann was working both his heart and his mind. His yin and yang.

"So you have read his *N'ei Ching Su Wen?*" Ann asked, impressed that Desaix had studied the earliest chronicler of traditional Chinese sex practices. Most likely when Desaix was a medical student, she thought, since the Yellow Emperor had written his book as part of a more extensive study of medicine and philosophy.

Desaix looked around as they walked. The Forbidden City reminded him of the medieval European fortress-cities of southern France. Thirty-foot-high walls. Guard towers. Immense wooden gates.

Insisting she was fine, Ann slipped her arm through Desaix's. They walked through the entrance tunnel of the Tiananmen Gate and continued arm-in-arm down a long path that led through Tuan Men Gate and the Meridian Gate. They soon found themselves directly on the grounds of the Inner Palace. Ann pointed to the Five Phoenixes, five pavilions from which past emperors had presided over military parades and ceremonies.

"The Jin Shui He, the Golden Water Stream, running just in front of us, crosses in a gentle arc from east to west." As she spoke, Ann reached up and caressed Desaix's face.

Desaix instinctively pulled back from her. He knew better than to be enticed into what the KGB called a "honey trap," a compromising love relationship.

"What's wrong?" Ann asked in a reassuring voice.

Desaix looked nervously around the paved courtyard. There was something surrealistic about the whole scene. A senior State Department official being sexually enticed by the beautiful Prime Minister of China in the Forbidden City while a war between their two countries was imminent. If he didn't recognize when he was being expertly sandbagged by an extremely shrewd, manipulative woman he had better turn in his psychiatric shingle. This wasn't the first time a head of state had tried to compromise him into a honey trap. All of his significant negotiations with senior officials of the Blue House, the Korean counterpart to the White House, had taken place in a Korean Central Intelligence Agency–controlled whorehouse. Throughout the entire meal two hostesses catered to his every whim—food, drink, and companionship—while the hostess watched and orchestrated the proceedings. But this was different, Desaix thought. Ann was acting as both the conductor and orchestra player. And he wasn't sure that he enjoyed a woman having so much control.

"Your eyes tell me one thing. But your body tells me something else." Ann held him at arm's length. "Perhaps we may be proceeding too quickly."

"I think it's simply a matter of jet lag," Desaix said, noticing that her protective detail had disappeared.

"Don't worry, no one is around. Simply you and me," Ann replied. "Romantic isn't it?"

"Ann, we're treading on very dangerous ground," Desaix responded, torn between a rush of desire and the feeling that he was being set up to be compromised later on. Yet he couldn't help himself. Something about her drew him to her against his better judgment.

"I thought you enjoyed danger," she replied, attracted by the dark, deep-set eyes that reminded her of her father's.

"The only thing on my mind right now," Desaix said, hoping he could contain his emotions, "is to accomplish the task that I was sent to do—stop a potential war." He gazed around the courtyard, trying to locate whoever was out there watching them.

"Trust is not one of your strong suits, is it?" she asked laughing.

"Trust is not a commodity that can easily be bought or sold," Desaix replied, wondering whether a female Prime Minister who, despite the fact that she was elected by a plurality, nevertheless ruled over two billion Chinese through force, intimidation, and terror could ever be considered trustworthy.

"But it is a commodity that can be manipulated," she replied.

"If the hen announces the dawn," Desaix recited,

> *"Instead of the cock,*
> *If the affairs of State*
> *Are in the hands of women,*
> *If the prince in bed*
> *Is the one to be mounted,*
> *Then will the Empire fall apart."*

As he finished the second-century Chinese poem, Desaix bowed from the waist. At least he could try to end her seduction by entertaining her.

"Yang Chen is one of my favorite poets," Ann replied, clapping her hands together enthusiastically. "Are you trying to tell me something?"

"As I recall," Desaix responded, "this poem was written as a warning to the Emperor of the Celestial Empire to be wary of women who had too much influence over him, for they might succeed to the Dragon Throne by cunning."

"And, my learned one," Ann asked provocatively, "do you know what these nefarious women did when they attained the Dragon Throne?"

"They promoted other women and eunuchs to ruling positions," Desaix replied. "I am familiar with the story of Empress Wu Zhao, an eighth-century ruler who rose to power from the position of Fifth Grade Concubine at the court of Emperor Taizung."

"Really?" Ann asked disingenuously.

"At the mature age of sixteen years she was appointed one of the palace maids to the Royal Toilet," Desaix continued, staring into Ann's incredible eyes. "Upon entering the harem, she was given the name of Most Beautiful Wu and the job of standing by the Emperor's side while he urinated, holding a bowl of water so that he could immediately rinse his fingers." Desaix paused, carefully assessing Ann's riveted attention. "The Sung Dynasty records show that on one occasion he carelessly urinated over the hem of his gown and the Most Beautiful Wu instantly ordered his servants to fetch him a change of clothing. Her sweetness caused him to ask her to raise her face, which she had modestly kept lowered, and he noticed her fresh beauty. He was so impressed by her that he flicked at the liquid in the basin she was holding, saying: 'I splash water on your powdered cheeks.' As you and I know, Ann, this was one of the traditional phrases for indicating desire. And the virgin immediately gave the appropriate reply: "I will welcome the Celestial Rain and Mist.' "

"Please continue," Ann said, eager to hear the end of the story she knew all too well. She liked the sound of his resonant voice and the way he took his time to make a very subtle point. She was impressed by the fact that Desaix could convey his attitude about women in power through the classic Chinese technique of recounting parables. He also revealed more about himself than even he probably knew— his basic mistrust of women and their use of sex to attain power. His message to her was clear: stay away. But she knew she couldn't.

"Where was I?" Desaix asked, distracted by a fleeting shadow that disappeared behind the terraced palace. Was this the setup? he wondered. Is this where he would be assaulted by her guards on the pretext that he had molested or endangered the Prime Minister?

"You were talking about the Celestial Rain and Mist," Ann reminded him.

"Ah, yes. The Most Beautiful Wu received the Rain and Mist on the couch in the toilet," Desaix added, as he continued to scan the cobblestone courtyard, "and the Emperor promoted her to Third Grade Concubine, which gave her the new title of Most Elegant

Beauty Wu. But as a Third Grade Concubine her chances of further promotion were limited because the competition was greater. And as the Emperor fell ill, her chances of another Regal Coitus markedly diminished. So through guile and deception she met the Crown Prince and bore him a male son. But according to custom, a new Emperor was forbidden to take over his predecessor's harem and wives. So at the insistence of his other wives, the new Emperor, named Gaozong, shaved off Wu's hair and banished her to the Buddhist convent of Kan Yen.

"However, the Emperor Gaozong was so distraught by her banishment," Desaix continued, "that he forced his ministers to revoke the old customs and have her released. Once Most Elegant Beauty Wu was again in the palace, this time with the high rank of Consort, she set out to revenge her humiliation and destroy the Emperor's powerful wives. When her son died under strange circumstances, she accused the two jealous wives, who were not able to bear children, of murdering her son. The wives were punished in a manner appropriate to the period. They were beaten with a cudgel, had their hands and feet chopped off, and were dropped into large wine vats and left to die. Once Wu learned that her husband was dying, she consolidated her position through a reign of terror. Installed as Empress, she began intrigues against possible rivals. Anyone who might have the slightest claim to the throne was immediately exterminated, including the relatives of her late husband and her own brothers, sisters, parents, and cousins. The rest you know. She became Empress Wu Zhao, the first woman to rise to that exalted rank."

"That's certainly an inspirational story," Ann replied. "But you forgot the part about her having appointed a Celestial Sex-Selector, whose primary function was to choose, from personal knowledge, those men most likely to please the Empress. It is written that the Sex-Selector 'interviewed' the three thousand men of the Palace Guard, and finally petitioned the Empress with the following words: 'My parts are so tender that I am unable to sit, my mouth so sore that it is impossible to eat, and my body aches so much that I am denied even sleep.' "

"I don't think I ever knew that part of the story," Desaix lied, wondering about Ann's purpose in recounting it.

"I had hoped that by now you would realize that an Empress has needs . . . " Ann said, pulling him toward her.

Against his judgment, Desaix felt his body respond to hers. How many times could he warn himself against her overtures? Whatever thoughts he invoked to dissuade himself from proceeding any further could not overcome the power of her palpable sensuality that drew him to her. His arms embraced her thin waist. He kissed her neck lightly, teasingly. His fingers wandered over the delicate curves of her back. He could feel her body blend into his, warm and inviting.

After a long, searching kiss, Ann looked into his eyes with tears streaming down her face. "Please, help me to escape from them."

"What do you mean?" Desaix asked, completely flabbergasted.

"Chang is holding me hostage," she replied trembling.

CHAPTER FIFTEEN

Y ou're a hostage to Chang?" Desaix asked incredulously. "What do you mean?"

"If I don't support his position . . . and escalate this crisis into a full-blown war . . . " Ann replied in a shaky voice, "he has threatened to overthrow me and push China into civil war, pitting my supporters against his." Pausing to catch her breath, she added, "He even orchestrated a train wreck involving nuclear weapons in order to embarrass me. You have no doubt seen those photographs by now."

"What do you want me to do?" Desaix asked, satisfied that parts of the puzzle were finally falling into place.

"You must convince Secretary of State Moffat to support me publicly," Ann said, "and use your government's well-known methods to get rid of—"

"We don't . . . " Desaix hesitated to say the word, "assassinate world leaders—"

"Of course you don't," Chang said, interrupting their conversation. His PLA soldiers, who had surreptitiously surrounded them, separated Ann and Desaix. Ann screamed obscenities at the soldiers who forced her down a path toward an unmarked van.

"Wait a minute," Desaix exclaimed as the PLA soldiers shoved him toward a waiting car. "What are you doing?" he asked Chang, who was already in the back seat of the limousine.

"Something that I should have done many hours ago," Chang said in excellent English. He handed Desaix a few glossy pictures.

"What's going to happen to her?" Desaix asked, glancing at the familiar photographs of the train wreck.

"I strongly suggest that you worry about your own well-being," Chang said. "We'll take care of her in our way."

"You can't get away with this," Desaix said. "My government will never tolerate this kind of behavior."

"But they do tolerate *this* kind of irresponsible behavior," Chang replied, pointing to the photographs Desaix was holding. "She alone bears full responsibility for these pictures. But I'm certain that it would be futile to try to convince you of that since it is obvious that she has already co-opted you."

"Are you trying to tell me that my talks with the Prime Minister have just been terminated?" Desaix asked.

"My personal advice to you," Chang said, emboldened by the notion that Desaix was a personal enemy, "is that you leave the country as soon as possible. Otherwise, I am afraid that the Chinese government will not be able to guarantee your safety." The car stopped. Chang unlocked the back door and motioned to Desaix to step out. "You have exactly twelve hours to leave the country. I will make certain that you will be safely escorted to the airport. You will be picked up at your embassy."

Before Desaix could respond, the limousine pulled away from Desaix's hotel, the Holiday Inn in downtown Beijing. As Desaix walked through the empty lobby, he glanced at his watch. It was three o'clock in the morning. Desaix had until three in the afternoon to find Ann and turn a deteriorating situation around.

Not surprisingly, his room was a mess. His clothes and toiletries were strewn everywhere. He picked through his possessions and packed everything in his suitcase. As far as he could see nothing was damaged or missing. The message was clear: get out!

Certain that his phone calls were monitored, he nevertheless placed a call into the embassy with instructions to the night duty officer to send a car for him at eight A.M. and to inform Ambassador Cartwright that he, Desaix, wanted to see him at eight-thirty. And to have a secured call placed to the Sec State by nine o'clock. That was all Desaix knew he could do for the moment, except to get some sleep.

As he lay down on the bed, his mind was again flooded with the same strange images, sounds, and smells he had experienced the night before. Once again, he was entering the world of dreams in which words, meanings, and emotions had their own syntax and logic to be deciphered at some later time. In the background, he could hear those little iron triangles clanking together.

His hands shaking, the nine-year-old boy placed the silver tray stacked with expensive Wedgwood china teacups and saucers on the veranda table. The boy felt overwhelmed by the splendor of the house and the responsibility that was entrusted to him. He heard his mother yelling at him: "Be careful! Don't break the china! You have to pay special attention. You know you're a bad boy, mischievous and irresponsible. Don't let your mind wander. Focus your attention on what you're doing." The boy wanted to scream back that he hadn't done anything wrong, but every time he opened his mouth no sound came out. He was being blamed for something that he hadn't done. Yet he knew he was about to commit an infraction. No amount of good intentions or careful attention paid to his task could stop him from getting into trouble. He felt frustrated and helpless. There was no one he could turn to. His father was busy reading the newspaper. His sisters and brother were playing among themselves. His mother was too occupied yelling at him to listen to his concerns and fears. He was all alone.

The only place he felt safe was in the family's crowded flower garden, filled with the waxen-barked crape myrtles with their airy blossoms of red, purple, pink, and white, nestled alongside the sweet magnolia. As he bent down to smell the flowers a bee stung him on the back. He ran screaming onto the veranda, tears streaming down his cheeks, bumping into the table and knocking over the tray of china. The precious cups and saucers crashed onto the floor, shattering into tiny pieces. His father said and did nothing. He continued to rock back and forth, reading his paper. His brother and sisters laughed. His mother ran out of the kitchen screaming, "You broke china! You allowed it to happen. It was not a time to smell the flowers. The garden is swarming with bees."

Startled by the dream, Desaix bolted upright and saw that it was already seven-thirty in the morning. He tried to steady his shaking hands as he went about his morning rituals. What was it about the dream that made him so frightened? Was it the feeling that he was alone and vulnerable? Or was it the fact that despite his mother's warning to pay attention to what he was doing, he still got into the trouble he hoped to avoid? He broke the china. Hadn't he been warned not to break it? Yet despite all the forewarning and his careful attentiveness, he broke the china. That was it, he thought as he showered and dressed himself. No matter what he did he could not prevent the disastrous outcome.

Desaix checked out of the hotel and sat in the back of the embassy car mulling over the meaning of his anxiety-ridden dream. As a psychiatrist, he knew that dreams were the expression of unresolved emotional conflicts as well as the creative expression of the day's residue of activity. For the most part, he rarely dreamed. But the last time he had a dream anywhere similar to the one he had twice this week occurred when he was sent to Italy in the 1970s to negotiate the safe release of kidnapped Prime Minister Aldo Moro. Throughout the six-week ordeal, which ended in the brutal murder of Moro, Desaix had dreamed of having accidentally torn up his mother's expensive Venetian lace, for which he was severely punished by her. When he had put the dream in perspective, he realized that the issue of trust was at the core of his nightmares. He had felt all along that he couldn't trust anyone with whom he was working, including his own ambassador, a career female FSO who was both a coward and incompetent. A year after the Prime Minister's assassination, he discovered that the Italian officials with whom he had been working—the military generals, the intelligence officers, and the politicians—had all been part of a conspiracy to overthrow the enfeebled Christian Democratic government. He had concluded that he should have interpreted his dreams as a warning. He had been working in an environment replete with duplicity, betrayal, and hidden political agendas. Only his dreams knew it before he did.

As they drove down Jianguomen Avenue, Desaix gazed beyond the bicyclists riding alongside him. He realized that he didn't have to be a shrink to know his recurring dream about breaking china revolved around the unspoken fear he had from the very beginning of his involvement in the crisis—that he was not in control.

When the car pulled up in front of the embassy, Desaix headed straight toward Cartwright's office.

"Are you all right?" Cartwright asked, holding the phone in the air. "Just as you requested, Moffat is on the phone."

Desaix picked up the telephone and listened to his friend berate him. "Persona non grata?" he repeated calmly, as he paced in front of Cartwright's desk.

"That's right." Moffat's voice boomed from the speaker box attached to the telephone. "You've been PNG'd out of China by none other than the Prime Minister herself. Wayne," Moffat said to the ambassador, "would you please tell me again what happened after you and Desaix terminated what you described as a successful negotiation?"

Cartwright looked at Desaix and shook his head disapprovingly. "It's hard to describe an evening of so much drama. Isn't that the problem, Desaix?"

Desaix shrugged his shoulders in resignation. He was feeling both confused and angry, but he wanted to collect his thoughts before he said anything that he might later regret.

"As I explained to you earlier, Jim," Cartwright responded, motioning to Desaix to sit down and relax, "our internationally renowned crisis manager, the man whom we've come to respect and admire for his cool, dispassionate analytical skills, found himself alone with the Honorable Chinese Prime Minister Ms. Lee Ann Wu. The Prime Minister was doing all she could to seduce our Cajun Lothario, in a show of true Chinese hospitality. But by an equally strong show of American character and purpose, Desaix refused to be compromised by Her Majesty's sexual favors, honoring neither the well-known Hovering Butterflies or Silkworm Spinning positions."

"Oh, come on guys!" Desaix shouted. "Give me a break!"

"How the hell did you let him get away from you?" Moffat asked. "Didn't I tell you to keep an eye on him at all times?"

"Wait a minute!" Desaix exclaimed. "What's going on here? When did I ever need a nursemaid?"

"Didn't you think that she might be setting you up, Doctor?" Moffat asked, clearly irritated.

"That's all I thought about," Desaix replied contritely, holding back on his own defense until he heard everything Moffat wanted to say.

"Well, it's pretty clear what you have to do," Moffat said.

"And what is that?" Desaix asked provocatively.

"I don't think there is any question," Moffat replied, "but that you have to return home as soon as possible."

"Why?" Desaix asked, purposely not mentioning General Chang's threat to him. A lot could happen before three P.M.

"Why?" Moffat screamed into the telephone. "You know as well as I do that a PNG means that you are no longer under the protection of the American embassy and must leave the country within twenty-four hours. Tell me, Wayne, has Desaix fallen on his head?"

"No, Jim," Cartwright replied. "But he has had a rough evening." Knowing Desaix, he suspected that Desaix hadn't told Moffat everything.

"First of all, you have to return home because I said so," Moffat screamed into the phone. "Second, you have to return home because I said so. Third, you have to return home because China seems to be saying so. And fourth, if there is a war with China, I need you here, on this side of the ocean. Get my drift?"

"Hey, Jim," Cartwright asked, "what about me? Am I disposable cannon fodder?"

"No career ambassador is disposable," Moffat replied, in a hurt tone of voice. "You should know that by now."

"The answer is yes, Wayne," Desaix replied. "You and I are extremely disposable. Our job is to provide the President and Sec State with seemingly high-quality verbiage . . . and cannon fodder."

"Oh . . . oh . . . do I detect a note of Cajun peevishness?" Moffat asked.

"I read the message loud and clear," Desaix replied.

"Good! Then I can expect you here by tomorrow evening, right?" Moffat asked, ready to sign off.

"I can't leave, Jim. I can't tell you why, but you have to trust me,"

Desaix said, sensing that the time was right for him to respond in full.

"Listen, I put my ass on the line with the President," Moffat said. "He never wanted you to go to China. He figured, correctly I might add, that you would end up causing more problems than it was worth. Now that you've put me in a shit-ass position you're telling me that you're not coming back and you refuse to follow my orders? What the hell am I supposed to tell him?"

"Tell him that you couldn't find me," Desaix replied, pantomiming to Cartwright to get Phoebe Hill.

"Desaix, remember what I told you before you left?" Moffat asked, in a voice he was obviously having difficulty controlling. "*Quanxi.* Remember? Friendship. Relationships."

"That's exactly why I have to stay, Jim," Desaix replied hesitantly. "I've begun to establish some *quanxi* with the Prime Minister. I just need more time."

"In my book, six inches of coitus interruptus does not constitute *quanxi,* or anything else for that matter," Moffat replied, hoping that Desaix would quickly come to his senses.

Desaix, beginning to anger, forced himself to reply in a calm, soothing voice. "Jim, I don't think that she was the one who precipitated the crisis." He paused, hoping for the right words. "I think she's in a lot of trouble . . . and needs my . . . our . . . help."

"You've really flipped out," Moffat responded, in a controlled rage. "Are you trying to tell me that Desaix Clark is now a knight in charming armor going to rescue a damsel in distress?"

"I think," Cartwright interjected, "that you're being too hard on him, Jim. Give him a chance to explain."

"Thanks, Wayne," Desaix said.

"Desaix, please don't tell me that you're willing to jeopardize little things like your career . . . your life . . . or our national security because you've really got a hard-on for a woman with whom you can't play your usual games," Moffat said.

"All I can tell you is that I believe I can stop a war if I can help Ann escape from the grip of General Chang and whoever else is controlling her," Desaix replied. "They want a war. She doesn't."

"Is that all?" Moffat asked, disgusted. "Are you certain that you are not a prisoner of your own delusions? Or hers?"

"Maybe," Desaix replied. "But when Chang personally threatened me—" He decided to say nothing about Ann's accusations concerning Chang and the photos. It might only reinforce Moffat's argument that Desaix was enraptured with her.

"He threatened you?" Moffat interrupted. "That's even more reason why you should get out of China ASAP. Do you hear me?"

"Yes," Desaix replied. "But just give me a chance, Jim. If you make an official demarche to the Chinese ambassador in Washington, I have a feeling that Chang and the others would back off and let me stay. I'm telling you she needs my help."

"Leave it alone," Cartwright said, "and get ready to go. According to her office, they're sending someone over to accompany you to the airport to make certain that you leave the country. It seems that your grand paramour doesn't trust us one iota."

"Desaix, listen to me," Moffat said quietly. "I know how important the concept of love is to you. But wanting an unobtainable seductress, and having rescue fantasies, is not a good thing right now. So just keep your wits about you and your zipper closed for at least twenty-four hours. That alone will do more to promote world peace than any other action you might undertake."

Desaix looked up to see Phoebe Hill standing at the doorway holding a stack of highly classified folders. Cartwright beckoned her forward, instructing her to keep silent.

"I need updated Operation Codes and Psychological Profiles on the Empress Dowager, Defense Minister Chang, and Japanese Prime Minister Mori," Desaix whispered to her.

"I have them right here," Phoebe replied, "plus some very interesting intel on the dissident who tried to kill her."

"Desaix, did you hear me?" Moffat shouted. "Are you flying back this evening? Just tell me yes or no."

"Phoebe, you're a gem," Desaix said, his interest piqued by her comment.

"Yes or no?" Moffat shouted. "Desaix, do you hear me?"

"That young student who attempted to kill Prime Minister Lee Ann Wu . . . " Phoebe paused, hoping to enhance the dramatic moment, "is named Jin Bo Newton." She searched Cartwright's face for some guidance.

"So?" Desaix asked, impatiently.

"He is the Prime Minister's younger brother," Phoebe replied.

Desaix hung up the phone without answering the Secretary of State.

CHAPTER SIXTEEN

Jin Bo Newton?" Desaix repeated, uncertain whether he was more intrigued with the alleged assassin or with his name.

"In your profession," Cartwright quipped, "doesn't shooting your sister constitute major-league sibling rivalry?"

"Where was he taken?" Desaix asked, ignoring Cartwright's version of psychoanalytic theory. An onslaught of questions rushed through his head. Was Ann's brother acting alone? What were his motives? Where did he fit into the politics of China?

"General Chang personally took him to the Gongabu at the Department of Public Security on Beichizi Street," Phoebe replied, certain that Desaix knew the building to be a repository of torture and misery.

"And that's where they're going to take you, if you don't get the hell out of here soon," Cartwright interjected.

"Tell me about him," Desaix asked, once again avoiding Cartwright's warning.

"He is in his early thirties," Phoebe read from her papers, as if she were reciting the ingredients of a cake batter—simple, direct, matter-of-fact. "He, unlike his older sister, was born in Shaoshan city, Hunan Province."

"Mao's hometown," Desaix interjected. "Must be something in the drinking water that fosters revolutionaries."

"Before he entered politics," Phoebe continued, "he was an outstanding chemist who taught at the Chinese People's University in Beijing. As a tribute to his favorite scientist, Sir Isaac Newton, he added the name Newton. As far as we know, he has spent no time working in the formal political party. Unlike his sister, he is considered to be guileless, dedicated to his profession and extremely honest. What is interesting is that he has a long history of engaging in nonviolent, anti-government demonstrations all over Asia. In China, Myanmar, Thailand, Vietnam, Cambodia, and Japan. But this is the first time he has resorted to violence of any kind."

"Events seem to be getting out of hand very quickly," Cartwright said, glancing at his watch. "This is one more reason why you should get out of here soon."

"What do you make of it?" Desaix asked Phoebe, interested in her assessment of the situation.

"I find it extremely unusual that someone who is an avowed Buddhist and practices passive resistance should decide to use a weapon against his own sister," Phoebe replied. "Furthermore, whenever he was arrested in the past by the Gongabu for anti-government demonstrations, his sister would immediately intervene to effect his release. This time, our sources at the Ministry tell us that he is under the complete control of General Chang, and that she hasn't made any effort to see him."

"What's so strange about that?" Cartwright asked, determined not to be ignored. "I'd be pretty pissed off if my brother or sister tried to kill me." He looked to Desaix for a response, but received none. Desaix was totally focused on Phoebe.

"If they had been close in the past," Desaix concluded, "it wouldn't have made any difference to her whatever he did. Blood runs deeper than turbulence."

"That's precisely what I think, Dr. Clark," Phoebe said, pleased that Desaix had very quickly reached her own conclusions. "But here comes the ominous part. The Prime Minister has personally ordered a

massive crackdown throughout China. Security is tightened everywhere. The PLA is on maximum alert. And the universities will be
closed soon."

"How do you know that the Empress ordered this herself?" Desaix
asked, eager to find some shred of evidence that might redeem Ann in
the eyes of everyone in the room.

"Soon after you both were escorted from the Forbidden City she
was taken to her office in the Zhongnanhai, the government com-
pound a half mile from Tiananmen," Phoebe replied, carefully monitoring Desaix's face for any sign of incredulity. "She met with General
Chang after he dropped you off at the Holiday Inn, and they both
took a long walk around Nanhair Lake later that night. It's there that
we think she instructed him to carry out her orders."

"How do you know all this?" Desaix asked, wary that Phoebe always seemed to know so much. Everyone had been monitoring his activities from the very first moment he had arrived in Beijing. But
why? Did Phoebe know more than she let on? He sensed that she had
her own hidden agenda. But what was it? And for whom was she really working? Clearly, she was more than a mere political counselor at
the embassy. Cartwright hadn't told him anything about her or her
activities. If anything, he seemed to defer to her.

"As you know, Dr. Clark, the National Security Agency at Fort
Meade can detect the number of a license plate from a satellite several
miles up," Phoebe said, and then couldn't resist adding, "Big Brother
is everywhere. In the beginning, the intel community was completely
perplexed by what you and the Prime Minister were doing when you
went to the Forbidden City. But soon, I can assure you, you had the
undivided attention of over one hundred and twenty different listening posts around the world."

"I see," Desaix replied, suspiciously. There was only one problem
with her explanation. The NSA is forbidden by law from sweeping,
that is, eavesdropping, any international incident that may involve a
U.S. citizen, unless they were specifically tasked to do so by someone
very high up with the authority to waive the legal restrictions. Like
the Sec State, the CIA Director, or the President.

"Dr. Clark, you asked me to bring you updated Op Codes and Political Profiles for . . . " Phoebe paused, careful to avoid using the term Empress Dowager, "the Prime Minister, Chang, and Mori."

"Listen," Cartwright interrupted, "I'm really concerned that you won't have enough time to pack. Moffat is expecting you—"

"My bags are downstairs," Desaix replied. "Take your time, Ms. Hill, and summarize whatever you think is relevant. Particularly any inconsistencies."

Inconsistencies of facts, thoughts, values, emotions, and behavior, Desaix knew, were the backbone of identifying discrete patterns of political thought and action. A leader who propounded democracy while practicing an authoritarian style had to be able to constrain the truth and propagate the Big Lie at the same time. Suppressing truth required an effective security apparatus to terrify and intimidate the citizenry: an organization of hooligans, sociopaths, and sophisticated psychological manipulators who were completely beholden to the leader through ethnic bloodlines, ideological fanaticism, or opportunism.

Additionally, the ability to disseminate the Big Lie required a strong personal commitment to betray a public trust without any remorse. And an incredibly selective memory to explain away contradictions. But the most important factor in lying was the *entitlement* to lie, cheat, deceive, and betray. For most world leaders, Desaix had discovered, there was almost a spiritual quality to the compunction of lying that masked an elaborate rationalization of personal interests and venal intentions.

"This is the Op Code and Psych Profile on Lee Ann Wu," Phoebe began, grateful that Desaix had both the willingness and patience to listen to the material her colleagues across the river, at the CIA, had prepared at her request several months ago. She had correctly anticipated that as the political counselor in Beijing she would one day deal directly with the Assistant Secretary of State for East Asian and Pacific Affairs on one of his many routine trips to China. And he would ask her for precisely what Desaix had requested.

She opened up a file labeled with bold black letters: **OPERATIONAL CODE/PSYCHOLOGICAL POLITICAL PROFILES: CLASSIFIED TOP SECRET/HUMINT/NO FORN/NO DIS/ELINT/EYES ONLY.** Only a few top senior administration officials could read this sensitive, highly classified material, and then only on a NEED TO KNOW BASIS.

"I didn't realize that you had access to this material, Ms. Hill," Desaix said, wondering how she could have gotten these files when he hadn't been allowed to have them.

"We do if there is a pressing need," Phoebe replied perfunctorily, realizing that her response was completely unconvincing. But she was betting on the fact that the information she provided him with would distract his attention away from any further suspicions. She glanced at Cartwright, who looked quickly away, busying himself with the filing of some insignificant papers.

"Okay, tell me what you know and don't know," Desaix replied impatiently, confused by the strange glances between Phoebe and Cartwright. He caught a glimpse of his own watch and realized that time was running out.

"Cutting to the bottom line," Phoebe replied, "the Prime Minister is a narcissistic, highly dependent woman, who early in her life abandoned her mother, father, and brother. Through guile, deceit, betrayal, and ruthlessness she climbed up the greasy pole of politics."

"Nothing special there," Desaix replied, an edge of disappointment in his voice. "She sounds like any other ambitious politician anywhere in the world." Phoebe's presentation was typical of the briefings prepared by the CIA's Center for the Study of Political Leadership, affectionately known as "sluts and nuts," since most of the material usually included prurient information concerning world leaders' mental status and sexual aberrations. The material she had just presented could have been abstracted from *Time* or *Newsweek.* Phoebe had better make it more informative and interesting, Desaix thought, if she wanted to keep his attention.

"Of course, I'm certain that you are aware of all that," Phoebe replied, sensing his disappointment. She had expected his response and was prepared.

"Folks," Cartwright interjected, looking up from his paperwork, "a minor reminder that we're in a hurry. We have to start making motions as if we're leaving for the airport."

"Clearly, the Prime Minister demonstrates the classic Chinese ambivalence to authority," Phoebe continued, scrutinizing Desaix's face to see whether he was happy with the psychological approach she had decided to take. "On the one hand, she believes in the autocratic values of Confucianism, which bestows authority and power to the elders of the family and to the party. On the other hand, having been trained in the States for several years, she has acquired a deep respect for the rights of the individual. In graduate school she was a staunch feminist who believed that a woman had as much right to decide her own fate as any man did. She discarded her many lovers with a ruthlessness that any man would envy." Phoebe paused again to assess Desaix's reaction. She had a distinct feeling that he was analyzing her as well as the material she was presenting. "In graduate school she had an affair with one of her professors, a prominent Chinese scholar who left his wife for her. But once he was free of familial obligations, she left him for another man."

"Do we know anything about the professor?" Desaix asked.

"No," Phoebe lied. She wanted Desaix to work his way through her presentation, point by point, until the moment was right. "We do know that he was older than she was, and that they were madly in love."

"What in God's name does that mean, 'madly in love'?" Desaix asked, clearly agitated by her statement.

"Goddamn it, Desaix!" Cartwright blurted out. "Instead of worrying about making your plane, you're worried about whom a part-time seductress made it with twenty years ago. What real difference does it make that she may have had some type of relationship with one of her professors at Berkeley?"

"If it's an older man or a mentor," Desaix replied, with more seriousness than Cartwright had anticipated, "she might have what the textbooks call an unresolved Electra complex, which in plain English means that throughout her life she continuously plays out a neurotic need to be with an older man—or teacher—who represents the all-powerful, all-caring father she never had. This might explain, in part, her political alliances with General Chang, or Prime Minister Mori." Yet he wondered how that would explain her having warned him that she was Chang's hostage. Could it be, thought Desaix, that Ann had developed an identification with the aggressor or a Patty Hearst syndrome? In this psychological phenomenon, the hostage makes a strong emotional bond and unconscious alliance with the terrorist who is holding her against her own will as a way of protecting her against any further torture. In other words, although Ann had warned Desaix about Chang, she was really ambivalent about Chang, acting as both the victim and the terrorist at one and the same time.

"Or it may explain why you were sent here," Phoebe added provocatively.

"What do you mean?" Desaix asked, piqued by her innuendo. Clearly, Phoebe knew more than she revealed.

"Why do you think you were sent here?" Phoebe asked, ignoring the increasingly exasperated Cartwright. She couldn't stop now. She now had only one chance to help Desaix, and in the process help herself.

"What kind of games are we playing?" Desaix answered, annoyed. "You know that as Assistant Secretary of State I had an obligation to do whatever was necessary to stop an international crisis that could lead to a major war." Desaix was disturbed that he sounded so pompous and self-important. In fact, his answer was only part of the truth. He was here as much for his own need to impact on history and to satisfy his own quotient of action.

"That's true," Phoebe replied, unconvinced. "But why not entrust your good friend Wayne Cartwright, an extremely competent ambassador, to handle this matter? Could it be that you might not consider him senior enough or experienced enough to manage this crisis—or more precisely, to manipulate Prime Minister Lee Ann Wu?"

"Okay, Phoebe," Cartwright interjected, in an angry voice, "I think that's enough. You're here to do a briefing, not a character analysis of us."

"No, Wayne," Desaix replied. "She's doing exactly what I would want her to do. She's covering my downsides. If I trust her to tell me the truth about my adversaries, why then should I not trust her to tell me the truth about my allies—"

Desaix was interrupted by the ring of the telephone, informing Cartwright that a car to the airport had been sent by General Chang and was waiting at the gate.

"I'll cut to the chase," Phoebe responded, "with the *Reader's Digest* version of the Prime Minister's Op Code." Phoebe spoke quickly, ignoring Cartwright's attempts to have her stop. "It goes something like this: your Empress Dowager avoids any form of conflict, preferring to manipulate the actors and situations indirectly; she's extremely pragmatic and believes that the ends justify the means; she believes that only a few self-selected individuals determine the outcome of history and act in a predictably rational, self-interested fashion; power is a basic political commodity that should be carefully nurtured and harvested."

"All right, that's enough, we've got to go," Cartwright said, as he walked toward the door. "I'll see Desaix out, Ms. Hill."

"What's her weakness?" Desaix called back to her from down the corridor, as she stood in the doorway of Cartwright's office.

"Despite all her good intentions, she's unable to follow through and implement her plans," Phoebe shouted down the hallway. "She's frequently paralyzed by her own fears and doubts."

"Is that it? Was I sent here to act as her shrink?" Desaix asked Cartwright as they walked down the stairs.

CHAPTER SEVENTEEN

W hat the hell is going on?" Desaix asked Cartwright as they sat in the back seat of the black Russian-made Zil limousine, speeding down tree-lined Jichang Lu toward Beijing airport. An English-speaking Chinese PLA major sat in the front seat next to the driver, glancing frequently in the rear-view mirror at the two men as they talked. The major was pleased that General Chang had approved his request to allow the insistent American ambassador to accompany Dr. Clark to the plane.

"The Chinese are playing games and we're caught in the middle," Cartwright replied, hurt by the accusatory tone in his friend's voice.

"What do you mean games?" Desaix asked.

"They set you up with the classic good cop–bad cop routine," Cartwright replied, fully aware that the driver was overhearing their conversation and would report it back to his superiors. "The Prime Minister set up the honey trap while the general threatened you. It's their way of telling our mutual friend Moffat to forget his peace initiative. They're intent on invading Taiwan and in the process engaging us in a confrontation."

"I'm not talking about them," Desaix replied brusquely. "I'm talking about what's going on between you and Ms. Phoebe Hill."

"What are you talking about?"

"Oh come on, Wayne," Desaix replied, disgusted. "You know what the hell I'm talking about. I've got a supposed political counselor, let's say at tops an FSO-2, who meets me by accident at the museum, tracks my every movement through normally illegal NSA sweeps, not to mention the fact that she has incredible access to highly restricted intel to which even I'm not allowed, and, at the same time, is able to intimidate my good friend and her supposed superior, Ambassador Wayne Cartwright."

"It's that obvious?" Cartwright responded dejectedly.

"Yes," Desaix replied angrily. "It's that obvious. The only thing she doesn't have is both of our nuts on a silver tray." Interesting imagery, he thought.

"She's the SRO," Cartwright responded, using the initials for Special Regional Officer, the CIA Station Chief.

"I thought we didn't have one here since our institutional reorganizations a few years ago," Desaix asked surprised. "The CIA claimed they would no longer place people in major embassies around the world."

"For the most part that has been true," Cartwright responded, motioning to the two Chinese in the front seat, reminding Desaix that they should be discreet. "But there have been one or two exceptions. And this is one of them."

"Why wasn't I informed of this?" Desaix asked, concerned about what other important information he was not told.

"I was specifically prohibited by you-know-who," Cartwright replied defensively, "because of your poor relationship with Phoebe's employer."

"Moffat instructed you to keep me out of the intel loop?" Desaix was incredulous. "What else did he tell you not to include me in?"

"Desaix, please," Cartwright said, pointing to the men in the front seat, "Can't we talk about this at another time?"

"They're probably better informed than I am," Desaix said indignantly. "Why would he do that?"

"Because of your intense mistrust and distrust for her organization," Cartwright replied, "he feared that you would refuse their request to assign her here. So he preempted the whole issue by taking matters into his own hands."

"He was probably right about that," Desaix replied in a reflective tone. It was true. Had the Agency come to him with a request to put a Station Chief in Beijing he would have turned them down. Since the major reorganization of the intelligence community several years ago, Desaix had alienated the Agency by insisting that they could not assign covert agents overseas as long as they would not share their intel or place their HUMINT assets at the disposal of the State Department bureaucracy.

He excluded the Agency and all its personnel from his embassies, assigning the FSO political counselors at each embassy to the job of collecting and interpreting primary intelligence. Desaix knew this was a highly controversial, unpopular move, but at least it allowed him to control and verify his intelligence source. But what Wayne had just told him meant that Moffat had been undermining and dismantling Desaix's intel system behind his back. What else had Moffat done? Desaix wondered. Without his own intel people overseas, Desaix was handicapped, bereft of the necessary "senses" to make an intelligent policy decision. Worst of all, Moffat was taking away Desaix's only way, other than ELINT/SIGINT, to reality-test a crisis.

Arriving at the airport, the major quickly rushed out and ushered both Desaix and Cartwright toward the VIP lounge. As usual, the dismal, unfinished airport was crowded with people carrying everything from bloated cardboard cartons held together with string to unbridled livestock.

"I still don't get it," Desaix said as they passed through customs and walked down the long, dark corridor toward the Air China flight to Tokyo, where he would then transfer to the obligatory American air carrier for his flight back to the States. "Why does the PRC want to invade Taiwan?"

"Taiwan, the 'silver tray' of the Orient," Cartwright replied, half seriously, "is a convenient pretext for precipitating a conflict in which the U.S. would be forced to join. Think of it as their coming-out party as a superpower. What better way than to challenge the only other superpower—the U.S.?"

"There's got to be more compelling reasons than their need to assert themselves by taking on the U.S.," Desaix said.

"Historically, they have always felt that they should be the center of world commerce and culture," Cartwright responded. "Five thousand years of this Middle Kingdom complex compels them to create a confrontation with Western values."

"So China versus America," Desaix interjected, "is really a contest between which moral, ethical, and religious philosophy will dominate the world—Oriental or Occidental."

"Crassly stated," Cartwright replied, "this confrontation will determine whether we eat won ton soup or a Big Mac."

"But there are also significant geopolitical and realpolitik reasons for their desire to take us on," Desaix said.

"Like the Greater East Asian Co-Prosperity Sphere?" Cartwright asked, looking at his watch.

"Sure. That hypothetical strategy that's been floating around the State Department for quite a while which no one in national security ever took seriously," Desaix replied. "China and Japan bring peace and prosperity to the entire Far East, making the area forever independent of the economic and military colonialism of the Western superpowers. Of course, when the plan first came out twenty years ago there were two superpowers—the USSR and the U.S. And despite the flurry of activity from Western Europe, their efforts for a fully integrated Economic Community came to a big zero."

"But now there is only one superpower," Cartwright continued. "The United States. And from the Chinese point of view it is completely muscle-bound, barely able to handle anything other than its own deteriorating economy. The Chinese believe that we prefer to deal with our foreign policy obligations through surrogate nations like China in the Far East, Israel in the Middle East, Germany in Western Europe, and Poland in Eastern Europe."

"So China and Japan strike a deal," Desaix said. "The Japanese navy and air force will protect a Chinese landing on Taiwan. Japan will be the acknowledged leader and protector of the overseas territories. She will have access to Indonesian oil and Malaysian tin and rubber. And China's two billion people will become Japan's market for these new resources and manufactured goods."

"But instead of allowing Japan to become the new leader in the Far East," Cartwright concluded, "the Chinese leaders substitute China as the sole protector of the Far East. From the Chinese point of view it's an easy and morally correct substitution, because as we all know, every single country in East Asia detests the Japanese for the atrocities they committed during World War II."

"It's a pretty ambitious plan," Desaix responded, as he rushed briskly down the walkway toward the Boeing 747, the major following about ten feet behind.

"In order to make it work," Cartwright replied, "they have to defeat the U.S., their major opponent to this expansionism." Catching his breath, he added, "They have an inspiring name for this strategy of hegemony."

"What is it?" Desaix asked, handing his boarding card to the flight attendant.

"Pax Pacifica," Cartwright replied, flashing his ID to the attendant.

"Sounds ominous," Desaix said, walking down the aisle.

With their customary beatific smiles, two Chinese flight attendants showed Desaix to his window seat in first class. He could see the major standing at the doorway of the plane.

"Well, at least I did one thing right today," Cartwright said as he hugged Desaix, "I got you on board the plane and safely out of this country."

"Thanks for all of your help," Desaix said. "And for your spasms of honesty."

"Don't be too hard on our friend," Cartwright added, walking toward the exit. "He's got a lot of big-picture issues that he has to keep to himself, no matter how close you two guys are. That's part of being a good Sec State. Remember that."

Cartwright waved good-bye as the plane pulled away from the terminal and he accompanied the Chinese major back to the waiting limousine.

"I will," Desaix said to himself, settling back into his seat as the plane rolled slowly down the tarmac. He wondered why Cartwright had called Taiwan the "silver tray" of the Orient. From the recesses of his mind he knew that he had heard that expression once before. Of course, in Chinese "Taiwan" literally means "Big Bay." And the term referred to the fact that Taiwan, like a silver tray, had taken all the wealthy Chinese Nationalists, or "silver clients," off the mainland after their defeat by the Communists.

Desaix was suddenly clear about what he would do once he got back to the States. He began to catalogue his course of action as the Boeing 747 approached the runway. He would reinstitute his own intelligence network by sending over some of his more trusted operatives, reporting directly to him. He would monitor both Ann's and Chang's behavior, letting them play out their games, until he could strike back more directly at them. He would convene a meeting of the Washington representatives of ASEAN, the Association of Southeast Asian Nations, those Asian countries with the greatest financial stake in the Far East, urging them to formulate a plan of action where they could act as mediators to negotiate a peaceful settlement of the crisis. At the same time, Desaix would ask Moffat to convene an emergency meeting of the Permanent Five Members of the UN—England, France, Russia, China, and the U.S.—to assess the international reaction to this confrontation. Suspecting that the Western European countries would oppose any further Chinese expansionism or military confrontation, he would then request them to authorize an immediate deployment of UN peacekeeping troops to both the PRC and Taiwan to act as a deterrent to any imminent invasion. From his experience with the International Peace-Keeping Force, Desaix knew they could deploy several brigades within forty-eight hours. He would then activate the public diplomacy machinery at State, which he had helped to develop, and saturate the media with pinpoint information that would embarrass both the PRC and Japan. In short, he would put in place a political action campaign that would mobilize international support against the aggressors, initiating an international embargo and freezing their extensive assets in the U.S.

As Assistant Secretary of State for East Asian and Pacific Affairs, Desaix had the authority and the bureaucratic capacity to implement this international strategy as well as the ability to convene a meeting of the Deputy Directors Committee, where he alone could task the different national security agencies to develop contingent military and intelligence plans to handle this crisis. DOD would be asked to develop a military options paper for both a war with China and the defense of Taiwan. The NSA would be ordered through the National Reconnaissance Office in DOD to redirect all their satellites for East Asian SIGINT and ELINT collection. The CIA and the INR bureau at State would be requested to draw up plans for covert operations against China, including Black Box Operations, Psywar, and a disinformation campaign. This part of his plan would take the greatest amount of time and effort, possibly weeks. By law, Desaix or Moffat was obligated to request a finding from both the Senate and the House intelligence committees in order to authorize any special operations against a foreign government. But the hidden beauty of the U.S. government, Desaix thought, was that during an international crisis of such magnitude and severity, one person, like himself, could do so much with such limited resources and authority. Desaix always worked on the assumption that the national security bureaucracy naturally gravitated to the leadership of that one person, other than the President, who was willing to provide a clearly stated plan of action for which he would take full responsibility if it failed. It was only during the normal downtimes that the bureaucracy was at its worst. Desaix was determined to do whatever it would take to prevent war.

Looking out the dirty window, he realized that the plane had come to a complete stop on the runway. Desaix saw three military trucks approach and five PLA soldiers climb a portable ladder into the first-class compartment.

"Come with us!" a PLA captain barked.

Desaix looked around and realized he was trapped. Four soldiers were converging on him. He climbed over the empty seat in front of him and ran down the aisle pushing aside two attendants. He ran to the cockpit, trying to force open the door. But before anyone could respond, three of the soldiers grabbed Desaix and bound his hands, blindfolded him, and hustled him down the ladder and into a waiting truck.

From the increasing sounds of traffic, Desaix deduced that after their forty-minute ride over bumpy roads they were entering a heavily congested area, possibly a city. None of the occupants with him in the back of the truck spoke to him or to one another. But as far as he was concerned, the less said the better off he was until they arrived at their destination. Then he would find out what it was that they wanted from him and why they had pulled this stupid stunt.

When the truck stopped, Desaix was led out into a building, and then down several flights of stairs that he assumed went into a basement. From the cacophony of human screams, it was evident he had been taken to some sort of detention center. When his hands were untied and his blindfold was removed, General Y. K. Chang stood somberly in front of him. Without any explanations or formalities of greeting, he started to walk down the dark hall, beckoning Desaix to accompany him.

Desaix followed. For the first time, he noted Chang's slight hunched back and the imperceptible grimace of pain he evinced every time he swung his arms. Was Chang the torturer or the victim?

"*Hsi nao.* Brainwash." Chang enunciated clearly, making certain that Desaix heard him above the screams.

The two men walked through the fetid, humid subterranean corridors of what Desaix finally realized was the Gongabu.

"The word literally means to wash one's brain," Chang said. "As you know, Dr. Clark, our penal policy emphasizes reform first, production second."

Desaix tried to maintain his composure as Chang catalogued the diversity, ingenuity, and expertise the Public Security Bureau had developed in the art of inflicting pain. Walking beneath the decrepit arches of the seemingly collapsing building, Desaix was forced to bear witness to threats, beatings, electrical torture, and mutilations. The intent was always the same: to break down the psychological and physical defenses of a willful individual. The Gongabu was a veritable cornucopia of man's inhumanity to man.

If Chang was trying to scare him with this show-and-tell visit, Desaix thought, he was succeeding. But how much longer was it to last? As far as Cartwright or anyone else knew, Desaix was on his way back home. When Cartwright discovered that Desaix had not arrived at his final destination—probably the next day—he would initiate an inquiry and then lodge a protest with the Chinese Foreign Ministry. But that would take at least forty-eight hours. Later, the embassy would apply diplomatic pressures. To no avail, of course. *Quelle blague,* what a joke, Desaix thought. What a fucking joke. Sure, he hadn't wanted to leave China. But now he was certain he didn't want to stay.

Gagging on the foul smells of urine, feces, vomit, and perspiration, Desaix thought it ironic that in many ways the culture of torture was the only truly universal human experience. Unlike religion, ideology, or mercantilism, torture could bridge the gaps that existed between the Zairean internal security officer forcing his prisoner to drink his own urine, and the Chilean policeman using the telephone book to beat his victim's ears. Torture had become the common bond that united those in power in a perverse brotherhood that made certain that those without power could never rise beyond personal helplessness, economic desperation, and political futility.

As a physician, Desaix could appreciate the medical paradox within which all torturers had to operate: they were only as effective as their victim's precarious health. If the victim died during interrogation, then the torturer lost his ultimate leverage of disseminating fear throughout the community of dissidents. If the victim refused to break and provide information, then the torturer had spent his time without eliciting any benefits.

As a psychiatrist, Desaix appreciated the fact that the effectiveness of torture could only be measured within the province of individual psychologies. It reflected the intent of the one willing to inflict pain, pitted against the victim's will to resist—a psychological *mano a mano.* But contrary to popular mythology, Desaix knew that torture was not the product of a sadistic mind. It was nothing more than part of the rational calculus of a state-controlled machinery designed to suppress dissent. Concentrated in the torturer's electrode or syringe was the collective power and responsibility of the state. How typically hypocritical, thought Desaix, that most governments which practiced torture, including the U.S. through their Third World public-security technical assistance programs, were more than eager to ratify the Geneva Conventions that designate torture as a crime in domestic and international conflicts.

Desaix knew he had to inure himself to the sights and sounds around him. The naked male body suspended from a meat hook, arms bent backward. The woman screaming in pain as a man beat the soles of her feet with a cane. Otherwise Chang would have accomplished his goal of breaking down Desaix's resistance without even subjecting him to any direct punishment. Desaix tried to numb his senses by making believe that he was on a Surgical Grand Rounds on the oncology ward at Children's Hospital, where he had trained himself to treat dying children in severe pain without remorse, sadness, or pity. Otherwise, he would have lost his effectiveness as a physician.

"We are proud of our eclecticism," Chang said, surprised that Desaix, a man of such diverse experience, would flinch at such sights. "I am particularly honored that we have professional representatives working with us from several Middle Eastern, Latin American, European, and Asian countries. Each one contributes a very particular skill. It's a sad commentary on man's primordial instincts that we can acquire a greater diversity of countries to assist us in our . . . information-gathering activities . . . than the United Nations can for a peacekeeping nation."

"You're right," Desaix replied sarcastically. "I'd hate to think where we would be without aggression or sadism."

"Bored," Chang said.

They walked through low-ceilinged, arched corridors bracketed by small rooms illuminated by naked light bulbs dangling precariously from rusted metal chains. Hollywood couldn't have created a more perfect set, thought Desaix. He was reminded of a Kafkaesque Grand Central Station, populated by a mosaic of uniforms rushing about with a frightening sense of urgency and purpose, completely oblivious to the presence of either Chang or Desaix. Or a Willy Wonka version of a torture factory. Instead of chocolates, the inventory was frightened human souls, the product was information, the laborer was the interrogator, and the working capital was provided by the state in the form of different instruments of torture and an endless supply of political dissidents. The factory's sales representatives were the elite Psychological Operations Officers of the Gongabu, peddling their wares selectively to the senior leadership in order to curry favor and advance their careers. It was capitalism working at its finest in the guise of a controlled state economy.

"They will live a long life," Chang said, implying that no matter how brutal the torture might appear, the victim would eventually recover.

Both men knew that without the presence of a physician before, during, and after the punishment, the act of torture would not be possible. Cynical, thought Desaix, yet nevertheless accurate.

"I see that you are a full-service shop," Desaix said. "Do you also provide psychotherapy for your clients, once you've destroyed them?"

"As a matter of fact," Chang replied, "I think you would be quite surprised to learn that we have a very sophisticated program of treating the patient once we are finished with the initial phase of our . . . operation."

The two men walked toward what looked to Desaix like a group of Japanese military officers giving orders to Chinese soldiers. The obvious leader of the Japanese, an inordinately tall colonel with short-cropped hair and a taut physique, glared at Desaix and then at Chang. He didn't have to say a word. His contempt for both men was etched into the haughty expression on his face. Clearly, he was waiting for an apology for the intrusion.

Desaix was impressed that Chang remained unperturbed.

"Apologize!" the colonel shouted at Desaix in English.

"May I remind you, Colonel," Chang interjected in an authoritative voice, "that you are still a guest in our country. As is this gentleman."

The colonel's angular features tensed up into a threatening, hatchet-shaped gesture of defiance. His four associates assumed a posture of physical readiness. Desaix stepped backward, hoping to defuse the tension. But he was curious to see how this ridiculous confrontation between two ostensible allies would play itself out. If it was any indication of the state of the alliance, then the mutual antagonism between the Chinese and the Japanese was as strong as it was during World War II. Any perceived Chinese-Japanese alliance was, at best, fragile. At worst, nonexistent.

"I am sorry, General Chang, for my inexcusable effrontery," the colonel said, bowing from the waist.

"I and my American guest accept your apologies," Chang replied.

"Thank you," the colonel responded, and motioned to his colleagues to proceed down the corridor.

"Tell me, Dr. Clark," Chang asked, when the Japanese had disappeared into another corridor, "do you think that he was trying to threaten me?" His face broke into a smile, giving his potato face the deceptive appearance of a happily inebriated drunkard.

How unusual, thought Desaix, that he would be willing to share his concerns about the colonel with him. Could he be signaling to him that all was not well between the Japanese and the Chinese? Was this the reason he was brought here? But this had been a chance meeting. Or was it?

"I think," Desaix replied, choosing his words carefully, "you should be very careful." He paused to gauge Chang's skeptical expression. "I'm reminded of the Chinese myth about the tiger who descended from the mountains of Khun-lun, the Western Paradise. In the beginning, the tiger played joyfully with the Chinese peasants who tilled the soil in that region. Then one day, without warning, the tiger turned violently against those same farmers and devoured them. It is believed that the tiger ate those innocent farmers in order to make their souls a slave to his evil intentions, and so he could prey on other equally decent farmers without frightening them first."

"Very interesting, Dr. Clark," Chang replied. "Very interesting."

Chang led Desaix into a brightly lit, relatively clean room, with a long metal table in the middle. A set of surgical instruments was splayed out on a nearby stand. Four Chinese men in white surgical gowns, wearing gauze face masks, stood silently around the table. There was no doubt in Desaix's mind that this was an ersatz operating room.

"As a trained physician," Chang said, "I'm certain that you will appreciate a new surgical technique we have adopted from the old Chinese medical textbooks."

Desaix chose not to respond.

"In the Celestial Kingdom it was said that the only misfortune greater than that of being a female was to become a eunuch," Chang said calmly, prodding Desaix gently forward. "Although this would not necessarily apply to those who were honored by a high position at court."

"Yes, I know," Desaix replied anxiously. "They were often described as 'court rats' or 'flapping crows.' "

"Then you must be familiar with the ancient Book of Odes," Chang said, reciting a poem from the book:

> *"Not Heaven but Women and Eunuchs*
> *Bring Misfortune to Mankind.*
> *Wives and those without balls*
> *Bleat with similar voices."*

CHAPTER EIGHTEEN

Desaix watched as a moon-faced young man in his early thirties was dragged into the room. He saw his intense, darting eyes scan the faces of his captors with the silent desperation of a rat caught in a trap from which there is no exit.

"Castrate the horse," Chang said, "and it stops prancing about, but can still be put to work."

"Do you really need to do this?" Desaix asked.

"Castrate the bull," Chang continued, "and it loses its fury but remains as strong as ever."

Desaix watched as the four attendants strapped the youth onto the shining steel table.

"Castrate the dog and it never roams around, preferring to stay at its master's heel," Chang concluded.

"I think your point has been well made," Desaix replied, angry at the intimation that Chang was going to castrate this young man, right here, in front of him. Was this Chang's way of telling Desaix that this is what could happen to him? Or was this standard operating procedure, with the youth sent home a eunuch as a reminder to other dissidents that their cause was futile. The clearest implication of all, thought Desaix, was that the United States government was impotent to affect the outcome of the mounting crisis between the two countries.

Desaix felt disgusted and started to walk out of the room.

"Please don't leave, Dr. Clark," Chang said sternly, "for there is no place for you to go. I strongly urge you to watch this most unusual procedure, which, as an aficionado of Chinese culture, I am certain you will enjoy."

"I think I have had enough Chinese culture," Desaix replied, stopped at the door by several PLA guards.

"One can never have enough Chinese culture," Chang replied brusquely, motioning to the attendants to begin. "I think you miss the subtlety of our culture if you don't appreciate the nuances of character change that arise as a result of this operation." He waited until Desaix was returned to his side. "As a psychiatrist you should find it extremely interesting that the castrated servant, the *hsing-ch'en,* may lose his virility and many of his male characteristics. But as a person he acquires different and infinitely more complex feelings. Fascinating, isn't it?"

"Absolutely fascinating," Desaix replied sarcastically, as one of the attendants slipped an intravenous catheter into the young man's left arm. A nurse injected a syringe labeled "Valium" into a Y joint of the plastic tube hanging from the D5W intravenous bottle. "Wait a minute, you can't do that!" Desaix shouted, as the youth writhed in pain on the table. Chang was planning to operate without benefit of an anesthetic.

The doctor, wearing a faded escutcheon icon on his blood-streaked frock, wiped the youth's groin region with a foul-smelling, clear-colored antiseptic and began placing a handful of acupuncture needles along his arms, legs, and shoulder areas.

"Don't forget, Doctor, our acupuncture skills are equal to those of any Western anesthetician," Chang said.

"Why did you bring me here?" Desaix asked. "You've already made your point several times over: those people you don't like—or don't like you—you torture. What kind of privileged information do you think you will get from him? Or me?"

"Please, Dr. Clark, you have no cause to be alarmed," Chang said in a reassuring voice. "I think you will uncover a very unusual perspective on this mounting international crisis that you so bravely tackled head-on, as your football fans would say."

"Are you trying to tell me," Desaix paused, "that what you are about to do now will be helpful in the resolution of the crisis between the U.S. and China?"

"You be the judge, Dr. Clark. Before we begin," Chang said, "I am going to read you the details of this operation described by an authority on Chinese court life as it appeared in the *Journal of the Royal Asiatic Society* in 1877."

"Please spare me the details," Desaix replied, with disgust. "I can well imagine what is about to happen."

"No," Chang replied, motioning to one of the nurses. "I insist. It's for your edification."

"That's extremely considerate of you," Desaix said. Something was going on that Desaix didn't understand. Why was Chang torturing Ann's attempted assassin, albeit her brother, when he, Chang, was her ostensible adversary? Desaix recalled the old Arab proverb that the enemy of my enemy is my friend. But for reasons he didn't understand that didn't seem to apply here.

"The operation is performed in this manner. White ligatures or bandages are bound tightly around the lower part of the belly and the upper parts of the thigh to prevent too much hemorrhaging." Chang walked over to Newton. "*Éechyèh dō hǎo ma,* Jin Bo? How are things, Jin Bo?"

"*Léekī!* Go away!" Newton shouted as the doctor approached him with a set of bandages. But the more Newton pulled at his four-point leather restraints, the more he felt bound. The doctor started to wrap the bandages tightly around the lower part of his abdomen.

"*Kūnchóng!* Insect!" Newton shouted.

"So Jin Bo speaks!" Chang chortled. "That's an improvement. As we Chinese like to say, a major confession begins with one simple word." He turned toward Desaix and smiled. "The parts about to be operated on are then bathed three times with hot pepper water."

The doctor picked up a basin of scalding water and poured it carefully around Newton's groin. Desaix turned his head aside as Newton screamed.

"When the parts have been sufficiently bathed," Chang continued, "they are cut off as closely as possible with a small curved knife, something in the shape of a sickle." Nodding his head, Chang instructed the doctor to proceed with the operation.

The doctor picked up a small scalpel and started to measure the imaginary length of the incision line.

"No!" Newton shouted in English. His voice was frail and reedy. "Stop!"

"After the emasculation is completed," Chang continued reading, oblivious to Newton's protest, "the wound is then covered with paper saturated in cold water and is carefully bound up. After the wound is dressed the patient is made to walk about the room, supported by two knifers for two or three hours when he is allowed to lie down." Chang paused to watch the doctor begin cutting along the right inguinal line.

Newton's scream reverberated throughout the room.

"The patient is not allowed to drink anything for three days, during which time he often suffers great agony, not only from thirst but from intense pain and from the impossibility of relieving nature during that period."

"General Chang," Desaix interrupted, "you've made your point. Let him go." Desaix wanted to rush to the table and physically restrain the surgeon but that would only exacerbate the problem. He was trapped.

"At the end of three days," Chang kept reading, "the bandage is taken off and the sufferer obtains relief. If this takes place satisfactorily, the patient is considered out of danger and congratulated upon it. But if the unfortunate wretch cannot make water, he is doomed to a death of agony, for the passages have become swollen and nothing can save him."

"She made me do it," Newton screamed.

"Who?" Chang asked indifferently, as if he already knew the answer.

"My sister," Newton replied, his face and body writhing in pain. "She wanted to create a groundswell of support for herself among the peasants."

"What's he talking about?" Desaix asked. "Can we stop this and listen to him?"

"Of course, Dr. Clark. If that is your wish." Chang nodded his head and the doctor put down his scalpel. "All good things come to those who watch, wait, and listen," Chang said sardonically. "Not unlike your very own psychotherapy."

The guards in the room released Newton from his restraints.

"Can they clean his wound and give him some painkillers?" Desaix walked over to the trembling youth. Only now did he realize that the doctor had made an incision barely the length of a postage stamp. The implied procedure had had a far greater psychological effect on Newton than the actual incision could have had. "Son of a bitch!" Desaix muttered, looking at Chang.

"Would you have preferred that we actually cut him up?" Chang asked.

"Newton, my name is Dr. Desaix Clark," Desaix said as he watched the doctor bandage the superficial wound. Desaix helped the frail-looking Newton off the table, holding him tightly for support as he walked him over to a wooden chair.

"I know who you are," Newton replied in perfect English, exhausted. "My sister told me all about you. She said you would help her . . . " He suddenly became faint and appeared to be falling from the chair. Chang motioned for the doctor, who revived him with ginseng.

"What did she mean?" Chang asked.

"Mean?" Newton repeated, looking confused and disoriented.

"You just told Dr. Clark," Chang replied, "that your sister—"

"My sister," Newton screamed, trying to stand up, "my sister will kill me—she will kill you." He rocked back and forth on the balls of his feet, agitated. "She will stop at nothing."

"Well, Doctor, what do you make of his statements?" Chang asked Desaix, gloating. "See what strange and wonderful mysteries are unraveling."

"General Chang," Desaix replied, "do you really expect me to accept the rantings of a delusional prisoner who has just been tortured?"

"As I understand the concept of delusion," Chang repeated the word slowly, as if it encapsulated some magical properties, "one is convinced of an obsessional thought that could be based on fiction or truth."

"Very good, General," Desaix replied. "Now tell me which of his statements are based on reality."

"Jin Bo," Chang said with familiarity, continuing his conversation in English, "can you understand what I'm asking you?"

"My sister . . . Lee Ann Wu," Newton muttered, as he watched the doctor draw up medication in a syringe. "She wants to destroy China."

"Tell the good doctor how your sister, the Prime Minister, is going about destroying China." Even Chang had to admit that he sounded rehearsed. But he realized that Ann had already co-opted Desaix, so that he had only a few hours to give Desaix an alternative perspective. He was determined that Desaix should hear the truth. Otherwise, China would suffer irretrievably.

"She has . . . " Newton spoke haltingly. Looking into Chang's squeezed and acerbic face, he knew he had little hope of kindness or understanding.

"What did she do, Jin Bo?" Chang asked, beckoning the physician to administer a tranquilizer.

"She met with Mori," Newton replied, uncertain who he was about to condemn.

"What about Mori?" Desaix asked. "What did she say to him?"

"She asked Mori to fight alongside her," Newton replied.

"And who else?" Chang asked, unable to disguise his impatience.

"Chang and his military traitors, as she calls them," Newton replied.

"I don't understand, Newton," Desaix said, with a clear edge of frustration in his voice. Suddenly the logic of good and bad, black and white became cylindrical and confusing. He didn't know whom to trust—Ann, Chang, or Newton. Or none of them.

"Perhaps we should let Newton rest for a while," Chang said. "There are too many relationships that he must recall and too many alliances to discuss. We will begin again after he has rested. When his mind is clear."

Chang nodded to the others in the room, and each began what now appeared to Desaix as a frequently performed role. The doctor put his instruments of torture on the small table and left with the nurses after they had cleared the room of everything that had been brought to it. The guards carefully lifted Newton from his seat and slowly walked him out. Within minutes, the room was empty, except for Chang and Desaix. Just like a theater, thought Desaix, after the performance of a play.

"Things are not so clear to you now, are they, Dr. Clark?" Chang asked.

"I prefer to see things simply," Desaix replied. "And speaking simply, it appears that someone is trying to destroy someone else. But right now, I'm not clear who is doing what to whom."

"A very intelligent conclusion, Dr. Clark," Chang said. "I would like to think that you will try to discover whether I am creating this crisis between our two countries or whether the Prime Minister is."

"And if I uncover the truth," Desaix replied, "what difference will it make?"

"Time is running out," Chang replied impatiently. "We know that the Prime Minister has told you in a moment of passion that she was my hostage and wanted you to help her escape from my hold over her."

Desaix didn't respond.

"The simple truth is that I, you, Jin Bo, and all of China are hostage to the Prime Minister's ruthless, insane ambitions." Chang spoke with a combination of disgust and anger. "With the help of your President, who is strongly influenced by your Secretary of State, she has built the Chinese military into a formidable machine. She has forged an alliance with Japanese Prime Minister Mori, placing pressure on me and the Chinese military to carry out her expansionist ambitions of developing complete hegemony over the Pacific Basin. When I tried to defy her she put me in my place by inviting elite Japanese military units to visit Manchuria and engage in joint military exercises."

"Why didn't she simply have you sent away or killed?"

"Three million PLA members loyal to me is an effective deterrent to any precipitous action on her part," Chang replied, soberly.

"Then why don't you overthrow her?"

"Believe it or not, Dr. Clark," Chang replied defensively, "despite what you see here today, we Chinese are proud of the fact that we are entering a period of prosperity, peace, and democracy. Certainly not the kind of Western democracy that you have in the States. But one, nevertheless, that allows for the checks and balances between a popularly elected civilian head of government, like the Prime Minister, and a nonelected general like me."

"In short," Desaix said, "there is very little you can do against her because she is extremely popular. And because you don't want another Tiananmen Square."

"Precisely!" Chang replied. "That's why Newton's foolish act is nothing more than an attempt on her part to rile up the peasants who support her because she panders to their every need . . . "

" . . . and to ridicule you and your commanders for not being able to deter an assassination attempt," Desaix finished Chang's thought, "which was always intended to be a failure."

"And all for only one small wound to the shoulder," Chang said.

"Is this why you brought me here?" Desaix asked. "To hear your version?"

"Yes," Chang replied. "In part."

"Did you sabotage *huoche* 217 and take those pictures that were sent to Moffat?" Desaix asked hesitantly.

Chang didn't respond, screwing his face into an expression of disdain.

"Can I assume that's a yes?" Desaix asked, certain that Chang would not confirm it for fear that it might have consequences he could not anticipate. Desaix was always surprised how military contenders to power were extremely sensitive to the perception other world leaders had of them. Desaix knew that Chang would be concerned that he, instead of Ann, would be held personally responsible for introducing the massive shipment of nuclear weapons into the Middle East. "Does that mean that I can leave now?"

"What do you think, Dr. Clark?" Chang asked.

"I think that you will keep me here," Desaix replied, "because basically you do not trust me. And I could present a serious problem to you."

"As you know, Dr. Clark, war is a game of deception," Chang replied pensively. "The strong should feign weakness and the weak should try to appear strong."

"I think I can recognize the words of Sun Tzu," Desaix replied, contemptuous of Chang's patronizing attitude. Modern Chinese leaders, as far back as Mao, were ardent followers of the master strategist's *Art of War*, which reaffirms the basic tenet that battles are fought and won in the minds of men and not on the battlefield.

"If you remain as my house guest, your leaders will think that it is the Prime Minister who has taken you captive, despite her formal protestations," Chang replied. "When they turn against her, I and the PLA will become the rightful heirs to lead China without having to precipitate a civil war or fire a shot against our own people."

"What if I am perceived as dispensable?" Desaix asked.

"Then your long-standing *quanxi* with the Secretary of State will have turned out to have been a mockery," Chang replied, "and you, I, and China will have to pay the unfortunate price."

CHAPTER NINETEEN

"Well, Newton, it looks as if we are going to be roommates," Desaix said, examining the dark, musty cell.

"It could have been worse," Newton replied, adjusting the plastic frames on his glasses.

"You mean we could have been one of those poor creatures being tortured right now." Desaix tested the mattress on the rusted metal bed and scratched the mortar of the thick stone wall with his fingernail.

"At that rate," Newton said, "it would take two centuries of our working together to reach the outside."

"No windows." Escape was futile.

"There's no way out of here other than through the front door," Newton said. "I know, I've been here several times before."

"How did you get out?" Desaix asked, surprised by Newton's seeming acceptance of the situation. "And call me Desaix."

"My sister would come here and order General Chang to release me," Newton replied nonchalantly. "He would protest, citing some civil or criminal infraction. Then, after a little bit of horsetrading, he would release me. Several days later, Chang would receive money to spend on the military."

"So Chang and Ann have been playing this hostage game for quite some time," Desaix said. "And that castration scene . . . "

"From the very first day that they fell in love . . . politically . . . " Newton replied, "they knew that it was the only way they could control each other. So they kidnap and exact tribute. Occasionally, however, they get a bit too carried away—like today. But everyone is released eventually. They just have to agree upon the price."

"From my conversation with Chang," Desaix said, "I get the feeling that he thinks my government will blame your sister for my imprisonment, bail me out, and switch its alliance away from her to him."

"Could be," Newton replied as he urinated into a small hole in the back of the cell. "We can always count on you Americans to overread our actions and then overreact."

"What do you mean?" Desaix asked, irritated.

"I am only stating what has always been true. You are the crisis expert. I am only a Chinese heathen whom you have to educate and reform."

"Newton," Desaix responded, "this is clearly some game that you, your sister, and Chang enjoy playing. But from my point of view, it has to stop. I can assure you that my President and Sec State will be on a warpath headed in this direction unless someone here in China convinces them that Taiwan is in no danger of attack. I don't care whether it's your sister or Chang who stops this goddamn military escalation. Do you understand?"

"I can assure you that when we get out of here my sister will help you. But as you Americans always say: what's in it for me?"

"Your life," Desaix replied, with disgust. Somehow he had expected something more noble from someone named Newton.

"Sorry, Dr. Clark," Newton replied. "No tickee, no shirtee." He paused to assess the extent of Desaix's frustration. "Saving my life is too hyperbolic a concept to me. It doesn't translate into anything practical."

"What is it that you want?" Desaix replied.

"If I get you out of here," Newton replied, "I want you to help me become an important broker for U.S. arms shipped to China."

Desaix was flabbergasted by Newton's audacity. This mild-mannered youth with an intellectual look—had a greed that was obviously limitless. He wondered if Newton knew that the shipment of arms was patronage usually given to close friends of the President for services rendered beyond the call of duty. That arms dealing was something that the "bag boys" in the White House would have to approve. "I'm not sure I can help you . . . "

"Then you take the upper cot," Newton replied, kicking the frame of the cot with his ersatz cowboy boots. "I'll take the lower one and we can both sit out the war." He jumped onto the cot, folded his arms beneath his head, and pretended to doze off.

"And what if I tell you I will help you . . . ?"

"Then that is a good beginning . . . Desaix. Now you're beginning to understand the Chinese way of doing things." Newton extended his hand to Desaix to seal the deal.

"How do you know that I'm not lying to you?" Desaix asked, shaking hands.

"Does it really matter at this point in time?" Newton asked. "All I wanted to know was what you would say or do to get out of here."

Desaix smiled when he realized that that was also the way of China. Just tell them what they want to hear and worry later about fulfilling your obligation.

"But I warn you, Desaix," Newton said. "At some point there will be a call for payment and when it comes . . . "

Newton walked over to the cell door and shouted something. Ten minutes later a guard stood outside the door and listened carefully to instructions Newton gave him. When the guard had gone, Newton took off his right shoe and smashed its heel against the wall. From a hollowed-out cavity in the rubber heel he pulled out American money. Twenty minutes later, when a round-faced Mongolian in an oversized green uniform entered the cell, Newton handed the money to him. With no further formalities, the guard unlocked the cell door and checked the hallways. He ordered Desaix and Newton to raise their hands in the air and walk slowly down the corridor.

Desaix was surprised that they encountered no one as they retraced his earlier steps with Chang. Their "escape" couldn't have been less eventful. This was probably a frequent charade the guards played out.

A hostage-for-cash ransom. Standard operating procedure, with greed overtaking any other serious consideration—security, ideology, information, or adversarial differences. Cash-n-carry. The prevailing commodity of discourse and transaction. Desaix smiled to himself. All of his Psychological Profiles and Operational Codes could be replaced by two simple words—how much?

"Let's get out of here fast," Newton said to Desaix as they reached the front door of the Gongabu.

"Where are we going?" Desaix asked, following Newton down a poorly lit alley toward a street with all-night stores.

"We can talk later," Newton said, starting to run.

Desaix easily kept up with Newton, who panted heavily as they raced down a flight of stairs into the subway station. He was amazed to see how many people were in the station at this late hour, pushing, coughing, and spitting on the platform. He felt like covering his nose and mouth with a handkerchief, as if he were on an ambulatory tuberculosis ward. Only when the train had finally closed its doors behind them did he see Newton relax.

"Why did we need to run?" Desaix asked. "Everything seemed to have worked out with the guard. He got the money. We got our freedom. There was no one chasing us."

"Any American businessman knows that every monetary transaction is limited," Newton replied, slightly patronizing. "Once my money exchanged hands, and we reached the door, we were on our own. But now we have a major problem."

"What might that be?" Desaix asked, realizing that the person he had originally thought was an ideologically driven youth, filled with democratic ideals, would probably be able to hold his own with the finest con men on Wall Street. Newton was both the bag man for his sister, prepared to do anything and go everywhere for the proper amount of money, and her fixer.

"I violated the first rule of the hostage game," Newton replied. "I didn't wait for the ritual exchange to be made. Chang didn't get his. Now he'll come out in full force and try to capture me, you, and even my sister until he can extract a proper payment."

"And what might that be?" Desaix asked.

"Everything and anything. Rest assured that we are now being hunted by hundreds of PLA and security officials under the direct orders of General Chang."

For the next few minutes they rode in silence, crushed by the boisterous, foul-smelling subway riders.

So this is the next generation of rulers, thought Desaix as he carefully studied Newton. From corruption to corruption. Desaix recalled that when Mao became senile and retreated from public view in the early 1970s, he delegated his powers to Jiang Qing, his ambitious, ruthless, venal wife. His niece and nephew also became powerful, claiming to be able to interpret Mao's unintelligible grunts and make them into national policy. Ten years later, during the Deng Xiaoping era, Deng's two daughters played a central role in dislodging the hard-liners in the Central Committee and helped their father push through economic reforms that had made China the economic miracle it was today. Not surprisingly, in the process of implementing a progressive economic policy, both daughters, as well as a handicapped brother, amassed an absolute fortune brokering joint venture deals between China and foreign companies. At the same time, they were able to mold both domestic and foreign policy by acting as their father's official interpreter, explaining Deng's senile, inarticulate words, blurred by his strong Sichuan accent. As the sisters became older they came to rely on their niece by marriage, Lee Ann Wu, as their personal confidante. They admired her beauty, ambition, and innate political talents. Once she was of age, they sent her to the United States to obtain a graduate education in political economics. They wanted her to learn to think like an American, since they understood that the destiny of China was intimately tied to that of the United States. And now Jin Bo Newton was the confidant and interpreter of his sister, the newly styled Empress Dowager. The mandala was complete, thought Desaix. Nepotism and corruption in one generation had begotten nepotism and corruption in the next.

"Where are we going?" Desaix asked, noticing the large number of policemen in dark khaki uniforms passing through the train.

"We'll get out next stop," Newton replied. "I'm going to have to make a phone call. You just keep a lookout," Newton added laughing, "like in the old gangster movies."

"I think we should part company," Desaix said. "I'll head toward the U.S. embassy."

"By now, Chang has surrounded your embassy. He expects you to return there. Not a smart move."

When the train stopped at a relatively empty station, Newton and Desaix walked the long corridor at an unhurried gait, climbed the stairs, and reached the relative sanctity of a deserted bus terminal. The steel girder Desaix stood behind while Newton made two telephone calls was decorated with graffiti denouncing government corruption.

For the first time since he had arrived in China, Desaix felt vulnerable. Every principle of his well-stated precepts of crisis management—control, control, and more control—had been violated. Every piece of information or intelligence he was processing was either incomplete, distorted, or both. Everyone who was part of this disastrous trip, including Moffat, Wayne, Phoebe, Ann, Chang, and Newton, had a hidden agenda that was, like his dream, encoded with such complexity that he was unable to recognize any pattern or develop any strategy to deal with them. In one way or another, everyone was lying to him. And to one another. It seemed to be a game of deception, duplicity, and continuous betrayal, in which all the major players, except himself, seemed to understand the rules. They seemed to know who their true adversaries were and how to play them off, one against the other. They seemed to know when to discount or act upon an adversary's statement or action. Most alarmingly, they seemed to understand one another's intentions and motivations better than he did. In short, he felt at a major disadvantage, unable to fathom the encoded information he gathered and fearful that he was incapable of interpreting this reality called the new China.

His fate might very well be in the hands of a tempestuous, wily young man whose duplicitous sister was the reason for his having been PNG'd out of China and placed in the precarious position of being hunted by the Chinese military. He had already failed in his intended mission to prevent the escalation of a crisis. He had ignored every warning Moffat had given. Don't get involved in China's internal affairs. Don't get personally involved with Ann. Just deliver the official U.S. message of restraint and conflict resolution.

Now Desaix found himself concerned about only one thing: getting out of China alive. Right now, his fate lay with Newton, whose fate, in turn, depended on Ann. For a man who prided himself on the good old American virtues of self-reliance and autonomy, dependency was psychologically anathema. Now, like hundreds of millions of Chinese, he, too, was dependent on one man to negotiate through the simple necessities of existence. Like most other mortals, he had no other choice than to make a Mephistophelian deal in order to save his body. As far as he knew, his soul had already been discarded in the human ether of self-preservation and fear. Where once uncertainty had been a trusted emotional companion, it had suddenly become an unwelcome burden.

He decided to call Cartwright as soon as Newton finished his telephone calls.

"What's the story?" Desaix asked Newton, as he tried to warm his hands against the cold night.

"Keep your voice down," Newton whispered. "I'm talking to my sister, who just informed me that you have been declared officially dead."

"How did I die?" Desaix asked, laughing nervously.

"You died in a car accident on the way to the airport," Newton answered. "According to Chang's statements, the remains of your mutilated body were identified by your ambassador. My sister said, however, that your ambassador has left the embassy and gone into hiding somewhere in China."

"Chang certainly doesn't waste much time cranking up his disinformation machinery," Desaix said. "As long as I'm officially dead then anything can happen to me without attracting world attention. It doesn't seem to me that Chang's kidding around anymore."

"Let's get out of here before we attract attention," Newton said as he hung up the telephone. "I tried the embassy for you but there was no response." He walked over to a group of bicycles that were locked up on a rack, opened his jackknife, and pried the locks on two bicycles. Now Desaix had become an accomplice to a crime.

"We have just acquired a cheap means of transportation," Newton pronounced. "Here, you take this Phoenix and I'll take the other. Remember, keep your light off."

They mounted the bicycles and rode down a series of dark streets and alleys. From time to time, they passed a group of poorly dressed men huddled around a makeshift fire in a trash can, trying to stay warm. For the most part, they appeared destitute but harmless. But as they approached one group of relatively young men, Desaix could smell danger.

"Don't stop!" Newton shouted. "Just keep pedaling. They won't bother you if they think that you know where you are going."

But Newton's words were lost on Desaix. All he could think of was how to end-run the three large peasants approaching him. Shit, thought Desaix, three against two. As he pedaled forward, the largest of the men took hold of his handlebar.

Newton stopped riding his bicycle and shouted at the men in Chinese. From what Desaix could gather, the men wanted his much valued Phoenix, the Mercedes of the line. As Desaix appraised the situation, he had only two choices: relinquish the bicycle or fight for it.

Just as Desaix expected, the large man holding the handlebar started to pull on it, trying to shake it free. Desaix, in turn, lifted both feet off the pedals and rammed them straight into the peasant's face, knocking him to the ground. The blood flowing from the man's head scared his two companions, who started to flee. But after a day of humiliation and fear, Desaix wanted more than his ounce of revenge. He circled his bicycle around the smallest of the men, who, with his missing front teeth, looked like a Halloween pumpkin, while Newton cornered the third one.

Desaix aimed his bicycle directly at the man and forced him to back up into a large pothole in the street. When he fell backward into it, Desaix ran his bicycle over him. The man screamed as his head smashed against the stone-hewn edge of the hole.

Newton raced over to Desaix and grabbed the bicycle, preventing him from running over the man a second time.

"You're dangerous when you're angry," Newton said, as they both started to pedal away.

"What would make you think that I was angry, Jin Bo?"

CHAPTER TWENTY

M ake a left on Dazhalan," Newton said as they approached a street that, during the day, was one of the most crowded shopping areas of Beijing. Newton got off his bicycle and pushed it into a group of already parked ones. "We'll leave the bicycles here so they will be inconspicuous."

As Desaix tried to clean some of the blood off the front fender, a convoy of military trucks passed by. Both men ducked in between the bicycles.

"If you don't mind being a little less compulsive," Newton said facetiously, "I would strongly recommend that we proceed with haste."

"You mean that convoy was looking for us?" Desaix asked, as he followed Newton down the dimly lit street.

"Chang doesn't waste time," Newton responded, distracted. "Tell me if you see number eighteen."

"I don't read Chinese very well."

"My sister neglected to mention that," Newton said, stopping in front of a doorway littered with torn brown paper wrappings, broken cardboard boxes, and smashed wooden crates.

"What the hell are we doing here?" Desaix asked. He read the English translation on the storefront window out loud. "Enamel and Lacquerware. Ornaments and Jade. Embroidered Silk Garments. Carpets. Chinese Calligraphy and Paintings. Stone Carvings and Engravings. Tourist Souvenirs."

Newton forced open the door, the bone-dry wooden door frame easily giving way. "Follow me," Newton said, "and try not to stumble into anything. Don't open the light or strike a match."

Desaix held on to Newton's jacket as they walked cautiously through the store. Desaix imagined the crashing sound of porcelain and ivory. But Newton knew his way through the maze of objects. Clearly, he had been here before.

"We have to pick out the proper gift for the gods in order to appease them," Newton said.

"What?" For a minute Desaix was caught off guard by Newton's remark. It sounded plausible. The Chinese were highly superstitious people, continually trying to please one god or another, depending on the occasion. But Newton was too irreverent to be anything but atheistic. It was his version of humor, Desaix decided.

At the end of the long store Newton stopped before a curtain that concealed a metal door.

"Desaix, you're bigger than I am," Newton said. "Push against this door with your shoulder. See if you can shove it open." He paused, adding, "I don't want to put you under too much pressure, but time is running out."

"I don't know what you're talking about." Desaix grunted as he pressed all his weight against the rusted door.

"Good," Newton said. "You're less dangerous that way." But he could see that Desaix was not having any success. And they had to get through the door before daylight when the store opened for business.

Desaix looked around in the dark shop for something that could be used to pry open the door. "What about this mother over here?" Desaix asked, approaching a five-foot-long ivory elephant tusk. He grabbed it with both hands and managed to drag it over to the metal door.

"Be careful with that. It's very valuable," Newton warned.

"Why do I get the feeling that you are more worried about my destroying this tusk than about it destroying me?" Desaix asked, angry.

Newton laughed. "My sister is part owner of this store . . . as well as all the other stores on this block . . . as well as eighty percent of all the privately owned stores in Beijing. She would be furious with me if I destroyed her precious tusks, even if it was to save your life."

Together they pushed a carpet up against the door to deaden the sound of impact. Holding one end of the tusk, they rushed the door with the other end and it gave way. Beyond the door was a steep flight of narrow metal stairs. After resealing the door they descended in almost total darkness. Once they reached a landing Newton turned on a small ceiling light.

In front of them stood a large room containing two long rectangular tables, each covered with a food-stained white tablecloth and several dusty artificial flower arrangements. Metal folding chairs surrounded the tables, making the room look as if it were being prepared for a banquet.

Newton walked over to a large painting of the Great Wall of China hanging over a filthy fireplace, and took it off the wall.

"Don't tell me," Desaix said, "that this is where the great art treasures of China are hidden." But as he looked more closely at the painting, he realized that it could have been obtained years ago from a Sears catalogue.

Newton smiled at Desaix's attempt at humor while he untaped a back corner of the painting. He separated the brown paper backing from the picture and pulled out a folded paper.

"This map," Newton said, as he unfolded the thin sheet and flattened it out on one of the tables, "identifies the underground tunnels and civil defense bunkers that honeycomb Beijing and the countryside. So if it is good to us it will tell us how to get out of here without being captured." He looked up into Desaix's surprised face. "This is a tourist shop with a great deal of information, if one only asks the proper question."

"Point well made, Jin Bo," Desaix said respectfully.

Newton quickly scanned the map, refolded it, and put it in his jacket pocket. He walked over to a small door at the far end of the room. "Follow me," he said.

"Do I have any choice?" Desaix asked, feeling like a young boy at the entrance to his first roller-coaster ride. At some point, he was sure he would get queasy. But until then, he might as well try to enjoy the ride.

They descended another flight of rickety wooden stairs. At the landing, Newton felt around the wall until he found the light switch. A few flickers later a series of long fluorescent lights illuminated what seemed to be an endless corridor with a fourteen-foot ceiling.

"Welcome to the network of corridors under Beijing," Newton said. "It was built by Mao as a civil defense shelter against potential Russian and American imperialism."

Newton led Desaix through an endless series of crisscrossing hallways leading everywhere and nowhere. Desaix couldn't believe the extent of construction that was undertaken to prepare the Chinese people against an invasion that was always more fiction than reality. The hallways reminded Desaix of the worst of the psychiatric hospitals he had worked in. The walls were painted a putrid green. Exposed pipes and ducts ran the full length of the walls. Cold white fluorescent lights highlighted every imperfection in the peeling plaster walls. The hallway reeked with the musty odor of neglect, humidity, and urine.

Every few feet Desaix noticed a room filled with ten bunk beds upon which rested blankets and frayed towels. They passed communal bathrooms, containing endless rows of sinks, urinals, and toilets, looking as if they had never been washed or properly maintained. In one hallway hung a sign in both Chinese and English that read: HOSPITAL. Bunk beds lined the perimeter of the ten-by-ten room next to the sign, along with a rusted green oxygen tank and a large brown metal trunk with a large red cross stenciled on top of it. Further down the hallway Desaix saw large metal casings on which were written in small English letters: VENTILATION AND POLLUTION FILTERS.

"This was a present from the British," Newton said sardonically, "who figured that they might be the only ones to survive a nuclear holocaust. They wanted to make certain that the senior Chinese officials didn't forget the humanitarian concern that England had expressed."

As they approached a turn in the corridor they heard voices coming from around the bend. Newton switched off the overhead lights and motioned to Desaix to step inside one of the rooms with beds. They each stood silent, flattened against a dark wall, waiting apprehensively as the voices came closer.

"Stop!" Newton shouted, and ran out into the dark corridor. "Put your hands up! I have a gun pointing at you."

"Oh, stop that Hollywood nonsense, Jin Bo." The familiar female voice responded in English. "It's us."

"Why didn't you announce yourselves?" Newton asked as he flicked the lights on again.

"Who would have thought that you would start playing cops and robbers at a time like this," Ann said, hugging her brother. "I told you that you were making your head soft with all those movies."

"Hello, Ann," Desaix said, hesitantly stepping forward.

"Good to see you, Desaix," she replied flatly.

He walked toward her with both arms extended.

She stepped back, cold and distant.

"Is something wrong?" But as the words left his mouth he realized that the day before they had engaged in a self-designed ritual of affection and emotion based on nothing more than the imperatives of the moment. Yesterday, she had needed him. But today the slate was clean, so to speak. Starting from this moment onward, all emotions and entitlements would have to be recalibrated.

He had to admit that he was hurt. For a brief moment he had convinced himself that the Empress Dowager of China was attracted to him. But perhaps the real pain came from the fact that, more often than not, he was the one who inflicted pain. Not vice versa. So it was a matter of pride. He recalled a silly, but meaningful, episode in his youth. As a kid, he had taught himself, through trial and error, to appreciate the mildly spiced andouille sausage of his hometown. He had spat out his first taste of the spiced pork, which flavored gumbos, red beans and rice, and jambalayas, hating it. But it was a matter of pride that, as a native son of the bayous, he should be able to appreciate the biting flavors of his dying heritage. So he had taught himself, through forced servings, to appreciate the dish. It was a matter of pride. In the same way that Ann's rebuke was a matter of pride.

"Hey, what about me," interrupted Phoebe, "don't I get a hug? Or at least a handshake?"

"What in God's name are you doing here?" Desaix asked, hesitating, uncertain as to whether it would be appropriate. Then he pulled her toward him and held her tightly. She felt good and he was pleased to see her. Unlike Ann, there was no cutesy game playing. In that way, she was very much American—direct, goal-oriented, and no-nonsense. But more than that, she felt full—physically and emotionally. And he was feeling starved.

"After Jin Bo called Ann, she called me, informing me that you two were out. And I just had to see how my Assistant Secretary was doing," she replied, trying not to sound worried. She could see the deep, dark lines under his eyes and wondered what he had endured over the past twelve hours.

"How did you get here?" Desaix asked in a caring tone that quickly switched to indignation. "And why are you here? Given the days that have elapsed since I arrived, and my untimely death, the embassy should have closed by now. You should have been evacuated from the country."

"Give me a chance to explain." Phoebe said. "Once Cartwright confirmed through sources in the Gongabu that you were still alive, he felt comfortable in evacuating the embassy when the order came from Moffat. I refused to go. You know the Sec State needs someone with strong political contacts below the ambassadorial level to remain here. So I volunteered. And here I am."

"Is a war about to start?" Desaix asked, fearful of the answer.

"No," Phoebe replied. "Believe it or not, your disappearance is preventing one from beginning. No one bought your death story. Moffat suspected that you were pulling one of your magic-hat tricks, so he convinced the President to hold off our strike force. Chang was pissed off that you and Newton had gotten away. Fearful that he would be accused of being the aggressor, rather than Ann, Chang is holding off any action until he can find you and Newton and, of course, Ann."

"It seems that I'm far more effective at conflict resolution if I'm not around."

"I'm afraid that's what it amounts to," Phoebe replied, hoping he wouldn't guess that one of the reasons she hadn't left was to make sure he was safe. And she was supposed to be a professional who never let her private life interfere with her professional performance. Damn him!

"You're quite amazing," Desaix said, finally thrilled that Phoebe was far more than a political counselor at the embassy.

"I take that as a compliment," Phoebe said, trying desperately not to flush.

"Not bad for the first female CIA Station Chief in Beijing," Desaix whispered in her ear. "You even fooled me."

CHAPTER TWENTY-ONE

I can neither confirm nor deny," Phoebe said, lying to conceal her overly warm feelings for Desaix. It also would not have looked good on her record if she had lost an Assistant Secretary during her tenure as Station Chief.

Desaix was still fuming over the fact that Moffat and Cartwright, and who knew who else, had hidden that information from him. As pleased as he was to see Phoebe, and as attracted as he was to her, he was now completely distrustful of her explanations or intentions. He would have to draw her out carefully to uncover her real agenda.

"Why did you bring the Prime Minister with you?" Desaix asked.

"Her life is in danger," Phoebe responded, detecting a sudden frosty tone in his voice. "Since your escape from prison, General Chang has issued an order to the military to arrest her as an enemy of the state for instigating domestic unrest and promoting subversive activities. He's even offered a bounty of one million American dollars for her safe apprehension." She looked at the skepticism written all over Desaix's face and realized that despite his warm greeting, she would have to expend a lot of time and energy convincing him that she was trustworthy.

"Have you received any orders?" Desaix asked, suspecting that she had not acted on her own initiative.

"My instructions from Moffat are as follows," Phoebe replied cautiously. "Get the Prime Minister out of Beijing and bring her to the port of Shanghai in three days. Rendezvous with Ambassador Cartwright, who will hopefully have a boat waiting for us on the Huangpu River."

"Why take two to three days when Shanghai is only a three-hour airplane flight away?" Desaix asked, incredulous that anyone would take so much time in the middle of a crisis that at any moment could flare into a war. On the other hand, Phoebe had mentioned that his absence was delaying Chang's declaration of war. Yet Chang had assured him while he was in prison that he didn't want the war. It was the Prime Minister, he said, who wanted to invade Taiwan. Now Ann was ostensibly fleeing from Chang with the help of none other than Phoebe Hill of the CIA. Extremely interesting, he thought. And totally confusing. He had a feeling that as events unfolded there would be many more unusual twists and turns. And the only thing he could do right now was to take them like an Olympic bobsledder, banking as carefully as possible without crashing.

"Because every major airport and minor airstrip in this country is being closely watched by Chang's troops," Phoebe replied calmly.

"Is there any chance of flying her out of Beijing incognito?"

"No way," Phoebe replied. "Airport security and domestic passport controls have tightened up significantly in the last twelve hours."

"Train?"

"Possible," Phoebe replied. "Even though the railroad stations are covered, we might have a chance. The thousands of peasants who use the trains each day make it hard for the authorities to control the passenger manifest."

"But it's a helluva train ride from Beijing to Shanghai," Desaix said, concerned about the amount of time that they would be exposed to searches.

"If we book second-class passage, which is the safest," Phoebe replied with measured caution, "I estimate that it should take about twenty-four hours to reach Shanghai. We'd head straight south through Nanjing, Zhenjiang, Wuxi, and Suzhou. Once we're in Suzhou, we can take a boat or continue on the train."

"And the road?" Desaix asked.

"Too great an exposure and much too long," Phoebe replied. "I would hate to have to sit out a war in China."

"So they intend to use Ann to stop the war?" Desaix asked, jealous that in only twelve hours he was already out of the information loop. Now he would have to depend entirely on Phoebe to know what was or was not permissible. It was not a situation that lent itself to his need to be in control.

"As best as I can understand it," Phoebe answered, "Ann is to be used as a political counterweight to Chang. She will be cast in the role of the wise stateswoman who has been physically and psychologically abused by her ruthless military leaders over whom she has little control. Using an international forum as a backdrop, either the United Nations or the ASEAN countries, we intend to broadcast a televised message for civil disobedience to her fellow Chinese citizens and, at the same time, disseminate a message for world peace."

"A very interesting strategy," Desaix said. "I'll certainly help you in whatever way possible." Desaix was lying, but he had no other choice. The strategy that Phoebe had just proposed was seriously flawed, if not outright insane. There was no way that Chang or his operatives would allow Ann to portray herself as a helpless victim of military brutality. If nothing else, the Chinese Ministry of Propaganda was already in full swing convincing the world of Ann's harsh reign, including the incarceration of innocent students and political dissidents. Furthermore, Moffat would never expose Ann to such a crass public campaign. He was a lot more subtle in the way he used people and wielded power. If anything, Moffat would have wanted to keep Ann inside China and work with her from some covert base to mobilize her Chinese constituency, utilizing TV and radio broadcasts, pamphlets, and public diplomacy to manipulate international coalitions against Chang.

Staring at Phoebe's expressionless face, Desaix realized that she could have told him anything she wanted. From this moment on, he could not believe her. He would just have to watch the game evolve, depending on no one. Not even Cartwright or Moffat. From this point forward, his strategy for survival was that of a Taoist warrior: conserve

one's energy while inducing others to dissipate theirs. Instead of fighting this conundrum of deception and betrayal, he would adhere to the
principles of the famous warrior-philosopher, Sun Tzu, who stated the
basic tenet of victory: "To win without fighting is best." To face this
situation of lies, half truths, convoluted relationships, and complicated dynamics, the best strategy, Desaix decided, was to assume Sun
Tzu's prescription of arriving at a state of "formlessness and fluidity,"
just like water, which has no constant shape. In adapting and changing according to the enemies' vagaries, Sun Tzu believed that one
could get enemies to spread themselves thin, in the process revealing
their strengths, weaknesses, and intentions, while remaining unknown oneself. At the right moment, he would strike. But until then
he would watch and wait, allowing himself to "go with the flow."

Looking at Desaix's expression, Phoebe realized that his pride had
been hurt. She was not in charge. In diplomacy, as in most highly
technical fields, information was king. And she was the last person to
be briefed by the Sec State before the embassy officially closed. That
made her the de facto Chief of Mission and the most senior U.S. government official in China. Those were the rules of the diplomatic
game and not even an iconoclast like Desaix would dare to tamper
with them. Especially when he was persona non grata in China.

"I am sure that I am going to need your improvisational skill and
creativity," Phoebe said.

"Thanks, Phoebe," Desaix responded coldly. "I appreciate that."

"What's going on over here?" Newton asked, as he and Ann returned from the end of the corridor. "A conspiracy?"

"Hardly," Phoebe replied, trying to diffuse any we-they mentality
that might be building. "I just briefed Desaix about what Ann and I
decided would have to be done in the next few days."

"First of all," Ann said brusquely, "we must get out of this infernal
tunnel. It's making me anxious."

Despite the damp coldness in the tunnel, Desaix noticed small
drops of perspiration over Ann's brow.

"Are you all right?" Desaix asked. He walked over to her and felt
her forehead. It felt cool. Clearly, she didn't have a temperature.

All of a sudden, Ann was all smiles, holding Desaix's hand against
her head. "That feels extremely comforting, Doctor."

"I think that we're going to have to start to move," Phoebe said, conscious of a twinge of jealousy. "But first we are going to change our appearance as much as possible."

"Phoebe, if you think we can fool Chang, forget it," Newton said.

"We can try," Phoebe replied, dumping the contents of her large pocketbook onto the floor. "Makeup, scissors, hair dye, fake travel papers. Take a look at the photo in each of your internal documents and see how closely you can make yourself look like that fuzzy picture." Phoebe handed a set of papers to everyone.

"I'm always amazed how efficient American women can be," Ann said, scowling as she looked at the picture in her document. Within minutes she had made her face look at least ten years older by accentuating the natural crease lines along her forehead, eyes, and mouth with dark powder. Then she took the pair of scissors, flipped her head forward, and started to cut her hair. "Well, what do you think?" she asked when she was through.

"I'd say that I don't even recognize my own sister," Newton replied, replacing his wire-rimmed glasses with contact lenses.

"You look like a fifty-year-old farmer's wife from Harbin," Desaix said, trying to lighten up the dark features on his own angular face, and powder his hair color to a lighter shade of brown.

"Thank you," Ann said, "that's just what every woman wants to hear." She searched through one of the rooms and found some old clothing in a trunk.

Phoebe braided her own hair into pigtails, which made her look much younger and more like a student.

"I see that you chose the youth motif for yourself," Ann said as she finished dressing.

Desaix noted the increasing tension between the two women and wondered about its source. Jealousy? Rivalry? Dependency?

"Women!" Newton mumbled to himself. He greased his hair and combed it into Mao's swept-back fashion. He changed his denim outfit for navy blue cotton baggy pants and a loose-fitting, frayed navy blue jacket that he found in one of the rusted trunks.

"Jin Bo," Ann asked curtly, "have you forgotten to whom you are talking?"

Ann suddenly seemed agitated. She continuously adjusted and
readjusted her makeup. She wiped off the dark pencil lines that made
her look older and reapplied the very same lines to the same place,
with an obsessiveness that worried Desaix. She was obviously dissatis-
fied with the persona she had to assume. Through the magic of
makeup she was turning into the image of a person who seemed to
frighten her. One of the multitude of nonentities. One of several hundred million elderly Chinese women who tilled the soil and eked their
meager living from selling turnips, radishes, or cracked brown eggs.
What was she really frightened of, wondered Desaix. She was beginning to manifest the clinical signs of an acute anxiety attack.

None of the behavior was lost on Phoebe and Newton either. But
neither one said or did anything. They simply continued their preparation for the trip and made believe that Ann was having a hard time
adjusting to the reality of being a fugitive.

"Ann, are you all right?" Desaix asked, placing his arm around her
shoulder.

"Of course I'm all right," she responded angrily, and threw his arm
off her back. "Don't patronize me with that soothing . . . understanding . . . shrink voice of yours."

"Is there anything that I can do?" Desaix asked, stepping out of her
way and trying to assess her mood swings.

"Don't mind her, Desaix." Newton said. "She just doesn't want to
play an old woman. Even when we were kids, she made me dress as
the older person in all of our plays. She has this thing about age and
growing older."

"Shut up!" Ann shouted in a shrill voice that resonated throughout
the tunnel. "What do you know about anything, little brother? You
were still wetting your diapers when I became the Executive Secretary
of the Central Committee. I didn't have a mother or father to hold my
hand every time someone tried to compromise me or get rid of me. I
did it all on my own, Jin Bo."

"If everyone is ready, we'd better be on our way," Phoebe interrupted, realizing that the situation was about to get out of control. "I
hear sounds of people moving about upstairs."

"You're right. It's soon time for the shops to open." As Newton
checked his watch, an expensive Patek Philipe, he realized it would be

best if he just threw it away. But he couldn't bring himself to do it. It had been given to him by one of his French business associates as a thank-you for influencing Ann's selection of his company for a major construction contract in the Pudong Free Trade Zone in Shanghai.

Phoebe started down the poorly lit hallway. From her previous explorations of the Dazhalan Street maze of tunnels she knew that it would be safe to exit onto Kangji Road, just north of the main Beijing train station. But she was concerned about the myriad shops, restaurants, hotels, and movie theaters above ground that had exits into the tunnels, however infrequently used. Chang's men could intercept them at any point if they were not careful. But she was counting on the fact that no one used these tunnels.

"Let me help you, Ann," Desaix said, trying to lead her in the semi-darkness.

"Stop touching me!" Ann shouted, pulling away from him. She started to rub off her makeup again. "You think that by playing Halloween, we can avoid Chang? If you do, then you have seriously underestimated him."

"Ann," Desaix said in a soothing voice, "you're upset right now. Try to pull yourself together. Each one of our lives depends on our ability to escape from this tunnel. It's not pleasant for any of us. But I remind you that in order to make you the legitimate ruler of China again we have to get you to Shanghai."

"Does that mean I am really going to be the Prime Minister of China without having to worry about General Chang?" she asked in a suddenly childish tone of voice.

"Yes, Ann," Desaix replied, surprised to hear himself responding to a plaintive schoolgirl, begging for reassurance that no harm would come to her if she left home. Only a day before, he had almost been seduced by a self-assured temptress who was clearly in control of her own emotions. And fully capable of manipulating his. Now he faced a woman who was starting to fall apart psychologically, losing control of her emotions, thought processes, and impulses. In addition to the obvious psychological regression, Ann had begun to engage in a series of ritual behaviors: putting on and removing the makeup, walking around in small circles, compulsively touching the sides of the tunnel walls. She was exhibiting all the elements of what was known in the

psychiatric community as obsessive-compulsive disorder, a mental illness in which a person becomes trapped in a pattern of repetitive
thoughts and behaviors that are senseless and distressing but extremely difficult to overcome. Most of the patients whom Desaix had
seen with OCD could, with treatment, recognize that their obsessive
thoughts were senseless and their compulsive behaviors were unnecessary. Unfortunately, their insights were not sufficient to enable them
to break free of the behaviors. They were able to keep their symptoms
under control only when they operated in a familiar structure, such as
work. But in an unknown situation, they could unravel quickly.

What bothered Desaix was that Ann's mental problems had not
been picked up by her Psychological Profile and Operational Code.
Equally disturbing was the fact that neither Moffat, Wayne, nor
Phoebe had even mentioned any serious personality problems. If it
was OCD, Ann must have had it since adolescence. Which meant that
Jin Bo would have known about it, so did Chang, as well as those in
the U.S. government who had been tracking her for years.

Desaix was trying to understand why no one had warned him about
Ann's condition when the sound of gunshots reverberated through the
tunnel.

CHAPTER TWENTY-TWO

As the gunfire became increasingly louder, Ann covered her ears with her hands. "Tell them to stop! I can't stand it." She ran into Desaix's outstretched arms and he cradled her like a child.

"Ann, you must try to be strong," Newton screamed at her, embarrassed.

"I'm trying to, Jin Bo," Ann replied, her face completely frozen in a mask of terror.

"We must move faster," Phoebe yelled to them from the front of the line. "In a few minutes we are going to have a lot of company in this rat-infested hole." As soon as she uttered those last words, Phoebe realized her mistake.

"Rats?" Ann screamed. "What rats?" Her body trembled with fear.

"Don't worry," Desaix said, and tightened his hold around her. "It was just a figure of speech. Take a deep breath and let it out slowly."

While Desaix wondered how far his powers of psychology might go in lieu of adequate medication, Newton walked up to them and smacked his sister across the face, yelling something at her in Chinese. Within seconds Ann had composed herself.

"Something someone should have done from the very beginning," Phoebe thought to herself as the group started forward once again.

The tunnel had suddenly become an inferno of sounds. Whichever direction Phoebe decided to take she knew that they could easily encounter Chang's soldiers. But if they left the tunnel through one of the shop exits they might have to provide too many explanations and fight their way through now crowded streets. Meanwhile, time was running out. They had only an hour to get to the station and board the express train to Shanghai.

Phoebe started to run, but as she turned a corner she saw four soldiers waiting at the other end of the next hallway, about three hundred feet away. She quickly drew back and motioned to the group to stop.

"We can't go down there. We'll have to either go back or get out here," Phoebe said. "What's upstairs?"

"That door leads to a restaurant," Newton said, pointing to the only door in their corridor.

"Are you certain?" Phoebe asked.

"I should be," Newton replied. "When I worked there as a student, I used to bring the garbage down here instead of taking it to the dump six blocks away."

"How do you think Ann is doing?" Phoebe whispered to Desaix.

"Quite frankly," Desaix answered, "I don't know. She could have another anxiety attack at any time. If I could find some tranquilizers in those medical trunks I would feel better about the situation."

"My guess," Phoebe said, "is that anything in those trunks is at least forty years old. Is that right, Jin Bo?"

"Give or take ten years," Newton replied, peeking around the corner at the loitering soldiers. "It would be useless."

Newton took the lead and led the group back down the hall, through a rusted metal door propped open by a tin bucket. Everyone side-stepped the remnants of garbage in the area surrounding the door. They managed to wend their way without incident up a narrow metal staircase cluttered with brooms and empty bottles to a wooden door with faded Chinese letters.

"Here we are," Newton said. "What a pity to walk through one of the finest vegetarian restaurants in China without even ordering Beijing duck—made of bamboo, of course."

"I'll give you a rain check," Phoebe said and smiled.

"When we enter the restaurant," Newton continued, "do not be surprised if you find many people, even though it is morning. Perhaps you have had our noodle soup for breakfast . . . ? We will just walk in, nod to the owner, and take a seat. I know the owner. He should have no difficulty with an old peasant woman, her son, and his friends."

"And if we get into any problems?" Desaix asked, holding Ann's arm. "What do we do then?"

"Start a food fight!" Newton replied smiling. "Only kidding. I have seen your movie *Animal House* many times."

Desaix laughed. There was something infectious about Newton's humor, a combination of adolescent defiance and youthful enthusiasm. In contrast, Ann had retired into a protective shell of silence and gloomy uncertainty. Although she said nothing, he knew she was aware of what was happening around her. The question for him, however, was what would snap her out of her condition.

As Newton opened the door to the restaurant, shouting and singing filled the air. At the tables near the door sat six Public Security officers, distinctive in their green uniforms, obviously celebrating. Desaix wondered why in God's name people would be drunk so early in the morning in a restaurant.

Newton took a step backward, trying to close the door before his motley group was spotted, but Phoebe pushed him forward.

"*Gānbēi!* Cheers!" a tall thin soldier shouted, and raised a glass toward Newton.

"*Gānbēi!*" Newton shouted back.

"Won't you join us," the soldier shouted, grabbing Newton by his shoulder and dragging him into the group of carousing soldiers. Another soldier motioned to Phoebe, drunkenly offering her food and drink.

Phoebe smiled and shrugged her shoulders as if she didn't understand.

Desaix and Ann remained silent on the steps in the shadow of the door.

"What brings you here, my young friend?" the soldier asked, offering Newton food. "What is your name?"

"Jin Bo," Newton replied.

"Jin Bo," the soldier said, "my name is Lee Yang, and we are all here to celebrate our commander's birthday." He placed his fingers to his lips in a conspiratorial way. "We are supposed to be looking for a very important person who is fleeing the country with many of China's treasures."

"I like your round-eyed friend," Yang said, grabbing Phoebe away from the officer who was regaling her. He smacked Phoebe's behind playfully.

"*Hǎochīr.* Delicious." Phoebe said, raising a steaming bowl of shark fin soup in a mock toast of appreciation, and spilling it clumsily all over Yang.

"*Hǎochīr,*" Yang repeated, wiping the soup off his green tunic. "Jin Bo, I like this spirited woman. Please invite your other friends over here. I want them to join us."

"Which friends?" Jin Bo asked nervously.

Yang beckoned to Desaix and Ann. "My friends and I want to meet your friends in the shadows." Pausing to collect his thoughts, Yang uttered what he thought was a brilliant insight. "Your friends, the shadow people." He flailed his arms about, as if he were conducting a choir, and he and his friends started to chant, "Bring out the shadow people. Bring out the shadow people."

"Okay . . . okay," Newton responded. He walked hesitantly toward the door and brought Desaix and Ann back to the table with him.

"*Née hǎo.* Hello," Desaix said, extending his hand in a gesture of friendship, to ingratiate himself as quickly as possible with Yang and his inebriated colleagues. To divert attention away from Ann, Desaix pointed to Phoebe and said in English, "She is my wife." Desaix pulled Phoebe to him and smiled at the group.

Newton translated Desaix's words. A glance at Ann confirmed that she had psychologically withdrawn from the present situation.

"*Gānbēi.*" Yang and his friends raised their glasses again and broke out into a song that glorified the virtues of marriage.

"*Gānbēi.*" Desaix shouted, raising a glass of what he now recognized as *máotáī jǐu*. By the number of empty bottles and glasses on the table, Desaix was certain that most of the soldiers were already drunk.

"Let me see who this quiet friend is," Yang said, staggering over to Ann. He stood in front of the old disheveled woman, trying to focus his glassy eyes. Something about her looked familiar. But he wasn't sure what it was. Everything in his brain seemed to be working in slow motion.

He continued to stare at her eyes, too sharp and penetrating for her age. Her high-cheek-boned face, too smooth. Vague images passed through a hazy filter of remembrance. Her bearing, hidden beneath layers of baggy, ragged clothing, was too stately.

Suddenly it all became clear to him.

"The Prime Minister," Yang said and grabbed her.

"No . . . no," Ann responded, pulling back.

"Of course you are!" Yang shouted boisterously. "Of course you are the Prime Minister."

"My dear friend," Newton interjected, "I think the drink has clouded your judgment. This old woman is my great-aunt." Newton pried Ann's arm away from the soldier. "How can a man of your taste compare this hag to the beautiful Lee Ann Wu?"

"Please, old mother, do not be offended," Phoebe said, trying to support Newton's claim, "you are not in good health."

"Yes, you are right," Ann murmured. "I will try to act my age. Am I fifty-seven? Sixty-seven? Is that how old I am?"

The soldiers laughed at her confusion.

"You see," Yang shouted, "the old woman doesn't even know how old she is. Here, grandmother, drink something with us. Perhaps it will help your memory in the same way it blots mine."

Ann took the glass offered to her and stared at its contents.

Newton placed his arm around Yang's shoulder and tried to turn him away from her. But he wouldn't budge. Yang insisted on examining Ann more closely.

"Comrades," Yang shouted to his colleagues. "Arrest this woman!"

The singing and shouting stopped at once. The drunken officers looked at one another, confused.

"If no one will arrest this woman, then I will," Yang shouted, pulling out his gun and aiming it straight at Ann. "I accuse you of being the Prime Minister."

Desaix drew Ann close to him. Phoebe darted in front of them, directly in the line of fire. Newton tried to cajole Yang into putting the gun down. His colleagues were still too inebriated to take him seriously.

"Yang, is this any way to show your hospitality to my friends?" Newton asked in a petulant tone. "You wanted me to join you, and I did. And then you insisted that my friends and relatives join you as well." He paused to look around the room, ascertaining that most of the soldiers were more interested in enjoying themselves than in carrying out orders. "So I brought them over to celebrate with you. And what do you do?" Newton watched Yang's face closely for signs of anger. "First you insult my friend by giving unwanted attention to his wife. Then you frighten my great-aunt. And now you confuse her by telling her she is the Prime Minister. It is not at all proper to take out your gun and threaten us when we are all celebrating together."

The officers in the room broke out into spontaneous applause and cheers. Yang looked around and realized what a fool he had made of himself. He put his gun down by his side and looked ashamed.

"You are right, my friend," Yang said contritely. "I have disgraced myself in front of your friends and your great-aunt. Please excuse me."

"I accept your apology," Ann said in a frail voice. "But youth is not to be wasted so frivolously."

"You know," Yang replied, in a sad tone, relaxing his grip on the gun, "I only meant—"

"I understand that you meant no offense," Ann said, grabbing the gun before he realized what had happened.

Desaix tried to hold her back, but he was too late.

"Remember, son," she said, in her normal voice, "respect for the elderly is the essence of our society. Without reverence to those who are older, Confucius teaches us that you end up without any respect for any authority . . . And that we must not have."

Desaix tried to grab the gun but before he could a shot reverberated throughout the room. Yang fell backward onto the floor, blood trickling down the back of his head.

CHAPTER TWENTY-THREE

Yang lay moaning on the floor of the restaurant. Ann's bullet had missed him entirely, but he had smashed his head against the corner of a table as he tried to avoid a potential second shot. None of his colleagues made a move for their weapons. They were too stunned. As far as they were concerned, a crazy old lady had been insulted by their friend and had tried to shame him.

"Give me the gun," Desaix said calmly, reaching out to Ann. "We have to get out of here before all hell breaks loose."

Ann turned toward Desaix and pointed the gun directly at his head. She stared at him, wondering whether this was the opportunity for which she had waited. She had resented Desaix since she had first met him. Spurning her sexual advances. Cocky in his feeling of Western superiority. Pretending to be her protector, as if she were ill. So what if an Assistant Secretary of State was found dead, killed by a drunken Chinese soldier. She would be free to pursue her goals without any interference from the meddlesome Dr. Clark or his sanctimonious boss. And it could all happen with one bullet. Only Phoebe would know who had done what to whom. Very clever, Ann thought, for Phoebe to have called Desaix into the crisis.

"Give me the gun," Desaix said again, extending his right arm toward her. "You and I know that won't solve anything. You will have to kill everyone in the room. And you're not that self-destructive."

"According to you I'm crazy. Isn't that right?" Ann said. "Why shouldn't I benefit from the merits of being insane?"

"Because you and I know that you wear the cloak of insanity at your convenience," Desaix replied, telling her a half truth. She did have a mental disorder. But she was also highly manipulative in using it to her advantage.

Newton walked over to her and grabbed the gun. "This isn't going to work." He added in a whisper, "What you want to do is really crazy. Don't you realize that we still need them?"

As the shock of the situation wore off and the soldiers quickly sobered up, several of them started to reach for their guns. Newton waved Yang's pistol in the air, shouting that he would kill the first person who tried to stop them. He pushed Ann ahead of him, toward the door to the street. Desaix and Phoebe followed, racing through the restaurant to the already crowded sidewalk.

They each took a bicycle from a nearby stand. Phoebe led the group. Newton followed Phoebe with Desaix making certain that Ann rode in front of him. They pedaled toward the train station on the outskirts of Beijing where Phoebe felt they could pick up the Shanghai express with less risk of being caught than at the main station.

"I know who you are!" Yang shouted, following the intruders out of the restaurant. "You're the Empress Dowager!" He ordered his drunken colleagues to pursue the fleeing bicyclists now already two blocks away.

They pedaled down Dazhalan Street through a maze of bicycle riders. Yang's colleagues screamed to passers-by to stop them, but for the most part the drunken and disheveled soldiers found themselves the object of derision. "Who?" the people asked. "The ones on the black bicycles or the ones on the other black bicycles?" Frustrated and humiliated, several soldiers threw cyclists from their bikes in an attempt to follow their suspects. The remaining soldiers radioed for assistance, informing headquarters that the Prime Minister had been discovered and was being followed.

Looking back at the soldiers in disarray behind them, Phoebe had to laugh at the absurdity of the situation. She was in the middle of a Chinese version of a Mack Sennett Keystone Kops movie, where the bumbling villains were being pursued by an equally bumbling group of policemen. But as in those movies, she knew that eventually the soldiers would catch up to them.

There was only one way to lose them, she decided, and that was in the Bei Hai Lake and park area where she had spent many Sundays walking the countless forest paths. From there they could get a public bus headed toward the Great Wall and then board the Shanghai express at the small station.

Pedaling through the Southwest Gate of Bei Hai Lake, Phoebe led the group toward the Bai Ta, the White Pagoda, a pleasure palace built over a thousand years ago and now a tourist attraction. When she could no longer see any soldiers following them, the group stopped to rest.

"Ah, the Bai Ta," Ann said as she lay her bicycle on the ground. "How kind of you to stop here at one of my ancestral homes."

"Don't start your stories, Ann," Newton said angrily. "Don't play the part of the Grand Empress with her fictitious Mongol forefathers."

"Jin Bo, aren't you being too harsh . . . " Desaix said as he dismounted from his bicycle, deciding that he might have a better chance of gaining Ann's trust again if could exploit the underlying tension between Newton and his sister.

"What she did back there was inexcusable," Newton replied. "She almost had all of us killed because of her stupid pride."

"I don't understand you, Jin Bo," Ann responded in a thin, hurt voice. "You more than anyone should know why I would want to kill that soldier—"

"We don't have much time," Phoebe interrupted. "Let's get something to eat and be on our way."

They walked over to a group of vendors selling their products from small carts and tables. Common vegetables such as spinach, tomatoes, and sweet potatoes were displayed alongside the more colorful, exotic sheepfoot onion, *jiaobai,* stem of wild rice, and ivory radish. Everything from glazed geese hanging from strings to bamboo basketware stocked one on top of the other beckoned them with a full bouquet of colors, tastes, smells, and textures. As if that were not enough, each vendor hawked his goods with the frenzied enthusiasm of a commodity trader, shouting out his price and then lowering it before there was even a response, in order to ensure selling off his entire inventory by the end of the day.

Ann ordered a *jianbingguotai* from a jagged-toothed young man who spread a thin batter over the rounded top of a makeshift stove heated by a pellet of coal.

Never taking his eyes off Ann, Desaix ordered the same, thinking that the resulting pancake stuffed with eggs, mushrooms, onions, and scallions was China's answer to McDonald's Egg McMuffin. Despite the overwhelming demands of two billion people, he knew that very few went hungry or homeless. Somehow, everyone possessed the few yuan needed to buy the minimal essentials for sustenance. Here in China the beggar was looked down upon because he brought shame to his people. While Ann had imposed an authoritarian regime, she had also shaped a basically lazy and disorganized people into a productive, economic international giant. It had taken discipline, force, ambition, and, yes, even terror. But it had worked—in spite of all her personal peccadilloes.

"It's time to go," Phoebe said, watching Newton eat a stick of small candied apples, *bingtanghulu.* No wonder Jin Bo had such oddly shaped yellow teeth, she thought. Like most Chinese he had terrible nutritional habits and probably even worse dental hygiene.

"Phoebe, take a look down the road," Desaix said, pointing toward the North Lake Bridge that led from the Southwest Gate. Several armored personnel carriers were heading toward them. Two MI-24 Russian-built helicopters hovered overhead. This time, if he were captured, Desaix was certain it would not be just a gentlemanly discourse on the necessity of maintaining law and order.

"I have an idea." Desaix said, spying a sign in both Chinese and English. "Follow me." He pushed his way through a path littered with Chinese tourists and purchased four tickets to the dog zoo. The ticket seller tried to tell him that the zoo was out of bounds to everyone but native Chinese. But he slipped her a few extra yuan and received the tickets.

"What are we doing in a dog pound?" Phoebe asked, following Desaix around a gravel path that twisted around chicken-wire fencing that caged hundreds of dogs.

"I want all of these gates opened," Desaix said. "Let the dogs out. I want to create some havoc that will buy us the necessary time to escape."

"Are you nuts?" Phoebe asked, passing an emaciated white Samoyed lying languidly in an outdoor cage next to a boxer whose ribs almost protruded through his skin. Three matted cocker spaniels yelped to be released. Several German shepherds raced inside their cages barking at the running visitors. These were the sorriest dogs she had ever seen.

Phoebe had heard of the dog zoo but had never visited it. The zoo's very existence was a sensitive subject for the Chinese government because Chinese citizens who lived in the cities were forbidden to possess a dog. They were considered an unnecessary luxury that required money and effort to maintain. So the government, years prior to Ann's rule, had created a place that the people could visit and learn what a dog looked like and how it behaved. Glancing over the yelping, unkempt, starving collies, sheepdogs, German shepherds, and French poodles, Phoebe decided that the government was probably a major violator of every American standard for the humane care and feeding of animals.

The four of them ran through the zoo, opening gates. Hundreds of dogs walked and ran from their claustrophobic areas, barking, yelping, biting, licking, and jumping on both the tourists and the soldiers coming through the entrance.

"Oh look how cute these Pekingese are," Ann said, stooping down to pet two yapping, snub-nosed dogs.

"You love them because the first Empress Dowager used to collect them," Newton said, pushing her on.

"Help me!" Phoebe shouted. An emaciated German shepherd stood alert, growling, ready to jump. Phoebe had nowhere to go, pinned up against a metal fence.

"Don't move!" Desaix shouted. He took off his jacket, wrapped it around his right arm, and walked cautiously toward her. As he waved his right arm toward the dog in a threatening manner, he distracted the dog's attention away from her toward him as Phoebe managed to walk slowly away. Once Desaix saw that Phoebe was no longer in danger, he grabbed Newton's unfinished stick of candied apples and threw it toward the dog who immediately started to lick it.

"Let's get out of here," Desaix said as they ran.

"You owe me one *bingtanghulu,*" Newton said, running alongside Desaix and shooing away the dogs that jumped up at them.

On the far side of the exit gate, Desaix noticed a group of Chinese tourists entering one of many dilapidated parked buses. It reminded him of the little yellow school buses used throughout America.

"Jin Bo," Desaix asked. "What does the sign on the bus say?"

"It says that its destination is the Great Wall."

"Tell the driver we want four tickets. And give him this." Desaix handed Newton a fifty-dollar bill.

Within seconds of Newton's conversation with the bus driver, the four were seated in the last row of the filthy, crowded bus, their laps filled with children, animals, and oversized packages.

CHAPTER TWENTY-FOUR

W*an Li Chang Cheng*. The Great Wall of China." Ann shook her head in disgust as she lumbered up the twisting, steep, cobblestone path built five hundred years ago over long sections of northern China's barren hills.

"Try to act like a tourist for the next few hours and enjoy this marvel of human endeavor." Desaix rubbed his hands together, trying vainly to warm them in twenty-mile-an-hour winds carrying a chill factor of ten degrees above zero.

"How long do we have to wait here?" Ann asked, slapping her sides with her hands.

"About two hours," Phoebe replied, rocking back and forth on the balls of her feet. "The Great Wall is the last place that Chang would look for us. And the railroad station is only a few hundred feet from the Badaling portion of the wall."

"Listen to this," Newton said excitedly, reading from a guidebook and eating yet another *bingtanghulu*. "The Great Wall is the only manmade structure that is visible from the moon 240,000 miles away."

"That's a myth propagated by a magazine article written in 1983," Ann retorted.

"Why don't you take a bite of some sweetness from these candied apples," Newton said, extending the stick to her. "It would do you good. Your cynicism and bitterness are getting impossible to tolerate. Lighten up, my dear sister, as the Americans say. Try to make the best of a bad situation."

"Ann has a point," Phoebe said, checking her watch to see if they had enough time to reach the station. "There are a lot of legends associated with this Great Wall—"

"As there are about China," Ann interjected, glaring at Phoebe.

Desaix suspected that there was much more that transpired between the two women than met the eye. Ann seemed to resent the fact that Phoebe was in control, yet accorded her a certain undefined legitimacy in her role. There were certain aspects of their relationship that mirrored the covert ambivalence and hostility between a psychiatrist and his patient, or a professor and his students, or between two lovers, or a control officer and his agent. Most probably both Ann and Newton were working with Phoebe, he concluded, which meant that they might even be on the CIA payroll. But what intrinsic interest did the Agency have in China? he wondered. Since the 1970s they were no longer in the business of overthrowing world leaders because they had acquired a pretty poor performance record and Congress had stripped them of their authority for what was euphemistically called "political action." Over the subsequent thirty years it had evolved into a bloated and rather tame organization that gathered intelligence, analyzed it, and disseminated the information to its principal clients, the President, the Sec State, and the Def Sec. From time to time, a Station Chief in some part of the world would work directly for the Sec State or the Assistant Secretary for that region, in place of the ambassador, because of greater competence or impressive access. But that was the exception these days and not the rule.

Desaix looked at Phoebe trying to keep warm. He wasn't sure exactly when the thought hit him, but at some point during their escape into the tunnels under Beijing he had concluded that Phoebe was working directly for Moffat. It was Moffat who had told her to keep track of him. It was Moffat who had instructed her to sweep his negotiations with Ann. It was Moffat who had instructed her to save Ann and Newton from Chang's revenge. And it was Moffat who wanted Ann in Shanghai.

Desaix did believe Phoebe's initial assertion that she was implementing Moffat's grand strategy of removing Chang from his position of power and replacing him with Ann as the undisputed leader of China. So it was probably Moffat who was controlling a major part of the Chinese side of the current crisis. But who was controlling Chang? Clearly it would have to be someone Moffat opposed. But who?

Suddenly Desaix's dream came back to him with a jolt. Desaix had to laugh to himself. In retrospect, it was so obvious. He was only surprised that it had taken him so long to figure it out. Was the dream warning him that Moffat was the source of all the "bees" or betrayals surrounding him in his "family garden"? But how was Moffat betraying him? By setting him up in this enigmatic world of distorted truths, half truths, and deceit? To what end? Who had really dropped the "silver tray" that was Taiwan? Desaix or Moffat? And who was responsible for "breaking china"? Desaix shuddered, not from the cold, but from his inability to shake off his unwanted thoughts. Was Moffat responsible for the crisis between Taiwan and China?

"The first sections of the Great Wall," Newton continued to read, "were built as early as the fifth century B.C. when a number of Chinese states were fighting against the Mongolian barbarians. In 221 B.C. a ruthless emperor put hundreds of thousands of workers to the grueling task of connecting the earthen walls and creating a great military roadway. A brace of five horses could gallop side by side on top of the wall conveying soldiers, armaments, and supplies. From the sixth century to the fourteenth, the wall was abandoned and fell into disuse. After the Mongols were repulsed by the Ming dynasty in 1368, the emperor decided to rebuild the wall. However, when the Manchu armies captured China and the Qing Dynasty ruled from 1644 to 1911, the wall was again abandoned and fell into ruin."

"That's all nonsense," Ann said. "The wall didn't exist for two thousand years after the date that everyone quotes as the beginning."

"So, history is off a few thousand years," Newton said angrily. "What difference does it make whether the wall can or cannot be seen from the moon or was built two thousand years later than everyone had thought?"

"What difference does it make, my little brother?" Ann asked like a supercilious teenager intent on proving her point. "It's the difference between education and propaganda."

"Propaganda?" Desaix asked, intrigued by her insightful point. He watched with interest as Phoebe looked around nervously. For the moment their safety seemed relatively assured with the crowd of people gathered about them.

"Yes, propaganda," Ann replied impatiently. She wondered if Desaix wasn't more naive than everyone suspected. "The Great Wall was used as a political symbol of national unity and historical legitimacy by Mao Zedong and Deng Xiaoping."

"There's too much cynicism here for one day," Phoebe said, eager to change the conversation.

"Ann's got a point," Desaix said, thinking that in the distance he spotted a soldier with the distinctive green uniform of the Public Security Bureau.

"It's all one big myth," Ann suddenly shouted in English to the mass of tourists around them. "The Great Wall of China cannot be seen from the moon. Astronauts have reported that all they could see, miles above the earth, were the hazy outlines of the continents." She paused to determine whether the crowd was listening to what she had to say. "The Great Wall never marked the northern border of China. It was a lousy deterrent to invasion by barbarian hordes. And no one can even agree how long it is." Ann stopped to catch her breath, pleased to be able to debunk sacred cows again. Her ability to brazenly tell the truth had allowed her to claw her way through the political network. It had established her reputation as a fearless politician. But truth to Ann was little more than an instrument of political expediency. She had no illusions about herself or Desaix or Phoebe. Given the appropriate circumstances, any one of them would lie. But like most Americans, they would always couch their lies in terms of rationalizations about national security interests.

At least she didn't fool herself, Ann thought. She rarely had to invoke anything more than her own persona as a ruler. Even the appearance of madness had distinct advantages. It allowed her, like many of her infamous predecessors in other countries, to commit acts of duplicity, terror, and violence with impunity. How convenient for Stalin to have executed over twenty million of his fellow citizens as a "paranoid megalomaniac," she thought. No one dared to confront him directly with his barbarous acts. Instead, he was dismissed as a "madman" with whom one had no other choice but to deal as if he were "crazy." Ann had concluded a long time ago that the international community found it convenient to accept ruthless world leaders like Mao, Pol Pot, Saddam Hussein, Assad, Milosevic as long as the psychiatric labels of "crazy" or "mad" were attached to them. These labels allowed the responsible world leaders to absolve themselves from making the "madman" accountable for his or her treacherous deeds.

"I think it's time to go," Desaix said, gently taking her arm and trying to pull her away from the gathering crowd. Although few of the onlookers understood English, Ann's hostile, haughty manner seemed to agitate those around her.

"Leave me alone," Ann shouted, pulling her arm free from his hold. "These are my people and they understand me."

"They don't. And they don't know who you are," Desaix whispered firmly. As a physician he was concerned that she might start to fall apart, but as a crisis manager he was aware of the way she was using her illness to manipulate everyone around her. And he was determined to limit her behavior before she wound up harming them.

"Desaix is right," Newton said, finishing his last candied apple. "You are becoming a freak show."

"So now I'm a freak, "Ann said, newly determined to continue her monologue. "The Great Wall cannot represent strength or progress or glory because it is a symbol of confinement, conservatism, impotent defense, and cowardice in the face of invasion."

Desaix anxiously glanced around. Now he could see several soldiers in the distance, approaching.

"Let's get out of here," Desaix said, grabbing Ann's arm. He pushed her up the cobblestone steps, followed by Phoebe and Newton, toward the watch tower.

"Let go of me," Ann said, trying to pull away from Desaix. "I can't go any further. I'm exhausted."

Desaix looked behind him and could see that Newton and Phoebe were also having trouble. But Chang's soldiers were gaining on them, effortlessly taking the steps two-by-two in cleated boots that prevented them from slipping.

Desaix and Ann stopped to catch their breath at a landing on which two Mongolian vendors wrapped in heavy fur coats were selling Great Wall T-shirts and memorabilia from a rickshaw bicycle.

"Ask them how much they want for all of their merchandise, including that run-down rickshaw," Desaix said to Ann. He figured that three people would just barely be able to sit in the back seat.

"Wait a minute," Ann said, her chest heaving up and down.

"Damnit! Ask them!" Desaix screamed, desperate to try anything that would put some distance between them and the approaching soldiers. Catching up to them, Newton asked the question for his sister. The two vendors smiled and conferred with each other. This was the opportunity they had dreamed of—a wealthy foreigner offering them whatever they wanted for their goods.

"We'd better hurry up," Phoebe said.

"Here, Jin Bo," Desaix said, reaching into his pocket and handing him money. "Give them a hundred dollars. Tell them that I don't have any time to negotiate the price."

Once the money changed hands, Desaix threw the memorabilia to the ground and placed Ann in the back seat, squeezing her in between Newton and Phoebe. He mounted the torn bicycle seat and started to pedal the rickshaw down the cobblestone steps. If only Moffat or Cartwright were here, he thought. They would have appreciated the ingenuity behind his Great Wall Rickshaw Escape.

The rickshaw sped down the steps on its airless tires. Using the faulty handbrakes, Desaix tried to slow down the momentum of their increasingly greater acceleration, but without too much success. The oncoming tourists hugged the sides of the Great Wall in disbelief, grateful for a chance to stop their exhausting climb for a short while as the rickshaw sped by them.

"On the count of three," Desaix yelled back to them as they approached the bottom. "Phoebe has to jump out first. Then throw your sister off, Newton, and jump off last. There's no way to stop this thing."

Ann didn't reply. But she couldn't help being impressed with Desaix's ingenuity.

"One . . . two . . . " Desaix counted, knowing that he had to be very precise to avoid crashing into the stone wall at the bottom of the steps.

"Watch out!" Ann shouted, realizing that there was no way they could avoid becoming entangled in a group of soldiers just starting their trek up the steps.

Chapter Twenty-five

General Chang," Ann said, spitting out the words as if they were snake venom, "you will never get away with detaining us without any formal charges."

"I think you are right," Chang said as he led his four captives around the seemingly abandoned detention center, whose handful of rusted, corrugated Quonset huts and wooden guard towers had been built at the end of World War II. "Renounce your office as Prime Minister, stop this impending war, and I will set you and your companions free."

"I will give up my post as Prime Minister," Ann replied, firmly, "if you walk away from your position as Supreme Commander of the People's Liberation Army."

"That sounds fair to me," Desaix said.

"Fair?" Chang repeated the word with a tone of disgust. "Dr. Clark, I think I have been more than fair with you. At the Public Safety Bureau I gave you the opportunity to choose between me and Ann, a political charlatan." Chang's face squeezed into a grimace of discomfort. "I tried to explain to you that it was she, not I, who created the military crisis over Taiwan." He pointed an accusatory finger at her and shouted, "She wants to draw the United States into a confrontation with China. She even drew the Japanese into a reluctant partnership with her. And it all serves her own schemes of expansionism over the entire Pacific Rim. Her own Pax Pacifica, with my help or without it." He paused to assess the reaction of the group, huddled closely together to counter the effects of the biting winds from the Gobi Desert. "Fair, Dr. Clark? I have been more than fair. Some of my people now consider me foolish for having thought that I could have persuaded Ann to be reasonable. Or you."

"What purpose does holding us in this detention camp serve?" Desaix asked, looking to an inordinately silent Phoebe for support. "We have the means to rectify your grievances."

Chang smiled with incredulity. "If I let you all leave here, you would have me believe that once you reached your destination, you would present a fair picture of what I have just told you? And as a result of my compelling arguments, your senior government officials, especially your good friend Moffat," Chang continued sarcastically, "might change his support from Ann to me?"

"I can guarantee that you would get an impartial hearing," Desaix said, hoping that his own misgivings weren't apparent in his voice. What did Chang mean when he said that Moffat was supporting Ann? As far as Desaix knew there were never any discussions on the seventh floor of the State Department concerning whom Moffat supported, and there was still no official tilt one way or the other. But Phoebe's support for Ann did belie that impartiality.

"And what do you say to Dr. Clark's guarantee, Ms. Hill?" Chang asked sardonically.

"I think that Dr. Clark is to be taken at his word," Phoebe replied.

"What guarantees could you give me, Ms. Hill, that I would receive a fair hearing from Secretary of State Moffat?" Chang asked.

Desaix wondered why Chang would ask Phoebe for her opinion. Wasn't it sufficient that an Assistant Secretary of State gave his word? Why would Chang seek corroboration from her? Desaix's suspicions of Phoebe deepened. It was she who might hold the solution to which of the two ruthless politicians Desaix should trust.

Desaix had to laugh at himself. Trusting a politician was a contradiction in terms. Desaix had often wondered why he, himself, didn't run for office since he had chosen to work in the politician's world of deception and posturing. But he had come to the conclusion that by temperament he was ill suited to spend a good part of his life involved in a series of trade-offs in order to pass legislation. Like Ann and Chang, he preferred an autocratic approach to decision-making. So he had entered the world of politics through the back door, manipulating people, ideas, and emotions without being accountable to anything more than vague remembrances.

"As you know, General Chang," Phoebe said in a subdued voice, "the U.S. government doesn't make any political or monetary concessions to kidnappers or hostage takers. But our policy is to discuss anything and everything with leaders . . . and potential leaders . . . of their country."

"Again I state that I will guarantee you a fair hearing from Secretary of State Moffat," Desaix said angrily, bothered by the fact that both Ann and Chang were acting like two feuding siblings vying for the approval of an American Secretary of State. Not the President, but the Secretary of State. Something was very wrong. And he, Desaix, was perceived by both of them as having a secondary position of importance to Phoebe. He felt as if he were watching a school play written and produced by Moffat with Phoebe directing the actors. He would have to let the play evolve through its standard three acts before he could try to influence the finale.

Desaix saw Chang again look to Phoebe for bona fides.

"Don't let him rile you, Desaix," Ann said, standing behind him for protection against the wind. "He's an expert at playing off one ally against another."

"That's a joke," Chang uttered. "It's your Empress Dowager who knows how to make two brothers fight each other. Even I must admit that her skills are admirable."

"Why not invite General Chang to travel with us?" Phoebe suggested unexpectedly. Looking at Desaix's face, she saw that she had caught him off guard.

"Well, General Chang?" Desaix asked. "What do you think of that suggestion?" He was impressed by Phoebe's quick mind. She didn't miss a beat. And nothing seemed to fluster her. Definitely comfortable in the world of power and personality. As a matter of fact, too comfortable. He needed to draw her out to see exactly what she knew.

"I will consider your invitation," Chang said.

"We were headed to Shanghai when your escort arrived at the Great Wall," Desaix offered, hoping that his show of good faith would pay off.

"Thank you, Dr. Clark, for your confidence in me," Chang said. He straightened his body as much as his hunched back would allow and led the group into a small metal hut filled with broken furniture and fragments of rusted farm machinery. The room had the distinct stale odor of neglect and disuse.

As you might imagine," Chang went on, "I already suspected where you were heading. As Ann can confirm, our intelligence is quite good."

"Is it a deal?" Desaix asked, hoping to resolve the matter before Chang did anything that could never be forgiven by the U.S. government.

"I will have nothing to do with this criminal," Ann screamed. "Article 43-52 of Criminal Procedure Law states that he must interrogate us within twenty-four hours of detention. And the detainee's family, in this case the people of China, should be informed of the circumstances of my detention within forty-eight hours."

Newton whispered something in his sister's ear.

"Don't tell the Prime Minister of China what she can or cannot do," Ann shouted at him, agitated. "General Chang, have you informed the Procuratorate of our detention?"

"Take hold of yourself, Madame Prime Minister," Chang replied blandly. "Look about you. No one other than yourself is so distraught."

"Don't provoke him," Desaix whispered to Ann.

"Leave me alone, you hypocrite," Ann said, pulling away. "You have insulted me by suggesting that my words should be arbitrated by a third party in order to determine who is lying."

Chang pushed aside a rusted metal cabinet that was concealing a metal door. Opening it, he escorted the group down a narrow set of stairs that led into a well-lit area, half the size of a baseball field, teeming with armed soldiers and what seemed to be civilian laborers working on heavy machinery. At the far side of the room were offices.

"Crimes of counterrevolution are dealt with under Article 90-104 of the criminal law," Ann said, hoping Chang would be forced to admit that they were being detained for criminal activity. Then she could request legal recourse to a public trial, something Chang of course would want to avoid.

"Ann, please let Desaix handle Chang," Phoebe said soothingly.

"Get away, you traitor!" Ann shouted, shoving Phoebe. "Chang's your puppet, not mine."

"What do you mean by that?" Desaix asked, grabbing Ann by her shoulders.

"Ask your compatriot, Ms. Phoebe Hill," Ann replied caustically, shaking his hands away. "I'm certain she can tell you whatever you may want to know."

"Please, Ann, don't say things that you might later regret," Phoebe said, glancing at Desaix.

"Arrest me, General Chang!" Ann yelled. "Charge me with treason. No, arrest me for spreading counterrevolutionary propaganda." Her voice was drowned out by the noise of the machines.

"In the spirit of friendly cooperation," Chang said, ignoring Ann, "I would like you to see our detention center. This way you can report to the American public that we are not the barbarians that your media portray us to be."

"General," Newton asked, "couldn't we dispense with this? Please allow my sister and us to eat something and take a much needed rest."

"All in its proper time, Jin Bo," Chang replied. "Dr. Clark, I know you would be interested to learn that Chinese penal policy considers labor to be an integral part of personal rehabilitation."

"Are all these workers political prisoners?" Desaix asked, resenting the fact that he felt like a pawn thrust in the middle of a political chess game played by two masters. Ann's fluctuations in behavior in the service of political self-preservation reminded him of President Donald Westview's misguided attempt to increase his popularity by staging a fake coup against himself. Fortunately, Westview's stratagem backfired and contributed to his own political demise.

"It would be foolish of me to deny that the people you see are not political prisoners," Chang replied, "considering that our beloved Prime Minister Lee Ann Wu placed them here."

"Nonsense," Ann replied. "China no longer has political prisoners."

"Officially our Prime Minister is correct," Chang answered quietly. "China does not have political prisoners. Then why am I forced to house and feed over one million counterrevolutionaries who have committed crimes against the state such as organizing demonstrations, disclosing information to foreigners, and disseminating treasonous material? I do not know what to label these people, since we have no political prisoners. But I think that you will find as a result of our tour that these 'workers' are treated well."

"Our human rights bureau has received numerous complaints," Desaix interrupted, "about the use of cattle prods, electrodes, beatings, shackles, and prolonged periods of solitary confinement and being held incommunicado . . . "

Chang responded to Desaix's assertions by pulling an emaciated, frightened laborer away from his lathe. He spoke to the prisoner in Chinese and the man removed his shirt. "As you can see from the extensive black-and-blue marks on his back, this man has been beaten quite severely. I could lie to you and tell you that it was done by one of the other prisoners over some minor matter. But I will not insult your intelligence. As some people here might want me to." Chang paused and stared at Ann. "The truth is that this man physically attacked a guard with a homemade knife. The guard almost lost his life. In order to teach the other prisoners a lesson, this man was whipped in front of the other prisoners. This is your so-called torture. But that is more the exception than the rule."

"Do you mind if I pick the next prisoner?" Desaix asked, feeling that he had been set up by Chang.

"Not at all," Chang replied confidently. "Pick anyone you want."

Desaix looked around the makeshift factory. It was like many he had seen in China, filthy and disorganized. Rusted water pipes hung loosely from the ceiling. Frayed electrical wiring wound itself in and around the building and machines alike. In order to save electricity, the ceiling was covered with alternately lit flickering fluorescent lights. The room smelled like an unwashed urinal in a sweat-filled gymnasium. In fact, the factory reminded Desaix of some of the psychiatric back wards for chronic patients in which he had worked in Louisiana before joining the State Department. Like the patients on those wards, the prisoners looked lobotomized. They worked in a methodical, automaton-like way, as if they were on high doses of a tranquilizer.

"General," Desaix said, "would you please take off your shirt?"

The question caught Chang and the others by surprise. Desaix could almost see Chang's blood pressure rise as his face reddened. But with a sneer on his face, Chang meticulously unbuttoned his shirt. Turning slowly around, he revealed a back scarred with fibrous tissue, obviously the result of beatings.

"How did you know?" Ann asked, trying to hide the admiration of Desaix she felt.

"Careful observation of human behavior," Desaix replied, examining Chang's back. "The more I thought about the general's hunched walk and how painful it seems for him to rub against a hard surface—"

"We have millions of Chinese men who have some sort of structural deformity in their back," Ann interrupted, realizing that Desaix was now essential to her survival. A man with such acute powers of observation was to be taken very seriously. She wondered what he had concluded about her.

"His is not a skeletal deformity," Desaix replied, examining a faded tattoo on the back of the general's left shoulder. "General Chang avoids accentuating the lingering pain by keeping his back slightly hunched. I suspect that these scarred welts are the result of systematic beatings over a long period of time," Desaix continued. "Could those whippings have been a lesson to his fellow officers from his beautiful Prime Minister? Just a reminder that any act of disloyalty to her would be severely punished." Desaix turned to Ann. "One of your hostage games, I presume." He looked to Newton, who lowered his eyes. When Desaix glared at Phoebe, she also looked away.

"Since you are clearly an astute observer of human behavior," Ann said sarcastically, "tell me what else you have deduced about my poor, good general."

"On the basis of his speech and mannerisms," Desaix replied, "he wasn't born or reared in China. General Chang is a native Taiwanese." The Tiger Eel tattoo he saw on Chang's shoulder would remain Desaix's secret.

CHAPTER TWENTY-SIX

M r. Secretary," Renee Rydell said calmly, "we have just been placed on Def Con One. We are now in a maximum state of military alert." The frail Deputy Assistant Secretary was surrounded by Edwin Rittenhouse and William Toland of the East Asian and Pacific bureau crisis staff.

"And it's about time," Edwin responded. The rotund FSO served as the official Pol-Mil liaison between State and DOD. "Any longer and the People's Liberation Army would have called our bluff."

"What type of aircraft has DOD dedicated to the attack on China—or should I more correctly say the defense of Taiwan?" Moffat asked, staring at the marked-up map of East Asia hanging on the wall of the Op Center.

"Four AWACS are already in place," Rydell replied, "providing the necessary airborne surveillance, warning, and combat control. In addition, we have the usual assortment of F-117A, F-15, and F-16 air-combat fighters ready to engage the Chinese MiG-21s and MiG-29s. Our long-ranger bombers, the F-111 and the Stealth B-1, are prepared to penetrate deep into the People's Republic and knock out the Frog and Scud missile sites, command centers, and petroleum, lubricant, and oil depots. DOD has already placed on line the High-Speed Anti-Radiation missile to explode their warheads. At the same time, DOD's portable Patriot tactical air defense system installed throughout Taiwan is designed to destroy incoming missiles and aircraft. And by the way, the Senate and House Foreign Relations Committees are waiting to assist you and the President in passing the appropriate authorization to intervene militarily."

"I presume that they are part of DOD's Stage One and Two offensive," Moffat responded, looking at Edwin for confirmation. He wasn't worried about the Hill. He had excellent relations with the key members, who trusted him implicitly and would give him whatever he needed.

"Yes, sir," Edwin said. "Stage One begins with a massive attack against the PLA's missile sites and command centers. Stage Two involves an air offensive against the PLA's rail lines, roads, ammunition, fuel depots, and other logistical targets. Stage Three, which would come only after our preliminary evaluations of Stages One and Two are done, is a concentrated air-ground attack against PLA ground forces including the elite troops stationed in Manchuria and Fujian provinces. Hopefully, we will never get to that point. China will have capitulated and Taiwan will accept a peace of sorts. Stage Four would be a more concentrated U.S. ground attack."

"What do you think, Mr. Toland?" Moffat asked William, Desaix's natty exec sec.

"Well, sir," Toland replied hesitantly, "I would feel a lot more comfortable if Dr. Desaix Clark weren't over there."

"Do we know where Desaix is?" Moffat asked. As both his best friend and his bureaucratic protector he wanted to make certain that he appeared to do whatever was necessary to extract Desaix from China before a war began. But Moffat wouldn't let himself be caught in the trap of having short-term tactical concerns dictate longer-term strategic outcomes. He recalled the Iran hostage siege, when the worry about the fate of the Americans paralyzed American foreign policy for three years and caused the downfall of President Jimmy Carter. Moffat knew that he couldn't hold military plans hostage to Desaix's well-being.

"NSA ELINT sweeps and HUMINT intel indicate that Desaix is

somewhere between Beijing and Shanghai," Toland replied. "Isn't there anything we can do to get him out?"

"What about it, Edwin?" Moffat asked in a concerned voice.

"We've already tasked the SEALs, the 82nd Airborne Division," Edwin responded, "the Rangers, the Green Berets, and Delta Force to prepare Special Ops plans to fly Dr. Clark out of the PRC—when located."

"Good," Moffat said, comfortable knowing that while he was flying to the Far East the Op Center would be managing the crisis effectively. In any case, he would be in constant contact with them from his airborne State Department. "Remember, absolutely no military action is to be initiated without my explicit consent. Is that understood?"

"Does that mean that the rules of engagement do not allow our planes to fire back," Edwin asked, "even if fired upon?"

"That's correct," Moffat replied, walking out of the Op Center. "No shots are to be fired under *any* condition."

"I don't get it," Edwin said. "We're simply shadowboxing."

"You heard the boss," Renee said. "No shooting. Make sure DOD understands that."

Toland broke into a huge grin. What a wonderful friendship, he thought. Moffat was holding up a war until Desaix could be gotten safely out of China.

"What the hell is going on here with Chang and Ann?" Desaix asked angrily, pulling Phoebe over to the side of the Quonset hut.

"Wait a minute," Phoebe said, trying to loosen his grip. "I don't know what you're talking about."

"Right," Desaix replied, "just like you didn't think I would uncover the fact that you've set me up." He hoped Phoebe wouldn't realize that he was on a Cajun fishing expedition, throwing in the garbage-eating catfish in order to catch the crawfish needed for his highly priced étouffée stew.

"Where do you come off telling China's Defense Minister that he's, in effect, a traitor?" Phoebe asked, fidgeting with her hands. "Do you want to have all of us killed?"

"No," Desaix replied coldly. "I don't want to get us all killed. But I am afraid that one of us, namely me, will end up conveniently dead in some out-of-the-way malaria-infested ditch unless I find out what is going on here. And I said that he was born in Taiwan, not that he was a traitor."

"Let's not quibble," Phoebe said. "You accused the Commander-in-Chief of the PLA of being Taiwanese in order to destroy his credibility in front of his men and his main political rival, little Miss Ann, who is intent on invading Taiwan. Very clever, Dr. Clark. But I don't think that your cheap psychological tricks will work. If you get him angry enough then he may do away with all of us."

"You sound like a goddamn apologist for him," Desaix said. "If I didn't know better, I would suspect that you were also his control officer."

"You've been working in China too long," Phoebe responded. "You're starting to think and act like *they* do—suspicious and mistrustful of everyone."

"The correct word for what you're telling me is paranoid," Desaix said.

"Okay, Dr. Clark," Phoebe replied, "if it makes you feel any better, I'm saying that you're paranoid, and unless you can contain your suspiciousness and wild accusations you're going to get us all killed."

"From day one at the museum you were calling the shots." Desaix mimicked her inviting, seductive voice: "Did you know that Chinese lice are yellow in color while North American lice are dark brown?"

"Oh, come on."

"Why didn't you tell me," Desaix asked, "that Ann has a serious mental problem?"

"Am I your social worker?" Phoebe replied defiantly.

"No," Desaix said, "but as the Beijing Station Chief you certainly were the person in charge of overseeing the preparation of Ann's Psychological Profile and Operational Code. I found it strange that no mention was made of her OCD. Or even her mercurial temper. So I began to ask myself why?" He paused to order his thoughts before they were completely overtaken by his rage. "I asked myself who would benefit from such a serious omission."

"And . . . ?" Phoebe asked, knowing that she would have to hear him out even though there was no more time.

" . . . and I came to the conclusion that someone wanted me at a serious disadvantage in dealing with the Chinese Prime Minister," Desaix said. "I could envision a scenario where you hoped I would turn against Ann and commit myself to getting rid of her."

"But you're a psychiatrist," Phoebe replied. "You are the best person to understand her and deal with her." He was cunning, she thought. He knew more than she had suspected but not as much as he might want to.

"Very clever, Phoebe," Desaix replied. "But you knew from my own history in the department that the minute I picked up the fact that she wasn't all there mentally I would return to the States and tell Moffat that we should attempt to remove her. And short of any surprises to you, she would be replaced with none other than good old General Chang, who, I suspect, has been on your payroll for quite some time."

"You're losing me, Desaix," Phoebe said, quietly impressed with his ability to unravel the tangled ball of string she had handed him a few days ago.

"It's really very simple," Desaix said, relaxing a little bit now that he felt some sense of control again. "It boils down to an old-fashioned bureaucratic rivalry—the State Department supports the beautiful wicked witch, Ann, but the CIA wants macho man, General Chang, to become the new leader of China. According to your assessment, Ann is too volatile, too hard to handle. On the other hand, Chang is a good ole boy, probably trained in the States and with deep roots in our intelligence and security institutions. Admittedly, he's not quite as attractive or charismatic as Ann, but he's a helluva lot more dependable and controllable."

"I'm listening," Phoebe replied, knowing that Desaix had to get the anger out of his system before they could work together on their release.

"So it was your job as Station Chief to make sure that I switched my allegiance from Ann to Chang," Desaix said. "How am I doing?"

"Not bad," Phoebe replied, aware that even Desaix needed stroking. She wondered if this was a universal trait for all narcissistic men who find themselves, sooner or later, performing in front of a woman. "But how did you figure out that Chang had been Ann's prisoner?"

"First, it was clear that tension ran high between you and Ann. My clinical intuition told me that the hostility Ann felt toward you had a long history that antedated my arrival."

"Two women disliking each other is not exactly an epiphany," Phoebe replied, realizing that Desaix was more intuitive than intellectual. In a crunch, he would rely primarily on his gut feelings.

"No, it's not a revelation. On the other hand, two strong-willed women working with each other against a common enemy comes pretty close to a unique situation," Desaix replied. "But the fact that you brought her to the Dazhalan underground shelter told me that Newton is also on your payroll, along with Chang."

"I don't follow you," Phoebe said innocently.

"There was only one way that you could have known that I was incarcerated by Chang. Either he told you. Or Newton told you. Or both. Most likely, because of the tight security in the Gongabu, Newton was unable to reach you, and Chang told you that I was there. I am also assuming that neither Chang nor Newton knew that the other was working for the same spymaster—Ms. Phoebe Hill." As Desaix spoke, he was conscious of the outlines of a picture taking shape where there had previously been haze. "In part, Chang had me arrested in order to surface the proposition that is at the core of this whole mess—am I with him or am I with Ann? On a larger scale, the same question can be rephrased in strict realpolitik terms: Do U.S. government interests lie with Chang and his efforts to stop an impending war with Taiwan? If we believe that is what he wants to do. Or do our interests lie with Ann, a Machiavellian leader who is interested in expansionism? If we believe that is what she will do. Which leader will really prevent a war from occurring?"

"You've got a great sense of the dramatic, Desaix," Phoebe said smiling, "but I'm not ready to accept or deny your reasoning. Let's get down to the important issue. Which one *do* you support? Ann or Chang?"

"I want to prevent even the remotest possibility of a war that would eventually bring in the U.S.," Desaix replied. "And if that means I have to get Ann to Shanghai to defuse a crisis that she provoked for her own benefit, then that's what I will do."

"Since when does Desaix Clark simply follow seventh-floor orders?" Phoebe asked, trying to provoke him. "Aren't you the infamous iconoclast who makes his own rules and regulations?"

"Are you looking for trouble?" Desaix asked.

"Am I?" Phoebe replied, knowing that she had Desaix just where she wanted him. On the defensive. "You still haven't answered my question—Ann or Chang?"

"Is there a realistic choice?" Desaix asked, surprised at his own ambivalence. He just wasn't sure.

"You and I know that Moffat will listen to whatever you tell him," Phoebe said, her mouth increasingly dry. "You were right," she added, hoping that what she was about to tell him would gain his trust. "The CIA supports Chang. We believe that he can defuse a crisis that Ann created for her own reasons. We don't feel she is mentally stable enough to run a household, let alone to continue to run a country of two billion people. But your friend Moffat has the final ear of the President. So unless you convince him that Lee Ann Wu is not fit to rule there isn't a snowball's chance in hell that we can persuade Moffat away from supporting her."

"Why doesn't Chang just get rid of her?" Desaix asked, trying to assess Phoebe's candor.

"For the same reason that Ann never tried to eliminate Chang. It's the classic standoff. Each one has his own very powerful domestic and international constituency. So they play games. Intimidation. Kidnapping. Torture. Just to break down the other's will power. Every time Ann has had Chang flogged, he, in turn, has retaliated by kidnapping Newton or threatening the lives of others near to her. That was one of the reasons he took you captive." Sensing a sudden vulnerability in Desaix's face, she decided to make a bold, unorthodox move. She reached out to squeeze his hand. "I tried to stop him. I told him that it was a very serious mistake that could backfire." She wished that she didn't like touching Desaix. And she was aware that he took his time before removing his hand. "I know that you don't believe me. And there is no reason why you should right now. But I am afraid that we are entering a new phase. Chang no longer listens to me. Several weeks before you arrived the situation started getting completely out of control. And the ultimate outcome might be civil war."

"Why does Moffat support her?" Desaix asked, surprised that after all these years of friendship he wouldn't automatically know the answer to the question. "And why did he order you to help her, knowing your allegiance is to the CIA and Chang?"

"The stated reason is that she is the leader of China and a long-standing ally," Phoebe replied, sounding unconvinced herself. "But I think that Moffat genuinely believes she is the better of the two, despite her . . . handicaps."

"Moffat seems to trust you quite a lot," Desaix said, realizing that his friend had greater faith in this apparatchik than in his own best friend.

"You could say that," Phoebe said, suddenly sorry for Desaix.

"Stop playing mind games with me," Desaix said, stepping back from her into the sudden realization that she was manipulating him again. "I asked you why Moffat supports Ann."

"You tell me, Doctor," Phoebe replied defiantly. "He's your best friend. Isn't there lots of *quanxi* between the two of you, as we China hands like to say?"

"What the hell does *quanxi* have to do with any of this?" Desaix asked.

"Think, Desaix," Phoebe replied, as if she were a sixth-grade teacher encouraging one of her pupils to expand his intellectual horizons.

"I can't," Desaix responded, frustrated by his inability to comprehend what Phoebe might be hinting at. *Quanxi,* that magical, indefinable word. A word that he and Moffat always used to explain their special friendship to the outside world. A word that bound them both intellectually and emotionally. A word they both used to explain shifting power alliances that existed within the seniormost levels of any government. One simple word, so amorphous, so expressive, and yet so elusive, Desaix thought. But Phoebe had something very concrete in mind. Something that was only one memory synapse away.

"Concentrate, Desaix," Phoebe pleaded. "Why did Moffat send you here? What conceivable reason would he have to send his best friend into a crisis that was created by a mercurial long-term lady friend of his?"

"What did you say?" Desaix asked, stunned by Phoebe's last words.

"You heard me. Long-term lady friend." Once again, she felt sorry for Desaix. He looked both hurt and confused, trying to comprehend what his unconscious was dutifully protecting him from.

"Come with me, Dr. Clark," Chang said brusquely, physically separating Desaix and Phoebe. Two guards took Desaix into custody. "It's time for your reeducation program."

CHAPTER TWENTY-SEVEN

This is what will happen if you support Ann," Chang said, turning on the movie projector in the small darkened room in which Desaix, Ann, Phoebe, and Newton sat. "Civil war and a multitude of atrocities that even you, Dr. Clark, would find incredible."

"I don't have to be party to this propaganda," Ann shouted, standing up.

"Sit down!" Chang ordered. He nodded to the three guards standing by the door in the back of the room. One bolted the door and remained standing while the other two took seats behind Chang's "guests."

Desaix watched as a grainy black-and-white film appeared on the makeshift screen, a white sheet attached to the dirty wall behind it.

Chang began his narration as images of Chinese men and women, chased and murdered by what appeared to be other Chinese civilians, moved across the screen. "During Mao's Cultural Revolution of 1966 to 1976, ten million innocent Chinese people died because of an uncontrolled surge of ideological fervor, mass hysteria, and brutality. But even recently, acts of cannibalism have been reported in certain areas of China and Prime Minister Lee Ann Wu has done nothing to stop it."

"Lies," Ann screamed. "All lies. We didn't know anything about it."

"Official reports that I had prepared in the mid-1980s and updated in the mid-1990s were suppressed by the authorities," Chang continued. "They documented countless cases of cannibalism, especially in the Guangxi Autonomous Region in southern China."

"When I found out about these acts," Ann interrupted, "I ordered the local government officials to put a stop to them. But they were under Chang's control, not mine."

Ignoring the bickering between Ann and Chang, Desaix sat transfixed by the gruesome scenes of two dozen high school students attacking their principal, stabbing him repeatedly until his head rolled off his body onto the blood-stained cafeteria floor. He watched as a pretty, cherub-faced girl, wielding a sharp butcher's knife, peeled off a layer of skin from the principal's abdomen. She proudly announced in a high-pitched voice, translated in the English subtitles, that she was the former girlfriend of the principal's son. She said that she had no sympathy for him and that she was ideologically "correct." She then proceeded to eat the man's flesh to the resounding approval of her fellow students.

Desaix looked away. He had seen all kinds of barbarous acts from mutilation to torture, but this was the first time he had actually witnessed an act of cannibalism.

"Please, Dr. Clark," Chang said, "this is only one small example of what actually transpired. I strongly suggest you watch the rest of the film. I believe you will find it quite enlightening."

An official Chinese document appeared on the screen. Chang paraphrased it for the audience. "This document, prepared by Chinese government officials, is called 'The Diverse Varieties of Cannibalism.' It says that there were many varieties of cannibalism practiced in the provinces. Among them are killing someone and making a late dinner of it, slicing off the meat and having a big party, dividing up the flesh so each person takes a large chunk home to boil, roasting the liver and eating it for its medicinal properties."

Desaix watched as a heavyset student took the girl's knife and made a large incision in the dead man's chest and dragged the knife down through his abdomen.

Running to the side of the room, Newton threw up. Now the stench of vomit, as well as the hideous images, pervaded the room.

"Enough of this nonsense. I had no part in this," Ann shouted. "I'm getting out of here." As she started toward the door, a guard stepped forward.

"Please sit down, Madame Prime Minister," Chang said forcefully.

Ann acquiesced, returning to her seat.

"General Chang," Phoebe said, "I think your message is quite clear."

"Remember, Desaix, the different techniques that you used to teach in your psychological warfare course?" Chang asked.

Despite a sick feeling in the pit of his stomach, Desaix said nothing, not wanting to utter any sound that might give Chang the satisfaction of knowing that his *hsi nao,* brainwashing, was working. Chang's question also corroborated Desaix's suspicion that Chinese intelligence had developed extensive files on senior State Department officials. How else would Chang have learned about Desaix's early years in the State Department, when he used to teach an FSO course called Totalitarian Coercive Methods for Eliciting Individual Compliance. According to Desaix's own teachings, Chang was at the fifth level of coercion. "Degradation" through images of human barbarism. Desaix and his group had already experienced "threats," level four. Ironic, Desaix thought, how beautifully systematic forcing psychological compliance could be. None of that histrionic mad-scientist quality portrayed in movies was necessary.

"Madame Prime Minister," Chang said sardonically, "what do you think of your great white knight now? Do you think that he can help you? He seems totally paralyzed by a simple film."

"Why do you ask me these foolish questions?" Ann responded. "He's no concern of mine. Do what you want with him." She waved her hand dismissively. "Stop playing games with me. If you do not, rest assured I will try to kill you when the opportunity arises." She turned to her brother, who had come back to his seat.

"I'm sure you will," Chang replied, returning his attention to Desaix. "Well, Dr. Clark, have you reconsidered your allegiance? Is this callous woman the one whom you want to rule China?"

Desaix didn't respond. He tried to keep his mind occupied with thoughts of what he would say to Moffat when he met him again. He knew that if he focused on the film, he would become what Chang intended—both physically ill and mentally depressed.

"What is his other choice, General Chang?" Phoebe asked indignantly. "Accept the allegiance of a brutally sadistic military officer who has sworn to obey the humanitarian code of conduct provided to political prisoners by the United Nations Geneva Accords?"

"Oh, Ms. Hill," Chang replied, "please spare me the diplomatic hypocrisies."

"General," Phoebe replied sternly, "I must insist you release Dr. Clark and the three of us, immediately, otherwise . . . "

"Otherwise what, Ms. Hill?" Chang asked. "Otherwise you will have me assassinated? Neutralized? Overthrown? Remember, as far as China is concerned, Dr. Clark has no official status here. He was asked to leave the country days ago and has not complied with our request. He . . . and you . . . knew what the consequences of being persona non grata would be."

"You can't get away with this," Phoebe replied. "It's only a question of time before you will have no allies left." Chang's facial expression told her that she had hit on a crucial point and she decided to drive it home. "Remember, whatever happens to any one of us will be carefully watched and evaluated by those people who do support your efforts, General Chang. If this is the way you treat a senior official of an alleged ally, all China watchers will assume that you are not trustworthy, and are loyal only to your own personal ambitions. And that is neither strategically nor tactically smart."

Chang's face became expressionless. He hated to admit it, but she was correct in her assessment.

Desaix stood up, wondering what Phoebe meant when she referred to "those people" who would be watching Chang's every move. To whom could she be referring? The Agency? Mori? Moffat? The Taiwanese?

"Get him out of here!" Chang shouted to the guards. "And take that trollop and her puking pimp brother with him." Chang walked to where Phoebe sat and pointed his finger at her. "This is your last chance. Get them all out of here! You will have exactly thirty-six hours to accomplish what we had initially agreed upon. There will be no second chance for any of you."

"I need at least forty-eight hours," Phoebe shouted at Chang as he walked out of the room.

"I said thirty-six," Chang repeated.

"Forty-eight hours," Phoebe said, unperturbed. "And not one hour less."

"Forty-eight hours then," Chang conceded, breaking into a series of Cantonese expletives that even Phoebe could not understand.

"And there is one other thing," Phoebe said. "I want you to apologize to Dr. Clark for how you have treated him."

"Out of the question," Chang replied angrily. "Ms. Hill, you have exceeded the limits of my extreme patience."

"General Chang," Phoebe said in a conciliatory voice, "I am asking you to assume the role of diplomat that I know you want to be. Would a responsible statesman ever attempt to humiliate a senior official of an ally?" She paused to allow him a moment's reflection. "I know you were extremely frustrated by the situation. So was I. But for the official record, with me as a witness, I think that it would be wise for everyone in this room to forget and forgive. Is that clear?"

"Wait a minute," Desaix said angrily. "Are you also asking me to say that I forget and forgive what has happened to me? To all of us?"

"I think that's a correct interpretation," Phoebe replied. "It was all a misunderstanding."

"This is crazy," Desaix said. "I don't know what you've got going with him, but there is no way in hell—"

"Trust me," Phoebe said in a threatening tone.

Desaix stared into her cat eyes. Could he trust her to do what was best for the country? She might be a flagrant sociopath who knew how to manipulate him and everyone else, telling each one what they wanted to hear. Or she might know better than he what was appropriate for them to do, given the circumstances they were in. This time he could not rely on any sophisticated analytical tools for an evaluation of the situation. He had to rely on only his clinical skills and intuition. Did it feel right was the only question that he now had to answer for himself.

"I forget and forgive you, General Chang," Desaix called after the general.

Chang stood at the door for what seemed like several minutes, his back facing Desaix. "I apologize, Dr. Desaix Clark, for what I have done to you and your companions." Never turning around, he closed the door behind him as he left the room.

"Can you tell me what the hell just happened?" Desaix asked Phoebe.

"I'll explain all of it to you later," she replied. "But first we have to get out of this place before Chang changes his mind."

CHAPTER TWENTY-EIGHT

Sipping green tea from chipped and stained porcelain cups, Desaix and Phoebe sat facing each other on the soft-seat sleeper train headed toward Shanghai. Ann and Newton were eating dinner in the dining car. A continuing fog and the well-known mechanical problems of limited air flights had helped them make the decision to take the slower but more reliable train.

Unlike France's formidable TGV, Japan's high-speed bullet train from Tokyo to Kyoto, or the U.S.'s sleek Metroliner, China had not yet mastered the art of high-speed luxury train travel. But to Desaix the soft-seat compartment, a considerable improvement over the thinly padded vinyl-covered hard seats, gave him more comfort than he thought he'd ever feel again.

The hard-seat cars were typically stuffed with farmers, peasants, soldiers, students, and business people, all carrying an assortment of well-worn luggage, cord-wrapped packages, grocery bags brimming over with the food necessary for a twelve-hundred-mile trip, and live chickens that would at some point mysteriously disappear. The soft-seat compartment was generally populated by the elite of Chinese society. Only those individuals who had earned their position through privilege, nepotism, or corruption could afford one of these seats. In a way, thought Desaix, this section was a testimony to how hard new China was trying to evolve into an economic and political superpower, driven by the pent-up consumer needs of its people. The seats were amply padded to provide a comfortable ride. Above each of the two banks of seats, each long enough to sit three, were bunks that provided sleeping accommodations for two travelers. The floors were carpeted with handmade rugs from Wuhan, and pairs of plastic sandals, too small for most Americans, were placed beneath the seats. Small pillows, towels, and blankets, all riddled with holes, were neatly folded at the far corner of the seats. A small tar-stained table attached to the wall beneath a filthy window held a small lamp with a perforated hexagonal shade. Beneath the table sat a large thermos of hot water that was frequently checked on and refilled by a cabin attendant. For a few fen, he provided sachets of *chá,* tea.

Desaix calculated that it had been five hours since boarding the train at Badaling, the station located near the Great Wall. By now, after passing over the Yangtze River, they should be entering Nanjing, the tree-lined city that had served as the capital under the presidency of Dr. Sun Yat-sen. From there, they would stop at Suzhou, and continue eastward toward the East China Sea. All told, the trip to Shanghai would be about twenty hours.

"How are you feeling?" Phoebe asked.

"Right now, pretty good," Desaix replied calmly, "and pretty grateful for what you did back there."

"Think nothing of it," Phoebe said, flushed with embarrassment. "Just part of the job."

"No," Desaix said. "I mean it. If you hadn't been there to stop Chang, I would have been *bok choy,* cabbage, by now."

"Those were gruesome pictures," Phoebe said, sensing where Desaix's thoughts still were.

"I think that film," Desaix said, "was just the beginning of what would have been a very extensive effort on Chang's part to break my psychological and physical defenses until he had gotten me to write a statement of contrition and official support for him."

"Well, we have a long relaxing trip ahead of us," Phoebe responded, wanting to reach out and comfort him. "Why don't you just take it easy?"

"I would love to relax," Desaix replied warily, "but every time I try, something unexpected happens."

"What do you mean?" she asked nervously.

"Oh come on," Desaix responded with disgust. "I feel as if I'm on a merry-go-round and you're the one who's making it stop and go."

"What does that mean?"

"It's like I'm in an elaborately orchestrated shadowboxing match. Ann claimed she was kidnapped by Chang, but it turned out that she had herself wounded by her own brother, and then may or may not have helped orchestrate my kidnapping. Chang, who has frequently been physically beaten as a result of Ann's orders, arrested Newton and me, allowed us to escape, and then initiated an elaborate cat-and-mouse game to catch us. And what is most fascinating in this orchestrated ritual is the fact that everyone seems beholden to you. And then there is my dear friend Moffat . . . " he added contemptuously. "What the hell is going on?"

"You're supposed to be the expert in human behavior," Phoebe replied coldly. "Why don't you tell me what you think is happening."

"You want to know the truth?" Desaix asked. "I don't know."

"Well, that's quite a revelation from the infamous crisis manager."

"One thing I do know," Desaix said, "is that you know what's going on." What he hadn't told her was that he was beginning to discern a very clear pattern of "nondoing" or "nonhappening," as the Taoists call it. From the very beginning, his assignment was unclear. Was he sent to China to stop the war, assist Ann, or merely keep the game in play? Since arriving in China, no threat, action, or statement had had any sense of finality to it. His official negotiations with Ann seemed final, but they weren't. Newton's assassination attempt, contrived to create a swell of public sympathy and support for Ann, never seemed to have happened. Ann's kidnapping by the PLA was also a "nonevent." Chang was as much a hostage to her as she was to him. And then Chang had Desaix kidnapped in order to make his case for a fair hearing with Moffat. But Chang was already working for Phoebe, who could make a case with Moffat. So why did Chang have to try so hard to intimidate him, Desaix? It seemed as if Chang were simply prolonging the process of "nondoing" and everyone else was keeping the shadow forces of the crisis in perpetual motion through the use of half truths, distortions, and betrayals.

Staring at Phoebe, Desaix suddenly recalled an old Chinese story that seemed to clarify his understanding of what had been going on. According to the story, a lord of ancient China asked his physician, a member of a family of healers, which of them was the most skilled in the art of curing the ill. The physician replied, "My eldest brother sees the spirit of sickness and removes it before it takes shape, so his name does not get out of the house. My second brother cures sickness when it is still extremely minute, so his name does not get out of the neighborhood. As for me," the famous physician concluded, "I puncture veins, prescribe potions, and massage skin, so from time to time my name gets out and is heard among the lords." Desaix realized that the story captured the essence of Sun Tzu's *Art of War*. The healing arts and the martial arts were very similar in their approach to life—the less needed of either, the better. Just as the eldest brother in the story was unknown because of his acumen, Sun Tzu affirmed that the skilled warrior was clever enough to win early in the fray, when victory was still easy. And so while the victories of skilled warriors were not always known or rewarded, they were consistent with Sun Tzu's philosophy of winning without fighting. Accomplishing the most by doing the least.

"Right now you need me," Phoebe said, interrupting his thoughts. "So I would strongly advise you to stop your recriminations. I assure you that would be the best course of action at this point."

"I still have a lot of questions to ask you," Desaix said, sipping his tea slowly, "but something tells me I should heed your advice."

"Your sharply honed instincts are relaying the proper message," Phoebe responded, attempting to defuse Desaix's rancor with a conciliatory comment. "I appreciate the fact that you trusted me at a moment when it would have been very easy to dismiss me along with Chang. I wouldn't have expected that from the Desaix Clark I had been warned about."

"What was that Desaix Clark like?" Desaix asked, curious about the Agency's word on him.

"Oh, the Desaix Clark I was told to monitor had an interesting Operational Code," Phoebe replied. "He was a loner who trusted no one and proudly espoused the motto 'trust is good but control is better.' But as a professional who was trained to play with people's minds and feelings, he could be extremely ingratiating, charming, and smooth. In order to attain whatever it was that he wanted, of course. A policy—or a woman. He gave lip service to consensus building and group effort but that was simply a facade behind which he would work his two-track diplomacy, relying very heavily on covert manipulations and pressure tactics."

"Very impressive," Desaix said, wondering whether she was making up the analysis on the spot or whether there was in fact an Op Code on him at Langley, Virginia.

"Is that enough?" Phoebe asked, knowing full well that she had piqued his curiosity—and his narcissism.

"Please continue," Desaix said, sipping his tea and trying to believe her.

"That Desaix," Phoebe continued, "believed in the Machiavellian tenet of power that the ends justified the means and that it was more important to be feared than to be liked." She paused to clear her parched throat and sip some tea. "He was by temperament a man so much addicted to action that it was rumored he would start an international crisis just so he could continue the high adrenal game of crisis management." She paused to assess whether she had hit any raw spots. "Should I stop now?"

"Not at all," Desaix responded. "You're batting one thousand."

"But like all men who work alone," Phoebe continued, "his very strengths could be turned against him and used to manipulate him to effect an outcome that served his opponents' interests." She stopped, aware that she had entered a minefield she had been desperately trying to avoid. "My throat is dry," she said and poured another cup of tea.

"That's convenient," Desaix said, "just when you are telling me how I . . . I mean that other Desaix . . . could be manipulated." Desaix's mind raced with fear and excitement. He wasn't used to a situation where a woman held most of the playing cards.

"Loners like to imagine themselves as self-sufficient," Phoebe continued, "but the truth is that many of them need a cause greater than themselves to justify their existence. Then they feel that much more indispensable and, not surprisingly, self-contained."

"But the truth is that they are a patsy for just causes and women in distress," Desaix said.

"Something like that," Phoebe responded. "But inevitably, they feel hurt or deceived by those they assumed were closest to them." Phoebe's last words sent a cold shudder through Desaix. Was it Moffat, not he, who had knocked over the tray and broken the china in his dream? Had Moffat betrayed his friend? Desaix shuddered again and tried to push the thoughts from his mind. Dreams always had a habit of turning things upside down. How else could the silver tray support the much heavier chinaware? Could Taiwan, the smaller of the two countries, be supporting China? Perhaps, he thought. That was the key to the dream, the last missing part. A nervous spasm of coughing refocused Desaix's thoughts to Phoebe.

"Are you all right?" Desaix moved over to Phoebe's banquette and tapped her gently on the back.

"I'm okay," she replied. "Some tea went down the wrong pipe."

"Are you sure you're all right?" Desaix asked, examining her flushed face.

"Yes," she replied emphatically. "I'm fine."

"Are you trying to warn me that someone close to me is using me?"

"Don't we all use one another?" Phoebe felt distinctly uncomfortable with Desaix sitting so close to her. And she had said more than she had expected to. She didn't want to turn their first private moments together into a fishing expedition about who was doing what to whom.

"I'm trying to ask you whether I'm in danger from my enemies . . . or my friends . . . " Desaix said with seriousness, "but you don't seem to want to help me out."

"But I won't turn against you," Phoebe said, knowing that for someone like Desaix these were empty words.

"Deeds speak louder than words," Desaix replied, smoothing back the wayward strands of hair falling over Phoebe's shoulders. "You must realize that you have me at a disadvantage. You seem to know a great deal about me, but I don't know very much about you."

"There really isn't much more to tell you than when we met at the museum, that first day," Phoebe replied, flooded with a sensual warmth.

"You told me a lot of things that didn't quite bear out," Desaix said.

"You're right," she said, her voice increasingly more parched as he stroked her hair. "The truth is that I'm your typical all-American, born and bred in southern California. My father was an ex-navy fighter pilot who retired to become an investment banker. My mother is a talented painter who is both highly disciplined and free-spirited." She stopped when she thought it might sound too rehearsed.

"An unusual combination," Desaix said.

"That's true," Phoebe said. "Am I boring you?"

"Not at all," Desaix said. "Please go on."

"From the very first day they met," Phoebe continued, "my father loved and supported my mother in every one of her creative undertakings. And she felt extremely grateful that she married a man who could love her so unconditionally."

"Sounds simple," Desaix replied, withdrawing his hand from her hair. He thought of the battles between his own father and mother. Those wars had exacted a heavy price on his own psyche. "How did you get into this business?" he asked, changing the topic.

"You mean why didn't I become a financier like my father?" she replied, "or a painter like my mother?"

"Something like that," he responded, caressing the nape of her neck.

"It's very simple," she said, savoring the touch of his fingertips winding their way down her back. "I don't like working with numbers or playing with paint. So I decided on a career of adventure and intrigue."

"Why didn't you join the Foreign Service?" Desaix asked, gently massaging her shoulders.

"That feels wonderful," Phoebe said, reclining backward.

"You might have ended up working for me," he said.

"Or vice versa," she responded, laughing.

"Touché," Desaix said, chuckling. He liked the feel of her body. It was supple and inviting. Yet he sensed he had to proceed very carefully.

"I had an opportunity to go to State," she added, "but I felt it would be too confining, stuck in a cubbyhole as the desk officer for some Third World country. And I didn't think there were too many opportunities for women to become ambassadors."

"So you arranged that as Station Chief," Desaix said. "You became the de facto ambassador to China."

"I don't know if I would exactly say that," Phoebe said defensively, straightening her back and pulling away from him.

"I'm sorry if anything I said upset you," Desaix said, realizing that he had needlessly irked her. He touched his hand to her cheek.

"Deeds speak louder than words," Phoebe replied, mimicking Desaix.

"Is that the entrance price for getting involved?" Desaix asked, pulling her closer to him. He was aroused by both her tone of defiance and her inviting smile.

"I think so," Phoebe replied, feeling both excited and awkward in his arms.

"Do you realize that we're running out of conversation?" Desaix said, stroking her hair.

"What do you mean?" Phoebe asked, pressing her body against his.

"Each of us has been repeating the other person's words," Desaix replied.

"Does that mean that we have nothing to say to each other?" she asked, running her fingers through his curly hair.

"Maybe," he replied, as he bent his head toward her lips.

"A loss of conversation," Phoebe said breathlessly, "is such a terrible loss."

"I agree," Desaix responded as he kissed her gently on the lips.

The response of her body answered any questions left open to doubt. Desaix reached over to the compartment's latch and locked the door. He lay her carefully down across the seat and ran his fingers over her face, resting them on her lips. As he pressed his lips against her closed eyelids, he could feel her body quiver beneath his.

After they undressed each other, their torsos became a statue of intertwined legs and arms. Their groins arched up to meet each other in an embrace that moved slowly, rhythmically, and definitively. Desaix entered Phoebe with the grace and ease that only lovers who have practiced the mechanics of lovemaking could take for granted. Each was certain that the other had been there before.

When someone knocked on the door, they reluctantly separated. Before they could dress and open the door, Newton's voice came through it loud and clear. "Ann is gone."

CHAPTER TWENTY-NINE

Hurrying down the *hutungs,* narrow lanes, over cobblestone streets, Newton, Phoebe, and Desaix passed the whitewashed cottages that bracketed the black water canals snaking throughout Suzhou, a medium-sized city fifty miles west of Shanghai. Street vendors hawked their wares from makeshift pushcarts—raw sugar cane sticks, straw mats, and headboards for beds. Permanent stalls carried scarves, ties, and dresses, all made from silk, the product for which Suzhou was famous.

"Goddamn it, Jin Bo, how did you let Ann get away from you?" Phoebe asked, biting into her breakfast of *yŏutíao,* an unsugared doughnut that she had bought for ten fen from a street vendor. Smiling at Desaix, she couldn't help thinking that Ann had picked an inappropriate time to run away.

"For the thousandth time," Newton replied defensively, "she told me that she didn't feel well, got up from the table, and left to go to the bathroom. I followed her, of course."

"First you said that you didn't see where she went," Desaix reminded Newton, skeptical of the story and angry at Newton for having intruded into what had promised to be an evening of tender passions.

"The last I saw of her," Newton said, turning up the lapels of his jacket, "was when she entered the hard-seat compartment and simply disappeared in the crowd of people."

"Then why did you insist we get out of the train in Suzhou?" Phoebe asked, brushing up against Desaix.

"She kept on telling me that she didn't trust you after you made that deal with Chang to allow us to leave," Newton replied.

"What in God's name does that have to do with our being here?" Desaix asked, suspicious of Newton's motives. After all, he thought, Ann is Jin Bo's sister. He would choose to protect her from what appeared to be shifting alliances. Perhaps he had helped her to disappear, so that she could, like the phoenix, rise again. And take control. And now he was leading them on a wild goose chase through Suzhou in order to give her the time she needed.

Desaix noticed how similar the marshy countryside of Suzhou was to his ancestral Acadian country, thick with greening rice and lavender clover. Suzhou was encircled by the canals, stitched through with interlocking waterways upon which disheveled boatmen poled and sculled their sampans. The cottages on the embankments, like their inhabitants, showed two faces, one to the street and one to the canal.

Lafayette, the largest city in Acadia, was surrounded by a countryside dotted with centuries-old oaks with ragged gray buntings of Spanish moss that formed canopies over the paddlewheelers that kicked up froth on the bayous. Dirt country roads followed the contortions of the Teche, the largest bayou west of New Orleans, as it meandered through ancient Acadian villages. Cypress cabins rose up out of its waters on stilts, and moored fishing boats and pirogues, canoes, bobbed on the sluggish, bottle green waters. Both Acadia and Suzhou were regions where water seemed as prevalent as land.

"Throughout our dinner conversation," Newton said, "Ann kept quoting an old Chinese proverb: 'Above is Paradise, below are Hangzhou and Suzhou.' Then she mentioned something about the Humble Administrator's Garden. But quite frankly, she spent most of dinner accusing each of you of being traitors, kidnappers, and enemies of the state."

"So why aren't we in Hangzhou?" Desaix asked, pondering the meaning of the proverb. Ann may have suffered an acute panic attack since their encounter with Chang.

"Hangzhou is not on the train line toward Shanghai," Phoebe replied. "It's about three and a half hours south of here. And she didn't get off at Nanjing because Newton and she were eating in the dining car. And our first stop since Nanjing is Suzhou."

Although Phoebe had tried to sound positive, she had not yet ruled out the possibility that Ann might still be on the train to Shanghai. And the chances of finding her there were minimal. Ann just had to be in Suzhou, Phoebe decided.

Desaix convinced Phoebe and Newton they would save time if he investigated the Humble Administrator's Garden while they continued speaking to vendors and shopkeepers. He really didn't want to go alone, but he was worried that if Ann saw the three of them descending upon her, she would panic and run. After reassuring Phoebe that nothing would happen to him they agreed to meet in two hours at the railway station on Chezan Road.

Desaix meticulously followed the directions that Newton gave him and arrived at the Garden, ten acres of lush foliage and waterways. Originally constructed four hundred years ago for a famous Tang poet, the Garden eventually became the property of a wealthy court advisor to the Empress Dowager who retired from his powerful government position to lead a humble, contemplative life.

Once inside the Garden's walls, Desaix continued along the man-made streams that snaked around contorted, perforated boulders placed one on top of the other to resemble mountains. The garden was almost empty of visitors so early in the morning. A blue-stoned path that passed gnarled trees at every turn reminded him that he was entering a world of mental gamesmanship and illusion, a garden of carefully placed pieces of nature intended to suggest the insignificance of man. A large pond, spangled with lotus and bridged by several walkways, mirrored the contorted waterways surrounding Suzhou itself. The walking path around the pond led to a wall in which an opening was cut to simulate a window. Looking through the window, Desaix gazed at shaped bamboo, twisted pine trees, and unusual rock formations, optical illusions created to reflect the underlying unity and harmony of man and nature. He saw Ann, sitting quietly on a rock near a pond. No one else seemed to be in that part of the Garden.

"How did you find me here, Dr. Clark?" Ann asked, startled as Desaix came up to her. "Was it sheer luck? Or is it rude of me not to expect more impressive investigative skills from so great a diplomat, psychiatrist, and Chinese scholar?"

Desaix greeted her politely, turned off by her sarcasm but impressed by her composure. "I'm glad to see you again, Ann." Amidst the intricate beauty of the Garden, she looked as attractive and self-assured as on the first day he had met her.

"Have you figured out why I would flee here, to Zhuo Zeng Yuan?" Ann asked, leaving her seat and starting to circle Desaix like a cheetah ready to strike its prey. Any calm that she had absorbed from the Garden quickly vanished. "Or as you Americans prefer to call it, the Humble Administrator's Garden."

"You tell me why I would have figured out that you would come here," Desaix said.

"Let us not play games, Desaix," Ann said angrily. "My brother told you that I had been talking about this garden on the train. So you put two and two together. Not very complicated, my dear Watson." She paused to add, "You know as well as I do that the Garden's name comes from an old Chinese saying: "To cultivate the garden for a living is really the politics of a humble person.""

"I'm not clear about what you've said, Ann," Desaix replied. "Could you explain what you mean?"

"Don't start to patronize me," Ann said, biting her lower lip, "like you did that night—"

"Do you mean when I came to see you as an official of the United States government?" Desaix asked. "You thought that I was patronizing you?"

"Don't act so surprised," she replied, continuing to circle him as they spoke. "He sent you? Didn't he?"

"To whom are you referring?" Desaix asked, trying to calm her down with his own appearance of relaxation. Watching her circle him, he could almost see her ego boundaries dissolve into their primordial compartments of jealousy, rage, and paranoia. Were these the underlying emotions she was protecting herself against with her obsessive-compulsive rituals in the underground tunnels? When they failed her, he was certain, she would panic and regress to a state of extreme anger.

"Wouldn't you like to know?" Ann said, now coyly. "Why don't you tell me about you and Phoebe." She began a sickly laugh.

"There's nothing to tell," Desaix said in the voice he had always reserved for his psychiatric patients. "Is that why you ran away from us?" Desaix asked.

"Don't be so vain, Dr. Clark. I ran away, as you euphemistically call it, because I don't trust her, you, or my brother. My survival was best assured by leaving all of you."

"So you're angry with me for not being able to protect you," Desaix said, falling easily into his old familiar patter.

"You!" Ann replied. "Why should I be angry with you? You're not my lover."

"If you're not angry with me then why do you sound so angry?" Desaix asked. "With whom are you really angry?"

"It's pretty here, isn't it?" Ann asked, avoiding Desaix's question. "I used to come here whenever I felt upset or frustrated, just to remind myself that compared to the beauty of nature, my problems were really quite insignificant."

"What made you so angry that you fled from our protection?" Desaix asked, trying not to crowd her either physically or mentally. She was obviously jealous of Phoebe. But why would that upset her? Because she had attempted to seduce him and it hadn't worked? No, he thought. There is something else behind her jealousy. Something much deeper. And it involved someone else. Not him.

"Protection?" Ann said laughingly. "What protection? Against whom? Chang? He's in Phoebe's pocket. You? You're about to be co-opted by Phoebe. My dear, loyal brother? He's already straddling Chang, Phoebe, you, and me. The real question is to whom has he *not* pledged his allegiance. So please, Dr. Clark, don't speak to me about protection. I'm much better off alone. The only protection you can offer me is that of self-delusion."

"What do you mean, self-delusion?" Desaix asked, concerned that beneath her vitriolic statements were the lattices of truth.

"Self-delusion, as in the process of convincing oneself about something that has no correspondence with reality," Ann said. "Phoebe Hill really has my interests at heart? Or that we are going to Shanghai in order to sign a treaty that will stop the mounting crisis among China, Japan, and Taiwan—and inevitably with the U.S.?"

"I don't understand you. Why do you think Phoebe is going to all this trouble to take you out of China?"

"Don't you Americans have an old saying that 'when you hear hoof-beats, don't think of zebras'?" Ann said. "She's getting me out of China because that's the best way to get me out of the way. Period. It's as simple as all that, Dr. Clark." She rubbed her hands together, imitating a well-known American television commercial for a detergent. "No fuss, no bother, no mess. I sense that she has already convinced you that without me in China, Chang will be able to lead my country into an era of peace and prosperity."

Desaix was confused about who was telling the truth. A mentally handicapped, ruthless, but politically shrewd Chinese Prime Minister, or a manipulating, affectionate, but American-grounded CIA Station Chief? Or as Moffat was wont to say in his academic cadence—do you believe the Oriental or Occidental myth?

"Confusion," Ann said, reading his face, "is the first sign in the healing process. Isn't that what all you therapists tell your patients as they grapple with self-understanding?" She started to walk toward a group of empty sampans floating lazily in the pond, knowing that Desaix would follow her.

"You sound like you feel a lot better than before," Desaix said.

"Wouldn't you," Ann asked, "if you had control over your own destiny?"

"I assume so," Desaix replied. "Is that why you became so anxious underground?"

"Desaix," Ann said in a patronizing tone, "I do whatever it takes to stay alive. Two days ago, I felt I was in captivity. You psychiatrists tend to underestimate the value of mental illness as a moral expediency. I tried to shoot a soldier because he threatened my life. It was as simple as that. But it is a lot more convenient and compassionate to say that I didn't know what I was doing and tried to shoot him in a moment of insanity." She paused to examine the scull and awning of an empty black sampan. "To paraphrase one of your great American playwrights, Eugene O'Neill, 'Madness becomes Ann.' " She laughed. "Desaix, don't take yourself so seriously. I simply played out one of your mind games in order to protect myself from the more devious ones of your colleagues."

"That's a pretty strong indictment of Phoebe," Desaix replied, impressed with Ann's emotional fluidity. She was moving effortlessly out of intense seriousness and rage into self-assuredness and moral indignation.

"You forgot one other very important person," Ann replied. "The ultimate mind game player."

"Who's that?" Desaix asked.

"Oh come now," Ann said. "Remember, 'think of horses, not zebras.' "

Not Moffat, Desaix thought, trying to rid his mind of the idea as strongly as it chose to remain in it.

"Think of the obvious," Ann continued. "Ask yourself why your good friend Moffat sent you to see me."

"That was my role," Desaix replied defensively. "I am the Assistant Secretary—"

"I know all that," Ann interrupted him. "But what was the real purpose of your trip?"

"To stop an impending war," Desaix said, feigning indignation. He noticed that the pathways were starting to fill with tourists.

"You must think a great deal of yourself to think that one man could stop what many people had placed in motion," Ann said. "You must be suffering from a serious problem of self-importance."

"Moffat and I are the closest of friends," Desaix said, sensing that he was on the verge of evincing a painful truth. "He trusts me implicitly to complete the assignment."

"So the issue of trust was paramount in sending you. What else, Dr. Desaix Clark, Board-Certified Psychiatrist?"

"Being a psychiatrist?" Desaix asked, picking up on her heavy-handed statement.

"Very good, Doctor," Ann replied, pushing him to explore the unthinkable. "But why send a trusted psychiatrist?"

"I want to say for conflict resolution," Desaix answered, "but you say, 'Think of the obvious.'" All of a sudden, Desaix felt what it was like to be the patient and not the doctor.

"One possibility is to treat me for a mental illness that I may or may not have," Ann said.

"Moffat must have known about your problems and wanted me here to be able to help you during the crisis," Desaix said. "But that doesn't answer the question of why he never mentioned your condition to me."

"So what does that make you conclude, my dear Dr. Desaix Clark, trusted friend and advisor of the Secretary of State?" Ann demanded dramatically.

"He depended more on our *quanxi* than on anything else," Desaix said. "That was the last word he said to me before I came to China. 'Remember *quanxi*.'"

"And what do you think he meant?"

"He meant that one set of close relationships would lead to another set of close relationships," Desaix said. "If he trusted me, hopefully you, too, would trust me."

"Or vice versa," Ann said. "Try to forget your narcissism, Desaix. Not all relationships center around you. What he probably meant was that you would learn to trust me as he has learned to trust me. For the past twenty years."

"Let's stop playing games," Desaix said, feeling sufficiently used and tricked. What right did she have to make intimations about his friendship with Moffat?

"Where did your friend teach Asian studies?" Ann asked, not finished with her interrogation.

"University of California at Berkeley," Desaix replied, trying to ascertain why she was suddenly becoming so nervous.

"And where did I get my Ph.D.?" Ann asked rhetorically. "Berkeley. And who was my professor and thesis advisor?"

Desaix thought back to what Moffat had said about him and Ann having been at Berkeley at different times in their lives. He had never mentioned supervising any doctoral theses, although he had said that the only true students he ever taught were those who read his textbook on China. The rest he considered irrelevant.

"And like in most mentor-student relationships of which I'm certain you know more than I do," Ann said airily, "I fell in love with my professor."

"And how long did that last?" Desaix asked. Could she be making this all up?

"Who said it ever stopped?" Ann asked, enjoying the mixed expression of disbelief and confusion on Desaix's face. "Or maybe we weren't lovers, just simply friends. But what difference does it make. Whatever it may or may not have been, that was then. Now is now. In any case, I was extremely angry that he didn't come here himself. Perhaps that may explain my initial attempt to seduce you. I was trying to get back at him for not having come. Childish, but nevertheless understandable." She added reflectively, "And all the times you tried to help me I struck out at you verbally, emotionally, physically. Perhaps it was really Moffat I was trying to hurt, not you. Isn't that what you psychiatrists call acting out my ambivalence toward the primary love object? And displacing it onto the transference object, my therapist, you?"

"So he sent me to be your emotional football, to be kicked around if need be, to help you maintain your stability and leadership under an extremely stressful situation," Desaix responded.

"That's going too far. You underestimate your true value to him . . . and to me," Ann said, sorry if she had gone too far. "He wanted you to protect me against . . . my enemies—Chang, Newton, and Phoebe. He knew that they would try to remove me as Prime Minister. So our dear Moffat sent his best friend, Desaix Clark, to China to make certain that what happened to me over the past forty-eight hours shouldn't happen."

"Then why did he recall me to the States after our first meeting?" Desaix asked, suspicious of her logic but not certain where the fallacy lay.

"Moffat always told me that if you wanted Desaix to do something, make certain that you first forbid him from doing it," she replied smiling. "He said a challenge to you was just like sex. The more nos you heard, the more convinced you were that 'the lady protesteth too much.' "

"So you're telling me that I've screwed up in a big way," Desaix said. "Well, since you are the only one who seems to know what is going on, what do you think Moffat expects of me now?"

"It's really quite simple," Ann said, spotting Phoebe and Newton in the distance. "Your colleagues are coming this way. They must have followed you. You've got to decide whether you're coming with me to Shanghai in this sampan, or whether you're joining them." Ann stepped into the canoe-shaped boat and picked up a long wooden pole.

"This time I hope you'll make the right choice, Desaix. There's no room for mistakes anymore."

CHAPTER THIRTY

Flying low over the Straits of Formosa, separating Fujian Province and Taiwan, Moffat glanced outside the window of his modified Boeing 747. The water and air space were dotted with an incredible array of death-dealing machines. So this was what a crisis looked like up close, he thought, feeling a rush of adrenaline course through his body.

If Desaix were sitting alongside him, Moffat knew that they would be acting like children, pointing out the various weaponry and testing each other's knowledge. He could hear Desaix tell him that the squadron of F-22 Advanced Tactical Stealth Fighters accompanying the Secretary's plane were far superior to the F-15 Eagle and F-16 Falcon screeching above and below the Boeing 747 because of their supersonic speed and ability to fly through enemy radar undetected.

But Moffat knew he had to restrain himself from being too overwhelmed by the situation. It was now, more so than ever, that he had to assume the mantle of emotional restraint and judicious pronouncements. He was in the midst of a crisis that would define the course of history. He, not unlike Desaix, secretly harbored the belief that one man alone could really determine the course of history. But, unlike

Desaix, he would go out of his way to create the appearance that it was, in fact, a collective effort. He was the ringmaster calling forth death-defying acts.

"Excuse me sir," Toland said, exhausted from the twenty-hour flight, "Commander-in-Chief Pacific would like to know if they can commence their forty-eight-hour countdown."

"Tell them to proceed and to ready themselves to implement Stage One of the AirLand Battle Plan." Moffat was surprised by the high he was feeling. The momentum of the crisis was building to a crescendo that he alone controlled. And at the right moment and time, he would orchestrate the finale. But like any good ringmaster, he had to wait for the right cues.

As Desaix thrust the long bamboo pole into the black water, jets screeched across the golden skies of sundown. Baptized by the intimidating designations of MiG-29, MiG-21, and Tu-22M, these supersonic cranes were painted in daring colors of allegiance. Red for loyalty, thought Desaix. Black for boldness. White for treachery. Instruments of destruction feigning aggression and terror, like the actress in the Peking Opera who manipulated her feathers to convey anger and surprise while posturing gestures to symbolize deep thought, gaiety, or anticipation. Much like an operatic script, thought Desaix, these warriors of the heavens still followed a set choreography orchestrated by Sun Tzu some twenty-five hundred years ago: engage the enemy with *cheng,* orthodox force, while the *ch'i,* unorthodox force, disrupts the communications and supply routes by attacking the deep flanks and the rear. The crisis was approaching its denouement, thought Desaix. And he had very little time to find a resolution.

With thoughts of Phoebe set aside, Desaix sculled with his entire weight as the sampan floated down Suzhou Creek. The sampan wound its way through a serpentine gorge shrouded in fog and poetry, framed by a shameless display of verdant foliage flowing into the turgid waters. Desaix watched as scores of trackers strained on bamboo hawsers, half a mile long, pulling a three-awning junket upriver. They were urged on by drum and gong, at times by lash and cane, while other men in the boat exploded firecrackers to try to ward off the menacing gods of the dark waters. Further down, a boat loaded with silver carp rose from the river into the waiting arms of jubilant fishermen lining the serrated margins of the rocky banks. Ann purchased food and utensils from floating vendors who were pleased to find tourists on this waterway.

Further downriver, Desaix watched as cormorants dove for fish and brought them to their masters holding old wooden tubs. Much like the Chinese citizen, thought Desaix, these birds had choke collars around their necks, preventing them from swallowing the day's catch. The collar was only loosened to reward the bird. It was the Chinese version of behavior modification, Desaix decided.

As the sampan approached the Huangpu River, Desaix and Ann navigated their way gingerly through a maze of sailing vessels from the *fanchuan,* or sailing junk, with its multi-colored quilted sails, to the red-rusted barges laden with the black anthracite coal that brought upper respiratory disease to the Chinese people as it heated their houses.

"I'm glad you chose to come with me," Ann said as she offered him a cup of cold *chá* from a rusted thermos. "May I ask why?"

"Quite frankly, I'm not certain," Desaix replied, attracted by the quiet commanding presence that once again had settled over her.

"Then I should be flattered that you decided to go with me," Ann said hesitantly, "instead of—" She stopped herself from uttering Phoebe's name. Why create an unnecessary problem, she thought. The choice was self-evident and leave it at that.

"Instincts," he replied uncomfortably, sipping his tea slowly. He was sensing the same sexual tension he had experienced when they had first met.

"I see," she responded with a knowing smile. His choice to go with her had already spoken a thousand words. But she would have to be careful with him. He was as skittish as a kitten. At Berkeley she had learned that American men were extremely sensitive to a woman who appeared aggressively intrusive despite the fact that they prided themselves on being the sole possessors of that very attribute. But now was not the time to be persistent or argumentative. She was beginning to feel desirable once again. For a while she didn't have to play the role of the Empress Dowager. Or the old grandmother. She could be herself, a woman.

"Listen to those jet planes," Desaix interjected, trying to change the subject. "Soon we'll be hearing explosions. And then—"

"Let's try to forget the world around us for just a while," she said, placing her index finger on his mouth, silencing him. "We do owe it to ourselves."

"You're right," he responded, pulling away from her. After all they had gone through together, he wondered how he could trust her.

"Why don't I prepare our meal for us," Ann said, trying to mask the pain she felt in his rejection of her. "We'll call it a Huangpu banquet in honor of the pleasant memories we're going to create for ourselves, sailing down the river."

"Where do we start?" Desaix asked, eager to keep her in a pleasant mood.

"Take this knife," she said, picking up a rusted steel knife from the bamboo food crate in the middle of the sampan. She pointed it straight at him.

"Tempting?" he asked, standing steadfast.

"Chang wouldn't hesitate to drive it through your heart."

"I know," he said. "But what about you?"

"The real Empress Dowager," Ann responded, "would have delighted in making you quiver and then finished you off." She snapped her fingers. "Like that."

"And you?" he asked, concerned that both her mood and attitude had changed suddenly, as they had in the past.

"Me?" she asked, picking up a spoiled head of cabbage. "I just want you to chop this up into small pieces." She laughed. "So I can stir-fry it."

"How are you going to do that?" Desaix asked. "We don't have a wok."

"No wok," Ann responded with mock indignation. "Impossible."

"Why do you say that?" Desaix asked, impressed with her determination to prepare a meal on board the cluttered, dilapidated sampan.

"A wok is to a Chinese boatman," she replied, "as a can of beer is to your trucker. It's just always there." They both laughed.

"Oh, master chef," Desaix said, "what do you propose for tonight's dinner?"

"*Sù shíjǐn,*" she replied, rummaging through the bamboo crate.

"There, I told you I would find one." She raised a dark brown wok perforated with holes.

"I would say that looks more like a utensil that makes Swiss cheese," Desaix said, laughing.

"Now I have to find another essential ingredient," she said. "A can of vegetable oil."

"Isn't it going to be rancid?" Desaix asked, bringing over the handful of chopped cabbage.

"I see you don't cook very much," she responded with a laugh.

"Why?" he asked, watching her try to clean the wok with a wet cloth.

"It's very hard to spoil cooking oil," she said, as she dropped the cabbage pieces into the wok.

"Tell me again," he asked. "What is the delicacy which we are preparing?"

"It's called *sù shíjǐn,*" she replied, "or stir-fried assorted vegetables."

"I presume these are the assorted vegetables?" Desaix asked, pointing to the scraggly pieces of cabbage.

"If you look very carefully," she replied, shaking the wok, "you will see the different vegetables."

"I think I see what you mean," he said. "This rusted-stained piece of cabbage . . . "

" . . . is red pepper," she interjected. "And that yellowish morsel?"

"Squash," he responded enthusiastically.

"Very good," she said, realizing that the tight-edged features of his face belied an underlying warmth and free spirit that enjoyed playing and make-believe.

"That green one is . . . " he asked.

" . . . spinach," she answered, "And that dark brown . . . "

"Extremely spoiled cabbage," he responded, laughing.

"No," she said, squeezing his hand. "It's *mógū,* Chinese mushrooms, a true delicacy."

"Should I assume," he asked, "that the *sù shíjǐn* has been properly cooked and is ready to be eaten?"

"Absolutely," she replied with a laugh and picked at the various pieces of cabbage. "Nothing spoils a true delicacy like reality."

"So there is no cooking oil," Desaix said smiling, "rancid or not. Or kerosene."

"That is what makes this stir-fried dish so unique," she replied. "No oil. No cooking." She sat him down alongside her on a wooden bench in the back of the boat as it drifted lazily down the gentle currents of the Huangpu.

"Did you ever go to Carnival in New Orleans?" Desaix asked, absorbing the rich mosaic of a red dusk hovering over the bent verdant treetops.

"No," she replied. "I always wanted to go. But I never had the time while I was a student. What makes you think of it now?"

"For about two months, from January sixth to Ash Wednesday, the beginning of Lent," Desaix said, "we create a complete fantasy world. Not quite as extravagant as this one, of course—"

"You ingrate," she interjected, slapping him gently.

"—of parties, balls, and parades," Desaix continued, "in which the poor can dress and act like kings, the society ladies of Gardenia Street can release their sexual inhibitions, and the straitlaced businessmen can ride floats wearing pageboy wigs, gold crowns, jeweled tunics, and white tights. Beautiful ladies run alongside the floats shouting, 'Throw me something, mister!' And the only concern we have is 'Who found the baby in the king cake?' "

"It sounds simply wonderful," she said. "But what does that mean, 'Who found the baby in the King cake?' "

"During Carnival we overdose on king cake," he replied.

"King cake?" she asked.

"Yes," Desaix replied. "It's a sweet-dough coffee cake shaped like a wreath and topped with icing or sugar sprinkles in the Carnival colors of green, gold, and purple."

"It sounds delicious," she added, remembering her carefree Berkeley days when her only concern was good grades and self-indulgent hedonism.

"Baked inside of the king cake," Desaix continued, "is the mysterious baby, a fingernail-long pink plastic baby doll. Whoever bites into the baby is supposed to give the next king cake party or bring a cake to the office. Some New Orleanians prefer swallowing the baby rather than having to buy yet another king cake."

"And what happens if you don't find the baby?" she asked, her spirits high and her body relaxed for the first time in days.

"Then the next Carnival, you try twice as hard to find the baby in order to make up for the missed opportunity." Desaix stared into her almond-shaped eyes and placed his lips on hers, inhaling the warmth of his body against hers.

"Help me to overdose on your king cake," she said as she started to undress him.

"Don't forget tomorrow is Ash Wednesday," he replied, running his hands through her hair and down her body.

CHAPTER THIRTY-ONE

As they entered Shanghai harbor, Desaix helped Ann navigate around blunt-nosed steamers stuffed with passengers, tankers filled with heavy crude oil, and naval destroyers. When they reached Huangpu Park they tied the sampan to a makeshift dock consisting of half-cut rusted oil drums tied together.

"Welcome to Shanghai," Ann said, spreading her arms out.

"Like you, it's overwhelming," Desaix replied, reliving in his mind the unrelenting passion of their lovemaking.

"May I say, Dr. Clark, that it was a wonderful evening," she added, holding him around his waist, "I want to thank you for one night of Carnival."

Together they had created a magical moment in time in which both were open, frank, tender, and loving. If there was any deception, she thought, it was only the requisite lies that all lovers feel compelled to tell each other at the moment of intimacy, especially those that entail past exclusivity and future commitment.

"Did you find the baby in the king cake?" Desaix asked, pulling her tightly against him.

"Not this time," she replied, afraid to let him go, "but maybe next—"

"Then I hold you to that promise," Desaix interrupted.

"I swear that we will have a next time," she said.

"Remember, whatever else happens . . . " Desaix said, "we owe ourselves at least one more Carnival night."

Desaix found Ann, unlike Phoebe, to be more accessible in her feelings and sexual desires. In many ways Ann was far more American in her lovemaking than Phoebe, more willing to take risks, and freer to comment on what she did or did not like. She was not afraid to explore their mutual vulnerabilities with tenderness and respect. But as he looked around him, Desaix realized that the magic of the night would have to succumb to the surrounding pandemonium.

"What do you think of my most favorite city in the world?" she asked, holding his hand tightly as they wended their way through the unrelenting onslaught of people running about frantically.

"It has always reminded me of some of the more colorful Mediterranean cities blended into one," Desaix replied as they walked along the riverfront. To Desaix, Shanghai evoked the faded elegance of the Promenade Anglaise in Nice and the decadent nostalgia of Alexandria. And now there was added the grandeur of the newly constructed skyscrapers. But his memories did not include the palpable sense of tension that encompassed them. Clearly, a crisis was approaching. People moved through the streets quickly, with panic on their faces. Long lines along the docks told him that soon-to-be refugees were seeking passage on anything that could float or fly out of Shanghai. They were trying to get away from the clouds of war that were clearly rumbling in all about them. Every few minutes, the screech of MiG-29s and MiG-21s rattled the glass display windows of the Western-looking storefronts. Army trucks and armed soldiers clogged every street.

They stopped briefly to watch a television in the window of an appliance store. The anchorwoman of the news show was in the process of dismissing all rumors of Prime Minister Lee Ann Wu's disappearance as false. According to the broadcaster, both the Prime Minister and the Defense Minister had been sequestered behind closed doors for the past few days "working harmoniously together while brilliantly managing this American-inspired crisis." Desaix and Ann looked at each other knowingly. Last night's magic would never happen again if their appointment was not kept.

Eventually they came to Nanjing Road, Shanghai's equivalent of New York's Fifth Avenue, which housed the famous Heping, or Peace, Hotel, once the stately Cathay, an impressive Gothic mansion with a bronze green roof, owned by the famous Sephardic Jewish family, the Sassoons.

Shanghai, in its layout and architecture, reflected its history as a vanquished city divided into French, American, German, and British sectors, each under the jurisdiction and rule of its respective consuls. In the nineteenth century these countries had dominated China's banks, trading houses, shipping, industry, taxes, exports, and imports. Through the heavy-handed rule of their expeditionary forces and the aggressive proselytization of the Christian missionaries, the European imperialists had managed to make the Chinese even more submissive than they had been under their feuding warlords. By the turn of the twentieth century the Chinese had many masters, including one mercurial Empress Dowager. No wonder Mao Zedong helped found the Chinese Communist Party in 1921, Desaix thought, initiating a peasant-inspired, working-class revolution that would eventually drive out all foreigners, including the Japanese and the Chinese Nationalists. But Mao never really understood the true character of the Chinese. Above all else they were a collection of individualists who were born to prosper in the free-market system. The closest they came to accepting an ideology or religion was Confucianism, which was basically a system of thought, moral philosophy, and a hierarchical conduct of behavior. Mao had failed because he had tried to rectify the inequities of a feudal system through thought control and fear, never understanding the basic capitalistic nature of the ordinary Chinese.

Desaix and Ann hurried along Zhongshan Road onto the cobblestone streets of the Old Town.

"This is our infamous Blood Alley," Ann said, pointing to the maze of narrow alleys and small whitewashed shops, "where thousands of Chinese were beaten, tortured, mutilated, and killed in the 1920s."

"Very interesting," Desaix said, knowing exactly what had happened during the period of urban guerrilla warfare between General

Chiang Kai-shek's Nationalist soldiers and Mao Zedong's Communist agents. Their civil war had lasted twenty-five years. His attention was riveted to the Su-27/FLANKER escort and defense jets filling the already cluttered blue skies. The military juggernaut was beginning, and time was running out.

"What's wrong?" Ann asked, realizing that he was totally distracted.

"We have to get to the American consulate as quickly as possible. I need to talk with Moffat and find out what the hell is going on."

"Will you trust me for just a little longer?" Ann asked, as calmly yet firmly as she could.

"Do I have a choice?"

"I'm asking you as someone who cares about you very much and also happens to be the Prime Minister," she responded. "And I'm not being manipulative. And I promise that I won't go crazy on you."

Desaix looked down at her serious face. His intuition told him to let her play out her part in this ever-changing play. "A few minutes more delay won't determine the outcome of this crisis," he said.

"As you know, the Chinese Communists won only after a grueling war against both the Japanese and the Nationalists," Ann said. "But they eventually lost China to a nonideological form of capitalism, without firing a shot—ideological rigidity, extreme self-discipline, a bloated bureaucracy, massive corruption, and the absence of a charismatic leader."

"I gather your point is," Desaix responded, "that you are that charismatic leader who can prevent another civil war?"

"It's more serious than that, Desaix," Ann replied, as they continued west on Fuxing Road. "Chang controls a military that is ready to embark on an expansionist expedition with the Japanese military. And receives support from Phoebe Hill and your CIA. So he feels invincible. You saw that. He felt he could arrest me and even you with impunity. If he didn't have CIA protection, he would have been eliminated a long time ago."

"Wait just one minute, Madame Prime Minister," Desaix replied, recalling Phoebe's mirror-opposite explanation of the situation. "Are you trying to tell me that Chang is the one who is working with the Japanese? Unless I'm wrong, America is no longer in the business of military coups, destabilization, or counterinsurgency. We have a hard enough time these days figuring out who are our enemies."

"Maybe you have had some problems deciding what your country's interests are in the Far East," Ann said as inoffensively as she could, "but I can assure you that your President, Secretary of State, and Director of CIA are very clear on that matter.

"For a long time your President has been trying to mediate a quiet battle that has been raging between the Secretary of State and the Director of the Central Intelligence Agency," Ann continued as they approached a nondescript house on the corner of Shimen and Fuxing roads. "The issue is really quite simple: how does the U.S. stop Japanese commercial, political, and military expansion in the Far East? Yes, you heard me correctly. Not Chinese expansionism. Japanese."

"What in God's name are you talking about?" Desaix asked, following Ann up the cracked steps of Dr. Sun Yat-sen's former residence. As Desaix looked around the unremarkable stucco home, he realized why Ann had brought him. Bookshelves lined most of the walls of the foyer. The doctor's medical instruments were splayed out in the drawing room on a mahogany table that also served as his writing table. Pictures plastered the walls chronicling the physician's extensive political activities, including his role as the first President of the constitutional Chinese Republic, declared on January 1, 1912, after the death of the Empress Dowager and the fall of the Manchu Dynasty. After Dr. Sun Yat-sen's Kuomintang party was outlawed a year later by a military strongman who tried to establish himself as emperor, the country fell again into a civil war among regional warlords.

In a very subtle, caring way, Ann was pointing out that it was an American-trained medical doctor, like himself, who had involved himself in the political affairs of his country to effect change for the better. But the doctor had lost control of the power that had been mandated to him by the people and unwittingly threw his beloved China into civil war. In short, the road to hell was paved with good intentions.

"I know you find it difficult to believe," Ann said somberly, "to think that you were not in, what you diplomats call the loop, and for whatever reason, Phoebe was."

"Are you trying to tell me that a CIA Station Chief was privy to what an Assistant Secretary of State was not allowed to know?" Desaix said provocatively, as they walked through the other exhibition rooms. "Preposterous!"

"No, not preposterous. *Quanxi*," Ann replied, lowering her voice. "Is it so hard for you to believe that this time the bureaucratic network didn't include you? But it did include a highly select group that kept the issue a secret?" She smiled. "Think about it, Desaix. Your approach to foreign policy is one of compartmentalization and selectivity with secret one-man missions like the one that you are on now."

They left the house and walked toward the U.S. consulate on Huai-hai Road. "Just recall the highly secretive trips of Henry Kissinger," Ann continued. "When he was National Security Advisor, his own Secretary of State didn't know he was opening up relations with our country. I think you recall William Casey, Ollie North, George Bush, James Baker, Warren Christopher, and a host of other officials who thought that one-man diplomacy was the way to bring about world change. Of course they had a fancy term for it, 'two-track diplomacy.' But it was always the same old thing, a few senior officials refusing to share power with a wider body of officials, and frequently violating their own laws to do it. A strange habit for such an open, democratic society, don't you think?"

"Are you telling me," Desaix asked, "that the President wants to stop Japanese expansionism without directly confronting Japan? And that we are using China to do it? But to provide a convincing cover, the Sec State sends his Assistant Sec State to make it look as if the U.S. is actively involved in peacemaking activities while the U.S.— via the CIA—is really helping the Chinese military prepare for war? Very convenient and very imaginative. But I thought we stopped playing those games a long time ago."

"Hardly, Desaix," Ann replied. "Just remember back in the early 1990s when your government used a recently converted enemy, Syria, to attack a long-standing ally, Iraq." They skirted around a group of Chinese soldiers. "You tell me, Dr. Clark. Do you stop the Japanese by co-opting them into a military alliance with an ally like the Chinese, against an expendable ally like Taiwan, and then have the Chinese turn against the Japanese—"

"—or do you allow your Chinese ally to feign an attack against Taiwan," Desaix interrupted, "and then turn your formidable Chinese military forces against the already exposed and extended forces of Japan? A kind of surrogate preemptive strike against a duped Japan."

"Exactly," Ann answered proudly. "Your Secretary of State supported my strategy to dupe the Japanese into a joint military venture. The CIA backed General Chang and his desire to feign an attack against Taiwan. The result of either approach, however, is the same—the demise of Japan."

"Then this entire struggle between you and General Chang is really one glorified bureaucratic turf issue," Desaix concluded, sensing that somewhere in the verbiage was the nidus of an emerging truth. "Which tactical approach is the best one to use and which of you would be more effective in implementing it."

"I'm sorry if I have disappointed you," Ann replied as they approached a U.S. Marine guard standing alongside his Chinese counterpart in front of a little wooden booth outside the U.S. consulate. "But you are right. No matter which one of us gets your country's support, the outcome will be the same."

Desaix showed the marine guard his ID and he and Ann passed through the electronic metal detectors and entered the consulate grounds. "When I think about it, it's quite brilliant," Desaix said. "Get the Chinese to rid the U.S. of an economic and potential military enemy during a time when Japan-bashing is so rampant that it has been developed by the U.S. government and the media into a full-fledged public relations industry. On one level, every country would object to China's unprovoked aggression against Japan. But no one would step in to help Japan. In fact, practically every country in the world would be pleased to rid the world of arrogant, racist Japan."

"It's practiced by doctors all the time," Ann said. "You call it prophylactic medicine—cut out the benign tumor before it becomes malignant."

"Not quite..." Desaix said somberly. "We call what you're about to do malpractice. And the medical profession severely punishes those physicians who perform unnecessary procedures." But if the medical analogy held, who was to be the wrongfully accused sacrificial healer?

CHAPTER THIRTY-TWO

War is a nightmare comprised of magnificent machines," Japanese Prime Minister Sammy Mori said nervously, standing next to Moffat on the flight deck of the aircraft carrier *Thomas Jefferson*. He watched with mixed fascination and fear as the A-6 Tomcats catapulted into the air. Yesterday they had been enemies, today they were allies, but what about tomorrow? he wondered.

"We are not yet at war, Mr. Prime Minister," Moffat replied, trying to relieve Mori's palpable anxiety. "We are simply prepositioning our forces for the proper moment."

"When will we attack?" Mori asked, checking his watch, proud of the fact that this was the first time American and Japanese forces were fighting alongside each other.

"Within the next six hours."

"What about your Assistant Secretary of State?" Mori asked. "Have you found him yet?"

"I hope to hear from him quite soon," Moffat responded, reluctant to say anything more. For the past several days, Desaix's whereabouts were being tracked by human assets and ELINT. If everything went according to plans, Moffat thought, Desaix should be at the American consulate within a few hours, where he would hook up with Cartwright, who would then phone him. Only if needed, would he send the Special Ops forces to get Desaix and the rest of them out of China. Otherwise, he would simply send in a helicopter and fly them out directly to the aircraft carrier.

Mori beamed, delighted to see the *Shirane*, the pride of Japan's Maritime Self-Defense Force, a five-thousand-ton destroyer with two five-inch guns, two short-range SAM launchers, and one Asroc launcher, escorting the American aircraft carrier. For the first time in five decades, Japan and America would be sharing strategic objectives. First Taiwan, then the rest of Southeast Asia. China would provide the manpower. In turn, Japan would prosper from her economic and military support of China's expansionism. And America would profit from her relationship with stable political surrogates who could provide her with cheap goods. A marriage made in heaven, as the Americans would say.

"I'll be damned," Cartwright said, hugging Desaix. "I guess it takes more than a couple billion Chinese to kill off one mean Cajun." He tried to hide his concern about Desaix's haggard, disheveled appearance.

"Thanks for worrying about me," Desaix replied. "I was really touched by the efforts you and Jim made to find me." He looked around the nearly empty room. Only a government-issue metal desk, a color picture of the President of the United States, and a STU-3 secured telephone gave any indication that they were in the American consulate. He realized he was arriving at a denouement and yet he still didn't have a clear idea of who was doing what to whom.

In one corner of the room, Ann was hastily changing her clothes and reapplying her makeup, transforming once again into the young seductress.

"You ingrate," Cartwright said, tossing him a can of Tsintao beer. "Who do you think kept you alive? Mother Cabrini?"

"Phoebe Hill," Desaix responded without hesitation.

"Ouch." Ann said as she heard Desaix's response. She turned toward them, seeking their approval for the newly refurbished Prime Minister. "Talk about emotional insensitivity. I sacrifice my life to keep him alive and whom does he thank? Phoebe Hill. That serves you right, Ambassador Cartwright."

"We've got to get going," Cartwright said, checking his watch. "Everyone is waiting for us. And we certainly don't want to be late."

"Wait a minute," Desaix said. "Where are we going?" Although he feigned surprise, he was pleased to know that he would soon witness the finale of the play in which he had been performing an unusual—and unclear—role.

"Good question," Cartwright replied, reclaiming the can of beer from Desaix. "But I just don't have time to explain. Take my word," he said, mimicking the harried rabbit in *Alice in Wonderland*, "we're late, we're late for a very important date."

"I think you're going to need a little bit of empathy for our confused friend," Ann said to Cartwright, radiating the regained bravado of a woman once again in control of her life. She walked up to Desaix and touched his cheek in a gesture of sympathy. She felt hurt that he had chosen Phoebe over her. But she could understand the reason. He was reverting to his customary defensive posture, grabbing an American paramour, whom he thought he understood better—and could control more—than his mysterious Empress Dowager.

"Just make believe you're in the middle of a Pirandello play and someone in the audience screams out 'fire.'" Cartwright answered, holding the door open for everyone. "So you better get your ass out."

"Hold it," Desaix said, grabbing Cartwright by the lapels. "No one is going anywhere until someone tells me what the hell is going on." He had effectively used anger with Phoebe as a means of uncovering certain facts. Now it was Wayne's turn. Of course, even if Cartwright answered his questions, Desaix wouldn't know how to evaluate the veracity of the information. The only thing he could now rely upon with any sense of confidence was his sixth sense, his clinical intuition. Ironic, he thought, how much it always came down to his relying on the human intangibles—emotion, attitude, intent, belief—to discern the bare outlines of truth.

"Meet your savior, Desaix," Cartwright replied, pointing to Ann. "If it were not for her direct intervention, you would not be alive today."

"Wait a minute," Desaix said. "Are you trying to tell me that Ann, not Phoebe, saved my life?" Only a few days ago Wayne seemed to be allied to Phoebe. Now he was heaping accolades onto Ann.

Cartwright smiled and nodded his head. He enjoyed surprising his control freak friend. The whole scenario had played out even better than he had imagined it would.

"It's hard to buy that one," Desaix said, raising his voice in mock anger. "If anything, it was the other way around. If I hadn't helped get Ann out of Beijing and brought her down to Shanghai, General Chang would have made *moo shu* pork out of her."

"Are you certain?" Ann asked in an unassuming manner. She did not enjoy watching Desaix squirm, but it was presumptuous of him to think that she had not been in control of the situation at any point along the way.

"Pardon me, Madame Prime Minister," Desaix replied defensively, "but didn't you ask me to save you from General Chang?"

"Why would I ask you, a foreigner, to rescue me from someone who was my...employee?" Ann asked, feeling sorry for Desaix. It was clear that he still had no idea what had happened or why. The mindbender's perceptions had been twisted so many times and in so many different ways that he was dizzy from the shifting realities that had been imposed upon him. All she could do now was hope that his increasing frustration would force him to react unpredictably.

"We really have to get going," Cartwright replied impatiently.

"Chang arrested you on my orders," Ann tried to explain, "so that we could determine which of us you would align with in our ongoing bureaucratic wars. We also wanted to find out what Phoebe had told you about—"

"Are you telling me that these last few days were part of a charade acted out by both of you in concert?" Desaix interrupted, incredulous.

"Not quite," Ann responded. "It's just a system we Chinese have developed over centuries—mutual hostage taking with the promise of money or political favors."

"I get it," Desaix said. "Only neither one of you could be certain what Newton said to the other. So his omissions to each of you acted as my insurance of safety."

"You could say that," Ann said. "But believe it or not, Jin Bo grew fond of the 'hip American,' as he affectionately calls you."

"And last night?" he asked, unsure he wanted to hear the answer. "Was that also part of the elaborate charade?"

"No," Ann responded emphatically. "Especially not our Carnival night." She looked at him with all the tenderness she could muster in the middle of an empty room and prying ears.

"Unfortunately, the day after Carnival is Ash Wednesday," Desaix replied. "The day of reckoning." His mind was telling him that she was manipulating him. But his heart wanted to believe that she truly cared about him.

"But that's all a footnote in someone's Ph.D. dissertation," Ann said, glancing at her watch. "We must get going. Time is running out."

"I told you before. I'm not going anywhere until someone tells me what is really going on," Desaix responded, having difficulty controlling his mounting rage, resenting the fact that everyone had been so successful at keeping him in the dark.

"You'll see," Cartwright answered, taking his arm. "Trust me."

"I don't trust you," Desaix said. "So tell me now, before we step a foot outside this door."

"It's very simple, *mon vieux ami*, my old friend," Cartwright said. "China is about to embark on a war against Japan—on behalf of the United States." Cartwright paused to savor Desaix's quizzical expression. "Taiwan is the pretext that the Chinese will use to entrap the Japanese navy heading toward Taiwan. At the same time, the two hundred thousand Japanese soldiers who have been prepositioned in Manchuria for the invasion of Taiwan will be encircled by General Chang and his troops and taken prisoner as invaders of Manchuria. Ann's propaganda machinery has already fabricated the necessary disinformation material about the Japanese 'invasion' of Manchuria— pictures and all."

"Are you telling me that there never was a crisis between Taiwan and China?" Desaix said. "It was all a ruse to entrap the Japanese into a phony coalition with the Chinese?"

"As you see, it's really very easy to create an imaginary crisis. You should know that, Desaix," Cartwright replied. "Doctor up some State Department cables out of Beijing warning of increasing hostilities between China and Taiwan. Fabricate highly restricted intelligence reports that only the President and a few very closely trusted advisors can read. And then make certain that there are no media leaks. Of course, other than those selective bits of information you do want leaked. Mix it all together in the cauldron of TOP SECRET/NO DIS/EYES ONLY and *voilà,* you get a soufflé called a preemptive strike without the annoying intervention of Congress, whose key members have already been co-opted, of the American people, or of the UN. We like to think of it as a more sophisticated version of Desert Shield—a tightly managed aggression by the good guys."

"And send the Assistant Secretary of State for East Asian and Pacific Affairs over to China to create a false expectation that peace was at hand," Desaix added.

"Something like that," Cartwright replied, pleased that Desaix seemed to be taking their revelations so well.

"I still don't get it," Desaix said. "Why would the Japanese buy into a military coalition against Taiwan?"

"Manchukuo," Cartwright replied. "Remember the Japanese conquest of Manchuria in 1931?"

"Sure," Desaix said. "Japan saw Manchuria as a natural repository for badly needed resources—coal, minerals, lumber, rubber, cheap labor. In their eyes, Manchuria was theirs for the taking."

"Then it should be no surprise to you, Desaix," Ann said, impatient for them to leave. "National character, like personal dynamics, rarely changes."

"Meaning what?" Desaix asked, but knowing that she was right. It was an axiom of psychopolitical dynamics and international crisis management that neither world leaders nor nations change without some massive external intervention.

"You've heard of the Greater East Asian Co-Prosperity Sphere?" Cartwright asked.

"We now call it Pax Pacifica," Ann interrupted.

"Yes," Desaix replied. "Basically, China and Japan strike a deal to dominate the Orient together."

"So instead of togetherness," Ann said, "we substitute China as the sole protector of the Far East, acting of course as a responsible client for U.S. interests. It's an easy and morally correct substitution because, as we all know, every single country in East Asia still detests the Japanese for the atrocities they committed during World War II."

"You have to understand, Desaix," Cartwright said, "that unlike past invasions, in this case there is no aggression in the old sense of the word."

"What do you mean?" Desaix asked, once again stung by the realization of how much he had really been out of touch in Washington. True, he had never really learned to become a team player. Unlike Moffat, Desaix never went out of his way to cultivate the President's trust and friendship. No tennis on the White House courts. No contrived photo ops and public relations opportunities. While Moffat was cultivating the President, Desaix had been at home alone, listening to his Cajun music.

Although Desaix had heard all this information before, he suddenly saw some of Moffat's decisions over the past two years in a different context. In order to make the President appear committed to the growth and prosperity of China and the Pacific Basin, Moffat had encouraged the President to kill several significant protectionist policies, allowing China and other Asian countries to dump their finished goods onto the U.S. markets, undercutting their American competitors. Desaix had been tasked to undertake the difficult chore of enforcing both mercantile and human rights violations against China while the President and Moffat had been playing footsy with Prime Minister Lee Ann Wu. He had the role of bad cop, while Moffat, Cartwright, and the President had the role of good cop.

"I think it will work, Desaix," Cartwright responded. "We've gamed it out with the Joint Chiefs of Staff at the Department of Defense."

"Winning without fighting," Desaix added. "Intimidate your opponent with a show of force so that they have no alternative but to acquiesce." So that was the underlying dynamic of the crisis, replete with contradictions, deceptions, and betrayals. From the point of view of both Sun Tzu's philosophy and a modern Psyops campaign, he had to admit to himself that Moffat had designed an elegant piece of work. Desaix should have remembered that, like himself, Moffat was a student of Sun Tzu. But the issue of *quanxi* and the need to sacrifice it for a greater good still ripped through Desaix's thoughts. Why didn't Moffat bring him into his confidence? He would have played the game, had he known the rules. Or would he have?

"And not one bullet is fired," Cartwright exclaimed, with the enthusiasm of a young boy discovering a new G.I. Joe toy.

"So you're supposed to die of fright?" Desaix asked facetiously, masking the underlying pain of his mother's words in his dream. Moffat. Betrayal.

"All we have to do," Cartwright said, "is to wave the Samurai sword, not cut anyone's throat. In the old plan, the only overt act taken by China and Japan was a swift, bloodless invasion of Taiwan, the running down of the Republic of China's flag and the running up of the People's Republic of China banner on Taipei flagpoles. Beijing promised scarcely a stir in the economic climate of Taiwan. Japan then moves into Malaysia, Thailand, and Indonesia, demanding berthing privileges for its formidable navy, and renegotiating obscenely favorable commercial and security arrangements."

"But in the newly rewritten Pax Pacifica," Desaix said, "you intend to eliminate Japan and substitute China as the stealth invader, moving effortlessly from one country to another, intimidating each without firing a shot, extracting favorable commercial and security arrangements without disturbing the international money markets. In effect, China would establish a hegemony over the Pacific Rim." Desaix paused and then added, "The U.S. will be predictably ineffectual to prevent it. The UN doesn't have enough assets to mediate another regional conflict, having exhausted all of its money and political cachet in its ten-year history of costly, unsuccessful peacekeeping attempts in the former Yugoslavia, Cambodia, and South Africa."

"China, without the intervention of its good friend the U.S., will happily achieve the long-awaited dream of once again becoming the "Middle Kingdom," Ann said.

"Yes, the center of world trade to which the rest of the world," Desaix replied angrily, "including us barbarians, has to pay homage." He paused to make his point to Cartwright. "And that homage will cost us dearly."

"*Quanxi,*" Ann interjected. "You forget the recent history of friendship and intertwining relationships between the U.S. and China."

"*Quanxi,* of course, how stupid of me to forget," Desaix answered sarcastically. "What a convenient word to express the wonderfully varied attributes of the Chinese national character—friendship, networking, intellectual affinity, financial ties, family relationships, trust, understanding."

"I'm pleased that as a result of your brief but exciting stay here," Ann said, "you have been able to distill your varied impressions and experiences into the one word that is so important to the Chinese way of life. Because without *quanxi,* one can never become a friend of China."

"Paradoxically," Desaix said, "I have found *quanxi* to mean only one thing."

"And what is that?" Ann asked.

"Deception," Desaix replied sadly. "The certainty that what is said or done has no correspondence to the truth."

"Ah, you're still an idealist. I am surprised," Ann said jovially. "The condition of all men is to lie and deceive. There is very little that we can do about that." She didn't expect Desaix to be so sensitive and felt badly for him. But from this point onward there was very little, if anything, she could do for him as the Empress Dowager. Empathy was an extremely limited commodity in the game of international diplomacy, and friendship was at best a trace element.

"That's much too cynical for even me," Desaix said. "I would prefer to believe that China is simply scared of what she is becoming domestically and has deceived herself, with your help, into becoming something she is not—an international aggressor."

"What could China conceivably be afraid of?" Ann asked.

"*Luan.* Chaos," Desaix replied somberly.

The STU-3 rang. Cartwright picked it up and handed it to Desaix. "It's Moffat. He wants to talk to you."

"Hi, Jim," Desaix said hesitantly. "Thanks, I'm fine." He listened quietly to Moffat's profuse explanations and excuses for the prior two days, uncertain what he should say in return.

Desaix's side of the conversation was never heard by Moffat, however, for Chinese soldiers armed with semi-automatic weapons burst into the room and yanked the telephone from the wall. They forcibly ushered Wayne, Ann, and Desaix to a cordoned-off area of the street surrounding the consulate. At the curb, Chang and Phoebe sat on top of a refurbished Soviet-built T-72 tank with a 125mm gun barrel pointed directly at them.

CHAPTER THIRTY-THREE

W here are we going?" Desaix asked, riding in the back of the canvas-covered military transport truck through the center of the city. Soldiers were visible on every street corner. Trucks such as theirs moved rapidly down all the major streets. Whether this war was going to an exercise in Psyops, as Wayne maintained, or would involve massive death and destruction, Desaix was certain of one thing: he had to try to stop this crisis before it spun completely out of control. And time was running out.

"You'll see," Phoebe responded. The fact that Desaix had said very little to her as they all rode together in the truck told her that his trip from Suzhou to Shanghai with Ann had been eventful. She suspected that he had fallen in love with Ann and was jealous of both Ann and Desaix. But she was determined not to allow her personal feelings to interfere with her assignment to make certain Chang would become the new Prime Minister of China.

Cartwright sat inside in the truck with the driver, feeling as if he were celebrating VJ Day, the defeat of the Japanese in World War II.

"The old gang is back together again," Newton said, laughing. "Maybe we should have some kind of a reunion party."

"Be quiet, Jin Bo," Ann said, irritated by her brother's comment. She looked through a slit in the canvas and was impressed by the size of the military entourage. Although she had hoped to reach their destination without any interference from Chang or Phoebe, she resigned herself to at least arriving safely. And from the looks of the convoy they were well protected against any unforeseeable event. Staring at Desaix, who was avoiding her glance, she was concerned that she had damaged their relationship. She could not blame him for feeling betrayed by her participation in Pax Pacifica, but that was a matter of state that had to play itself out. There was nothing personal. She had been sworn to secrecy by Moffat, who, for all she knew, could be using her as a foil to an even greater deception. But that was part of the price she had to pay in order to play the game of international diplomacy.

"What are you thinking about, General Chang?" Desaix asked, responding to Chang's self-absorption. He needed to deflect the oppressive emotional tensions arising from Ann, Phoebe, and himself. Desaix was particularly intrigued by the fact that for a man who was on the verge of personal victory in his political contest with Ann, Chang seemed unusually preoccupied.

"We are about to enter into battle," Chang said, pensively. "And almost all battles are won by slaughter or strategic maneuver. The greater the general, the more he relies on strategy and the less on slaughter."

It sounded to Desaix that Chang was corroborating Wayne's prediction of a war without aggression. A Psyops war. Yet what if both Ann and Wayne were wrong? The situation could easily escalate into World War III.

"Oh my God," Phoebe exclaimed, piqued. "Just before the crucial moment, my general turns into Hamlet."

"I'm not your general, madame," Chang said, calmly. "I belong to all of the Chinas."

"All of the Chinas?" Desaix asked, stunned by the expression. "I haven't heard that since the days of Mao's Shanghai Communiqué, when that term included Taiwan."

"I'm certain that General Chang was referring to the fact that soon Taiwan will be part of mainland China," Phoebe interjected, checking the 9mm Glock 17 handgun tucked comfortably into the cradle of her back. It had been a while since she had carried a semi-automatic pistol, but there was too much at stake to leave to the vagaries of four whimsical personalities. But she questioned whether she could really use violent force against any of them, especially Desaix. Although she hated to admit it, there was something special about him. The night on the train was a joyous celebration of passion and tenderness. It had been a long time since she felt that way. Despite his mocking indifference to life's dangers, Desaix was sensitive and caring. Beneath that cynical and callous exterior was a man who was really concerned about things like fairness and justice. But if she wasn't careful, he could still upset the proverbial Chinese applecart.

Phoebe worried that Chang was becoming contemplative. She would have preferred that he act more decisively and self-assured, like Ann, even if it was only an act. She needed a charismatic leader for their mission, not a wistful philosopher.

"You were saying, General," Desaix said, "something about slaughter and strategy." Desaix watched Chang's pudgy features twist into a grimace of silent anguish and felt there was a substratum of truth straining to come out. What was it that Chang wanted? Did he really believe in this ersatz Pax Pacifica—this grandiose plan for China to dominate the Far East? If he did, then why didn't he just preempt everyone and take his loyal People's Liberation Army on a military expansionist expedition across Asia? He didn't need this charade that they were about to undertake. Unless, of course, thought Desaix, this was simply another ruse.

"A skillful general," Chang repeated, deep in thought, "relies far more on strategy than slaughter. Nearly all the battles of history that are regarded as masterpieces of military art have been battles of maneuver in which the enemy has found itself defeated by some novel device; some queer, swift, unexpected strategy. In such battles the losses to the victors have been small." He paused to assess his companions' interest and continued to remember something valuable from the past. "A great commander not only possesses common sense and strong powers of reasoning but also an element of imagination that leaves the enemy puzzled as well as defeated. Most of the maneuvers of battle rarely take place upon the battlefield. They are maneuvers of time, diplomacy, psychology, and most of all deception."

"That's right—you're a follower of Sun Tzu's concept of war," Desaix said. "Using *cheng* and *ch'i* tactics the superior commander confuses and disrupts the enemy's plans and alliances." As he talked, images of his mother's "silver tray" came into his head. But the tray seemed to be disproportionately larger than the elegant china tea set, which was receding rapidly from view. Was it Taiwan that was important, and not China? he wondered. The harder he tried to dismiss the image of the "silver tray," the larger it became. What was his subconscious trying to tell him? He gazed at Chang and thought about the faded tattoo of the eel wrapped around a sword. He recalled Toland's reference to Chang's secret meeting with Taiwanese officials. And then the image of the train wreck flashed through Desaix's mind. The "silver tray," Taiwan, the Tiger Eel, *huoche* 217, Chang, secret meetings between Chang and Taiwan, China, and Moffat were all related. But how?

"Yes, Desaix," Chang replied calmly. "One must be able to create divisiveness among the leadership, sow dissension, and completely subvert the opponent's position through the use of spies and agents." He glanced at Phoebe's expression of disapproval but continued nevertheless. "Above all else, the enemy has to be isolated, demoralized, and unwilling to fight anymore."

"As I remember Sun Tzu, wars are won before the battle even begins," Desaix said, unnerved by his glimpse of a gun handle peaking over Phoebe's belt. Why did she have to carry a gun, when they were surrounded by ostensibly loyal Chinese troops?

Too many assumptions, suspicions, and inconsistencies swirled around Desaix's mind. Although he was used to navigating through a world of mental shadows and half truths, he always found a time and a place in which he could anchor himself. But now, not even his current destination was a point of reality. He had learned no more than that they had to reach "somewhere," within the next couple of hours. Annoyingly indeterminate. Just like this phantom war with Taiwan. An aggressive posturing of military forces in order to induce capitulation without having to fire a single shot.

Strange, Desaix thought. Despite his initial assumptions to the contrary, the assumptions he had made in Moffat's office, Desaix now accepted the fact that China's history was one of inward aggression and annihilation. Civil wars. This crisis with Taiwan didn't make sense. Why should Moffat even suggest Taiwan as a potential invasion target when so much of its own financial resources were legitimately invested in mainland China? Sure Taiwan and China had been furiously building up their respective military forces for a decade, but technically both countries were part of one greater China. Taiwan had a staggering $100 billion trade surplus with Beijing. It owned most if not all of Guangzhou and Fujian provinces in the southeast of China, and had major investments in Shanghai, Singapore, Malaysia, and Hong Kong. Desaix imagined that the Japanese would have had a hard time accepting Taiwan as an intended target of aggression, given the fact that they knew everything Desaix knew. Something didn't make sense. He looked at his companions in the back of the truck again. Someone knew what the truth was, but it certainly wasn't him.

"There is an old Chinese proverb about Taiwan, General," Desaix said, determined to force more information out of him. "Every three years an uprising; every five years a rebellion."

"Desaix, you seem to have a morbid fixation on Taiwan," Phoebe said nervously, "just at the moment we are about to legitimize China's primacy over the Far East."

"Ignore me and my rantings," Desaix replied, hoping he had hit a raw nerve. Whatever else Pax Pacifica was, he decided, it contained one extremely important element that no one seemed to be paying enough attention to—Taiwan. The "silver tray," the Tiger Eel, Chang's secret Taiwan meetings, *huoche* 217, and the broken pieces of China finally came into clear focus. The truth lay within those disparate images. He could feel its palpable texture. It felt real and solid.

"I think that you should leave the general alone," Phoebe warned.

Newton sat quietly immersed in his own thoughts during all this. He wanted the entire affair to end as quickly as possible. It was too open now. Too much on the surface. Playing in the shadows of corruption and opportunism was much more fun and certainly more lucrative.

"Don't tell me that you're the general's new spokesperson?" Desaix asked, purposefully confrontational.

"Stop provoking me, Desaix," Phoebe replied. "It won't work. In

two hours Chang will announce, with the quiet support of your friend
Moffat, that Ann has graciously resigned from the post of Prime Minister and given it over to the one person who has the loyalty of both
the military and the people."

"Let me guess what comes next," Desaix replied, not entirely surprised at Phoebe's revelation. "Chang will then call a cessation to all
hostilities with Taiwan and reaffirm the importance of China's crucial
alliance with Japan in which Japan supplies the necessary monetary
and military expertise. And Chang goes on to lead his people in a
bloodless takeover of the continent through fear and intimidation."

"Over my dead body," Ann hissed. "It will never happen. I will remain the Prime Minister and Japan will be a militarily defeated nation."

"It's so therapeutic to air our differences in the open," Newton
quipped. "Isn't it, Dr. Clark?"

"It sounds to me as if the war we'll be part of is going to take place
when we reach our destination," Desaix said, looking back and forth
between Ann and Phoebe.

"Cool it," Phoebe snapped, afraid of losing control over the situation. Goddamn it, she thought, she had underestimated Desaix's cunning.

"Remember February 28?" Desaix asked Chang, recalling Moffat's
and his discussion after their escapade at Hurricane Alley. "Remember
how the Kuomintang massacred thousands of Taiwanese on February
28, 1947, murdering a generation of doctors, scholars, and political
leaders. As well as your family and friends?" He felt that Chang was a
prime subject for psychological manipulation, lost in his own memories.

"Shut up!" Phoebe screamed, pulling out her gun and waving it at
Desaix. As much as she disliked resorting to force, he was deliberately
backing her into an untenable corner.

"Defend Great Taiwan!" Chang murmured to himself. "Defend
Great Taiwan! Defend the sacred land for the national rebirth . . ."

As Chang recited the first verse of the popular Taiwanese poem, as
if in a dream, Desaix's understanding of his own dream was suddenly
clear. Chang was holding the large "silver tray" upon which were scattered the small pieces of the china tea set. But China wasn't leading a

sham invasion of Taiwan. It was completely the reverse—Taiwan would be invading China. Chang, the Supreme Commander of the PLA, was spearheading the Taiwanese invasion, masterminded by the CIA, under the direction of Phoebe. And created by Moffat. Of course, it was a plan that had all the brilliance of Moffat and the strategic ideals of Sun Tzu—a victory without war in which a smaller power achieves its goal through connivance, co-optation, and brilliant psychological manipulation. The ultimate deception campaign.

CHAPTER THIRTY-FOUR

Desaix lurched forward and grabbed Phoebe's weapon. At the sound of the commotion in the back of the truck, Cartwright ordered the convoy to stop. Soldiers barked out orders and quickly surrounded the truck.

"Sorry, ladies and gentlemen," Desaix said to his companions, "for any inconvenience I may have precipitated, but this show was strictly choreographed by Phoebe Hill, who thinks nothing of intimidating one of her own countrymen."

"Desaix, if I had wanted to kill you," Phoebe said calmly, "I would have."

"I'm certain of that," Desaix replied, pointing the gun at the group, "except that I don't want to run the risk of seeing how good a marksman you really are."

"Are you two going to stop playing with your toys?" Ann asked, annoyed. "We have an important meeting with Mori and Moffat in less than two hours. And we must arrive on time. The *Thomas Jefferson* will only wait for three hours before she leaves, with or without us."

"Oh, so I am finally privileged to know where we are going. Don't worry, Madame Prime Minister," Desaix said sarcastically, "I personally assure you that you will be there. No treaty ceremony is complete without the guest of honor." He wondered whether Ann had any idea that the meeting she was impatient to arrive at was the one in which she would be unceremoniously dumped. But he suspected that each person in the back of the truck might be very surprised to discover what Pax Pacifica would eventually turn out to be. Perhaps not quite what each had initially intended it to be. He looked around at all the nervous faces. "Take it easy. No one is going to get hurt—unless, of course, someone feels particularly self-destructive. You all will board that ship, except that I want to go there with a full deck of cards. And right now, each of you knows something that gives you some advantage over me. You see," Desaix concluded, "all I want to do is to fill in the missing pieces."

"This is a strange way to make a jigsaw puzzle," Newton quipped.

"General, Ann, Phoebe," Desaix said, pointing the gun at them, "I'm afraid that we're going to have to leave our lovely companion Jin Bo. But rest assured you will see him again—if we don't encounter any significant problems."

"Where are you taking us?" Phoebe asked, rising from her seat.

"I see all the rats are leaving the sinking ship," Newton said, impatient to proceed to the harbor even if he were alone.

"You're making a big mistake, Desaix," Ann interjected. "Let us continue to our destination."

"I hate to admit it, but she's right," Phoebe added. "Trust me."

"Trust you, Phoebe?" Desaix chuckled. "I think I've heard that before. What was brandishing this gun all about, your endearing love for me?"

"You pushed the wrong button," Phoebe replied, moving toward him.

"I'm certain of that," Desaix said, returning his attention to Chang. "General, I would like you, Ann, and Phoebe to come with me. Jin Bo, you will continue on. Tell Cartwright not to worry. God willing, we will join him on board ship in a couple of hours."

Chang jumped off the truck and told his soldiers that everything was fine. Ann, Phoebe, and Desaix followed closely behind him, Phoebe's gun in Desaix's pocket.

"Where do you want me to go?" Chang asked, unsuccessfully trying to convince his soldiers to put away their weapons. Guns drawn, they followed Desaix and the group. "Please don't shoot. Everything is all right."

"You tell me where we should go," Desaix answered, mindful of the fact that he had created a Mexican standoff. He held the group hostage while, in turn, the soldiers had him surrounded. And if he didn't succeed in his plan, Desaix knew he would be dead.

"I don't understand you," Chang said.

"I think you do, General Chang," Desaix said. "Let's try Dr. Sun Yat-sen's house."

"What?" Chang asked.

"Now's not the time to play games, Desaix," Ann interjected, checking her watch.

"You heard me," Desaix replied, noticing the tension in Chang's face, the surprise in Phoebe's expression, and the annoyance in Ann's voice.

"Why should we go there?" Phoebe asked.

"I think we'll find out once we get there," Desaix replied. "Won't we?"

"I'm confused," Chang said, his face twitching nervously.

"A completely understandable feeling," Desaix replied, pleased that he was now the one who had a clear sense of what was happening. "You were a very young boy on Taiwan when Generalissimo Chiang Kai-shek arrived with his defeated ragtag army of corrupt incompetents, cowards, and butchers, weren't you?"

"What if I was?" Chang asked, motioning to the surrounding soldiers not to fire.

"And you were there during the 2-28 Incident as the native Taiwanese call it. Weren't you?" Desaix asked, following Chang toward the Bund, near the harbor. "The day when thousands of native Taiwanese were massacred by the newly appointed governor, General Chen Yi, one of the Generalissimo's most brutal and incompetent senior military officers."

"My parents fled Shanghai a few years before the Generalissimo and his henchmen escaped from the mainland to the island," Chang said, his face grimacing with discomfort.

"That's a lie," Desaix said angrily, recalling Moffat's words. "They remained and you joined the Tiger Eels, one of Taiwan's nationalist gangs that fought both the Kuomintang's and Communists' attempts to conquer the island."

"What are you trying to say, Dr. Clark?" Chang demanded.

"Why don't you tell me, General," Desaix said, hearing the soldiers cock their guns. He jammed the Glock into Chang's back. "Tell them to back off."

"Please, Desaix," Ann said, both impressed and frightened by Desaix's foolhardy courage. "Put away your weapon, otherwise you'll get us all killed."

"You might as well tell Desaix the truth, Chang," Phoebe said, wondering which one would break first, Ann or Chang.

"I have nothing to say," Chang replied.

"Please, General Chang," Desaix said, cocking his gun. "Just as your control officer would have had no compunction about shooting me, I, too, can be equally cold-blooded."

"Desaix," Phoebe said, "he won't tell you anything. You yourself said he had been a member of the Tiger Eels. So you should know from their history that they are as stubborn and ruthless as they are committed to the cause of an independent Taiwan."

"Is that your way of telling me that you're willing to help?" Desaix asked, noticing that Phoebe radiated that same seductive glint in her eye that she had in the train compartment. She was clearly desperate enough to try anything.

"Maybe," Phoebe answered and then spoke to Chang in Chinese. He, in turn, ordered his men to step back as a gesture of good faith toward Desaix.

"What do you propose?" Desaix asked, uncocking his gun. He was amused by the fact that Phoebe never gave up on her desire to make a deal. Even to the end she was a professional, whose one mission was to make certain that she served her client, whoever that might be.

"It's now your turn to guess," Phoebe said smiling. "But I'll give you a hint. Think of the word 'fairness.' "

"By fairness you mean equal time," Desaix asked, "don't you?"

"Give me a chance to argue my case in front of Moffat," Phoebe said. "That's not very much to ask, is it?" Desaix shook his head in disbelief. Why would she want access to a person for whom she was already working? Could he have guessed wrong? Was Moffat not a part of a Taiwanese scenario that Desaix thought was brilliant? He decided to let her play out the last vestiges of her charade, to see where it would lead.

"Come on, Phoebe, that's a helluva lot to ask," Desaix replied. "Access to the right person at the right time is everything in our world of international power politics." In normal times Desaix's access to Moffat was worth his weight in gold. His effectiveness was constantly measured by his physical proximity to power. Or by how many times he did or did not brief a seventh-floor principal. In the world of State, both Desaix and Phoebe knew that the first one in and the last one out of the Secretary's office was the person you wanted to know.

"If I get you equal time with Moffat, then what evidence will you provide me to corroborate what we both know is your real agenda?" Desaix asked, hoping Phoebe wouldn't realize he was still confused.

"I have a feeling that you're not going to tell me what *your* real agenda is," Phoebe said coyly. "You're just going to see what I offer."

"Think of my agenda as my personal Rorschach test," Desaix replied. "You tell me or show me whatever you know that I need. If I think the evidence is compelling, and, I might add, timely, then I will agree to your deal. If I think you're jerking me around, then all is lost. And you and Chang lose your one and only chance to change the course of history." Clearly, she was playing out the last part of her game to save face in front of Chang. As long as it didn't conflict with his own interests, he would let her perform the final scene as she scripted it.

"I can accept that deal," Phoebe said, knowing she had no real alternative. "Follow me."

The four of them walked rapidly down Fuxing Road, past truck convoys headed for the docks. Phoebe led them to a house on the corner of Fuxing and Shimen roads.

"Just as I had hoped," Desaix exclaimed. "The residence of Dr. Sun Yat-sen."

"Why here?" Ann asked, her voice sounding shaky. "You have a lot more important things to do in the middle of a major crisis than to see this museum again."

"Do I really, Ann?" Desaix asked. "Then why do you seem so frightened?"

Ann looked nervously at Chang.

"Are we going inside?" Desaix asked, once again cocking his pistol.

Chapter Thirty-Five

I hope you know what you're doing," Phoebe warned Desaix. "Chang's soldiers won't let you out of here alive."

"We'll have to wait and see, won't we?" he responded, pointing his gun at Chang as two soldiers followed them up the flight of stairs.

"Please be careful, Desaix," Ann said, fearful that all of them could die in an unintended shoot-out. It was hard for her to imagine that the man who had made such tender love to her could also kill in cold blood. Despite her reputation as the ruthless Empress Dowager, she knew that she had neither the instincts nor desire to kill someone directly. True, she could order thousands of her troops to invade another country or her repressive security system to torture an entire community, but that was completely impersonal. And even then, she often found herself reluctant to execute orders involving brutality that her national security advisors would recommend. If truth be known, she thought, as she walked into the doctor's house, it was Chang who really proposed and executed most, if not all, of her policy initiatives that involved force or violence.

"I'm not going in," Chang said, stopping at the top of the steps.

"Phoebe, time is running out," Desaix said, checking his watch. "We have less than an hour."

"Then let's stop here," Phoebe implored. "If we lose the opportunity to reach the aircraft carrier, a war would start, and Moffat would have chosen, without us, either Ann to remain or Chang to become the new Prime Minister."

"That's always a possibility," Desaix said calmly, again checking his watch. "We have precisely fifty-three minutes."

Both Phoebe and Chang stood on the steps.

"Fifty-two . . .

"Fifty-one," Desaix said, looking coldly at Phoebe.

"Give this up, Desaix," Ann added. "It's not worth it. We'll all be killed."

Chang said something to Phoebe in Chinese.

"Forty-nine minutes left . . .

"Forty-eight . . . "

"Let's go in, General Chang," Phoebe said. In the long run, it was her instincts that had won out. She recalled Desaix's Operational Code—he was a high risk-taker who was not afraid of confrontations. And she certainly didn't want this to be one.

"Are you certain?" Chang asked.

"Please, General," Phoebe replied. "We're wasting valuable time."

"Forty-five minutes left," Desaix pronounced, accentuating the sense of urgency.

Chang somberly climbed the final steps. He trusted Phoebe. For years she had been of invaluable help to him. She had consistently placed his interests in the forefront, even at times when he was extremely vulnerable. And she kept him apprised of anything that might affect his political fortunes, at times coming very close to violating her own national security interests. She was in every sense a friend. There was *quanxi* between them. Phoebe walked over and spoke to a moon-faced elderly lady who both guarded the door of the home and sold tickets to tourists. When their conversation ended, the elderly lady went indoors and informed the few tourists inside that the house was closing early and that they would have to leave the premises immediately. After all the visitors were gone the elderly lady ushered Desaix's group, including the soldiers, into the residence.

Once inside, she locked the doors and tapped in code on the mahogany floor in the foyer with her right shoe. A few minutes later, a young man in his early twenties appeared in a doorway leading down to the basement. Without a word, he led Phoebe, Desaix, Chang, Ann, and the soldiers down what seemed like an unending set of stairs into the bowels of the earth.

"Before we go inside," Phoebe said, "tell me how you knew to come here."

"When Ann brought me here a few hours ago," Desaix replied, "I asked myself why. I concluded that she was testing me, trying to see if I knew anything about this house other than the fact that it is a museum. After I figured out what Chang's and your involvement really was in this ersatz invasion, I decided that the nerve center of this whole operation had to be somewhere in Shangha309i. Otherwise, why would you be so eager to come to this city and why would Chang be so willing to let all of us leave the prison camp? I figured that Ann knew about this operation, since everyone in China seems to know everything about everyone else's activities. Everyone, of course, except me. And since she had brought me here for no ostensible reason, I surmised that headquarters had to be here. QED." But he had purposely left out his most important reason for coming back—Ann's unconscious reason for bringing him here in the first place.

"In short, you weren't really certain," Phoebe said, "were you?" She glowered at Ann. If she hadn't brought him here the first time this would never have happened.

"No, not really," he replied smiling. "But I am now."

When they reached the third landing, Phoebe pointed to a huge room filled with charts, telephones, and people sitting at computer terminals. "Welcome to the command and control center of Greater China," she said. "In this room, you will find communication links with Taiwan, Singapore, and Hong Kong, and over two hundred and fifty million Chinese living outside the mainland."

Desaix was impressed by what he saw. It reminded him of a smaller version of the State Department's Operations Center, which could control the dynamics of a crisis in over a hundred and twenty countries around the world.

"This is my shadow government," Chang said proudly. "Our government within a government."

Ann remained silent. She was waiting to see what Desaix would do next.

"Of course all of this was sponsored and financed by none other than our beloved CIA," Desaix said sarcastically yet admiringly. "It's ironic that the museum has been revered for the wrong reasons."

"Let's just say that like all things Chinese," Phoebe said smiling, "there is always more than one side to any phenomenon." She led them and the soldiers through the neatly arranged rows of high-tech equipment and eager young people speaking in Chinese, English, Japanese, and French. "For those who desire to be passively instructed, this house is a tribute to a venerable, yet questionable, Chinese leader. But to those others who would like to leverage the history of China into a promising future, this house connects Chinese government officials, businessmen, organizations, and intelligence agencies all over the world—a Greater China led by Taiwan."

"Why haven't you just closed this all down, Ann?" Desaix asked, but already suspecting the answer.

"Why should I?" she replied. "If I ultimately win our bureaucratic fight, I will simply request that Chang turn over everything produced here—the intelligence reports, financial and business data, as well as the most sophisticated outreach network in the world. Not to mention trade profits."

"In short, why kill the golden goose if it can feed more than one master," Phoebe added sarcastically. "Don't forget, Desaix, Ann is above all else the Empress Dowager and must concern herself with what's best for China." Pausing to assess Desaix's reaction to her verbal attack on Ann, she then added, "Think of what happened to Hong Kong when the mainland Communist Chinese took over a few years ago."

"Nothing," Desaix responded, still mulling over her statement about Ann. "Hong Kong's differing ideology was simply viewed as a nuisance that had to be bypassed or ignored."

"Precisely," Phoebe said. "No one gains by destroying what has been valuable to the strength and viability of your opponent. Simply take it over when the time is right and try to improve it."

"So the real Pax Pacifica has nothing to do with the invasion of Taiwan or the destruction of Japan," Desaix said, glancing at charts on the wall that detailed the ownership of mainland Chinese companies by Taiwanese groups and front organizations.

"That's correct," Phoebe replied, pleased that Desaix had finally grasped the larger picture and hoping he didn't oppose it.

"Until very recently I had it all backward, didn't I?" Desaix asked, looking at Ann. He felt hurt. Once again, she had lied to him. Especially this last time at the consulate when she had expounded at length on how China would co-opt and destroy the Japanese on behalf of the U.S. Why did she have to lie continuously to him?

"Sometimes we have to say and do things that we know we will regret later on," Ann interjected contritely, suspecting what Desaix was thinking.

"Stop sounding so sanctimonious, Madame Prime Minister," Phoebe said, playing on the tension between Desaix and Ann. "You'll do whatever it takes to stay on as Prime Minister. Lying. Cheating. Isn't that part of the game?"

"Maybe you're right, Phoebe," Ann said, trying to control the tears welling up in her eyes. Above all else, she couldn't allow any of them to see any sign of weakness. This time she did not want to play the trump card—her convenient mental disorder. Instead, she had to remind herself that she was the Empress Dowager and she must act accordingly, even if she had to hurt herself in the process.

Chang didn't say a word. He sensed that something strange was happening to Ann. And it was best not to provoke her.

"So Pax Pacifica represents the long-cherished dream of the native Taiwanese to eventually take over mainland China," Desaix said to Chang. "Through peaceful means, of course. Taiwan has been doing it little by little for the past twenty years." Desaix smiled and shook his head in grudging appreciation of the cleverness of the enterprise. "Once the U.S. Secretary of State recognizes Chang as the new Prime Minister of China, Taiwan's continued financial invasion of the mainland, sponsored all along by our CIA, will become official. Even the Japanese will benefit from Taiwan's desire to maintain peace in the Far East as the already extensive trade between the two countries increases. Everyone will prosper. The idea is that nobody would really get hurt. The destruction of the Japanese was never anything more than a work of fiction, to be superseded by a war of financial domination led by Taiwan."

"Precisely!" Chang exclaimed, pleased to end the cat-and-mouse game he had been playing with Desaix.

"I'd say that was a pretty good summation," Phoebe said, uncertain how Desaix felt about what he had just uncovered. He seemed impressed. But that could be deceiving.

"Ironic, isn't it," Desaix said rhetorically, "that we Americans have a nasty tendency to be fooled by the obvious. A big country invading a small country is a natural. But no one thinks of a small country invading a bigger country. And through means other than war. It's all so counterintuitive. The Chinese make life so goddamn interesting."

"I would like to add a small but important correction, Desaix," Phoebe said. "Not all Americans believe in the obvious and the apparent."

"Yes, of course," Desaix said. "None of this would have been possible had the CIA not had the foresight and perseverance to develop Taiwan into a bastion of capitalism and anticommunism, from which the Agency could harass the mainland."

"I think all Americans can take pride in that unique accomplishment," Chang said, a broad smile creeping over his potato-like face.

"I hope you're right, General," Desaix said. "I hope America is prepared to deal with a Taiwanese-Chinese-dominated twenty-first century. We Americans have been so busy worrying about the Japanese that we completely forgot about China—or certainly the possibility of a Greater China."

"You have my government's word that there will always be *quanxi* between our two countries," Chang said, trying to be reassuring.

"That's precisely what I'm afraid of," Desaix replied somberly.

"May we leave now?" Ann asked nervously. "We have very little time left."

"That's the first true statement you've made all day," Desaix responded. "Except there are two unfinished pieces of business."

"What do you mean?" Chang asked.

"If you don't mind, General," Desaix said, checking his watch, "would you please ask your people to place two separate long-distance telephone calls."

"What are you trying to do, Desaix?" Phoebe asked.

"Phoebe, give Chang Moffat's telephone number on the aircraft carrier," Desaix ordered, "and have another call placed to the State Op Center that can be patched into Moffat's line. Ask for Deputy Assistant Secretary Rydell." He gave Phoebe the telephone number. "We have precisely five minutes left." Desaix stared at the Chinese soldiers, who were becoming agitated by the activity and uncertainty surrounding them.

Chang looked at Phoebe. Ann said nothing.

"Four minutes . . . " Desaix announced.

Phoebe nodded her head and Chang ordered both telephone calls to be placed. Desaix was impressed at the facility in English exhibited by Chang's telephone operators.

"Hello, Desaix," Moffat's familiar voice boomed over the loudspeaker for all to hear. "Where the hell are you?"

"I'm with Prime Minister Wu, General Chang, and Phoebe Hill in the Taiwan Command Center in Shanghai," Desaix responded.

"What the hell are you all doing there?" Moffat asked. "You should be here."

"We'll get there as soon as we can resolve a simple question," Desaix responded. "Who will rule China? Prime Minister Lee Ann Wu or General Chang?"

"Can't we decide this matter later?" Moffat asked.

"No, Jim," Desaix responded. "It has to be decided right now. Right here. I'm determined to stop this insane crisis from escalating out of control."

"I want you here immediately," Moffat ordered. "Prime Minister Mori is here with me. I'm afraid he'll proceed with the invasion of Taiwan if the Chinese delegation does not arrive. His men and guns are in place."

"It can't be your way this time, Jim. I'm in control now," Desaix responded. He covered the mouthpiece and turned to Phoebe. "Do you have Rydell on the phone?" Phoebe nodded in the affirmative, handing Desaix the receiver she was holding. "Renee, this is Desaix. I don't have much time to explain anything. But I want you to activate the official tape recorder system in the Op Center, the one you use when you're bugging all the seventh-floor principals."

"I'm afraid to ask you why," Renee responded, "but it's activated. Right now it's recording our conversation."

"Fine," Desaix said, instructing Chang's operators to patch Rydell's line into Moffat's. Desaix had designed a strategy that he hoped would resolve the crisis once and for all.

"Jim," Desaix said, "we have precisely five minutes. Without Ann or Chang at your meeting with Mori, a war will begin."

"Have you gone off your mind?" Moffat shouted.

"We have precisely four minutes," Desaix said calmly after a pause. "Whichever one of you," Desaix said, turning toward Ann and Chang, "can stop this crisis will be Prime Minister."

"How can you guarantee that?" Phoebe asked. "Only Moffat can."

"She's right," Ann concurred, sensing that Desaix had overplayed his hand.

"You bet," Moffat shouted through the speaker. "Only I will determine who will be the Prime Minister. Not you, Desaix. Or anyone else."

"Phoebe is going to guarantee my selection," Desaix responded. "She's going to tell Renee and the State Op Center tape-recording system who really authorized the illegal sabotage of *huoche* 217."

"What the hell are you talking about?" Moffat asked.

"Ladies and gentlemen," Desaix announced, "we have precisely two minutes for either Ann or Chang to come forward and stop a war. No Chinese invasion of Japan. No combined Japanese-Chinese invasion of Taiwan. No takeover of the mainland by Taiwan."

"What in heaven's name could I do to stop this crisis at this moment?" Chang asked.

"You could order the people in this command center to patch you to your field commanders in China and your allies in Taiwan and instruct them to cease and desist immediately," Desaix replied.

"And what could I do?" Ann asked, fascinated by Desaix's sheer audacity, which bordered on nothing less than insanity. He was determined to impose his own version of reality on events.

"One minute left," Desaix said, refusing to answer her question.

"Tell me what I can do that would prevent this war?" Ann asked again.

"Fifty seconds," Desaix responded. Ann knew that she could give the orders necessary to stop a war. But she risked the embarrassment that no one would obey her.

"Phoebe," Desaix said, "tell Renee who authorized that train wreck and who instructed you and your associate to take those pictures."

"This is crazy!" Moffat shouted. "I'm hanging up the phone."

"Don't, Jimboy," Desaix shouted back. "This crisis is going to be settled right now—my way. One of the two is going to walk out of this room the Prime Minister. And Phoebe's testimony will ensure your compliance. Understood?"

"I don't know what you're talking about," Moffat said, wanting to hang up the phone but knowing that Desaix had created a situation in which he had the upper hand. All Moffat could do now was play it out the way Desaix scripted it. Afterward he would have a chance to change it all—maybe. "Is this what you call crisis management?"

"Twenty-seconds . . . Nineteen . . . " Desaix counted, staring in turn at Ann, Chang, and Phoebe. "You each have your own responsibilities to stop a war."

"I can't!" Phoebe responded, knowing that her career would be ruined.

"Desaix, whatever else might happen," Moffat screamed, "you will pay for your insubordination."

"Ten seconds . . . nine . . . "

Ann stepped forward hesitantly, toward the bank of phones and computers. She glanced at Chang, who looked away.

"Five . . . four . . . " Desaix continued, staring at Ann, who he sensed was holding herself back. But why? he wondered.

"Three . . . Two . . . "

CHAPTER THIRTY-SIX

M y good friend," Moffat said, embracing Desaix as he stepped out of the helicopter onto the windswept deck of the *Thomas Jefferson*. "I'm glad to see you. You're just in time. In a few minutes, representatives of China, Taiwan, and Japan will lay the groundwork for a nonaggression treaty that we hope will lead them into the twenty-first century in an era of peace and prosperity. It's truly a momentous occasion."

As Moffat spoke military jets screeched across the golden skies of sundown, returning to their carriers. The heavens appeared to be devouring those colorful war machines. Even the herons, with their long tapered bills, could be seen trying to find their way back to their natural habitat along the marshes and riverbanks of the Huangpu River.

"It's good to see you, Mr. Secretary," Desaix said, conscious of the charade of which he was now a part. "I believe you already know General Y. K. Chang, former Commander-in-Chief of the People's Liberation Army and the new Prime Minister of China. Madame Lee Ann Wu has officially resigned her position and will not be joining us." Desaix winced inwardly as he spoke. The decision had been harder than he had imagined it would be. But personal feelings aside, he had decided that only General Chang could prevent chaos in China.

"Congratulations, Mr. Prime Minister," Moffat responded. He had many questions for Desaix but they would have to wait. There were too many more important things that had to be accomplished before the end of the day. It was sufficient for the moment that Desaix had worked things out, even if they were not exactly the way he, Moffat, might have them.

"Thank you, Mr. Secretary," Chang responded, shaking his hand. "I am certain we can work together just as productively as you did with my predecessor."

"Of course you know Phoebe Hill, our Beijing Station Chief," Desaix said, knowing that he had to move quickly. From the formidable Japanese and American armada displayed in front of him, it was clear that whatever invasion he had just stopped could easily be started up again at Moffat's behest. As far as Desaix could see, the East China Sea was dotted with destroyers. Ann had certainly been successful in luring the Japanese into a position from which they could be decimated by the Chinese. Coordinating with the American navy and air force, of course.

"Please follow me," Moffat said, leading them across the flight deck to a stateroom filled with Japanese, Chinese, Taiwanese, and American dignitaries.

"Dr. Clark," Toland said enthusiastically, "how are you?"

"Just fine," Desaix replied, wondering how he would get an opportunity to be alone with Moffat. "Please take care of Prime Minister Chang and Ms. Hill."

"My pleasure," Toland replied, leading Chang and Hill to a small group of senior American and Japanese officials. Toland couldn't believe that this was the same Chang about whom he had discovered the cable reporting the secret meeting with the Taiwanese. He imagined that in some indirect way he had contributed to the peaceful resolution of this crisis by having uncovered some esoteric piece of information that turned out to be invaluable.

"Jim," Desaix said, with a clear sense of urgency, "I must talk to you."

"Of course," Moffat replied impatiently. "But first I want you to greet Japanese Prime Minister Sammy Mori, whom I believe you have met before."

"I'm glad that you could be here on this propitious occasion," Mori said, bowing. Desaix hadn't seen him in quite a while. He was smaller than Desaix remembered, a man in his late seventies with a clipped bullet head, large tortoiseshell glasses, and an avuncular expression.

"Thank you," Desaix replied, aware of the small window of opportunity in which he could maneuver. He added provocatively, "I hope that we are all aware of what we are really doing here today." For the moment, Mori's confusion would buy Desaix some precious moments with Moffat, who, otherwise, would have dismissed Desaix.

"I'm sorry," Mori said, bewildered by Desaix's tone of voice, if not his words. "I don't understand what you mean."

"I think that Dr. Clark means that uncertainty looms in even the best of plans," Moffat interjected, trying to control his anger. Goddamn Desaix, he thought. Just when everything is ready to go.

"Not quite, Jim," Desaix replied, hoping to force Moffat into confronting him alone, before the meeting began. "Mr. Prime Minister, you know better than I that Japan has been treated poorly by the U.S. over the past ten years. Have you asked yourself why we suddenly want to include you in these talks with China?"

"Please explain yourself, Dr. Clark," Mori asked, his face flushed red.

"I will, sir," Desaix replied respectfully, "after my boss and I have a few words together about this very issue."

"Mr. Secretary," Mori said with concern in his voice, "I insist on an explanation of your Assistant Secretary of State's remarks."

"I assure you, Mr. Prime Minister," Moffat replied, "that you will receive both a satisfactory and immediate explanation after I speak privately with Dr. Clark."

Moffat led Desaix down a corridor, into a small cabin, and locked the door behind them.

"What the hell do you think you were doing in there?" Moffat screamed.

"I guess I finally managed to get your undivided attention," Desaix responded, looking at his friend for the first time without the smokescreen of friendship getting in his way.

"You'd better talk fast and convincingly," Moffat said. "You've got a lot of explaining to do in a very short time."

"Me? I think that you're the one who has the explaining to do. Remember *quanxi*?" Desaix asked, wishing he could throw a punch at Moffat's smug face. "Those were the last words of instruction you gave me before I left for China."

"Let's cut the horseshit, Desaix," Moffat said. "I have too much respect for your intelligence to begin playing mind games with you. Except you still don't have any idea about what the hell is going on."

"Then you tell me, oh wise one."

"It's not really very complicated," Moffat replied. "Even for you. Over the years I've funneled matériel, money, and weapons to Ann so that she could draw the Japanese into a conspiracy against Taiwan, which would eventually be Japan's undoing. Her idea of Pax Pacifica was to create a mainland China that dominated all the Far East and the Pacific. And I don't think she cared two cents how she accomplished it. Anyone and everyone—including me—was expendable. Now, I hope, General Chang will be equally cooperative."

"But what about the CIA and their efforts to build up Taiwan so that it could take over mainland China?" Desaix asked, starting to sense that something was wrong. "I was talking to you from General Chang's secret operations headquarters for his Pax Pacifica for Taiwan. I thought you approved."

"Of course I did," Moffat said, wondering how Desaix was going to feel when he realized he had been outwitted. "Did you really think that the CIA could covertly build up a country like Taiwan without my knowing about it?"

Desaix didn't respond. He was suddenly afraid of the direction their conversation was taking.

"Oh come on, Desaix," Moffat said. "The ultimate skeptic and mind reader couldn't really believe that I wouldn't know about a Beijing Station Chief supporting General Chang, Ann's arch rival for power."

"Don't tell me that you and Phoebe . . . ?" Desaix began, afraid to hear the answer.

"That night in the train compartment when you *quanxi*'d her,"

Moffat said laughingly, "you know you suspected she was working for me. As was Ann."

"You're telling me," Desaix said, "that Phoebe was also one of your graduate students?"

"Neither one was my graduate student," Moffat replied, checking his watch. "As a matter of fact, my relationship with both of them has been purely professional. I met and worked with each at different times during my twenty years in and out of government, academia, and think tanks. Several years ago, I introduced them to each other because I felt it would be mutually advantageous. And so it was, until their ongoing personal rivalry and petty jealousies became counterproductive."

"Did you order Phoebe to help Chang blow up *huoche* 217 in order to embarrass Ann's administration?" Desaix asked.

"It served its purpose," Moffat replied blithely.

"To increase the tension between Ann and Chang?" Desaix asked. "You realize that you illegally authorized an act of sabotage by not first obtaining a congressional finding, don't you? That's a criminal offense punishable by several years of imprisonment."

"You've never heard of a presidential pardon?" Moffat responded. "Are you trying to threaten me, Desaix?"

"Now I see why you sent me to China." Desaix said, ignoring Moffat's question. "It certainly wasn't to stop any crisis."

"You're right on that one," Moffat replied nervously, wondering whether Desaix would ever use his evidence against him. He had to bluff Desaix into backing off. Moffat knew he couldn't trust the President to support him, especially if there was too much heat generated by the media. And Desaix was extremely effective at managing the press.

"You goddamn, manipulative, deceitful—" Desaix began, stopping to laugh at himself. "You engineered the whole crisis between Taiwan and the mainland, the bureaucratic fight between Chang and Ann, the long-standing rivalry between Ann and Phoebe. You sent me to China to keep everyone fighting with one another just a little bit longer until you decided to arrange your own little Pax Pacifica. Just to keep the clients in play, so to speak. Very clever."

"You forgot the old adage, my friend, that nations don't have friends or enemies, simply shifting interests. I certainly couldn't be certain of what was going to happen once you arrived in China. But I knew my characters and I thought they would figure out how to . . . how should I say it . . . entertain each other for a while," Moffat said, sorry that he had to sacrifice his friendship with Desaix to accomplish his own goals. "You know Asia almost as well as I do. Remember the reason Thailand was never invaded by Burma, or Cambodia, or Laos for over a hundred years?"

"Sure," Desaix replied. "Thailand made sure that there was always a low level of strife and tension with her neighbors on each of her borders because it was a great way of deterring an all-out invasion by any one of them."

"And . . . " Moffat asked, pressing Desaix to continue.

" . . . and Thailand just kept shifting its alliances as any one conflict got too difficult to handle," Desaix responded. "Even with small wars, local corruption, and regional destabilization, Thailand was always in control, always pitting one enemy against another. And therefore never invaded."

"Your memory is as good as ever, Desaix. Now just try to see my version of Pax Pacifica as an American version of the Thai model. The meeting that you so rudely interrupted is just the first in a long, perhaps endless series to come. Chang is here, just as Ann would have been, in the hope that he can continue to con the Japanese into remaining his ally. With a war as bait, or without war. At the same time, both Phoebe and Chang, as you know, are going to try to do anything they can to advance Taiwan's interests. And financial strength. Now, instead of playing on only one side of the table, they will be playing on both sides without any greater effort. Mori . . . well, when hasn't Japan tried to extend its influence wherever it could?"

"And the military buildup?" Desaix asked, fidgeting with the tape cassette in his pocket.

"Think of it as no more than an instrument of psychological warfare," Moffat replied. "This time you were able to stop it. But remember, I can raise and lower our military alert status, and those of our allies, at will . . . within hours."

"Nothing really changes," Desaix responded. "Does it?"

"Don't you Cajuns have an expression?" Moffat asked. *"Plus ça change, plus c'est la même chose.* The more things change, the less they change."

"And you?" Desaix asked in disgust. "What is it that the United States—or should I say, Moffat wants?"

"You're really not as clever as you've intimidated everyone into thinking you are, are you?" Moffat asked laughing. "Can't you see yet that there will never be a Pax Pacifica? I am orchestrating a diplomatic-military process over which, for the first time, America will be in charge. There will be no invasions. Japan won't be destroyed. Taiwan won't be dominant. Nor will China. But America will fuel, manipulate, and control a constantly shifting set of alliances among those competing powers. Ultimately, it will ensure our own power in the Far East . . ."

". . . with Moffat acting as the American Mandarin," Desaix added. "American diplomacy but with an Asian mind. Controlling world tensions the Asian way."

"You got it," Moffat exclaimed. "We keep all the parties busy with one another, spinning like tops. But we're controlling the spin." Moffat couldn't help the self-satisfied grin on his face. "To overcome another's armies without conflict is the best of all skills."

"Sun Tzu," Desaix responded. "The *Art of War.*"

"You and I have certainly talked about his principles of war for years. I've just managed to put them into practice," Moffat said. "Doesn't the master strategist warn us to be extremely subtle? Even to the point of formlessness. And to be extremely mysterious, to the point of soundlessness. Thereby you can be the director of all of your opponents' fates."

Desaix was amazed at Moffat's accomplishment.

"I was waiting to see how long it would take you to figure that out," Moffat said. "Did you forget the most important of all Sun Tzu's lessons, that wars, and for that matter crises, are won not on the battlefield, but in the minds of men? It was all there from the very beginning."

"Starting with the train wreck and the photos," Desaix said, "then the supposed attack on you at Hurricane Alley by some fictitious Tiger Eel, to the doctoring and restriction of my intel to convince me that a major crisis was brewing. You even went so far as to suggest, reluctantly of course, that I might want to visit China to assess the situation firsthand. That was the infallible bait to get me into an action which was only intended to keep the Chinese pot brewing until you convened this meeting. And to add honey to the bait, you even provided me with a full set of tantalizing Operational Codes and Psychological Profiles on Ann and Chang that were, at best, inadequate."

"In diplomacy and crisis management," Moffat retorted, "like in the martial arts, Sun Tzu warns us that it is important that strategy be unfathomable, that form be concealed, and that movements be unexpected, so that your opponents will find it impossible to be prepared. He also tells us that a good general must have a modus operandi that leaves no tracks. Only the formless cannot be affected by opponents, he warns us, allowing the commander to hide his intent and actions in a series of contradictory actions, shifting alliances, and apparent betrayals."

"So Pax Pacifica is not only an elaborate exercise in Sun Tzu's strategies of war but the Taoist philosophy of nondoing as well."

"Desaix," Moffat replied "think of Pax Pacifica as a Cajun gumbo, a little bit of fish, an unknown amount of poultry and game meats, a variety of vegetables. But is it a soup . . . ?"

" . . . or is it a stew?" Desaix finished.

"It's all a question of how much roux you add, the mixture of flour and fat," Moffat concluded. "And that's up to the chef, Desaix, isn't it? Then let me be the chef. You just enjoy the meal."

"And where does that leave me?" Desaix asked, realizing that Moffat had always intended him to feel like a fool.

"It leaves you jobless at the moment," Moffat responded. "Perhaps the only part of this business that I regret. Your resignation is the one act that will seal my continuing role as the master puppeteer. I can never trust you now—our *quanxi* is gone. Chang will never trust you because of the humiliations you have put him through. Phoebe . . . well, who does the CIA ever trust, anyway? And Mori has always seen you as pro-Chinese." Moffat hesitated, saddened by the look on Desaix's face. "So, my dear friend, you become expendable."

Desaix remained silent until he felt that he could walk out of the room without shaking. Even to the very end, the spirit of Sun Tzu had prevailed. Another of the important lessons of the Master's teachings was the emphasis he placed on the dynamic structure of a group in action, the manipulation of an opponent's vulnerabilities by organizational momentum. It was the organization and not the individual that was important in attaining success. And that left Desaix on the sidelines. He recalled Sun Tzu's precise words: "Good warriors seek effectiveness in battle from the force of momentum, *not from individuals.*" It was this emphasis on the power of the group that set the teachings of the Master apart from the idiosyncratic individualism of the Samurai swordsman of feudal Japan.

Desaix realized that from the very beginning of the crisis he had been doomed. He had gone into this crisis, as he had countless others, to seek personal glory, hoping to impact directly on history. In the past, he would immerse himself in the very essence of the crisis, controlling every piece of information, intelligence, access, and action. The success or failure of the crisis would be determined by Desaix's three inviolate rules: control, control, control. But this time around he had no control. Even when he attempted to gain it, it was by assuming the Taoist posture of nondoing. He had gone through the teachings of Taoism and Sun Tzu in his mind. But to no avail. Because to be a successful crisis warrior, according to the words of the Master, "Those who are good at battle do not become angry, those who are good at prevailing over opponents do not get involved."

It was the importance of operating outside the sphere of the self, ego, and the individual that Moffat was really trying to teach him, at the cost of their friendship and Desaix's resignation. But what about Moffat's ego? Desaix thought. What had all of Moffat's machinations led to, if not a situation in which he was in control?

Finally, the last part of Desaix's dream came into focus—his aloof father, rocking on the veranda reading a newspaper, indifferent to the surrounding commotion. If, as Freud contended, the child is father to the man, then it should have been clear to Desaix that it was he, and not his father, who should have sat impassively, unaffected by his mother's rantings.

"I will make your apologies to the group," Moffat suggested. "I'll say that you are totally exhausted and will not be able to join us today. When the news of your resignation reaches the papers—"

"Here's the present I promised you, Jimboy," Desaix said, handing him the tape cassette, and enjoying the surprised look on Moffat's face. "The original recording is back at the Op Center ready for the proper dissemination. I would strongly urge you to resign as well. The President can't afford to keep such a clever Secretary of State. It's much too dangerous for the country and the world."

Desaix left Moffat standing alone in the room. As he passed by the stateroom on his way to the deck Chang and Mori were all smiles, intent on their conversations. Only Phoebe noticed Desaix through the window and looked away.

Les jeux sont faits. The game is over, thought Desaix. But not quite. Moffat was right. He had to resign. And in its own way, it was so typically an Asian ending to his career. He was the biblical sacrificial lamb required to make his best friend Moffat appear ruthless, duplicitous, amoral, and Machiavellian—traits greatly respected as the pillars of enlightened leadership in the Far East. Desaix had to chuckle to himself. The essence of friendship was personal sacrifice for the greater good. But even still, he couldn't help feeling that despite his education, travels, languages, and international experiences, he had too high an expectation for trust, friendship, loyalty, and fair play. He was, after all, too American.

"*Quanxi,*" Desaix said, spitting the word into the winds whipping across the deck of the aircraft carrier.

CHAPTER THIRTY-SEVEN

Empress Dowager," Desaix said, inebriated by the wonderful madness and merriment of the New Orleans Carnival. Ann and Desaix stood on top of a float in the shape of a serpentine Chinese dragon, one of the twenty floats winding their way through the French Quarter. Theirs had been organized by the Phunny Phifty Phellows, a group of Carnival devotees who were in the habit of sponsoring the less than aristocratic balls held on streetcars, in protest to the more elegant debutante balls.

"Yes, Dr. Sun Yat-sen," Ann responded, amused by Desaix's high starched collar and tight double-breasted brown woolen suit, typical of a nineteenth-century Chinese gentleman. She threw out aluminum doubloons, or "throws," to the crowd of costumed men and women.

"I was true to my promise that we would spend one more Carnival night together," Desaix said, throwing handfuls of plastic beads and Go cups to a group of inebriated college students wearing Tulane sweatshirts and draped with layers of beads around their necks. In earlier times New Orleanians had mailed these trinkets to family members who had married Yankees and moved away from the city.

He couldn't help himself from staring at Ann's imposing, regal beauty. She was dressed in the prescribed fashion of a Manchu Empress. Her straight black hair was drawn back from the forehead and fastened in a bun. On top of this was pinned a square headdress, shaped like a mortar board, from which tassels hung on either side. Onto this severe background were pinned bright, colorful jewels and floral ornaments that matched her long pendant earrings. She was swathed from her neck to her feet in a long, straight satin gown fastened across her chest from the left to the right shoulder. Lavish embroidery patterns covered her sleeves, neckband, sideband, and hem.

"Yes," Ann replied, moving closer to him, kissing him on the lips. "But I'm going to tell you a little secret."

"What?" he asked, proud of the fact that Ann had just been appointed director of the prestigious Center for Asian Studies and professor of political science at Tulane University as well as a member of the board of directors of three Fortune 500 companies. As for himself, he would wait and see what opportunities might arise at State, academia, or Wall Street. For the moment, he wanted to immerse himself in a world in which both he and Ann could enjoy themselves without any outside distractions or obligations. And his ancestral home of New Orleans was a perfect backdrop for that endeavor.

Blowing her a kiss with his hand, Desaix still marveled at her beauty and intelligence. Ann was a woman of many talents and an uncanny sense of her own potential. His heart had compelled him to whisk her away from China and bring her to safety in the States. But his mind kept warning him that they would both have to work very hard to build the trust and intimacy required to sustain a long-term relationship. Passion dictated the present but pragmatism would determine the future.

"I always had a premonition that you would fulfill that promise you made to me that night on the Huangpu River," she said, ignoring the plaintive shouts for more throws.

"Is that why you hesitated when I asked either Chang or you to step forward and stop the crisis?" he asked, hoping to close one more question that had been gnawing at him for some time.

"What do you mean?" she asked disingenuously.

"You could have called up those commanders in the PLA who were loyal to you," Desaix responded in a more serious tone, "or you could have informed the Central Committee in Beijing to mobilize the peasants to demand an end to the crisis. Or you could have called up the same Taiwanese officials who were loyal to Chang and inform them that the deal was off. But instead you let Chang take the initiative."

"Why do you think?" she asked, squeezing his hand.

"As much as my ego would like to think that it was out of desire to leave China and live with me happily ever after," Desaix said laughing, "I think it came down to the fact that you weren't certain that you had any political support, from either the peasants, your political appointees, or your PLA commanders."

"And that explains why I lied to you at the U.S. consulate when I told you that Pax Pacifica was simply a ruse to destroy the Japanese," she said. "And why I didn't say anything about the museum being Chang's Taiwanese Command Center."

"You didn't have to tell me," Desaix said. "The fact that you took me there was enough."

"What do you mean?" she asked, pleased that he understood her so well.

"Without saying a word," Desaix continued, "you informed me that the museum was serving a function far beyond that of a showcase for Sun Yat-sen's life. After having me followed by the Public Security Bureau on my first day in Beijing, when I went to the Museum of the Chinese Revolution, you knew that I would pick up on the one most important fact and historical pattern that would repeat itself." He paused to assess her reaction. It was admiring of him. "When the Empress Dowager died, it was Dr. Sun Yat-sen, who, as the founder of the Kuomintang party, eventually took over the reigns of power and whose party then ruled China for a quarter of a century. Perhaps I am being too psychological. Or you were being too Oriental. But since we are both avid students of history, I think you were trying to tell me that, in time, you, too, would have to relinquish your power to the inevitable Kuomintang rulers from Taiwan. Represented by none other than General Chang and his cronies. So the outcome was already predetermined by fate and the inevitable forces of history. You had no other choice but to bow out silently and graciously. As usual, you were quite eloquent and informative in your silence. And quite Chinese."

"You can understand how uncertain and impotent I felt," she said ruefully. "I wasn't certain that I represented any constituency any longer. So I wanted the crisis to play out the way Moffat had originally planned in order that I could continue."

"Except I interrupted his plans for a Pax Pacifica," Desaix said, picking up one of the many king cakes strewn over the float. He pulled off a piece of the green, gold, and purple wreath-shaped cake topped with multi-colored icing.

"I'm quite certain that Moffat didn't expect Chang to become the new Prime Minister," she responded, taking a bite of the king cake, "and he didn't expect you to stop the crisis." She munched carefully on the cake. "Ironically, Chang will, in time, become an excellent leader for the new China. He was correct at the prison camp when he said that he, more so than I, was the only one who could prevent the dreaded chaos in China."

"Aren't you afraid of the Taiwanese influence on the evolution of this new China?" he asked, eating some of the cake as well.

"There is only one China," she replied, "whether it's called the People's Republic of China or Taiwan. We Chinese are very flexible and have accommodated to differences for centuries. For instance, we speak two quite separate languages in China. In the south we speak Cantonese, and in the north we speak Mandarin. No one speaking Cantonese really understands anyone speaking Mandarin. But we've managed to overcome our differences through a common written language . . . and a heritage of combating outside aggressors together. So having the former Kuomintang and Taiwanese on the mainland will simply add one more culture for us to incorporate into the Middle Kingdom."

"But there was one other reason you decided not to challenge Chang," Desaix said, pulling off another piece of cake. "Wasn't there?"

"Okay, Dr. Clark, former Assistant Secretary of State and crisis manger par excellence," Ann said teasingly. "You tell me what it is."

"You had already decided that you no longer wanted to be the Prime Minister. Am I right, Empress Dowager?"

"And why would I no longer have wanted power, fame, or prestige?" she asked, slipping a piece of one-inch plastic from her mouth to his.

"Make me feel good. Could it be that you wanted to spend one night of Carnival in New Orleans with me?" he asked, examining the piece of plastic. "Christ, you found the baby doll. That means you've got to give the king cake party at next year's Carnival."

"I didn't find it in my mouth," Ann replied, holding him tightly. "You found it in your mouth." She had made her choice. The Empress Dowager was a costume to be worn, not a role to play for her whole life. She had no regrets. Desaix made her feel complete, and she knew she wanted to spend the next few years of her life with him.

"All right," he said. "This time I'll accept the baby. But next time—"

"Throw me something, mister!" Newton shouted from the sidewalk as he threw a handful of plastic beads and doubloons at Desaix and Ann to attract their attention.

"Jump on board, Jin Bo," Desaix shouted, grasping Newton's arms and pulling him up. He had to laugh at the way Newton was dressed. He wore a pageboy wig, a gold crown, jeweled tunic, and white tights. He looked like the typical prosperous New Orleans businessman who once a year let his hair down. "Or should I address you as King of the Carnival?" With Desaix's help, Jin Bo had found a lucrative position with a New Orleans trading company exporting to the Far East.

"Hi, guys," Newton said exuberantly. "I brought you tomorrow's edition of the *New Orleans Times-Picayune*, which I thought you would want to see right away."

"Is it that important?" Ann asked.

"Take a look at it yourself," Newton replied.

"Secretary of State James Moffat resigns," Desaix read out loud. He asked Ann teasingly, "Should I continue?"

"No," she replied, her voice quivering.

"You're not kidding," Desaix said. "Are you?"

"I'm afraid, Desaix," she responded, holding tightly on to him. He could feel her hands shaking. "I don't want Ash Wednesday to come so soon."

"Ann," Newton said, "let him read it."

"Go ahead," she replied, clenching her fists.

"Basically it says that Moffat resigned for personal reasons and will go to work for some Wall Street firm," Desaix said after skimming the article.

"Does it say why he resigned?" she asked nervously, concerned that she might be mentioned. Many of her colleagues at the university had reservations about her appointment, and the last thing she needed was uncontrolled publicity.

"Not exactly," Desaix responded, offering her the newspaper, which she refused to read.

"What do you mean?" Ann asked.

"The article says that Wayne Cartwright III has just been confirmed as Assistant Secretary of State for East Asian and Pacific Affairs," Desaix said, "and Phoebe Hill was appointed National Intelligence Officer for East Asia."

"But how does that relate to Moffat's resignation?" Ann asked.

"Knowing the President's past behavior in such matters," Desaix responded, "I suspect that he conducted a secret investigation of Moffat's unauthorized illegal sabotage of the train. I'm certain that the President used my tape in which Moffat confessed his involvement in the train wreck. In exchange for Phoebe's testimony against Moffat, she was exonerated of any wrongdoing and promoted. Instead of pressing criminal charges against Moffat, the President asked him to resign."

"Why didn't the President have him prosecuted?" Newton asked. "Or have him fired?"

"That's not the way we work," Desaix replied. "Moffat's future in the national security area is pretty much over. By now the word has already gotten out that he resigned under clouded circumstances."

"So Moffat will write a book," Ann added, "about his brilliant stewardship as Secretary of State and make millions of dollars."

"Of course. It's the American way. As the old song goes," Desaix said, "he'll be certain to accentuate the positive and eliminate the negative."

"In other words," Ann interjected, "he'll be writing fiction in the guise of history."

"But that's only the beginning," Desaix continued. "Then he'll become an elder statesman who pontificates on Sunday TV and vents his outrage and displays his sagacity in op ed pieces. And the good ole boy network perpetuates its corrupt mediocrity."

"What about the new Secretary of State?" Ann asked, her voice shaky. She wanted to grab the newspaper away from him. But she needed all her strength to keep herself together.

"Let me see," Desaix said, scanning the article. "There's nothing here about a new Secretary of State. It says that the Far East started to heat up again. This time, the Little Tigers, in particular Thailand and Singapore, are stirring up trouble in the countries surrounding China. They fear Chang and his Taiwanese minion: But what's new? You told me that within six months that would happen. You were only off by two months."

"Oh, Desaix," Ann said, tears welling up in her eyes.

"Why don't you call up the Prez," Newton said, "and offer your services?"

"Can you see me behind a desk," Desaix replied, "managing four thousand FSOs, all of whom think they can be a better Sec State than I?"

As he heard his own words, Desaix knew he had made the right decision. If he returned to State, as the President had asked him to prior to his coming to New Orleans, he preferred a position of influence rather than authority. Not one that would place him directly in the spotlight. Under Secretary of State for Political Affairs, the number three slot, would be high enough, he thought—and low enough—to let him be himself.

"I'm glad you feel that way," Ann said, searching Desaix's face for any sign of disappointment. "I would hate to think that in some way I have limited your career."

"Don't tell me you would be willing to give up that position to be with my sister here in New Orleans?" Newton asked.

"Jin Bo!" Ann shouted.

"I'm certain that your sister and I will live in interesting times,"

Desaix responded, echoing the famous Confucius saying and tearing up the newspaper.

"Or as we New Orleanians like to say," Ann said, "*Laisser les bons temps rouler*. Let the good times roll."

As he drew Ann's lips toward his, Desaix threw the shredded paper into the confetti night.